HER MAJESTY'S CAPTAIN

Books by Derek Wilson

A TUDOR TAPESTRY:
MEN, WOMEN & SOCIETY IN REFORMATION ENGLAND

THE WORLD ENCOMPASSED:
DRAKE'S GREAT VOYAGE 1577–1580

THE TOWER OF LONDON 1078–1978

HER MAJESTY'S CAPTAIN

HER MAJESTY'S CAPTAIN

Being the Manuscript of Robert Dudley,
Duke of Northumberland, Earl of Warwick
and Earl of Leicester in the Holy Roman Empire,
From His Own Hand

A NOVEL BY

DEREK WILSON

LITTLE, BROWN AND COMPANY   BOSTON, TORONTO

FIRST AMERICAN EDITION

Library of Congress Cataloging in Publication Data

Wilson, Derek A.
    Her Majesty's captain.

    British ed. published in 1978 under title: The bear's whelp.
    1.   Dudley, Robert, Sir, 1574-1649 — Fiction.
I.   Title.
PZ4.W7472He   1979   [PR6073.I463]   823'.9'14   78-24309
ISBN 0-316-94497-1

PRINTED IN THE UNITED STATES OF AMERICA

Select Pedigree of Robert Dudley,

sole heir of Robert, Earl of Leicester and Ambrose, Earl of Warwick

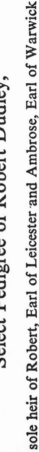

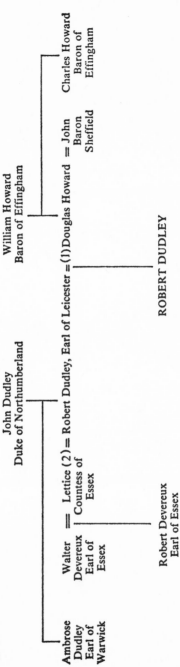

John Dudley
Duke of Northumberland

William Howard
Baron of Effingham

Ambrose
Dudley
Earl of
Warwick

Walter
Devereux
Earl of
Essex

Lettice (2) = Robert Dudley, Earl of Leicester = (1)Douglas Howard = John
Countess of   Baron
Essex   Sheffield

Charles Howard
Baron of
Effingham

Robert Devereux
Earl of Essex

ROBERT DUDLEY

HER MAJESTY'S CAPTAIN

PROLOGUE

My end, it seems, must follow the pattern of my beginning. The daydreaming child, spoiled by wealth but untouched by love, is become the aged exile enclosed in a world of splendour with only memories for companions.

Well, so be it. The years between have held enough of excitement and happiness, passion and tumult to satisfy a dozen men and setting down this account of those years will be for me like a pleasurable voyage of rediscovery. I cannot find it in myself to agree with Florence's greatest son, *'Nessun maggior dolore, che ricordarsi del tempo felice, nella miseria'*, 'The greatest of all sorrows is to recall times of happiness in the midst of misery.'

As I sit here looking down on Dante's city or playing host to those of his countrymen who climb the vineyard-hung slopes of Pertaia to visit the Villa Castello, I am constantly amused by the embarrassed half-recognition of these Tuscans. They stand awestruck before Botticelli's sparkling *Primavera* and *Birth of Venus*. They take their enchanted ease among Niccolo Tribolo's fountains, grottoes, shaded walks and bronze statuary. Then they catch a glimpse of the tall, stooping old man shambling like a drab ghost among the living splendours, or they stumble upon him suddenly as he sits scribbling in his favourite arbour. They exchange puzzled glances and as they wander away I hear snatches of whispered conversation about the strange Englishman, the *Duca di Nortumbria*. They are recalling tales told by their fathers about my adventures on the high seas, my many services to the Medicis or, more probably, the scandals that have always attached themselves to my name.

I

Does it matter what they say about me? When I am laid to rest beside my beloved Elizabeth in the Church of San Pancrazio, will my spirit concern itself with the colourful legends, and the obscene calumnies that men speak about Robert Dudley? I onces sacrificed everything – wealth, position, country, friends, the respect of those whose opinion I valued – and for what, if not for truth? Through more than three score years I have debated with the world's greatest scholars, punished my eyes in the study of books, wrestled with the enigmas of the universe, and truth has ever been the object of my quest. If I were to leave the world knowing that posterity will dub me 'libertine', 'traitor', 'false friend', 'imposter', I would be committing an offence, not against the name of Robert Dudley, but against truth.

Mother of God, how I ramble! Has my passion for order and precision deserted me in my dotage? Or is the sheer volume of material – this *cassone* full of old papers, letters and journals – so intimidating that I shrink from the task? I must not delay any longer. I am, thank God, in excellent health, but at seventy-four it would be foolish to imagine that I have a limitless amount of time to complete my memoirs. I must make a start. Whoever you are who read this in years to come know that I, Robert Dudley, Duke of Northumberland, Earl of Warwick and Earl of Leicester, wrote this accurate account in the year 1648 in the seventy-fifth year of his age while resident in the Villa Castello in the Grand Duchy of Tuscany, the realm of His Most Serene Highness Ferdinando II de' Medici. You may be aware of other memorials I have left to posterity – the port of Livorno, the fair acres of reclaimed farmland between Pisa and the sea, the finest fleet in the Mediterranean, cures for pleurisy, toothache and the bloody flux, the greatest book yet written on navigation and mercantile affairs. These are as nothing beside my most important legacy – a full life well lived, its sorrows borne, its misfortunes conquered, its achievements freely shared. I want the world to know the truth about that life.

1

The first fact I have to record is the one of which I have always been the most proud: I was born on 7 August 1574, the only son of Robert Dudley, Earl of Leicester. No Englishman ever had nobler ancestry. My father was for thirty years general, councillor and closest companion of Queen Elizabeth. His father, John Dudley, Duke of Northumberland, was the finest soldier in the service of Henry VIII and Edward VI. As Lord Admiral he laid the foundations of England's navy. As the young King Edward's most trusted adviser he held the government of his country for three years. My uncle Ambrose, 'the good Lord Warwick' as men called him, as well as being friend and councillor to his sovereign and serving her faithfully by sea and land, was one of the most cultured men of his day, a patron of artists, playwrights, explorers and philosophers. For generations before them the house of Dudley had been one of the firmest supports of the English throne and the Bear and Ragged Staff one of the proudest and most famous family emblems. It was ever my wish to continue that tradition. However ... No, I must not anticipate.

You would expect the son of such a great man to be brought up in palaces amidst the bustle and glamour of royal and noble courts, pampered by parents, relatives and servants. It was not so in my case for one simple and sufficient reason; I was a bastard. All the world knows that Elizabeth and Leicester were in love. Many times the Queen contemplated marriage with her favourite. For years, decades, my father was kept faithful by the promise of wedlock dangled before him. But the dessicated greybeards of the Council were set against the match, and the Queen heeded them rather than her heart. Leicester's position was impossible for any warm-blooded man (and no one has ever found the Dudleys lacking in passion). Elizabeth demanded his total fidelity and devotion but would not commit herself to him in return. Naturally, he had to find outlets for his desires in secret – very secret – liaisons. One such liaison was with Douglas Howard, a woman of high birth and great beauty with whom he shared a happy relationship for many years. I was the result of that relationship.

My few childhood memories are like flashes of light in a darkness of loneliness and misery. I was brought up in various houses by tutors and servants without any companions of my own age. 'Mother' was no more than a painful and puzzling sense of loss, for I had been taken away from her at the age of four. 'Father' was a magnificent, richly dressed man who visited occasionally, striking terror into the servants and scarcely less than terror into me.

One of those happy flashes of light was my first acquaintance with the sea. I was about eight years old and had been sent to live at my father's manor at Offington on the South Downs – a large friendless house, full of dark corners. The people who looked after me – a tutor, a housekeeper and half a dozen servants – were kind enough but frightened of exceeding their orders, which did not include taking me down to the sea. In its sheltered hollow the building might have been a hundred miles from the coast but lodged in the top branches of my favourite oak in a corner of the grounds I had a clear view southwards. For hours I used to sit there watching the crested breakers and the mysterious ships beating slowly up the Channel.

I suppose the sea was in my blood. I had two great Lord Admirals in my ancestry. I have already mentioned my grandfather; my mother's brother was Lord Charles Howard of Effingham, he who was to put Spanish Philip's Armada to flight. It was an age when all small boys were captivated by the lure of maritime adventure. The great news of the day had penetrated even the stout walls of my confined world: Francis Drake had circumnavigated the globe, to return laden with Peruvian treasure and Moluccan spices. I plagued my tutor to tell me all he could

4

discover about the voyage and I was very proud to hear that one of Drake's main backers was the Earl of Leicester. High in my oaken eyrie I too fitted out fine ships and sailed them to the lands of cinnamon and gold, to Tierra del Fuego, Ternate and fabled Cathay. One day, one golden day of summer sunshine such as only occur in childhood, as I sat among the leaves I made a solemn vow that I would lead an expedition around the world. I do not suppose I was unique in this resolve; all over England little boys were making up their minds to emulate the great Francis Drake. Yet, I suspect I was the only one to put the scheme into immediate effect. I simply climbed over the garden wall and walked the mile or so to the beach. I can still feel the sting of sand, blown by a stiff breeze as I stumbled across the dunes and ran triumphantly down to the water's edge.

Nearby there was a fisherman and two boys about my own age working at nets beside a boat drawn up on the sand. I walked straight up to them and said, 'Take me out in your boat.' Most of the people in my life were servants, paid to take orders, and I had no reason to suppose that these fisherfolk would fail to do my bidding. The man looked at me and laughed.

'If you want to ride in a fisherman's boat, youngster, you must do fisherman's work.' He held up the bone needle and the pitched twine he was working with.

'Very well,' I said, seating myself beside him.

At that he laughed more heartily, though his sons scowled at the intruder. But they showed me what to do and soon I was busily spreading out the net, and looking carefully for tears to be mended. When the work was done, I helped fold the stiff, sticky mesh and stow it in the boat. I got my reward; the fisherman took me out over the shimmering water, let me take a turn on the oars and even showed me how to catch mackerel with a line and a metal lure. It was a child's heaven. The freedom of the sea, the uncomplicated cheerfulness of my new friend made me feel as happy as the gulls which screamed and soared above us.

Afterwards I went back with them to their home to eat the fish I had caught. The man lived with his wife and sons in an old hulk beached at the edge of the dunes. Now, I know it was a

5

miserable, cold, dirty hovel and its inhabitants wretchedly poor. Then, it was an enchanted world – smoke blackened timbers, chairs made of old barrels, a plank stretched across from wall to wall which served as a trestle table, a bed built into the ship's bow and screened by a curtain of old sacking, and in the middle, the open fire over which the food was cooked. I had never enjoyed a meal as much as the coarse bread and the fish – my own fish – I ate that day. And as my host dined he told me stories, stories of great storms, of sea monsters and of men he knew who had been round the world with Drake. I listened, I ate, I absorbed the atmosphere. I had never been happier – but then I had never been in a family.

How I got back to the house and what happened when I did are matters on which my memory is mercifully blank. I was guarded more securely after that and never saw my fisher friends again but I often thought about what I had learned. I envied them the freedom of the limitless sea with its thrilling dangers and boundless opportunities and I wondered why I could not share a life like theirs which seemed much more full of purpose and normal than my own.

Of course, my destiny could never be so simple. Both my parents eventually married: my mother went off to Paris as the wife of the English ambassador, and Leicester at last braved the Queen's wrath by bestowing his name on Lettice Knollys, the Earl of Essex's widow. The new Countess certainly did not want her husband's bastard in her household, so I continued to lead the life of a pampered but unwanted embarrassment. When I reached the age at which I could dimly understand my situation I realised and, I suppose, accepted that when my education was finished I would be provided with a suitable country estate and a suitable wife and be consigned to a life of rural insignificance.

But in her unhurried way fate was changing my role. My father was born one of eight brothers. Acts of God and acts of Tudors had long since removed from this world all but him and my uncle Ambrose, Earl of Warwick. Neither of them sired a legitimate heir. So Leicester's 'base son' as he often called me, became the last of the line, the sole survivor of the richest family in England.

I remember very clearly the day my father explained all this to me. It began inauspiciously with his unexpected arrival at Stoke Newington manor, where I was currently billeted. He found me not brushed and dressed, ready to greet him with some well-conned Latin oration, as was the custom, but hot, scruffy and bad-tempered in a half empty barn which was my own secret place. The reason for my frustration was my lack of progress with a galleon I was modelling from a block of wood. Not until he laughed was I aware of him.

'So, we are to have another admiral in the family, are we?'

I spun round and saw him, a splendid figure in rich court clothes, leaning incongruously against some sacks of barley. I thrust the model behind my back as I stumbled to my feet, ashamed of my lack of skill.

'No, lad, let me see. Ah, look, here's where it's going wrong; the prow is too long and the forecastle set too far forward. Here, give me the knife.'

We sat side by side and I watched, fascinated, as he improved upon my rough work. And with his attention focused on the knife and the wood my father talked to me as he had never talked before. The task made it easier; there was no need for our eyes to meet. We both pretended we were making a model galleon; in fact we were fashioning a new relationship. From stories of ships and mariners and great voyages the conversation flowed easily to reminiscences about my father's own childhood and his family. There were tales of the great Baron Dudley who had fought in the wars of Lancaster and York a century before and of my grandfather's exploits by sea and land. As the day blossomed and faded outside I sat enthralled in the dusty coolness of the barn and heard all about my father's imprisonment in the Tower of London by Queen Mary and of the friendship forged there with the captive Princess Elizabeth; of the restoration of our family's fortunes by that pale princess when she became queen; of the Dudley lands, manors and great houses throughout England which would one day be mine.

I told my father all about my life, such as it was, and especially

7

of my passion for the sea which had grown steadily over the years. At last I raised the courage to ask the question I had, in imagination, asked him a thousand times.

'Father, may I have a ship and take her round the world?'

I had prepared myself for every reaction from laughter to stern refusal. I had not expected the raised eyebrow, and the long, pondering silence. At last he took me by the shoulders and spoke very seriously.

'Robert, England will soon need fine captains, for war with Spain cannot be much longer delayed. Then there will be no better way for you to serve your sovereign than as commander of an English galleon. But never forget that you have another loyalty. You are a Dudley. You have a great inheritance and you must pass it on to your son.' He laughed. 'We cannot have the last of the Dudleys dying full of arrows on some savage South Sea island, can we?'

I was excited and delighted by his reaction, but not too excited to ask for a new tutor, someone skilled in navigation, geography and astronomy.

Leicester stood up, a tall, dark figure, his features indistinct now in the deepening gloom. Again he laughed.

'Yes, we will indeed find someone to make a sailor of you. But first we must make you into a gentleman. Come, let us discuss all that at supper.'

With his arm round my shoulder we went together into the house.

After that day the pattern of my life changed. My father was as good as his word; he did send me a new tutor, a swarthy Welshman who had learned navigation and astronomy from the great Dr John Dee. He was a strange fellow, and, like all the rest of the household, I was more than a little afraid of him. His chamber was filled with books and alchemical paraphernalia. He cast horoscopes and used the money this brought him to buy more strange equipment. When I displeased him or was slow in learning my exercises he did not beat me. Instead, he threatened to call up demons to afflict me with boils or fill my nights with terrible dreams. It was an effective means of punishing a highly impressionable boy. Yet, I learned much from the 'Welsh wizard' as the servants called him. The movements of earth, moon and planets, the calculation of tides and latitude, the properties of lodestones and compasses and the reading of charts. I was genuinely sorry when Master Huw was jailed by the local magistrates at the suit of a local farmer to whom the 'wizard' had contracted himself to find buried treasure by magical means. That was when scepticism began to seep into my soul. I was shocked that the man whose mind was such a wonderful treasure-house of fascinating information could also be a charlatan. The truth occurred to me, dimly at first, that there was a distinction between real 'science' – things that can be observed, proved and deduced – and the hocus-pocus that clever, unscrupulous men could pass off as esoteric knowledge with superstitious folk who lacked the intellectual equipment to reject it. Even as quite a young man I surprised and horrified many of my friends and acquaintances by my scoffing at stories of ghosts, demons, familiar spirits, sea monsters and the assortment of magical beings who, in their opinion, inhabited the world just beyond the frontiers of everyday experience. The unknown came to be for me a place that should be explored, not feared. Frequently moved, as I was, from billet to billet, I had abundant opportunity to put this philosophy to the test. At each new house I familiarised myself immediately with every room, loft, cellar and barn. I forced myself to walk candleless along unlit passages and up pitch-black stair-cases. I took immense pleasure in proving to myself that the dark held no terrors. There have been many times in my life when I have been afraid but always I have known the thing which en-gendered my fear. For that I suppose I must largely thank a lonely childhood and a Welsh 'magician'.

Master Huw's departure was the moment chosen for me to be sent to Oxford. Once again my father selected the ideal mentor for me. I was lodged at Christchurch under the tutelage of Thomas Chaloner. Dear Thomas. I have known men – like Galileo – of more brilliant and original mind. I have known men – like Descartes – who were more subtle. But no one surpassed Thomas as an enthusiast. He did not just teach us students; he made us want to learn. His lectures inspired us all to a love of mathematics and cosmography and many were the long discussions we had, walking beside the river or drinking late into the night at our favourite alehouse.

We were a serious crowd and our talk turned often to religion and the current state of the world. We deplored the activities of the Inquisition and the fate of mariners like John Oxenham who had fallen foul of the Catholic torture-masters. For hours together we quizzed Thomas Chaloner on modern developments in navigation, argued about the relative strengths of the English and Spanish navies, and debated the best kind of fighting ships for use in the Channel and the Atlantic. If we were earnest, practical-minded young men it was because those were troubled times. Everyone knew that the mighty, ponderous power of the Hapsburgs was being directed towards our island, that Philip II was gathering an invasion fleet in the harbours of Spain and Portugal and an army in the Low Countries. Drake foiled him in 1587 by his famous attack on Cadiz and I have cause to remember the event and the way we celebrated it in Oxford, for it was the first time I ever got blind drunk.

There was little scope for mindless rejoicing in the following months. Fear and panic grew as rumours spread of massive invasion preparations across the Channel and of Catholic plots at home. Study was impossible and I wrote to my father asking for permission to join Lord Howard's fleet in the Medway. Impatiently I waited for my messenger's return. Weeks passed and I heard nothing. Leicester had been appointed Captain General and was, I knew, very busy mustering troops to face the invaders. Yet I could not help fretting at the thought that no place was to be found for me alongside my countrymen. I was nearly fourteen and was convinced that my services were indispensable. Then, when the festering heat of summer had brought plague to Oxford to add to our miseries, a messenger arrived from Tilbury. I was to report to the garrison there to take up a commission as colonel of a regiment of foot.

I shudder to think what the great Tilly or Gustavus Adolphus, whose commissariats were always impeccable, would have said about the hastily constructed camp at Tilbury. The half-trained English shire levies stumbled about in a misdirected and dis-organised manner, trying to dig trenches with only one shovel or pick between three men; they put up tents and then took them down again because some nobleman had decided he wanted them in the shade or farther from the river. Yet my youthful and uncritical eyes saw not the poor administration but only the bustle and excitement of men preparing to defend their homeland. I wore my new authority as self-consciously as my part armour, strutting about the camp with my officer colleagues, and riding proudly in my father's entourage. Leicester had aged rapidly in recent years; his remaining fringe of hair, like his beard, was quite white but he carried himself as erect as ever and no man sat a horse better.

I had been at Tilbury three or four days when, coming into my father's tent, I found him in conversation with a flamboyantly-dressed young man of about twenty. From the dust on his boots I knew that the visitor had recently arrived and, to judge from the quantity of wine he was consuming, the ride had been a long and thirsty one.

'Come in, come in Robert,' said Leicester. 'Here is someone you must meet. Be friends with him if you can, for he is the most powerful man in England.'

'Only if you are the greatest liar in England,' said the young man, turning towards me with a smile.

I had never seen my stepbrother before, only heard about him and hero-worshipped him – but I knew instantly that this must be he. The long, pale face had an almost girlish beauty and was framed by ringlets of black hair. There was nothing in the least effeminate about his greeting.

'So this is the bear's whelp!' He clapped me on the shoulder. 'Why have you kept him hidden so long, my lord?'

He steered me towards the long trestle table.

'Come, you shall sit by me and tell me all about yourself. That old bear Leicester is not deserving of so fine looking a youngster.'

Such was my first meeting with Robin Devereux, Earl of Essex, and I was overwhelmed that he should have admitted me so readily to his friendship. For Essex was, simply, the hero of the younger generation of Englishmen. He was Lettice Knollys' son by her former marriage, and at court his charm, wit and boisterous vitality had won him the affection of the Queen. By 1588 he was Master of the Horse and the brightest star in the royal firmament. His escapades were the talk of the court and the City. He had served with conspicuous recklessness in the Low Countries. He fought duels on dubious points of honour. He claimed the hearts – and not only the hearts – of several of the Queen's ladies. He roistered with his friends in London inns wreaking such havoc that many landlords closed their doors to him. But it was his attitude towards Spain that captured the imagination of warm-blooded Englishmen. While the penny-pinching dotards of the Council debated the cheapest and easiest way of keeping the peace, Essex demanded action. 'Strike first and strike hard' was his motto and there were thousands who would have followed him if the Queen had given him a fleet of ships. In fact, a fleet was virtually the only toy Elizabeth did not give him. She was bewitched by her latest charmer. Whatever outrage he committed he was forgiven, for the ageing Queen seemed to suck vitality and vigour from him and would not deny herself his company.

Supper on that warm summer's evening was a long and happy affair. I basked ingenuously in the flattering attention of my new friend and believed every word of the outrageous stories he told about the court and about the greatest men and women in the land. Afterwards Robin insisted that I join him and his friends in a riverside tavern. How the night ended I can more vividly imagine than remember.

Three days later – three hectic days of preparation when the gentlemen had to strip to the waist and work beside the troops to ensure that all was ready – the Queen came to Tilbury. Like the majority of Englishmen present on that large square of trampled grass I had never before seen my sovereign. Like them, I was overwhelmed by the vision of stateliness and splendour as the Queen rode slowly along the lines of soldiers. I suppose I had more cause than most to be impressed and delighted by the spectacle, for Elizabeth had chosen to come among her troops attended only by two trusted companions. One was my father and the other was my new-found friend. They both looked splendid in their gleaming armour and black horses which were designed to show off to best advantage the vivid white of the Queen's dress and her silver cuirass. The effect was magical: we were looking at a theatrically overdressed old woman on a grey horse but what we saw was Gloriana, Diana, Minerva and Judith all combined in one to lead her people to victory. I cheered as wildly as the rest and when our 'goddess' made a speech telling us she would lay down her life rather than see Philip of Spain set foot in England the spell was complete.

After dinner I was presented to the Queen along with the other captains. We all stood in a fidgeting bunch outside the Captain General's tent like nervous athletes before a race, and waited as our names were called one by one. I had more cause to be apprehensive than most of my peers. I knew that my father had told Elizabeth all about me and that he was waiting for a suitable opportunity to introduce me at court. All my hopes for the future rested on my making a good impression.

My name was called and I moved forward into the pavilion. The Queen sat in a tall chair flanked, as before, by my father and Robin. Leicester solemnly announced my name. Essex grinned broadly and winked. I knelt and kissed the cold, thin hand extended to me.

'Arise, Master Dudley.'

I stood awkwardly before the Queen and was subjected to a long, careful scrutiny.

'So, this is Leicester's base son. Well, boy, do you take after your father?'

'I believe so, your Majesty, especially in loyalty to my Queen.' It was not a brilliant reply but it amused her. She smiled and the rearrangement of her features dislodged some flecks of white paint which fell onto her bosom.

'Then we must put your loyalty to the test. Are you bringing him to court, Leicester?'

'If it please your Majesty.'

13

She tilted her head to one side and eyed me quizzically.

'It might, my lord. It might.'

With that I had to be content for the time being. After a few weeks of drilling and boredom at Tilbury the camp was broken up. My uncle's fleet had defeated the Great Armada, and the invasion had not materialised. I returned to Oxford. Leicester promised to visit me there in the near future to arrange for my presentation at court. That was at the beginning of August. On 4 September, while travelling towards Buxton to take the waters, my father died suddenly.

It was a great shock and a genuine grief, though mingled with my sorrow there was, inevitably, a degree of self-pity. The only fixed point in my life had been removed. What was to become of me?

I had no taste for the lavish official mourning which I knew would accompany the funeral, though I knew equally well that I would have to be present. In order to pay my respects privately I rode to Warwick a couple of days before the ceremony. I shall never forget my first intimate acquaintance with death. As I stepped inside St Mary's Church the door closed with a solemn muffled thud on the bustling world of the living. My footsteps on the ancient flags awoke no echo, for the massive piers and round arches were all hung with black drapes which sucked every sound from the air. Not an inch of bare stone was to be seen. The Dudley arms were prominently displayed but their heraldic tints were also stifled in sombre sarsenet. Even the hundred wavering spikes of candle-flame served only to draw my gaze towards the monumental bier rather than to invest the scene with inappropriate brilliance. I seemed to be choked, entombed, forced to share the eternal loneliness of death as I shuffled forwards to kneel before the canopied hearse. Black velvet almost slimy in its smoothness covered the coffin and above it my father's waxen image clothed in armour.

For perhaps half an hour I struggled with my thoughts but the proper sentiments and memories would not be bidden. At last, feeling nothing but a neutral emptiness, I rose to my feet and walked slowly from the pavilion of death. As I reached the door

I felt a hand on my arm and heard a quiet voice.

'He was a fine man, Bear cub; we shall all miss him.'

Only one person called me 'Bear cub' in those early days so I knew without turning that it was Robin Devereux who had been concealed in St Mary's shadows. For some minutes we walked in silence towards the castle through the dark grey October evening. Then Robin spoke in a tone much closer to his usual boisterousness.

'Come on, Bear cub, you need a cup of hot clary.'

He steered me down the hill and soon we were sitting before a fire in a tavern beside the west gate, sipping the spiced and honeyed wine. The warm drink and Robin's cheerful company soon lifted my spirits. Then he let slip a comment that filled me with alarm.

'You must pay no attention to rumours. When my father died there were stories that he, too, had been poisoned.'

'Poisoned? Do you mean that people are saying . . .'

'That Leicester's death was not natural. Yes, did you not know? How foolish of me, I should not have mentioned it. Well, whatever men say, you must take no notice; it is quite the accepted custom to suspect murder or witchcraft when a great man dies.'

'But who would want to kill my father?'

Robin shook his head.

'God's blood, Bear cub, but you are naive. I can see I've much to teach you about the wicked ways of the court. Leicester had many enemies. So have I. So has every man close to the Queen.'

'But why?'

'Jealousy, supposed grievance, discontent with the way the country is governed, religious fanaticism, personal rivalry – oh, there are many reasons why men hire assassins or buy potions. In the case of your father's death the motive is supposed to be adulterous passion.'

I must have looked a picture of comical, open-mouthed astonishment, for Robin laughed aloud.

'Oh yes, it is my loving mother, your respected stepmother, who is supposed to have made away with Leicester.'

'But why?'

15

Essex turned towards the fire. I could not read his face but the nonchalant ring had gone out of his voice.

'The Countess of Leicester has taken a lover. A man half her age . . . a servant.'

I had not the slightest idea how to respond. I expect I mumbled something incoherent.

'His name is Blount and he looks after her horses. God's blood, I could laugh if it did not make me feel so sick.'

Then, just as suddenly his mood changed again.

'But your problems must be our chief concern, young Bear cub, not mine. What are we going to do with you?'

I started to explain that I had not had time to make any plans but he cut me short.

'You don't suppose royal wards are free to make their own plans, do you? For that is what you are now, a royal ward, and the Queen is very interested in you.'

'Why should the Queen be interested in me?'

'She has two passions in life. Well, she has lost one of them. Do you know she shut herself in her rooms for ten days and refused to see anyone when she heard of Leicester's death? She needs someone to remind her of her old love and you are remarkably like your father. You also have that other thing she craves.'

'Money?'

Robin laughed again.

'So you are not as simple as you would have me believe. Yes, money. You are the richest heir in the kingdom and when Warwick dies you will be richer still. So the Queen will keep a very close watch on you. Nor will she be the only one. There will be merchants wanting you to sink money in risky ventures, courtiers wooing you to marry their daughters.'

Again the surprise and dismay on my face amused him.

'Well may you look worried, master Oxford scholar. You can bid farewell to your quiet life and your books. From now on you will be glad if you can snatch a few moments' solitude in a day. The court is a crowded place and every man and woman in it is only there for what he can get.'

'The court? But...'

'The court, of course. Where else? It was your father's wish that you should be introduced there and I have been sent here to take you back to Westminster after the funeral.'

2

And so the lonely boy became a courtier, pitchforked into the bewildering world of the royal household. My few previous glimpses of that world had been dazzling. Now I was to learn what close attendance on the Queen really meant.

I was very impressionable and quite uncritical, yet I think I can honestly say that I have never since been in a court so frenziedly gorgeous and gay. The daily routine was a perpetual masque in which each courtier played his assigned part and all had to provide a protective barrier of flattery for the old woman who had the leading role. Elizabeth surrounded herself with young people. She obliged them to live at a fast pace and then tried to outdo them. She spent long hours in the hunting field; she would dance galliards and voltas far into the night; she took her court on endless progresses around the houses of the nobility.

I was a very insignificant actor in that perpetual performance. By day I was at the beck and call of the ladies and gentlemen of the Queen's apartments. I carried messages, brought flagons of wine up to private rooms, conveyed platters of food into the banqueting hall and generally served those who served the Queen. By night I slept in a great bed with five or six other young lads whose families had bought them places at court. But I had an advantage over my colleagues, for Robin really did take a very close, protective interest in me. Our relationship was, I suppose, something between that of brothers and friends. He took his wide-eyed protégé hawking, hunting, on visits to the bull ring, the City taverns and the playhouses across the river. It was all very flattering and I paid little attention to the jealous taunts of 'Essex's darling' which were inevitably flung across the table in the great kitchen where we boys ate. We talked much about the important matters of the day; Robin often told me about Council chamber quarrels and what great men were in and out of favour. He made me feel that I was in his confidence, a member of his group, his faction. We were the men of the future. We were the ones who would establish England's greatness. We would oust Spain from the golden lands of the New World. We would explore unknown territories. We would open up the ocean routes to Cathay and the Spice Islands and bring vast commercial wealth to London.

There was no better time for ambitious young men. In those months after the Great Armada, when sporadic reports reached London of King Philip's proud ships dashed to pieces along the western coasts, all the great captains were beseeching the Queen for permission to launch a massive reprisal raid; an attack on Spanish fleets and harbours which would annihilate Spain as a maritime power. And they had their way. Sir Francis Drake himself was put in charge of the expedition and from all over England young men crowded to the court, using whatever influence they had to secure places in the great admiral's ships.

We fine gallants of the royal household assumed, of course, that positions in the fleet were ours for the asking. We talked excitedly of the forthcoming battles and the plunder we would bring home. Robin had promised to take me on his ship, which I never doubted for a moment would be one of the finest vessels involved in the enterprise. Throughout the winter the massive fleet was made ready in every harbour from Thames to Falmouth. It was the largest ever assembled in England and all her great mariners were given commands.

But not Robin. No place was found for him. Day after day he petitioned the Queen. Always the answer was the same: her Majesty could not excuse the Master of the Horse from his regular duties. When Robin presented my request to be allowed to sail with the fleet he was told that I was too young. Too young? I knew lads of eleven and twelve who had already left for Southampton and Plymouth to become pages or ship's boys. Two of my own colleagues rode off along the Dover road one day in

March while the rest of us watched them go in jealous silence.

My own disappointment and damaged pride were nothing compared with Robin's. He was usually very careful in what he said to me about the Queen but now he cursed her roundly as a possessive old woman who wanted to keep him within her grasp like a hooded hawk. I was angry, too; angry at the shame of it, the noble Earl of Essex detained at home while others won the glory that was his by right. There was another reason for my anger : when Robin was crossed a terrible change came over him. Despair casts most men into a lethargy; it elevated him into a state of savage exuberance. His talk was irresponsible: he picked quarrels with his friends and was haughtily rude to almost everyone. Even his appearance was wild: he went about the court with doublet unfastened, points hanging loose. In these black rages he became a frightening stranger to me, and I resented that bitterly.

One evening in early April I was stumbling back from the kitchens after serving supper. It was already dark and I was weary. I was also sore. I had spilled some wine over one of the Chancellor's men and been well thrashed for my carelessness. As I stepped within the greater darkness of an archway a hand reached out and grabbed my arm. Before I had time to cry out a whispered order checked me.

'Not a sound, Bear cub!'

'Robin, what . . .'

'Sh! Put this on.'

He pushed a bundle into my hands. With difficulty I unravelled a heavy cloak and fixed it around my shoulders.

'Here, you will need this, too.'

My fingers recognised a small sword with its belt and, fumbling, fixed it around my waist beneath the cloak.

'Now come with me.'

Ignoring my questions, Robin steered me around a moonlit courtyard, into the palace gardens and out through a small door which he unlocked with his own key. In a clump of trees a few yards away one of his men was holding two horses. Robin gave me a leg up, then mounted the other animal. Only then did he pause for a moment. Turning in the saddle, he said, 'I hope you are not tired, Bear cub. We have a long, fast ride ahead and no time to delay. If you fall behind I must leave you.'

'But Robin, where are we going?'

'To sea. Is not that what you have always wanted?'

His mare squealed as he spurred her straight into a canter.

How I kept in the saddle throughout that terrifying ride I do not know. All through the night we charged onwards with only occasional stops to change horses or gulp down a morsel of food. Fighting off sleep, I forced myself to watch for potholes and overhanging branches. Yet a hundred times I was taken unawares and all but unhorsed. Day brought no respite. Our mad flight continued. Robin spoke scarcely a word so that I was left to guess at our destination. I knew we were going westwards. Long before that awful ride ended I had ceased to care exactly where we were heading. I only wanted to dismount and lay my aching body on a bed, a floor, the damp ground – on anything as long as it was not moving.

Yet when at dusk we clattered into Plymouth a fresh excitement took possession of me and my weariness was instantly forgotten. It was a magical sight; black hulls and spars against the sky, ships' lanterns reflected in the rippling water, the smell of the sea. Soon Robin and I were sitting in the great cabin of the *Swiftsure* and I was being introduced to Captain Williams, Robin's friend and fellow conspirator.

'Welcome aboard, Master Dudley. I hope you have a taste for work. There's no room for passengers on this trip.'

Williams was a melancholy man and obviously worried about the escapade Essex had lured him into.

'You saw no sign of pursuers, my lord?'

Robin stretched his legs out beneath the table.

'No, I think we far outpaced the Queen's hounds, eh, Bear cub? Yet I fear they will be here by morning. When do we sail?'

Williams shook his head, gloomily.

'There's scarce a ha'penny breeze, my lord. I'll try to get her away on tonight's ebb but I make no promises.'

'And we make for Brest?'

'Aye, if we're not stopped by one of the Queen's ships.'

Williams spread a chart on the table, and we put our heads together over it.

The swinging lamp threw gently sliding shadows to and fro across the paper. The spidery outlines of land and the network of rhumb lines seemed to be constantly shifting. As the ponderous voices of the others melted into a constant drone which merged with the ship's steady breathing, I forced myself to extract details from the map's jumble of information. It was a vain struggle: darkness spread inwards like a stain from the edges of the paper.

I was cast out of sleep more abruptly than I had drifted into it.

'Come on, pretty boy, are you going to stay there all voyage?'

I was sprawled on the floor of the great cabin with a surly, one-eyed man standing over me. He had just pulled me from the bench bed where I had, somehow or other, fetched up the previous night. The man took a fistful of my hair and hauled me to my feet. He thrust his face close to mine.

'Some sailors like pretty boys, but I ain't that way inclined. Do you see what I mean, lad?'

He jerked my head into a nod.

'I only have pretty boys aboard my ship to work. Work is what the good Lord sends to keep our minds off other things. You can thank the Lord that you have a shipmaster who'll work you until you drop. So you won't ever let me catch you not working, will you?'

The fingers entwined in my hair twisted sharply from side to side.

'Because if I ever catch you not working I'll lay your back bare to the bones, won't I?'

Again the excruciating tug at my scalp.

'So we have a gentleman's agreement, haven't we, pretty boy? You promise to work all your waking hours and I promise not to flog you into small pieces. That's fair ain't it?'

This last speech was accompanied on my part with so many enforced nods that I expected to see all my hair lying loose in the master's hands. At last he let me go but it was only to grip me by the shoulder and fling me towards the open doorway.

'Now get down there and help the cook!'

I stumbled onto the main deck and looked about me. Dawn was already lighting a clear sky and the *Swiftsure* was moving crisply before a freshening breeze. The distant shore was no more than a grey line on the horizon astern. At last I was at sea in an English ship.

I had no more than a fleeting moment to relish what I had always imagined would be a sacred moment. The master's voice was bellowing in my ear again.

'I said help the cook, pretty boy. He's over there.'

A boot in the backside sent me flying across the deck. I barked my shin against a corner of the main hatch, stumbled and almost fell right into the firebox where the cook was stirring the contents of a steaming pot. I jumped quickly to my feet and found myself at the centre of a laughing circle of seamen and soldiers. The master's face was a lopsided mask of mockery and contempt. I dared venture no more than a sulky scowl but I vowed to myself that I would be even with the man.

The next few days gave me little leisure for planning revenge. As ship's boy I was at the beck of the captain, the master, the bosun and all the senior mariners. 'Fetch that.' 'Tell the master gunner this.' Clean out here.' 'Tidy up there.' And always the one eye of shipmaster Kendall following my every move. I had little time to myself, unlike the rest of the crew who were divided into watches. And yet I loved it. Whether I was clinging for very life to the ratlines far above the deck or seeking something in the stinking, slimy hold I knew that this was the life I wanted.

In one way I was far luckier than the seamen: I had access to the upper deck. I served meals at the great cabin table where Robin, Captain Williams and the other gentlemen ate. From what I learned there, and from what Robin told me on the rare occasions when we talked alone, I was able to gain some idea of what the expedition was all about. The *Swiftsure* had put to sea while the main fleet was still not ready to embark. It would, therefore, be some days before we could rendezvous with Drake off the Portuguese coast. When that happened we would be under the admiral's orders. Drake's first task was to wrest Portugal from

Spanish control by taking Lisbon and setting the pretender, Don Antonio, on the throne. Then he would visit the main Iberian seaports destroying whatever shipping he found there. Finally he would sail for the Azores to apprehend the homecoming treasure fleet from America. In all these exploits the 400 ton *Swiftsure* would have a vital role to play but until the meeting with the main fleet she was a free agent. Essex and Williams were determined to use those few days' grace for some grand enterprise, some daring coup which would justify their headstrong departure and assuage the Queen's wrath.

That was as far as my information went. Of our actual destination and what would happen when we reached it I knew nothing. I was not party to the plans made on the poop deck. Whenever important matters were discussed at table I was dismissed, and war councils always took place behind closed doors. Mine was a very frustrating position; I was neither confined to the lower decks nor fully accepted on the upper. Or perhaps it was just my overpowering curiosity about everything connected with naval command and naval warfare which made me so discontented with an aggravating half-knowledge. I suppose I could at a lifetime's distance find some justification for turning spy but I will content myself with simply stating that that is what I did become – a spy, a listener at cracks, a lurker in shadows.

My eavesdropping began innocently enough. One evening towards the end of supper in the main cabin I noticed that the wine flagons were both half empty. I poured the contents of one into its companion so as to leave the gentlemen a full flask while I went through into Essex's adjoining cabin to replenish the other from the cask of best canary Robin kept for his own use. The tap was stiff and I struggled with it for several minutes before obtaining a slow trickle of wine. Then the tap had to be turned off tightly again, so it was only after considerable delay that I stood up and balanced myself on the swaying deck before walking back into the main cabin. It was then that I became aware of the angry voices.

'And I say 'tis not possible, my lord.' Williams's voice had lost its usual slow mournfulness.

There was a murmur of agreement across which Robin's scornful reply cut.

'All the expert seamen told Drake it was not possible in '87.'

'Drake had thirty ships,' another voice replied. 'We have only one.'

'Aye, one ship, and obviously full of cowards, if you speak for them.'

Robin's retort was followed by an uproar of shouts and oaths. I was very thankful for that; it gave me the chance to set down the heavy flagon and settle myself into a more comfortable position behind the half-open door. In the heat of debate the gentlemen had obviously forgotten all about me. If I put in a sudden appearance now they would know I had been listening. Thus prudence as well as curiosity dictated my course of action. Now Essex was shouting above the others.

'Listen and you will see it is no mad scheme. In '87 the harbour was full of capital ships. It would have been folly, then, to go in alone. But where are those fine ships now? Keeping company with the fishes or lying crippled at Santander and Corunna.'

'Aye, and 'tis there we should be finishing them off or take them as prizes... my lord.' I knew Master Kendall's voice only too well.

'Not when we can win greater prizes...'

'What greater prizes?'

'Unarmed merchantmen loaded with supplies for the Netherlands' garrisons. A Portuguese fleet waiting to sail for the Indies with spices, cloth and wine.'

'Which will, I suppose, yield to us while the Matagorda and Hercules battery officers sit back and watch.'

This brought some empty-headed laughter. When Robin spoke again I could hear the tension in his voice.

'Gentlemen, I have explained my plan for surprising the garrisons. Master Kendall here approves the idea and he knows more about navigation than the rest of you put together.'

'Aye, my lord, it could work, with proper timing. But the fact is...'

'The fact is Master Kendall, that his lordship has only one

reason for attacking Cadiz. It has nothing to do with stopping Spanish supplies reaching the Low Countries or the Main. He simply wishes to prove that whatever Sir Francis Drake can do the Earl of Essex can do better.'

Robin shouted an oath. There was a hubbub of raised voices. Chairs scraped. Something crashed to the floor. And I panicked. If the meeting was breaking up Robin would soon be coming through the doorway to the inner cabin. There was nowhere I could hide and only one other exit from the room. As quick as thought I was out through the stern window and crouching on the narrow gallery outside.

The night was dark – and cold. Below, the ship's creamy wake gleamed. Above, the swaying wooden cliff of the *Swiftsure*'s stern rose sheer. As my heartbeat slowed and I reflected on my situation I began to wish I had stayed to face discovery and a beating instead of condemning myself to a freezing, cramped, sleepless night on the stern gallery.

I suppose I found some slumber in the hours before dawn arrived and I could climb quietly back into Robin's cabin to wake him as was my duty. But much of that night was spent in thought. A raid on Cadiz? Could it be done? And if so, how? What was Robin's plan for slipping, unobserved, past the harbour-mouth batteries? I wanted desperately to find out more. Could I persuade Robin to tell me his plans? Not without admitting I had eavesdropped. Then I realised that what I had done once, accidentally, I could do again whenever I pleased. All I needed was a short length of rope. I could fasten it to the poop deck rail any night after supper and let myself down to the stern gallery. It would be my own private access to the secret councils of my superiors.

And so I did. That was how I heard Robin persuade a majority of his colleagues to support his venture. Poring over maps which I could not see, he explained the details of his plan again and again. At first he only had Master Kendall's grudging support but, one by one, other members of the council came round to his side. Even Captain Williams at last conceded that there was just a chance his precious ship would not be blasted out of the water.

The scheme, as I listened from my vantage point, sounded like a brilliant piece of strategy. Under cover of darkness the *Swiftsure* would land two boatloads of men on the seaward side of the narrow Cadiz isthmus. The boats would be dragged inland and concealed on the wooded slopes above the beach. While most of the group stayed with the boats, a few men disguised as peasants would enter the city, make their way to the harbour, and select the most likely prizes. The following night the boats would be pulled the short distance to the inner shore of the isthmus and then rowed towards the harbour. If they were seen, little attention would be paid to them, for the Spaniards would not expect attackers to be coming away from the inner harbour. Silently our men would board the selected vessels, overpower the guards and wait. At dawn, just before the turn of the tide, the *Swiftsure* would sail into the outer harbour with all her guns blazing. If possible she would keep out of range of the shore batteries. This would be the signal for the crews of the prize ships to slip the cables, hoist sail and quit the harbour. The garrison commanders would assume that the ships were simply hastening to get away to sea to avoid capture. Only when they saw the *Swiftsure* turn to lead the Spanish vessels out between the sandbanks would they realise something was wrong. This would be the time of greatest danger. The prize ships would still be in range of the shore forts. If the artillery officers were quick-witted enough they would smash the unarmed merchantmen to splinters.

As the days passed and we drew steadily southwards my excitement mounted. I would soon be taking part in my first naval action and one which promised to be spectacular to say the least. I had made up my mind quite firmly that I would wangle a place with the shore party somehow, even if it meant disobeying orders and risking one of Master Kendall's celebrated floggings. I had made my own rough and ready chart which I kept folded up in the pocket of my leather jerkin. By skulking around the master of the watch when he took his astrolabe readings and by checking the charts in the great cabin whenever I was allowed a glimpse of them, I was able to keep a daily record of the ship's progress. We stood well out from land but by my reckoning twelve days' sailing brought us to the latitude of Cadiz. When, the next day, Captain Williams gave the order to alter course eastwards I knew I was right.

Nothing was said to the members of the lower deck but, equipped as I was with secret knowledge, I was able to interpret the various signs that pointed to imminent action. Robin now personally supervised the daily drilling of the soldiers instead of leaving the job to Sir John Frensham, the colonel. Grumbling seamen were set to stripping and recaulking the boats. And at our morning services the chaplain regularly worked himself into an eloquent frenzy against the popish Antichrist.

It was after these devotions one day that Captain Williams ordered the ship's company to stand fast. We were soon to see action, he said, and the Earl of Essex was now going to select men for a shore party. Robin, Williams and Sir John descended to the main deck and passed along the ranks stopping every few moments to note down a name. My stomach was a tight knot of excitement and apprehension as the general drew nearer. I edged forward slightly so as not to be overlooked. Robin came closer. He was in front of me. He stopped and smiled down at me.

'Not this time, Bear cub.'

As soon as the muster was dismissed I ran up the companion ladder to the poop deck. Robin was talking with his friends but I was too upset to worry about etiquette. I immediately began begging for a place in the boats. It was a stupid thing to do and it only annoyed Robin. He told me brusquely that it was out of the question for me to go. He needed trained men, not amateurs. Besides he had risked the Queen's anger in bringing me at all. If he should return home without me he would never be forgiven. I was aware that the other officers were looking at me with silly, patronising smiles on their faces, as though I were a spoilt little boy throwing a tantrum. I, who had overheard all their planning and squabbling, who knew the entire plan of the Cadiz raid. I was so angry and so hurt that I did exactly what a spoilt little boy would have done. I shouted at Robin.

'I care not for what you say. I am going and you shall not stop me.'

I turned to walk from the deck, but Robin reached out and caught me by the shoulder.

'Master Kendall!' he called.

The shipmaster came up from the main deck.

'Aye, my lord.'

'We shall need a sharp-eyed lookout to tell us when we are in sight of the Spanish coast. Master Dudley will do very well. Send him to the mast head, if you please. He is not to come down until I say so.'

If Robin thought that a few hours in the crow's nest would cool my head he was mistaken. From my vantage point I could see all the preparations being made below, and hear the lively bustle of men glad at last to be going into action. Isolated from this exciting activity, I had little to do but brood on Robin's unfair treatment and my own miserable plight. After the familiar relationship which we had enjoyed at court I found Robin's aloofness since the start of the voyage very strange. I knew that he had far more important things than me on his mind. I also knew that if I was eventually going to own and captain my own ships it was good for me to learn my craft the hard way. I shared the mariners' contempt for the gentlemen adventurers who strutted the poop deck but knew nothing about the workings of a ship. Yet this knowledge did not make my hard life and my disappointment easier to bear. I wished heartily that Master Kendall was not an ingredient in my apprenticeship. He had not, so far, made good his threat to take a lash to my back but there was scarcely a part of my body which did not bear a bruise inflicted by the shipmaster's large, hard hands and feet. The hair twisting had become a part of the bully's daily ritual. As for Robin's refusal to allow me to go on the Cadiz raid, I wondered how he could bring himself to be so hard. I had shared his own brave act of defiance, had run away from court with him rather than sit in idleness while there was man's work to be done. Now he was condemning me to helpless inactivity as soon as there was a prospect of real action.

These self-pitying reflections did not prevent me doing my job as a lookout. Twice I gave warning of the approach of other ships so that the master of the watch could alter course and keep the *Swiftsure* well away from inquisitive foreigners. I trained my eyes on the horizon ahead almost willing the straight edge of the ocean to crumple into the irregular outline of land but there was a fresh north-easterly breeze and the *Swiftsure* was making slow progress. The sun was more than half way down to the western horizon and the first watch well established before I was able to call out,

'Deck! Deck below! Land ahead on the larboard bow.'

With an hour of daylight left, we were close enough to the shore to anchor and send a yawl off to find a suitable landing place. Slowly, steadily darkness spread across the scene below. I could only hear the muffled sounds of soldiers mustering, arms being distributed and boats lowered. Just when I had convinced myself that I was going to be left in the crow's nest all night there was a creaking from the rigging just beneath me and a voice close at hand told me I was to come down and go straight to bed.

On the deck a line of men had already formed. One by one they went over the side into the waiting craft. I went straight to my bed space but sleep was the last thing I had in mind. I collected my sword and made my way to the after deck. Officers and crew were far too busy seeing the shore party away to pay any attention to me. I dragged my rope from its hiding place and went through the familiar routine of letting myself down to the stern gallery. My plan was a simple one. There was still another ten feet or so of rope, enough to take me close enough to the water. I would drop into the sea, swim around the side of the ship and cling, unobserved, to the back of one of the boats. Beyond that point I had not thought very clearly. What Robin might say or do I did not know; I only knew that he would not be able to send me back to the *Swiftsure*.

The first part of my scheme worked well enough. Though the water was cold and my limbs leaden with the cumbersome weight of soaked clothing, I was able to wallow around the ship's stern. Uncomfortable as I was, I consoled myself with the knowledge that I only had to swim a few strokes. I realised immediately that I had not made my bid any too soon. One boat had pulled away and the other was already well filled. Slowly and carefully, so as to make as little noise as possible, I moved towards the small dark mass. Clearly now I could hear all that was happening. A thud as another man landed in the boat's stern. Then a whispered conversation.

'You the last, then?'

'Yes.'

'Sit down, then – there.'

The same voice now raised into a hoarse shout.

'Casting off now.'

Panic seized me. I still had a few yards to make. The boat's bow had swung out from the ship. Careless of noise, I floundered towards the stern. Distinctly I heard the bosun's order.

'Oars forward.'

Then something cracked me hard across the side of the head. It was one of the oars being swung into position by a muscular seaman. I was only unconscious for a few seconds. When I came to I was under water, lungs bursting, arms and legs threshing wildly, head arching to find the surface. After what seemed several minutes I reached the air, coughing up salt water and wiping it from my eyes. I looked around for the boat and saw nothing. I could hear the steady dip of the oars but the vessel itself had merged with the night. I struck out in the direction of the sound. If I thought at all I must have deliberately shut from my mind the certainty that I could not hope to catch up with the boat. Within minutes I was alone in a total blackness of water and sky. There was neither sight nor sound of ship or boat. My head throbbed, my arms were tired, my legs were being pulled down by the weight of sodden clothes. And between me and the shore there was a mile or more of tumbling Atlantic. I trod water, tried to catch my breath and made myself think clearly. If I took it slowly and if tides and currents did not play me false I could, perhaps, do it. With some difficulty I divested myself of my heavy jerkin. Now, how to keep myself on course? The stars were my only points of reference so, singling out one close to the horizon and brighter than its fellows, I set off again with slow, irregular strokes.

31

How long I was in the water I do not know. I recollect the agony of my aching limbs, the choking brine in my mouth and nostrils, the dozens of times I stopped to listen, in vain, for the sound of breakers. Did I reach land before falling unconscious? Did I miraculously bump into some piece of flotsam which carried me ashore? I do not know. My next clear memory is of the sun on my back and my fingers flexing on warm, grey sand. That and a voice breaking into my brain.

'*Quién es usted?*'

Something was prodding my shoulder. Lifting my head slowly, I saw a sword point. Attached to the other end of the weapon was a bearded man in part armour and helmet. Another stood by his side. They were Spanish soldiers.

3

The prodding continued and the question (for I knew it must be a question, though I could not understand it) was repeated.

'Quién es usted?'

I groaned and tried to stagger to my feet. I made a poor job of it; my legs were too weak.

The soldiers held a brief conversation, then they grabbed me roughly, one by each arm and forced me, at a shambling march, up the beach. Beyond the sand a narrow track entered the belt of thick woodland which, as I already knew, covered most of the isthmus. Along the path we stumbled. I was gradually recovering from my exertions but deliberately gave no sign of this to my captors. Ahead of us, as I knew full well, lay Cadiz, prison and torture. Since I was in no hurry to encounter any of these I delayed progress as much as I could. I sagged drunkenly and tripped over every boulder and fallen branch which lay in my way.

My mind was working more clearly now. I realised that if I was to escape at all it must be somewhere in these woods. The Spaniards had obviously been taken in by my exaggerated exhaustion. They had not even bothered to remove my sword, so sure were they that I was too weak to use it. If I could muster a sudden spurt of energy I would take them by surprise and I might have just enough strength to lose them among the trees.

I looked more closely at my guards, trying to assess their relative capabilities. The thick-set heavily-jowled fellow on my right had a grip like the jaws of a terrier but I reckoned he would have no great speed or agility. His bearded companion was much more lithe. He balanced himself well on the balls of his feet and was constantly on the alert, glancing about him as he went. It would be no easy matter to outsmart him. I noticed that when the path became too narrow or when some obstacle obliged us to march in single file it was this smaller man who went ahead. I decided that I must try my luck on one of these occasions.

I was looking ahead to locate a suitable spot when suddenly the firm grip on my right arm was relaxed. The large man fell forward and lay writhing on the ground. A gash in his back was spurting blood. I turned. Two of the *Swiftsure*'s sailors stood on the track behind us, knives drawn. They had sprung from each side of the path behind us and had fatally surprised one of my guardians. The small Spaniard was too quick for them; moving with great agility he drew his sword and faced the attackers. He could have turned and run. Instead he threw me to the ground and faced the seamen across me with defiance and hatred.

I tried to scuttle out of the way but a kick in the chest sent me sprawling again. My comrades advanced slowly, their swords now drawn but I was in their way and the Spaniard's deft feints and passes kept them at bay. He was a fine swordsman, that Spanish soldier. He seemed to have three pairs of eyes and while engaging the blades of my would-be rescuers he kept me firmly under control. The sailors saw this, too.

'Tom, work your way round behind him through those bushes. He ain't got eyes in the back of his head.'

Tom did as he was bidden. My captor backed up against a wide tree trunk turning sideways on to the path so that he could watch both assailants. He kept one foot on my leg.

'Rush him now!'

From my strange viewpoint I saw the Spaniard with incredible speed lunge to the right, slashing Tom's upper arm while ducking to avoid the attack from the other direction. Then he turned to his left.

For the first time he momentarily forgot about me. I got to my knees. Snatching my sword from its sheath, I held the hilt in both hands and thrust upwards. I aimed for the stomach just below his corselet but my grip was unsteady. The point took him between the legs, went right up through his body and emerged at his neck. It was like spitting a chicken. His expression froze. Blood spouted freely. It cascaded down his armour. It flowed over my hands. For what seemed an age he did not move. Then, slowly, he toppled forward. I fell back on the path, my enemy's corpse pinning me to the ground. His parted lips brushed mine in a bloody, lifeless kiss. I screamed.

My mind was so numbed by the horror of my first killing that Robin's anger which burst on me half an hour or so later made little impression. Mechanically, I had helped the two sailors conceal the bodies in deep undergrowth and remove all trace of the struggle, then I had been taken to the place where the shore party was camped. In a small clearing stood the two upturned boats and around them clusters of men talking, dicing or sleeping. Robin, Sir John Frensham and the other gentlemen were, as usual in a group apart. I was marched up to them and my adventure was related.

Robin cursed me roundly for several minutes, revealing his embarrassment as well as his anger. Did I not realise I had probably jeopardised the expedition? What would happen when the two soldiers failed to report back to their barracks? The whole isthmus would be combed by troops. Even if we were not discovered the garrison would be on the alert.

The torrent of recrimination flowed on but I scarcely heard it. I was still wiping my lips with the back of my hand trying to remove the taste of death.

This infuriated Robin all the more. He reached out to grasp my arm but I backed away.

'By God, boy, I see I must teach you to do as you are told!'

I met his gaze.

'That will be hard, my lord. I have learned disobedience from a master of the craft.'

With those words I walked to the other side of the glade and threw myself down on a bed of ferns.

Robin's fears proved unfounded. Though extra guards were posted there was no sign of activity from the city. In mid-afternoon the two disguised men who had been sent to spy out the shipping in the harbour returned. They both spoke Spanish and had, to judge by the welcome they received from the gentlemen, done a useful job.

Shortly afterwards bread and beer were distributed. I did not go forward for mine but one of the sailors brought some over to me.

'Best eat, lad. No man can fight on an empty stomach.'

He sat on a rock beside me and made sure I followed his advice. He was a fatherly sort of man and when I discovered that I had an appetite after all it gave him as much satisfaction as me.

'Been hearing all about you, lad. You did a good job. I reckon every man who kills one of them papist bastards deserves a knighthood.'

He took a long draught of beer.

'I had a brother. Good seaman he was. Sailed with Drake once. Till he was caught by the Inquisition. Do you know what they did to poor Ned?'

He needed no reply, just someone to listen. And perhaps I needed someone to talk. Someone to tell me about the horrors of the Inquisition, the escapades of young Ned, the tribulations of Uncle Simon, the hard life of Dartmoor hill farmers, the ambitions of a forty-year-old sailor, hoping to return from a voyage rich in booty and buy his own land, so that his son ('just about your age, lad') would never have to go to sea.

At dusk the company was assembled. Weapons were checked and we formed up in our two boat companies. The upturned vessels were lying across the oars and with one man to each oar's end they were lifted quite easily. With much slithering, grunting and muffled cursing we made our way through the darkening wood towards the inner harbour.

We set the boats afloat without mishap. The oar blades were now wrapped in strips of cloth to muffle their sound. We embarked and pulled slowly towards Puntales Point overlooking the narrow strait between the two expanses of sheltered water. I knew that there was a guard post there. Unless the soldiers were asleep they must see us. Would they let us pass or would we be forced to land and silence them? We sailed close inshore so as not to appear suspicious. Squares of light revealed the position of the guard house. As we drew abreast a challenge rang out. Immediately the reply went back in Spanish.

'Men of the *San Felipe* returning from Puerto Real.'

'Have you left any women for us? Good night and good voyage.'

'Thank you. Peaceful watch. Good night.'

'Good night.'

Ahead of us we could now see the lights of the city and, less distinctly, the lamps of ships anchored offshore. We pulled into the centre of the channel. Our objective was three ships, already laden and moored in mid-stream awaiting armed escort before venturing into the pirate-infested ocean. Slowly we drew closer to our first victim, closer to the business of slaughter. I felt again those immobile, blood-moist lips on mine. Furiously I rubbed my mouth with my shirt sleeve. The sensation would not go away.

The shape of a large hull detached itself from the surrounding blackness. She was, I later learned, the *Santa Maria de Lisboa*, a Portuguese merchantman. The other boat disappeared into the deep shadow of the ship's side. Our rowers rested on their oars. We all strained our ears and just detected the faint sounds of barefooted men climbing aboard. For several minutes no noise competed with the soft licking of the waves. Then there was a whispered call from the *Santa Maria*'s deck. Once more the oars pulled at the water and we went in search of our next quarry.

The *San Felipe* was taken in the same way and the rest of us rowed on to find and win the third prize, the *Concepción*. As we drew near we heard singing and the screech of a viol. The few men left aboard were obviously enjoying themselves, which made it easier for us to bump alongside and clamber over the gunwale unheard. I found myself deliberately hanging back until urged forward by the men behind. The sounds of merriment had come to an abrupt end before I reached the deck. A lantern attached to the mainmast dimly lit up the swift movements of the Englishmen and the six Spaniards who would move no more. They had had no chance to defend themselves nor to cry out.

I kept in the shadows near the foredeck but there was no

37

escaping the Cyclops-like vigilance of Master Kendall, who led our boarding party.

'Come aft with me, boy.'

He entered the great cabin. Slowly I picked my way across the sprawled bodies on the slippery deck to follow him through the open door. In the dim interior I saw Kendall bending to peer under a table set against the far wall. I also saw what he did not, a Spaniard in the centre of the cabin with poniard raised above the master's arched back. Without hesitation I ran the man through. Kendall spun round, took in the scene, and strode from the cabin with a muttered, 'Good lad', as he passed me. Later that night, as we were clearing and washing the main deck, I found a broken viol in the lee scuppers. I kept it for many years as a reminder that even killing can become a habit.

The rest of Essex's plan worked almost to perfection. Before the first rays of the sun touched the mastheads men were posted on the spars ready to loose the sails. Others were all set with axes to sever the anchor cables. When the roar of the *Swiftsure*'s guns shattered the morning calm we rushed into action. First the *Santa Maria*, then our *Concepción* caught the offshore breeze and eased out into the centre of the bay. The harbour garrison had now opened fire on the English intruder. Between the boom of the guns I could clearly hear the shouts of the people on the waterfront and on the other ships. Looking back I beheld a scene of laughable confusion – the quayside filling with running, gesticulating figures, other vessels trying to follow our 'example' and getting hopelessly tangled up with each other in the process.

The *Swiftsure* turned to lead the way out between the deadly shoals of Las Puercas and El Diaman. Gathering speed by the minute we followed and a spontaneous cheer went up as we passed out of range of the harbour guns. The *San Felipe* was not so fortunate. She had difficulty finding a wind and was some half a mile astern of us as we struck the first waves beyond the harbour. The Matagorda battery opened up on her. For some minutes it seemed she might escape. Then we saw the top of her mainmast go overboard. She slewed sideways and we knew she was done for. There was no question of going back. We could only pray that our fifteen comrades would die in the fighting rather than fall into the hands of Philip's agents or the Grand Inquisitor.

For the loss of fifteen men we had obtained two very serviceable ships laden with wine, armaments and other supplies for which the Duke of Parma, Governor of the Spanish Netherlands, was anxiously waiting. It was not the gold and silver I had always dreamed of winning by maritime adventure but it was a useful haul in terms of the overall strategy of the Spanish war. Essex and the other leaders were well pleased and felt they could now cheerfully seek a rendezvous with Drake.

Their attitude towards me changed after the Cadiz raid. Not a word was said and I would be hard put to it to explain just how my status had altered. Yet altered it had; they knew and I knew that I had passed some informal initiation. No more was I summoned with the cry 'Pretty boy!' and when I asked questions about matters of navigation or warfare I found that Captain Williams and even Master Kendall were prepared to answer instead of sending me on my way with a throbbing ear. As for Robin, so far from holding my folly and insubordination against me, he seemed to take an almost paternal pride in my exploits.

After a few days westward and northward cruising our little flotilla came up with the main English force off Oporto. Robin had transferred to the *Santa Maria*, taking me with him and we stood together on the forecastle gazing at the brave sight of a hundred or more sail spread across the sea before us. I noticed that Robin was frowning and I guessed he was anxious about the forthcoming interview with the admiral.

'Robin, will you take me with you when you go over to the flagship?'

'You want to meet the great hero, do you?'

'Very much.'

'And if I say no you will doubtless swim across to the flagship anyway?'

We laughed, then Robin went on.

'Yes, you may come as my page. We will dress you up in some of those Spanish fineries from that chest in the captain's cabin. We must look our best for the great Sir Francis.'

'You sound as though you like him not.'

'Drake?' He pondered a moment. 'Have you seen Sir Christopher Hatton's pet monkey?'

'The one he sometimes has on a lead at court?'

'Yes. You know that monkey has at least a dozen changes of clothes, all made by the finest tailor in London. Well, Drake reminds me of that monkey. He wears his fame and wealth as badly as that poor beast wears his magnificent clothes. He makes a great show of culture and learning. Even at sea he dines off gold plate and is accompanied by a suite of servants and musicians. But beneath all the finery he is still a rural clod and he cannot hide it.'

'He is a brilliant navigator.'

'Yes, and a good captain. And for that I readily forgive him his airs and graces. I tell you all this so that you will not be disappointed.'

When, towards dusk, we stood on the poop deck of the *Revenge* and I was face to face, at last, with the greatest Englishman of the age, I was glad Robin had warned me. I might otherwise have been overcome by the incongruity of the luxury with which Drake surrounded himself.

It was a warm evening and an awning of yellow silk had been rigged up. Beneath this sat the admiral in a heavily carved armchair. Three liveried pages were ranged behind, ready to fulfil his slightest wish. Silver goblets and ewers stood before him on a table covered with a Turkey carpet. Several supernumeraries stood around in deferential silence. What tinged the whole setting with absurdity was the fact that Drake had no need of the impressive paraphernalia of power. Authority radiated from the man like heat from the sun. The penetrating eyes, the aggressive thrust of the beard, even the way the short, thickset body sat – not lolling, not relaxed, but alert, assertive, seeming ready to spring from the chair without warning – compelled respect. Here was a man to follow round the world, and back again.

I was soon dismissed, along with all other attendants, while Essex and Drake talked privately. At supper with the *Revenge*'s crew I made quite a nuisance of myself by firing question after question at Drake's men. What was he like to serve under? Had any of them fought the Armada with him? Were there any men there who had been round the world on the *Golden Hind*? Some of the mariners told their stories willingly enough and I listened with total fascination until the time came to return to my own ship.

As we were rowed back to the *Santa Maria*, Robin told me with no hint of dismay in his voice, that her Majesty was gravely displeased with us and demanded our immediate return.

'Drake is sending us back, then?' I was bitterly disappointed at the prospect of not seeing action under the admiral's leadership.

'Well, Bear cub, Sir Francis and I have reached an understanding. You see, he needs every man he can muster for the attack on Lisbon.'

'Lisbon?'

'Yes. In two days we take the coastal fortress at Peniche. Then we land the troops. They march to Lisbon with Don Antonio rallying his loyal people along the route. Meanwhile Drake takes the fleet up the Tagus. We mount a land and sea assault, enter the city and place Don Antonio on the throne.'

'And with Portugal independent again, King Philip loses half his navy and all his west coast ports.'

'Exactly. It is an excellent plan and I have no intention of not being part of it.'

'But how . . . ?'

'How, indeed. That is the question Drake has been asking himself. Fortunately, nature has answered it for him. It is quite obvious to Sir Francis and me that with these violent north-easterly squalls an immediate return to England is out of the question.'

We laughed as we looked ahead to the Portuguese prize whose limp sails and pennants drooped in the moonlight.

Peniche presented its boldest face to the sea. As the swarm of boats rode shorewards with the heavy swell, all that could be seen of the town was the severe, grey walls of the fortress topping a cliff of sheer crumbling sandstone. From this eminence the land fell unevenly away in thinly-grassed dunes. There was no sign of life on the battlements whose outline wavered in a slight heat haze. There was no sound above the soft thunder of the breakers.

Until the first boats were within fifty yards of the beach. Then the Spaniards opened up with all their artillery. The next boat to ours threw its stern in the air as a cannon ball smashed straight through the bows. All the men not killed by the impact quickly sank weighted down by armour and weapons. Everywhere I looked there were spouts of water, broken oars and struggling figures. Suddenly our boat was no longer surging forward. The oarsmen were out of sequence. Some, petrified with fear, had stopped rowing completely. Robin turned from his position in the bow. Shouting furious threats and waving his sword, he urged the frightened men back into action.

We were still a dozen yards from the breakers when Robin, with a cry of defiance leaped into the water. I followed him and was almost dragged down by the strong undertow. Seconds later, Robin and I stood side by side on the sand, the first Englishmen ashore. The gunfire had stopped. The defenders were shortening the range of their cannon. While they did so our men assembled in two groups, one under Essex, the other led by Sir John Norris.

Norris took his men off towards the dunes to the right. We ran forward to the cliff. Finding paths or making our own, we scrambled upward. It was hot, choking, dusty work. How the pikemen managed with their twelve foot long encumbrances I do not know. We arrived, panting and disorganised at the top to find a small detachment of Spanish soldiers lunging at us with swords and pikes. Many of our lads were sent crashing back down the rocks with gashed limbs and split heads. But we had fanned out in a long line for our climb and were able to turn the enemy's right flank.

The Spaniards fell back towards the town. We formed a solid square of pikemen and prepared to charge. Before we could do so Sir John Norris's men came marching up from the south. Seeing themselves greatly outnumbered the Spaniards turned and fled towards the gateway behind them. At that the English soldiers broke ranks and raced towards Peniche, shouting, jostling, elbowing each other out of the way in their anxiety to reach the town first. I turned to where Essex stood with his officers, standard bearer and trumpeters. Surely he would signal the retreat or somehow reassert authority over this rabble. He made no move; neither did Norris nor any of the other captains.

Minutes later we made our way into the town against a torrent of terrified civilians rushing out. Children, hobbling old men, screaming women with babies in their arms, a peasant trying to drag a reluctant goat to safety, a half-naked girl pursued by three soldiers, a priest with bloodstained face picking up the skirts of his cassock and running on shaky legs. As we walked the streets of the unimpressive little town I saw that not a single building remained unvisited by the victors. They made a bee-line for the churches, emerging with gilt crosses and chalices, jewelled reliquaries, altar frontals and vestments. They smashed the coloured windows and the statues of the Virgin. From shops and houses they grabbed whatever they could find, stuffing pouches and filling helmets with a variety of objects which would be evaluated later. When they had had their fill of looting and raping they repaired to the taverns and drank themselves stupid on free wine.

From a window in the house requisitioned by the officers I watched the debauchery and senseless violence in the streets below. Generals planned strategy, I reflected, and politicians talked of just and holy causes but in the last analysis this was what war was all about.

Next day we set out to march the forty-fives miles to Lisbon. Horses had been found for the officers and for the 'King' of Portugal who rode proudly at the head of the army. Poor Don Antonio, he was not a very impressive figure. A stocky man in his mid-fifties, he looked more like a prosperous grocer than a monarch invested with divine right. For years he had lived on Queen Elizabeth's charity, canvassing support among her ministers for his return to power. Now that his great day had come he was far from happy. He complained bitterly about the behaviour of the soldiers at Peniche – behaviour which was repeated at every town and village along the way. How could he obtain the support of his people, he demanded, if he came at the head of an army of heretics who destroyed churches and deflowered women?

Don Antonio and the English generals certainly had problems but soon I was oblivious to them. As we ambled along the hot, dusty road I became uncomfortably aware of a pain in my stomach and a throbbing head. The discomfort grew worse and when I hurriedly dismounted to relieve myself behind a pile of rocks I was seized with a violent fit of vomiting. Afterwards I had to be helped back onto my horse. I remember no more of the Lisbon campaign.

Fantasies and hazy images filled the next few weeks of my life. The only constant factors were searing heat, intolerable pain and a hearty longing for death. Then, suddenly, I was lying in my bed on the *Swiftsure* and I could see quite clearly all the features of the great cabin. I could also see the cheerful, weather-beaten face of the seaman sitting beside me.

'Feeling better, lad?'

I nodded weakly.

'You're among the lucky ones. Hundreds died of the flux in that damned hell hole.'

He stood up.

'I must go and report to the master of the watch. My orders are to let him know as soon as you wake.'

The master of the watch, as it turned out, was Kendall, scarcely the man I would have requested to sit by my sick-bed. He smiled down at me, an experience so unusual as to be alarming.

'Where are we?' I asked.

'In $43\frac{1}{2}$ degrees, off Corunna, bearing nor-nor-east. We should make Plymouth in a week.'

'How long . . .'

'Twenty-three days, lad.'

I struggled to remember.

'Then I missed the capture of Lisbon?'

Kendall laughed contemptuously.

'You missed nothing, lad, nothing except the most ungodly shambles that ever went under the name of a military campaign.'

He sat down and told me everything that had gone wrong.

Men falling like flies because they would guzzle themselves on stolen food and wine. The Portuguese peasants, who should have welcomed their deliverers with open arms, running away to hide in the hills. The generals blaming Don Antonio and Don Antonio blaming the generals. Lisbon proving impossible to take without cannon and the ships not arriving until the army was demoralised and decimated by fever and sunstroke. Drake ordering a withdrawal and Essex arguing with him angrily in front of the men. The *Swiftsure* sent home to return the troublesome earl to his anxious queen.

I must have fallen asleep at this point for the next thing I recall is Robin's face gazing down from the place where the Master's had been.

'You are a stubborn fighter, Bear cub. The surgeon gave you up days ago but I told him Dudleys don't die that easily.'

'Kendall tells me the Lisbon campaign was a mess.'

'Yes, your hero decided he would rather go off to the Azores to chase Spanish treasure ships.'

I decided on a tactful change of subject.

'Will the Queen be angry when we get back?'

Robin laughed heartily.

'Angry? Never. I promise you we shall be welcomed like a pair of prodigals – especially when she sees what presents we have brought her.'

'The prize ships?'

'Not only the ships.'

He stood up and walked through into his own cabin. Moments later he returned with a small bundle wrapped in silk. He sat down again and carefully removed the coverings of his parcel. I saw a small casket, gold or silver-gilt; it was difficult to tell in the half-light. It was studded all over with a profusion of jewels – emeralds, rubies, carbuncles, agates, pearls – set in no semblance of pattern.

'Is that not a royal gift, Bear cub? I found it in the garrison chapel at Peniche when we took the castle. It contained a few bits of dried out cedar wood. Some gibbering monk tried to tell me they were pieces of the true cross. "In that case," I said, "we will test their sanctity by fire." '

Robin chuckled.

'And do you know, when we threw those bits of wood on the brazier in the guard room they burned very prettily.'

He turned the box in his hands.

'Yes, this should salve her Majesty's indignation. These emeralds alone will make a magnificent necklace. Do you not think so?'

But my thinking was confused. I had images of drunken, uncontrolled soldiers, of fat priests living off the superstitions of the people, of desecrated churches, of solemn-faced chaplains urging men to fight for the true faith, of generations of simple peasants venerating centuries old relics, of generals who protested that war was a sacred calling for gentlemen and then used war to enrich themselves with gold and jewels. Were these the broken fragments of a picture which somehow interlocked? If so, I could not fit them together.

4

Robin was right about our welcome at court. The Queen was relieved to see her favourite safely returned and everyone in the palace was eager for first-hand news of the grand English armada. I found myself suddenly and unexpectedly the centre of attention, not least from some of the Queen's younger maids of honour. I had now much more to do with the men and women who were closest to the throne. The household was rather like one of the fascinating carved ivory globes which come from the Orient, in which a succession of hollow balls moves one inside the other. From the outside, glimpses of the innermost sphere can be gained but to observe its pattern in detail the observer would have to penetrate each of the intervening layers in turn. The court was just such an elegant succession of revolving spheres in which all members longed to be nearer the centre and only those at the centre really knew the Queen's private life and the people who influenced her public decisions. Shortly after my return I was appointed to the staff of the Privy Chamber. Now I was often present while the Queen entertained ministers, noblemen and ambassadors in private. I knew, or was in a position to know, everyone who had access to the royal presence. Most of them I had seen before but only through the ivory lattice.

Among those notables I saw at close quarters for the first time was Sir Walter Raleigh. I was disposed to dislike the man, for the little I knew about him was unappealing. He strutted like a peacock, gaudy and arrogant, losing no opportunity to display himself and assert his importance, though he must have known his absurd airs were a standing court joke. I especially despised him for his extravagant claims regarding maritime adventure and discovery which were based on the most meagre achievements. For what had he accomplished – an abortive attempt at English settlement in Virginia and the financing of some privateering captains who were indiscriminate in their plundering of ships on the high seas. Now, as everyone knew, he was bent on following up a wild mariner's tale about 'El Dorado', a gilded man who ruled some fabulous land of gold far up the Orinoco. But I had other reasons for being wary of Sir Walter: he had been no friend of my father and he and Robin were sworn enemies.

Robin's flight in the *Swiftsure* had been a godsend to his rival. Raleigh had ingratiated himself with Elizabeth and played upon her anger at the earl's disobedience. Robin's return to favour could only result in a direct clash. It was not long in coming.

One day in July the Queen was dining privately at Greenwich; which meant that there were no more than a dozen people at her board in the Privy Chamber. Old Lord Burghley was there in his usual place on her Majesty's right. Robin sat on her left. Raleigh was also of the company. I was busy, examining the dishes as they arrived after their long journey from the kitchens, making sure everything was clean, and the right temperature, ensuring that each course was accompanied by its appropriate relish. I paid little attention to the cheerful flow of conversation around the table, until I heard my own name mentioned.

Robin was regaling the company with the, much embellished, story of my escapade at Cadiz. His narrative was greeted by a clatter of applause. The Queen cast an appraising glance in my direction.

'The Bear's whelp grows quickly like his sire, Robin.'

'Indeed, your Majesty, he is a very Turk in battle.'

'Hush, Robin. See what a colour you are bringing to the lad's cheeks.'

At this point Raleigh made some remark to his neighbours which gave rise to a chorus of laughter at his end of the table. The Queen turned towards the noise.

'What is this, Sir Walter, some private joke, not for our ears?'

'It was nothing your Majesty.'

'Then we will hear this nothing.'

'I remarked, your Majesty, that Master Dudley might have some other cause for blushing.'

The Queen looked puzzled.

'Can you explain that enigmatic remark, cousin?'

'Your Majesty, would surely not press me to be so indelicate. We all know why my lord of Essex is always accompanied on campaign by fresh-faced young boys.'

Instantly Robin was on his feet, shouting that Raleigh was a foul-mouthed liar and that he would prove it with his sword.

His rival was unmoved. The very vehemence of Essex's denial, he suggested, might be taken by some as proving the common rumour true. At this, Robin made to move from his place. He was halted by the Queen's high-pitched voice.

'My lord, you forget yourself. Our Privy Chamber is no place for a tavern brawl.'

'Your Majesty, I cannot . . .'

'You can, Robin, if we so command.'

She smiled, revealing a row of discoloured teeth.

'We will resolve this matter in the garden. Sir Walter, my lord of Essex, you will walk with us there alone.'

The Queen rose. As the company made its bows and curtsies she walked slowly from the room flanked by her two gallants. I heard later that some sort of truce was patched up but it came as no surprise when, a few days later, Raleigh was sent off to join the army in Ireland.

This unpleasant incident was the prelude to my first *affaire de coeur*. The guests had left the room and I was supervising the clearing of the tables and buffets. Some of the Queen's ladies, unexpectedly discharged from attendance on her Majesty, apparently had nothing better to do than get in my way. Four of them danced around me giggling and taunting me.

'Little Turk!'

'Look at the fierce soldier!'

'Hush, my dear, you're making him blush!'

I ignored them as long as I could – which was about thirty seconds. Then – as of course they intended – I gave chase. I had already singled out the one I wanted and after a few breathless minutes of rushing through doorways and skidding past disapproving court dignitaries, I had her pinned against the clothes press in an unused bedchamber. She was a dark-haired, coquettish girl of my own age, a newcomer to the household, and her name was Margaret Cavendish. She looked up at me with mischievous eyes.

'Well, my victorious captain, what are you going to do now?'

And so the first, fumbling kiss of youth; the one still remembered when the thousands of more accomplished embraces are beyond recall. It was repaid at a usurious rate of interest, but when I fumbled my hand inside her dress she slipped out of my embrace.

'Oh no, my brave general, this citadel does not fall at the first salvo.'

She smiled and took my hand. Thus linked we wandered out into the gardens and down to the river. There, while coasters and merchant vessels sailed out of the estuary on an ebb tide, Margaret told me about herself, her home in Suffolk, her upbringing in the Earl of Oxford's household, how she had always wanted to be a boy – till now.

'Why did you want to be a boy?'

'Oh many reasons. I have no brothers, just two sisters, and we are a great disappointment to our father. Besides boys can do all kinds of things that girls cannot.'

'Such as?'

'Such as going to sea.'

I laughed so heartily at the thought of this pretty, dainty creature swaying about in the top of a ship's rigging that she became very cross and walked quickly away from me along the bank. When I caught up with her she looked at me her eyes aglow with reproach and brows furrowed.

'Girls may know nothing about the sea but Cavendishes do.'

'You mean Thomas Cavendish ...'

'He is my cousin. His family lives in the same village.'

If there had been any doubt a few minutes before, it now vanished; I knew I was in love with Margaret. Any girl who was related to the circumnavigator was worth knowing intimately. Thomas Cavendish had sailed into Plymouth within weeks of the defeat of the Armada, having been round the world in a mere twenty-six months. His achievement was the flourishing signature on the document of English naval supremacy written by Admiral Howard and his captains. I bombarded Margaret with questions until she petulantly remarked that I was more interested in her cousin than I was in her.

She was partly right. Though I was very fond of Margaret, I fervently hoped that one result of our relationship would be a meeting with Cousin Thomas. That meeting at last came about in the following winter. My Uncle Ambrose died in February 1590 and I was released from my duties at court for a short time in order to attend to the family and legal arrangements which now fell upon me. I moved immediately to my new house in the Strand. There I received visits from scores of people who came to offer their condolences and to satisfy their curiosity about the master of the Dudley estates.

Thus it was that Thomas Cavendish sat before me in the parlour of Bedford House one blustering March morning when the wind threw rain and hail against the casement. While he stretched long limbs towards the fire, expressing his family's gratitude for the kindnesses I had shown young Margaret and their sorrow at the double loss I had sustained in so short a time, I carefully studied the man who had seen sights and lands that were only legends to ordinary mortals. The contrast with Drake could scarcely have been more marked. Though he was twice my age his face was still youthful. His blue eyes were those of a dreamer. It was difficult to imagine this man hacking his way through ranks of painted American savages as he had done when helping to found the Virginia colony or severely confronting disgruntled mariners bent on mutiny. Yet what he lacked in inner strength he more than made up for in vision. On the subject of trade with the Orient he spoke with the fervour and reasoned conviction of a Jesuit priest. In that drab chamber whose fire did little to combat the chill draughts which rippled the rushes and stirred the heavy tapestries, he made me see sunlit clove plantations, the gaily-painted merchant ships of Cathay and the glittering open air courts of Javanese sultans. He stayed to dinner and well into the afternoon. Before he left we were firm friends and I had promised to visit him and his wife at their house at Chelsea.

In fact, throughout the following summer and autumn I paid several visits to Chelsea where the rambling, stone building and the riverside lawns rang with the boisterous laughter of Cavendish's three young sons. Sometimes Margaret and I were able to be absent from court together and could enjoy one another's company away from the sly winks and bawdy innuendoes of our colleagues.

Scarcely less delightful to me were the occasions when Margaret was not present. The afternoons were usually monopolised by Richard, Ned and Andrew who were indefatigable in devising games in which their 'Uncle Rob' was cast in the role of war horse, boat or hunted stag. The evenings were long and devoted by common consent to maritime affairs. Most of Thomas's other guests were men of the sea; some, like Captain Williams, I already knew, others such as John Davis and Matthew Baker – men who were to have a profound influence on my life – I met for the first time under Thomas's roof.

Davis and Baker were, in fact, the only others present at supper one evening the following December. The meal passed pleasantly, as usual, but I was aware of a slight tension in the atmosphere and this feeling was reinforced when, in the solar afterwards, Jane Cavendish made an excuse and left the room. No matter who was present she usually stayed and joined in the conversation. Sometimes she played to us on the virginals. But on this night she pointedly left the gentlemen alone with their wine. For some minutes we chatted inconsequentially. Then Thomas said, with a badly contrived nonchalance,

'John Davis and I are planning another expedition.'

I expressed my interest and waited to hear what else Thomas had to tell me.

'Two expeditions really. As you know John is anxious to find the North-West Passage round America.'

I knew well Captain Davis's passionate desire to discover the northern straits which would provide Englishmen with a short route to the Orient. I had read with fascination the accounts of his fearful experiences in the desolation of ice and snow beyond Greenland.

'We plan to journey together through the Straits of Magellan and up the western coast of America. Off Peru and New Spain we should find enough rich prizes to pay for all the costs of the expedition. Then, in about 35° we shall part company. John intends to continue northwards and find the Straits of Anian, the far end of the North-West Passage. I shall cross the Pacific to the Spice Islands and open up trade with all the princes who are longing to do business with England – Canton, Ternate, Java – Robert, it's an untapped source of wealth. If we can find the short route, then all the silks, porcelain and spices of Cathay and the eastern islands are open to us.'

'Aye, but Englishmen are too blind to see it.'

Davis's thick Devon accent was not easy to understand.

Thomas explained.

'John's right. We have spent months looking for backers.'

'But surely there are many gentlemen and courtiers who would be only too happy to take shares in such a venture.'

Davis's speech was always coarse. Now it was both coarse and bitter.

'God's blood, lad, are you so stupid you don't know that the strutting bastards of the court and the ermined pigs of the City are only interested in one thing – gold? There are no treasure galleons in the north Pacific so we can whistle for money. We can risk our lives, our ships, our men until we've opened the way to Cathay then they'll rush like swine to the swill bucket, these fine gentlemen, jostling each other to reach the riches of the East.'

He petered out in a string of oaths, then sat looking at me morosely. All three of them were looking at me. Slowly it dawned on me what was in their minds.

'So you want me . . .'

Thomas was quick to interrupt.

'Robert, you must not think we are just trying to take advantage of you because you are young and wealthy. But you see this venture must be properly equipped. That is why we have asked Matthew, here, to design ships especially for us. We could scrape together some sort of fleet but it would never come safe home. No, we must have at least three new capital ships of 400 tons or more. And for that, I fear, we need wealthy patrons.'

He looked so solemn and anxious – they all did – that I could scarcely refrain from laughing.

'My dear Thomas, you know how much I share your hopes and plans. I should be honoured to back your venture – on one condition.'

'Name it.'

'Take me with you.'

Thomas looked doubtful.

'Will the Queen allow you . . .'

'I think I can arrange that. Now, tell me more about your voyage.'

With mounting excitement I looked at their charts and maps and at the plans Matthew Baker had drawn up for the new ships. Baker, who was simply the finest shipwright in England, was a man of few words until the conversation turned to questions of the size and proportion of ships, their speed, sail area, sheathing, cargo-space and armament. Then everyone else fell silent and listened to the master. Before I was rowed back to Westminster late that night all our plans had been agreed in outline. It only remained for me to ask Robin to speak to the Queen on my behalf and I could make my own preparations to join the third great voyage of circumnavigation.

I fear I gave my friend little peace. As soon as I could get him alone I told him my news. He did not seem very enthusiastic but, at last, agreed to present my petition to her Majesty. After that, whenever I saw him I pestered him to know whether he had broached the subject. He told me to be patient. It was no use rushing these matters. One had to await the opportune moment.

Patience has never been among my virtues. It was certainly a stranger to me at the age of sixteen. At last Robin told me that if I trusted his judgement so little he would see me in hell before he assisted me in this matter. It was, in fact, about a fortnight later that I received a message late at night summoning me to Robin's quarters, adjacent to the Queen's.

I found him sprawled in a chair before the fire in his bed-chamber. He had been playing cards and drinking with the Queen and was very flushed. He waved me to a chair. When he spoke he did not look at me but stared at the glowing sea coals.

'I am sorry, Bear cub, the answer is no.'

The effect of those few words was shattering. It was as though they had drawn a heavy curtain across the bright future I had set out for myself. I felt shut in, excluded from the only thing in life that really mattered. Robin saw my intense disappointment.

'You must not take it to heart. She had good reasons for refusing.'

'What reasons?' I almost shouted the words at him.

'I cannot tell you.'

'What do you mean, you cannot tell me? The Queen wants to keep me at court like a useless lap-dog and you cannot tell me why.'

'She says you are too young.'

'But that is not the real reason?'

He did not reply immediately, but held a pomander to his nose, looked at me keenly while he sniffed it, then sat back and half closed his eyes. At last he said,

'If you want to know the truth, you are asking me to break a confidence: a royal confidence.' He got up and walked to the end of the room. 'That is something I would not do for any other man living.' He seemed to be trying to make up his mind whether or not to tell me what he knew. Finally he came slowly back and resumed his seat. When he spoke his voice was distant and dreamy.

'About a year ago I was alone with the Queen in her bed-chamber at Windsor. It was raining, she had a cold and was maudlin. I did my best to cheer her, but in vain: she kept on talking about the past, when she was young and could hunt all day and dance all night. She spoke a lot about Leicester. You know that she would have married your father if it hadn't been for Burghley and the Council?'

55

I nodded.

'Then she showed me a casket – a pretty little thing, gold and studded with pearls and emeralds. Did I not want to see her treasures, she asked. Of course I said that I was burning with curiosity.'

'And what were they, her treasures?'

'Letters. Nothing but letters – and all written by your father. Oh, yes, and in the bottom of the box his picture, done by Hilliard in a gold frame. She held it up, kissed it and laid it on the table. "There is my only true love," says she.'

'But the Queen loves you, all the world knows that,' I protested.

'Oh, Her Majesty's aged heart is wide.' He said this with a tone of scornful bitterness. 'Naturally, I pretended to be furious, telling her that she should live in the present, not the past. "Be sure that I *do*," she said, and fetched another portrait from her bedside, to lay next to Leicester's. And patting it, she says, "My Darling is not dead. Look."'

He stopped speaking, and I found him fixing me with a speculative stare.

'What then?'

He smiled wanly. 'The likeness is uncommon, Bear cub. You must look just as your father did when Elizabeth first fell in love with him.'

My head swam as I tried to sort out the implications of what I had just heard. If the Queen wanted to keep me near to remind her of her lost love I would be powerless to break away until I came of age – and that was nearly five years away. And what might happen in those five years. If Robin's description of the Queen's feelings for me were correct might not he and I unwillingly become rivals, insulting and plotting against each other just as he and Raleigh did now?

Robin came across and laid a hand on my shoulder.

'Get some sleep, Bear cub. Things will not look quite so black in the morning. After all, life at court is not that bad. There's always Margaret.'

As I recall things *did*, in fact, look pretty black for several days. I had to face my friends and tell them not only that the Queen

56

would not allow me to join the expedition but that she refused to allow me to invest in it. On this last part, however, I did have some success. I appealed directly to Lord Burghley, the Master of the Wards. He would not permit me to finance any new ships but he did agree that I might fit out the *Leicester*, a 400 ton vessel that had belonged to my father. Thus I kept a stake in the great voyage and was allowed to share in the plans of Cavendish and Davis right until the time of their departure the following August. I even went down to Plymouth to see them weigh anchor. I seriously contemplated repeating the escapade of my last visit to this port but I knew only too well how the Queen's vindictiveness might be brought to bear on my friends and their families. So, I returned to court, a frustrated youth longing to lay firm hands on his own destiny but unable to do so. I slipped back into the old routine and there were certainly many distractions – dances, banquets, masques, plays, hunting expeditions – to take a young man's mind off his troubles. And there was always Margaret.

5

My sweetest Lesbia let us live and love,
And, though the sager sort our deeds reprove,
    Let us not weigh them. Heaven's great lamps do dive
Into their west and straight again revive.
But soon as once set is our little light
Then we must sleep one ever during night,
    Ever during night.

That lovely song of Tom Campion's, one of Essex's protégés,
always comes to my mind when I think of Margaret. It was her
favourite and I often sang it to her, accompanying myself rather
clumsily on the lute. For we had embarked on the game of courtly
love, and all its rules had to be obeyed, its conventions strictly
observed. I had to assail her with songs and poems (some of my
own devising but more often commissioned from one of the
sonneteers who sought my patronage), ply her with trinkets and
posies, woo her with words and sighs. She responded by granting
or withholding favours, tantalising herself as well as me by
flaunting her charms and guarding her chastity.

The most delicious aspect of this self-imposed torture was the
secrecy which surrounded it. Our Virgin Queen would not tolerate
amours among her attendants: her ladies were expected to be as
chaste as she, her courtiers held in romantic thraldom by her
alone. Of course, Elizabeth knew what the coy looks and the
ecstatic gasps in darkened doorways signified. The rumours of
wantonings in the maids' dormitories did not escape her ears
alone. She knew as well as her minions what 'sickness' took a

lady suddenly from court and kept her in the country for several months. Yet officially she was ignorant of all this and whenever a scandal came into the open her rage was spontaneous and incalculable. So Margaret and I plotted secret meetings, inveigled confidants into acting as lookouts while we stole a few moments' dalliance in leafy arbours, snapped our fingers at the frowns of 'the sager sort', and found ourselves drawn closer together as much by conspiracy as passion.

Not that our relationship proceeded through the various stages of intimacy unhindered; quarrels, misunderstandings and rivalries were as much a part of the game as kisses and tearful reconciliations. And that calls to mind the mad, intoxicating affair at Elvetham. It was the spring of 1591 and the court was on progress. Every April the Queen left London before the plague arrived and bestowed upon specially selected gentlemen the expensive honour of entertaining her and her household. For a few, fresh, sunny days our itinerary took us to the Earl of Hertford's great Hampshire estate. Excited stories of the delights awaiting us passed back and forth along the royal entourage as we jogged past hedgerows in which the new growth was still only a green mist. Everyone knew that Hertford was desperate to make an impression. Twenty years before he had dared to marry without royal permission and had paid for his crime with a spell in the Tower followed by an indefinite period of social ostracism. Now that Elizabeth had at last condescended to accept his hospitality it was rumoured that the Earl had spent half his fortune on her entertainment. For once the stories were not exaggerated.

The procession halted in a large space that had been cleared before the main gateway to the estate. There stood the Earl and all his household, every one in expensive clothes or vivid livery, making deep obeisance before the Queen's carriage. A garlanded poet, clad all in green, stepped forth and recited a long, flattering Latin oration. Then Hertford approached the carriage and knelt before it proffering at the open doorway a velvet cushion on which lay a solid gold staff encrusted with jewels. He bade her Majesty accept this 'magic wand' and wave it towards the great iron gates. No sooner had she done so than there arose a fanfare from hidden trumpeters and the portals swung silently open.

The Queen's carriage started at a stately walk down the drive. Behind it the well-ordered cavalcade dissolved into an equestrian rabble as every rider pressed forward for a view of whatever 'conceits' were next to be presented. Robin, who as Master of the Horse was leading the Queen's charger, rode beside the carriage. As I was part of his personal retinue I was better positioned than most to see what happened next. A grotesque, horned figure in black and green darted forward and seized the lead horse's driving rein. He represented Envy and when he had successfully halted the procession he gleefully gambolled ahead placing 'obstacles' of painted board in the carriageway as he went. The inference was obvious: any barriers which had existed between Elizabeth and her loving subject had been the fault of neither but rather had been the result of lies and rumours spread by jealous rivals. No sooner had these symbolic rocks and briers been strewn than six startlingly beautiful maidens appeared from behind a large bush, singing a pretty song and removing the obstructions. They were accompanied by a small band of musicians concealed behind the bush which apparently was another artifice since it was obviously mounted on wheels and moved parallel to the procession.

The six maidens accompanied us all the way to the house, dancing and singing their welcome, their silken draperies floating beguilingly around them, their unfastened hair bobbing around their shoulders. Elvetham Hall itself had obviously been recently enlarged and nearby a new building of brick and timber suggested an extra banqueting chamber and accommodation for some members of the court. In front of the main entrance to the house lay a crescent-shaped lake, freshly dug, and within it three islands on which stood mysterious structures and pavilions all of which promised intriguing diversions. And everywhere, indoors and out, were garlands, flags, bunting and colourful drapes.

The entertainment fully lived up to the setting. Hertford's guests were allowed scarcely a moment's respite. The first evening – a banquet, dancing and a masque. We tumbled into our beds shortly before dawn. Soon after dawn we awoke to the sound of music; serenaders stood beneath her Majesty's window beseeching her to come forth and taste the delights of the chase. Off we went careering through the park in pursuit of deer and launching our hawks at doves and pigeons. The huntsmen cleverly arranged the sport so that at mid-morning, just as hunger was beginning to make itself felt, we were brought into a glade where food and wine were spread on grassy banks, and were served by 'Robin Hood' and his 'outlaws' dressed all in Sherwood green. Nor were we condemned to eat our meal in rural silence; the chorus of maidens appeared, dressed now as Diana and her huntresses in shimmering gold and olive, to delight us once more with dance and song.

Delight they certainly did – especially my young friends and me, as we cast appraising eyes over the Elvetham virgins and debated among ourselves on their assorted charms. At the end of their performance, the girls withdrew behind a brake of laurel close to where we gallants were reclining. The suggestion came immediately from one of our number that the ladies would appreciate a refreshing drink after their exertions. There was a hasty gathering together of ewers and goblets, of dishes of pasties and sweetmeats, and thus equipped we sidled into the undergrowth. The maidens were discovered fanning themselves and shedding some of their outer garments in a flimsy tiring-house of plaited branches. Their alarm at our appearance was easily assuaged by the presentation of our offerings and our impromptu feast was very soon a great success.

I fell to chatting with the shatteringly beautiful 'Diana'. With her short tunic, braided fair hair, athletic figure and quick, alert movements, she had for me totally personified the goddess, and I complimented her. But my admiration for her was as nothing compared with hers for me. When I told her my name her blue eyes opened wide.

'You are the one who went to Cadiz with the Earl of Essex! The one who killed all those Spaniards single-handed!'

I nodded modestly. What man under those delightful circumstances would have insisted rigidly on the truth?

'And now you are a great favourite with the Queen.'

I must have looked surprised at that, for she laughed.

'Oh, we know everything about you, Robert Dudley. We are not all uninformed simpletons in the country, you know.'

She lay back against an ash bole and closed her eyes.

'Oh, it must be wonderful to be at the court. All those fine people, and the dancing, and the lovely clothes, and brave soldiers coming back from the wars to lay their trophies at the Queen's feet.'

I agreed that it was, indeed, wonderful, far more wonderful and exciting than even my well-informed companion could possibly realise.

'Tell me about it.'

She leaned forward clutching her arms round her knees and gazing at me with frankly adoring eyes. A curl of hair had fallen across her forehead and she exuded such a simple, uncomplicated almost animal appeal that I could scarcely refrain from flinging myself upon her and grasping her in a tight embrace. Instead I answered all her questions, shamelessly exaggerating the delights of court life and my own importance.

My attentive audience was, I discovered, Kate Seymour, one of Hertford's nieces. Her family wanted to introduce her at court but the Earl's lack of favour had so far prevented this. They were obviously hoping that Kate would attract Elizabeth's attention during this visit to Elvetham. For my part I could not see how the Queen could fail to be dazzled by this delightful creature.

The private party was suddenly broken up by Hertford's master of revels, an agitated little man who stumbled into our bower distracted with anxiety and scolded the girls for not being at the lake and changed into their costumes for the afternoon's entertainment.

The water pageant was an elaborate, gorgeous spectacle in which sumptuous flattery was proffered to the Queen through sundry mythological personages. The Queen's chair of state was set up at the lakeside and she sat accompanied by Hertford, Essex and other dignitaries. I was among those ordered to close attendance on her Majesty which meant that, as well as having a good view of the proceedings, I could hold whispered conversations with Margaret. Elizabeth was enjoying herself greatly, watching the entertainment keenly, chatting with those around her and frequently breaking into her high-pitched shriek of a laugh. It was the mishaps that amused her as much as anything. These country-house diversions were often as under-rehearsed as they were over-ambitious. On this occasion the proceedings were opened by Nereus, the prophet of the sea, who waded across the lake accompanied by five Tritons who wore elaborate wigs and beards dyed many colours and whose torsos were wreathed in seaweed. As they approached they played a fanfare on their trumpets. Or, rather, they were supposed to play a fanfare. A few feet from the shore one of the Tritons lost his footing on the muddy bottom and fell forwards. The unfortunate fellow emerged spluttering, bedraggled and wigless and the Queen rocked with uncontrollable laughter. So did we all. The flustered sea-creature then decided to continue as though nothing had happened. He put his trumpet to his lips and blew. He blew for all he was worth. His bulging cheeks grew redder and redder. But his waterlogged instrument remained mute. By now most of the spectators were holding their sides. The determined performer would not give up. He shook his trumpet and renewed his efforts to coax a note from it. At last he succeeded. A fearful, gurgling wail filled the air, shattering the melody of the other players and causing the scarlet-faced Queen to gasp between gusts of laughter, 'Stop him, stop him. Oh, good my lord, stop him, for the love of heaven.'

Hertford waved to the performers who withdrew, crestfallen, to vent their embarrassed anger on their comrade in the privacy of the tiring house. The Earl turned anxiously to the Queen.

'Will it please your Majesty to see some more?'

Elizabeth dabbed her eyes with a kerchief and called me to bring her some wine.

'Yes, my lord, by all means, if you promise not to assassinate your sovereign with laughter.'

'Your Majesty, a thousand apologies. The man is a fool. He shall be punished...'

'Not so, my lord. He has pleased us greatly. Robin, have you your purse with you?'

Robin was schooled in this routine. He dropped on one knee before his royal mistress and held out to her his purse. Elizabeth's frond-like fingers probed the silken bag and emerged with a cache of gold coins. She handed them to one of her ladies.

'Go, find the sea monsters and give them these. Tell them we found their music ... interesting.'

As the girl curtsied and went on her errand Margaret plucked my sleeve.

'Poor Essex, the Queen is very generous with his money,' she whispered.

'Your pity is wasted there, sweetheart. He will win it back tonight at Primero.'

The Queen was speaking again.

'Well, Hertford, what have you for us now?'

'If it please, your Majesty, a sea battle twixt Neaera and Neptune. Then a masque of Silvanus and his Dryads. Tonight we have a play.'

He paused. Elizabeth regarded him with a raised eyebrow, apparently expecting him to say more. When he maintained an awkward silence, she spoke.

'Only a play tonight? Are we to have no dancing?'

Hertford looked uncomfortable.

'I thought your Majesty might wish to retire early. Tomorrow is May Day ...'

Elizabeth beamed and prodded him hard in the chest.

'Aha, we are to have a Maying.'

'If it please your Majesty.'

I caught hold of Margaret's hand under cover of the napkin which I had used to wipe the Queen's golden goblet. We exchanged smiles. A Maying! That promised all manner of delectable pleasures. It would allow us hours alone in the woods or whatever nook we could find for ourselves.

In the event, matters did not fall out thus. Long before dawn we were all awoken by the sweet sound of madrigals. The Earl's singers and musicians moved around the house and from chamber to chamber within. Each carried a lamp or candle and more lights were supplied to the yawning revellers as they assembled on the shadow-fringed lawn. Everyone waited impatiently for the Queen but first light was making an eastern horizon before she appeared with her giggling maiden escort.

Each man took a partner and to the sound of tabor and pipe the procession wound towards the woods. Margaret hugged my arm tightly as we entered the belt of trees. Our pathway was marked out by a thousand coloured lamps which twinkled on the bare boughs and cast an eerie glow on the mist which shifted among the grotesquely twisted trunks. The avenue led to a fairy grove where trees and bushes were hung with cloth of gold and where a band of children dressed as elves in green and red made obeisance as the Queen approached. Hertford led her to a silk-draped chair of state in the centre of the clearing and the tiny attendants danced around her in a fairy ring. Then the master of the revels stepped forward and invited all present to disperse through the woodlands to find posies and garlands to decorate the maypole. Hertford bowed and offered the Queen his hand. We all waited eagerly for permission to go through the dawn woods in search of our own pleasures. Elizabeth held up her hand.

'My good lord, we thank you for these delights but we have a mind to remain in this grotto to be entertained by your musicians and your charming fairies. Do you go a-Maying. We will stay here awhile with our maids of honour.'

Margaret stamped her foot.

'Oh, the polecat! She will not, so we must be denied.'

Then, as the Queen beckoned, she squeezed my hand and moved forward into the circle of light around the throne. Elizabeth dismissed the assembly with a wave of her hand and I was immediately caught up in a crowd of jostling, chattering people hurrying out of the glade. In the confusion a hand caught mine and I found myself being pulled along down one of the unlit paths leading deeper into the woods. All around the air was full of laughter, shouts and muttered oaths as revellers stumbled through the undergrowth bumping into each other and falling over roots and bushes. But I did not stumble even though I was rushed along at what seemed a reckless pace. My guide was obviously very familiar with the terrain. Gradually all other noises faded until I could hear only our own rapid breathing and the sound of our soft footfalls on the damp leaves.

At last we emerged into a clearing. In the sudden pale light I saw my companion clearly for the first time. A grey gown and loose, fair hair hanging down it, a lithe figure and a sure-footed, springing step. Kate turned to look at me and loosed my hand.

'This way, Bear cub.'

Laughing, she turned and stepped gracefully, carefully over the dewy grass, like a young deer. I followed her – because I wanted to and because I had no alternative; I would have wandered those woods for hours if I had lost sight of my guide. After another brief journey along dimly-discerned paths we came to the simple bower which had served the dancers as a tiring house the day before. Panting, Kate sank onto the bed of dry leaves.

'Oh, this is so exciting. It makes me feel wild and free, like the animals. Do you not feel the same, Robert?'

I knelt beside her. She gave me no time to answer, but reached her hand up round my neck and pulled me towards her until our lips met. Her passion was quiet but intense. She gave herself totally to lovemaking as she gave herself totally to dancing and as, I am sure, she gave herself totally to everything she did. And through that initial kiss she compelled my complete dedication also. I was under her spell, unable to resist either her or my own desire. My complete lack of experience was no obstacle; Kate initiated me so skilfully that not for one moment did I feel awkward. No words passed between us. We stood to remove our clothes and the first rays of the sun edged her in light. Her long neck, her arched back, the perfect hemispheres of her breasts – she seemed more than ever like a sculptured Greek goddess. But there was no suggestion of cold stone as she pressed herself into my arms. Her warmth and smoothness came almost as a shock. She kissed my mouth, my nose, my neck, my chest. She knelt to transfer her caresses to the rest of my body. I put my hands on her shoulders and forced her gently back onto the cloak I had spread over the ground. Now, slowly, savouring the tension tightening in both of us, I paid my homage. My fingers and lips

66

roved, explored and coaxed shivering sighs from within that lovely creature. When I reached the forest between her thighs she squirmed and arched upwards towards me. She held that position while I knelt between her legs and thrust deep inside her. She spread her arms wide and moved her head from side to side gasping as my drives became harder and faster. With a rush of purest delight, passion, like a shooting star, reached the zenith of its brilliance – and died. I was aware of the cold morning breeze across my sweating back.

Minutes later we clung tightly together wrapped in my long cloak. Kate was smiling triumphantly.

'Am I better than the court ladies, Robert?'

I could not tell her that I had not had any of the court ladies.

'You are different.'

'Would you like me to be at court?' She ran a finger along my spine. It was very disconcerting.

'Perhaps.'

Her eyes were wide and reproachful.

'Only perhaps?'

I was trapped.

'Certainly.'

'Then you will arrange it? You will speak to the Queen and ask for me to come?'

'It is not quite as easy as that.'

'Why not? You are a great favourite of hers. You told me so.'

'Yes that's true, of course. But I will have to wait for the right moment, when she is in a good humour. You know people are always seeking places for their daughters and their friends at court.'

She kissed me lightly on the lips.

'Have I pleased you, Robert?'

'Very much.'

'Then you will do this little thing to please me?'

I promised faithfully. I think it was the first promise I made that I had no intention of keeping. For weeks I was ashamed of myself.

But my own feelings of self-reproach were nothing compared

67

with the generous contempt which Margaret displayed for me. What she had heard about Kate and me I did not know but throughout that day she made a point of turning her head away when I smiled at her through the crowd, of being engrossed in conversation whenever I approached.

The great maypole was brought on an ox-cart to the main lawn at Elvetham and there we twined our fronds of birch and ivy around it, crowned it with nosegays of spring flowers and attached long, gaudy streamers before hoisting it into position. The day was given to feasting and dancing in the open air and that night there was a firework display by the lake. When at length we trooped wearily back into the great hall of the house most of the company were sated with revelry and longed only for their beds. But the Queen, it seemed, had no desire to sleep. She sat in her great chair on the dais at one end of the hall beneath a portrait of herself that Hertford had commissioned specially for the occasion and she called on members of the court to entertain her. Desperately swallowing my yawns I leaned against the panelling beside the great fireplace where a mountain of logs crackled and emitted a sleep-inducing warmth, and tried to listen as, one after another, the ladies and gentlemen sang ballads, declaimed poems and read speeches from the latest plays.

Suddenly, I was aware that Margaret was taking her seat at the virginals. My drowsiness left as, for the first time that day, she looked directly at me over the polished walnut as her fingers struck a melancholy chord and she began to sing.

> My love has vowed he will forsake me,
> And I am already sped
> For other promise he did make me
> When he had my maidenhead
> If such danger be in playing
> And sport must to earnest turn
> I will go no more a-Maying.
>
> Dissembling wretch, to gain my pleasure
> What didst thou not vow and swear.

So didst thou rob me of my treasure
Which for long I held so dear.
Now thou provst to me a stranger,
Such is the vile guise of men
When a woman is in danger.

Margaret's eyes scarcely once left me and I felt as though every-one in the room were looking at me. I was hot and uncomfortable, a condition which had nothing to do with the blazing fire. I did not want to hear the rest of Campion's bitter song but I did not dare draw attention to myself by leaving the room.

That heart is nearest to misfortune
That will trust a feigned tongue,
When flattering men our loves importune
They intend us deepest wrong.
If this shame of love's betraying
But this once I clearly shun,
I will go no more a-Maying.

There was a clatter of polite applause as Margaret walked back to her place near the Queen. Elizabeth eyed her shrewdly but spoke to the whole company.

'A pretty sentiment and a wise one. We hope all you men will take it to heart. 'Tis a foul misdeed to play with a woman's heart and one we would find difficult to forgive. Now, my lord of Hertford, let us have something merry – some rounds and catches, perhaps.'

As a hundred voices caught up the refrain of 'Hey Robin, Jolly Robin, tell me how thy lady doeth' and bandied it back and forth in playful counterpoint, I sidled from the room, gained my own tiny lodging and there passed an anxiety-haunted night of half-sleep.

The following day the royal cavalcade was on the road again. Leaving the Earl of Hertford to count the silver and to hope his immense expense had not been in vain, Elizabeth took her court northwards to sample the hospitality of yet another wealthy subject. After we had ridden an hour or more through intermittent sunshine and showers I managed to manoeuvre my horse alongside Margaret's. Having not received (and not expected) a greeting, I took the offensive.

'What do you mean by making a fool of me in front of everyone?'

'Sir, I know not what you mean. You speak in riddles.' She looked fixedly at the road ahead.

'You *do* know what I mean; that song ...'

She could not keep the aloof pose. She turned to flash me a look of concentrated venom.

'If the cap fits, Master Dudley!'

'Oh, and when did I ever have your maidenhead?'

'Never! Nor are ever like to. It is not an item for your collection.'

'Keep it! Keep it, and grow to be an old maid like your royal mistress!'

I did not realise I was shouting until the Bishop of London, riding some paces in front of us, turned and scowled. We rode in silence for some minutes. Then the rigid set of Margaret's shoulders relaxed. She shook her head.

'Oh, Robert, you are a fool.'

'I see; a fool, as well as a dissembling wretch.'

'I suppose you think she loves you.'

'You do not know what passed between us.'

Margaret laughed bitterly.

'Oh you simpleton. Do you not know with what relish that slut has been describing her adventure to whoever will listen?'

It had come on to rain heavily and water was trickling down the back of my neck. It did not cool the sudden heat of anger and embarrassment which came over me. The procession left the road to shelter in a small copse. When we had reined in beneath a broad-boughed ash I turned my fury on Margaret.

'You are only saying that because you are jealous.' I did not believe it but I could not stop myself saying it.

Margaret ignored the taunt.

'She wants a rich and high-born husband and now she thinks

she has a hold over you.'

'Then she is wrong.'

'And if she has a child? She could offer you the choice of scandal or marriage.'

It was a shock to hear my own anxieties so clearly expressed. 'But she cannot . . . there is little chance.'

'There is every chance. From what I hear of Mistress Seymour she is almost certain to have someone's baby before the year is out.'

'Then who will believe her if she tries to blame me?'

'Who will believe her? Why, the Queen. You know very well that chastity is her religion, and fornication to her is the foulest heresy. You think you will be able to clear yourself? Oh no, it will be "Master Dudley, marry the girl, take her to your home, and never come to our court again." '

The shower had passed, and my mare pawed the ground impatiently as the Queen's carriage and her escort of Gentlemen Pensioners moved back towards the road. I felt wretched and obviously looked it. Margaret stared at me with something like compassion in her face.

'You need not worry.'

'What do you mean?'

'Young Roger Manners, the Earl of Rutland, is besotted with your Kate. I introduced them and made sure they became very well acquainted.'

'But he is only a boy. He cannot be more than fourteen.'

'He is an earl. I am afraid that makes him more attractive to Mistress Seymour even than you.'

Margaret spurred her horse forward.

'So you see, Robert, a woman does not have to be on her back to perform favours.'

'But why, Margaret . . .'

She threw the answer back over her shoulder.

'If you do not know, Robert, you are an even bigger fool.'

The routine of court life continued on its inexorable round – summer progress through the southern counties, July and August at Windsor, triumphant return to Westminster in the autumn, Greenwich early in the new year, then sometime in spring or early summer the journeying around royal and private manors began all over again. It was like a tedious treadmill and one from which there seemed to be no escape. My total dependence on the Queen's favour kept me prisoner far more effectively than iron bars and bolted doors. I longed for news of Cavendish and Davis but none came. I took every opportunity of talking with ambassadors, captains and travellers who passed through the court. My reading was all of geography, navigation and foreign places. I thirsted for information about the wider world and especially newly-discovered lands. The court gossip that filled the minds of my friends and colleagues seemed utterly futile to me.

Continued service brought minor recompenses. When the court returned to Whitehall Palace in October 1591 I was allotted my own chamber and permitted a small establishment. For the first time I could enjoy occasional moments of privacy. Sometimes I was able to share them with Margaret. The maids of honour were forbidden to enter gentlemen's private apartments but, like most rules governing the conduct of the Queen's household, this one was cautiously ignored. Since the Elvetham affair there had been a new depth and stability in our relationship. Those moments in Kate Seymour's accomplished embraces had largely satisfied my adolescent curiosity and lust. They had shown me that whatever there was between Margaret and me was different and more important. And Margaret, who might justifiably have spurned me after my 'desertion', chose not to harbour wounded pride indefinitely.

I know our friends thought us a very solemn couple. We showed little interest in the latest play or fashion. We were indifferent to gossip but avid to learn the latest news when Drake or Frobisher, Howard or Hawkins returned from a voyage. There was nothing platonic about our love, yet when we were alone we often spent hours looking at maps and charts, speculating about distant lands and the people who lived in them. I confided in her my ambitions to sail ships to those lands and I knew that my secrets would not be giggled over in the maids' dormitory.

The most interesting news in the autumn of 1591 was the fate of Lord Thomas Howard's expedition to the Azores to intercept the Spanish silver fleet. Messengers up from the West Country told of the return of ships whose crews were decimated by the bloody flux and fever, of Howard's narrow escape from a superior enemy force. The admiral had been obliged to land all his men at Flores in order to careen and fumigate his leaking, disease-ridden vessels. He had thought there was plenty of time to complete this operation before the treasure fleet arrived from the Indies but he was caught unawares by a *flota* of Spanish warships fresh out of Cadiz. Howard barely got away with most of his ships and men; he was forced to leave the *Revenge*, trapped by a contrary wind, to face the enemy alone or seek some other means of escape. The court and, indeed, all England waited for news of Sir Richard Grenville's ship.

One afternoon towards the end of November Margaret came rushing into my chamber. Her story would not even wait for kisses. She wriggled out of my arms.

'No, Robert, there is not time. Come quickly.'

I hurried out after her and we ran through the tortuous passages towards the Queen's apartments.

'What is it, sweetheart?'

'A captured Spanish captain. Sir Walter Raleigh has just brought him here.'

The Privy Chamber was filled with councillors, household officials and others admitted to the inner circle of the court. Before the chair of state stood Raleigh, overdressed as usual in scarlet and silver. With him a dejected-looking little man in expensive black with iron grey hair and well-clipped beard. The Spaniard had every reason to look unhappy : not only was he a prisoner; he was standing in the presence of his master's heretical arch-enemy and being bombarded with questions by her and her confidants. Raleigh was narrating the story, occasionally calling on the captain for details and translating his replies for the benefit of those present who, unlike the Queen, spoke no Spanish. He was relishing his role to the full; all eyes were fixed on him as he unfolded the brave and melancholy account of the *Revenge*'s last fight.

'...and so Sir Richard offered battle to the whole Spanish fleet – fifty-five ships.'

Gasps of amazement.

'Undoubtedly he saved Lord Howard's contingent which drew steadily away till night and a favourable wind came on.'

The Queen leaned forward and glowered at Raleigh.

'Why did the *Revenge* not escape under cover of darkness?'

'She was already badly damaged, your Majesty. Before nightfall she had been grappled and boarded by two great galleons...' He exchanged a few words with the captain. 'Ah yes, the *San Felipe* and the *San Barnabe*. But, notwithstanding, Sir Richard battered them with broadsides hour upon hour, till the *San Felipe* sheered away, crippled and the *San Barnabe* sank.'

A flutter of excitement went through the audience. Sir Walter had them all in the grip of his eloquence.

'But for every ship that cringed away, another came forward to do battle. The 700 ton *Ascensión* caught fire and went to the bottom. Others exchanged shots and retired to lick their wounds. All night long the battle raged. As the morning light glinted on the water the battered Spanish fleet ringed the *Revenge* and she was a pitiable sight – masts gone, decks red with blood, powder spent, only a handful of men left and Grenville himself wounded...'

'Wounded?'

'Mortally wounded, your Majesty. When the Spaniards saw the *Revenge* had no more teeth they plucked up courage to board her. Sir Richard and the few survivors were taken onto the flagship, the *San Pablo*. The enemy thought they had a fine captive but Sir Richard Grenville denied them. Within the hour that brave admiral, that true friend and loyal subject of your Majesty yielded up his spirit to God and gave only his torn body to his foes.'

Raleigh paused, like an actor who wants the audience to savour his best lines. Slowly he drew a folded slip of paper from his sleeve.

'Will your Majesty permit me to read Sir Richard Grenville's last words?'

Elizabeth was far from being affected by this tale of bravery and sacrifice. For her Howard's abortive expedition was yet another expensive failure and the *Revenge* a good ship unnecessarily lost. Courageous gestures might stir the hearts of the people; they did not pay the government's debts.

'Did this mortally wounded loyal captain have the leisure to write letters on his deathbed?'

'No, your Majesty, but even with his last breath he flung defiance at his enemies and remembered his Queen. His words impressed even his captors and one of them wrote them down. I have your Majesty's permission?'

The Queen nodded expressionlessly and sat back among the cushions. Raleigh cleared his voice portentously.

'These, then, are Sir Richard's very words: "Here die I, Richard Grenville, with a joyful and quiet mind, for that I have ended my life as a true soldier ought to do, that hath fought for his country, Queen, religion and honour, whereby my soul most joyfully departs out of this body, and shall always leave behind it an everlasting fame of a valiant and true soldier who has done his duty as he was bound to do." '

There was a murmur of approval but all the Queen would say was, 'Very pretty, very pretty.' She was more interested when Raleigh and the Spanish captain went on to tell of the great Atlantic storm that had risen shortly after the capture of the *Revenge* and the losses suffered by Philip's treasure fleet. When Margaret and I slipped away again the little Spaniard was being closely questioned on the exact number of capital ships in the harbours of Spain and Portugal and on the King's preparation of a second Armada.

Back in my chamber Margaret seated herself on a joint-stool.

'Sir Walter should join the Lord Chamberlain's Company, I am sure he can out-bombast Burbage.'

'He would make a more convincing actor than a sailor. You know he should have been on the Azores expedition; his name was linked with Howard's as founder of the venture. Then, at the last moment, he withdrew. He may well talk of other men's bravery.'

'Be fair, Robert. It was the Queen who forbade him to go, just as she tried to keep Essex at home two years ago.'

'I'll not believe it. The man is a coward and a braggart.'

'No truly, Robert, it was so; the Queen stayed him. He amuses her and she has little enough to amuse her now, God knows.' She sighed. 'Poor Elizabeth, she will be very bitter when she learns of his latest treachery.'

'What "treachery" is that?'

'Why his marriage.'

'Raleigh is married?'

'Yes, several days since. Had you not heard?'

'Is it to Bess Throckmorton?'

'Who else? She is with child and threatened a scandal.'

A vision of Kate Seymour flashed before my eyes and I almost felt sorry for Raleigh.

'Poor, Sir Walter, so that is why he is hastily getting together another expedition to the Indies. He hopes to be a thousand miles away or, better still, home again with plunder before the truth is out.'

Margaret came over and put her arms round my neck.

'Must we talk of Raleigh? I can think of pleasanter ways to pass the time.'

But we had only a few moments to explore the possibilities. There was a deferential tap at the door and my page, Will Bradshaw, sidled in embarrassed at having defied my strict instructions that I was not to be disturbed.

'I beg your pardon, sir. Master Brindley is here again.'

'Well tell him to . . .'

'He says he must see you urgently, sir.'

Brindley was the executor of my late uncle's will and his visits were not unusual. He regarded it as part of his duties to educate me in the administration of my enormous estates and to this end he lost no opportunity to discuss with me every possible nicety of lands, tenancies and boundaries. The interviews were always tedious for the lawyer was totally lacking in humour and, though still a young man, affected the sonorous, plaintive tones of a greybeard.

'I suppose we shall have no peace till he has his way. Show him in.'

Will withdrew. A few seconds later a dry cough announced the lawyer's presence.

'Yes, Brindley, what is it today?'

He stood awkwardly in the middle of the room, holding out a rather worn piece of parchment, managing as was his special gift to look out of place and self-important at the same time.

'Well?'

'I found this letter among the late Earl's papers. It is addressed to you.'

'What does it say?'

'It is sealed, sir.' Brindley looked shocked.

'Oh.' I did not feel like dealing with legal matters and told him to put it down on the table. This obviously did not satisfy him.

'It ... er ... does not appear to be in the hand of the deceased.' He paused. 'I may be wrong, of course, but it seems more like your late father's hand ... and the seal ...'

Brindley had won; I took the document from him. It was true. There was no mistaking the bold characters, and the seal was not the bear and ragged staff but the double tailed lion which Leicester had always used for very personal letters. I tore it open impatiently. What could my father possibly have to say to me that could only be imparted from the grave?

'To my one surviving son, Robert Dudley.' The simple, direct words came as a sudden shock. My mind flashed back to the barn and the galleon and that rare moment of intimacy. Once more all I wanted was to be alone with my father. Brindley I had to tell to go away. Margaret stood up. She leaned over and kissed me.

'I will return later,' she whispered.

As the door closed I carried the letter over to the window-seat, and sat down to read.

To my one surviving son, Robert Dudley. By the time you read this not only I but also my brother Ambrose will be dead: and you, if it please God, will have attained sufficient wisdom to judge what action you must take when you have read these lines.

To the world you have ever been known as the Earl of Leicester's base son, the issue of an illicit union with Lady Douglas Sheffield. What I have to confess and explain to you is that this is not the truth; you were born in lawful wedlock and are the legitimate heir to the earldoms of Leicester and Warwick.

I met and fell in love with your mother when first she came to court. You will know enough of the Queen to understand that our liaison had to be kept secret, otherwise God knows what her Majesty would have done in her anger. After months of anguish your mother and I were married secretly at Esher, on 17 May 1573. The ceremony was performed by an ordained priest, according to the law and before witnesses. A year later you were born.

For four years Douglas and I were as happy as we could be under these difficult circumstances. I do not pretend that you will find it easy to accept what then happened – I can only say that it is seldom given to a man to love well and to love but once. Perhaps you have already found the truth of this and can believe me when I tell you that my love for Lettice Knollys implied no slight upon your mother. Lettice and I fell deeply in love and soon she was with child. Her kinsmen insisted on nothing less than open marriage. Your mother agreed to free me from a contract of which the world knew nothing, and Lettice and I were wed in September 1578. Thus, my poor son, did you become a 'bastard'.

It is for you to decide how you will use this knowledge. You bear an ancient name, and you may bear it with honour. It may be that in time you will be able to lay claim to all the dignities of Warwick and Leicester, as is your right.

Serve the Queen and her heirs faithfully. Pray for my soul and remember with affection the father who ever loved you dearly.

Leicester.

6

I cannot recall all the emotions that flooded over me as I read and re-read that extraordinary letter. Amazement, joy, pride, fear? Within a few minutes the whole basis of my life was changed. I had always accepted my illegitimacy. Indeed, it had been a spur to me, for it meant that any honours I attained would be achieved by my own efforts. Now that was no longer true; I was a real Dudley. I was Earl of Leicester, Earl of Warwick – titles to be respected and honoured.

The first thing I wanted to do was to tell Robin my news and discuss with him its implications. I picked up my cloak and set off in search of my friend. Down the broad stairs and into the courtyard. There was a light rain in the air but I scarcely noticed it as I ran across the grass. The implications of my new status were racing through my mind. I would have equal rank with Robin; perhaps a seat on the Council; great offices of state would be open to me – I might even be Lord High Admiral. I wondered how Robin would react.

Suddenly I stopped in my tracks only a few feet from the door leading to the wing where the Queen's apartments – and Robin's – were. With a hollow feeling in the pit of my stomach I suddenly realised that I could not tell Robin. I could not tell anyone. The letter had made no difference. I must keep my secret – or lose my honour. If the legality of my parents' union were established then my father's marriage to Lettice Knollys would automatically be exposed as bigamous. I felt little concern on my stepmother's behalf, but what of Robin? There were many jealous tongues about the court which would be only too delighted to pass on gossip which would embarrass the Queen's favourite. And what of my mother? She was happily married and had recently returned from Paris. I saw little of her but I certainly had no intention of causing her pain by raising old ghosts.

Yet had I the right to remain silent? Did I not have a duty to the name I bore? Could I see the dignities of Leicester and Warwick and all the proud titles honourably won by my ancestors pass into other hands because I was too squeamish to hurt a few people's feelings? What of my children yet unborn – could I give away their birthright? And myself – if I did nothing what would it mean for me? Years of living a lie, of being treated as something I was not. Slowly I began to grasp the enormity of the decision my father had bequeathed me.

I turned and slowly recrossed the courtyard. The rain was heavier now and water was trickling down my face. I regained my rooms and threw myself, wet as I was, onto the bed. From whatever angle I examined the dilemma, I could see no escape. Not for the first time in my life I wished I had some friend to confide in, a man or woman of wisdom and maturity. There was no one.

If there was a partial solution to my problem it was one that I sensed rather than thought out clearly. I seemed to have two overlapping lives, one centred on the court, the other on the sea. Now by intuition I realised that I must begin to make a choice. The first step was an easy one. I had made frequent visits to Matthew Baker's workshops in the royal shipyard at Deptford and been absorbed and fascinated by what I saw – the interlocking of intricate skills, the way concepts were converted into plans, plans into thousands of mathematical calculations, and those calculations into precisely-shaped pieces of wood and metal. I realised that all I knew about ships was theoretical and that if ever I was to sail one as it should be sailed I would have to understand its construction, its points of strength and weakness, its capabilities, the stresses and strains to which it was subject.

So, at a time when any ambitious courtier would have been seeking promotion to the rank of Gentleman of the Privy Chamber I began to absent myself from court and to pay others to do my duties. For several months I became an unofficial apprentice to Master Baker. He was an excellent and a hard taskmaster. In a long life on the waterfront he had developed a powerful arm and acquired a vocabulary as rich as it was foul. He used both freely and indiscriminately for he had neither patience with fools nor respect for rank.

With such a tutor I learned quickly how to trim and smooth timber with precision, how to assemble and adjust tackles, lanyards and deadeyes, how to make dowels fit perfectly, how to balance the tension of mast and rigging. I wrote pages and pages of notes on everything I learned. It was out of these that my diaries grew. I have the first one before me now, a ragged folio of dog-eared pages, covered in the impatient scrawl of youth. The first half of the book is crammed with sketches – 'stepping the main mast', 'carving treenails', 'lacing a bonnet', 'caulking – Master Baker's method', 'mast-housing'. Then the technical notes begin to be interspersed with entries of a personal nature – ideas for navigational aids, information culled from recently arrived sailors about the progress of Thomas Cavendish's expeditions, even news about events at court.

Sometimes Matthew Baker took me into the large rooms overlooking the yard where he made his drawings. Here I was on more equal terms with him, for though his understanding of practical shipbuilding enabled him to be constantly devising improvements I was a better mathematician and could calculate quickly the effects of varying the ratios of length to beam, of repositioning guns or increasing the spread of canvas.

Soon I was designing my own ships, and my rooms at court were littered with sheets of paper. It began as an academic exercise: I would set myself certain problems such as how to distribute cargo space in such a way so as to have the least effect on speed. Gradually I found myself drawing the sort of ships that I would like to own and sail. When summer came and the Queen went on progress my visits to Deptford had to stop but my own work did not. My papers, models and mathematical instruments went with me everywhere.

Poor Margaret, she now had a rival whose seductive power

was infinitely greater than Kate Seymour's. For all her genuine fascination with the sea and ships she could not grasp the many technicalities of rhumb lines, tide computation, the calculation of displacement to capacity ratios and the other matters in which I was now totally absorbed. Her interest in my designs dwindled as I grew impatient with her inability to grasp 'simple' principles and tired of trying to explain how sails were set or latitude reckoned. Our meetings became less frequent. Margaret had developed into a beautiful and vivacious young woman and did not lack for admirers. Whether she liked it or not her life was inevitably bound up with the court and its trivial concerns – the latest dance, the newest fashion, the current scandal. I was less and less a part of that world and looked forward avidly to my escape from it.

The scandal of Raleigh's marriage broke in the summer of 1592. He had spent every penny he had or could borrow in fitting out yet another privateering venture but in May just as the fleet was ready to sail Elizabeth ordered his return to court. According to Margaret, the Queen had known of her favourite's 'infidelity' for many weeks and was uncertain how to punish him. For the moment she was content to prevent his escape. Friends of the erring couple urged them to make abject confession and throw themselves on the royal clemency. They might as well have counselled the sea to catch fire as Raleigh to humble himself. It was his unremitting, brazenness that proved Sir Walter's undoing. He continued to strut around the court and pay flattering attention to his royal mistress as though nothing had happened. Elizabeth's patience snapped in early August. In the middle of a public audience she called Raleigh before her and raged at him for a full half hour. How dare he promise his undying fidelity to her, she demanded, when he already shared his home and his bed with another? In a crescendo of scarlet fury she ordered Sir Walter, his wife and child to the Tower of London. Even the older courtiers vowed they could not recall such a violent outburst of royal wrath. Fortunately for the disgraced favourite one of his ships returned to Dartmouth a few weeks later bringing with her a magnificent prize, the *Madre de Dios*, a great carrack carrying half a million in bullion. The Queen was somewhat appeased by her share of the plunder. She so far relented as to set the Raleighs at liberty but they remained banished from the court. All this was, of course, splendid news for Robin and his friends. I was happy for him but took little real interest in the sordid affair. I could not know that Sir Walter's indiscretion was the first in a sequence of events which would involve me very closely indeed.

In April 1593 the court was at Greenwich where the Queen, with a fortitude remarkable in a woman of her age, indulged in her favourite pastime of hunting. I was attending her one fresh, dewy morning when my page rode up to say that a gentleman had arrived and was asking to speak with me urgently. I was unable to leave immediately but as soon as I could I excused myself and cantered back towards the palace.

I scarcely recognised the man who confronted me in my chamber. The sallow complexion, the white hair, the sunken cheeks, this was surely not the John Davis I had bidden God speed to almost three years before. Even his voice was weaker and had quite lost its scornful abrasiveness. The man had obviously suffered the most appalling hardships and I imagined they had come his way in the arctic waters of the North-West Passage.

'No, Master Dudley, I have not been within ten thousand miles of the Arctic.'

I made him sit down and tell me his story in his own time.

'Well, Master Dudley, we made good time to Brazil and we were at the entrance to Magellan's Strait in six months. Then, as God's my judge, we met storms the like of which I never saw before, nor want to see again. Waves a hundred foot high. Twenty-three days without letting up. We lost seven men overboard in my ship alone. At last we got inside the Strait but things were no better there. Contrary winds and the men too weary and hungry to work properly. It was obvious we could not go on, Master Dudley.'

'What about Thomas; what did he do?'

'Poor Tom, the storm and the men's sufferings turned his head. Obsessed he was with the idea of getting to the Spice Islands.

Said if he couldn't go west he would go east, round Africa.'

Davis's eyes glistened with tears.

'Master Dudley, it was never possible. Five thousand miles and we with scarce no food and water. True we would have had the westerlies but five thousand miles...I had to tell him I would not go with him. For the sake of the men I had to make him turn back. You can see that can't you, sir?'

'Yes, John, you did the right thing.'

I thought of poor Thomas Cavendish, the man of vision. I could see those pale eyes gleaming as he spoke of Cathay and his dream of opening trade with that unknown land. That dream, that vision would, I could see, drive him to the brink of sanity... and perhaps beyond. Nothing else would matter, not the men, not the ships, not even Jane and those three lively boys. What decision, I wondered, would I have made in Thomas's place.

'So you turned for home. Thank God you are safe.'

Davis was making no attempt to restrain his tears.

'Aye, we turned back. Then one night in about 48°, off Port Desire we lost sight of the Admiral. Come daybreak we were alone on a calm sea with not a sight of another ship.'

He fixed me with a pitiable, intent gaze.

'I went about, Master Dudley. As God's my judge, I went about to look for Thomas, even though three-quarters of my own men were sick and all of us starving. Three months I patrolled back and forth off that God-forsaken coast and never anything except penguin and mussels to eat and the ship rotting under our feet. But there was never a sign of him, Master Dudley, not so much as a floating spar.'

I made Davis take some wine and recover himself before telling the rest of his story, wondering what horrors the sea had which could turn a tough, seasoned mariner into this quivering halfman. I soon discovered. Davis and his crew had taken ten months to get back to England from Port Desire. Day by day he had watched his comrades dying from scurvy and starvation. Twice, when landing parties went ashore to forage for food they were cut to pieces by Indians. The survivors had set out across the Atlantic from Brazil with only stale water and putrid penguin meat for sustenance. Within days they were eating rats, canvas, shoes, even the very timber of the ship. Some raged about the deck in delirium. No one was strong enough to set the sails; the ship drifted on with just the mainsail set, come storm or calm. When, by the Grace of God, the ship reached Ireland it contained sixteen men, all more dead than alive.

Thus ended the first great expedition in which I was involved. For some months there was a hope that Cavendish might have survived, might perhaps have continued with the journey as originally planned. Such hope gradually dwindled, and I had to accept the fact that my friend had perished with his men and the *Leicester* somewhere in the cruel waters about Cape Horn.

That tragedy far from curbing my lust for maritime adventure, helped to clarify my own ambitions. I knew now what I must do. I dedicated myself to completing Thomas Cavendish's task. I would make that journey to the eastern lands and islands and I would take up the trading concessions that he and Drake before him had pioneered. Within weeks I had commissioned two new ships from a Southampton yard. Before they were on the stocks I had named them – the *Bear* and the *Bear's Whelp*. They were not large; my flagship was only 200 tons but she was sleek and fast; she carried twenty cannon and was (on paper at least) more manoeuvrable than any other ship of her size afloat. I let Matthew Baker know that I was in the market for three smaller supply ships and that I would soon be recruiting men.

I was able to devote time and money to these preparations because I was growing older and the Master of the Wards agreed that I should have the disposition of a larger portion of my patrimony and also the time to devote to my many responsibilities. No doubt Lord Burghley thought that I was spending my months away from court touring my estates and talking earnestly with stewards about sheep prices and repairs to barns. In fact, my country houses and farms saw very little of me at this period of my life. I had been relieved of my Privy Chamber duties but my attendance at court was still required for long periods of the year.

The royal household returned to Greenwich for the autumn of 1593 instead of Westminster, for the plague raged late in London that year. One November day I received a message from Matthew Baker asking me to come without delay to a tavern on Queenhythe – I think it was the Swan. It was a strange summons, for the dismal waterfront alehouse was not one of Master Baker's regular haunts. On the other hand I knew he would not have sent the message without good reason. Probably he had found a ship for me to look at. Robin was with me when the messenger arrived. We spent very little time together now but we remained close friends. I showed him the piece of paper and asked him to excuse me because I would have to leave for Queenhythe immediately. He frowned.

'Do you think that's wise?'

'Yes, why ever not?'

I picked up my cloak and walked to the door.

'I did not like the look of the messenger and I have a feeling we have met before somewhere.'

'Robin, it is kind of you to be so concerned for me but I am nearly twenty years of age. I think I can take care of myself.'

I was, of course, very grateful to my friend for all he had done for me over many years. I owed a great deal to his support and protection. But sometimes I found his patronage irksome. This seemed to me like a typical example of his desire to have some say in every aspect of my life.

'You are right to chide me but make sure your claws are sharp, Bear cub.'

He joined me in the doorway.

'Will it upset you if I share your barge? I have to go to the City myself.'

So we made the journey upriver together and were set down at Billingsgate wharf in the middle of an overcast, dank afternoon. We had declined the waterman's usual offer to 'shoot the bridge for sixpence', preferring to walk the short distance which took us past London Bridge and its swirling rapids. In any case I liked dirty, bustling Billingsgate, the highest point on the river for large, sea-going vessels. I lingered there after I had taken my leave of Robin and picked my way happily through the busy, colourful world of London's waterfront – a scene so active and various as

86

to make any spirited young man yearn to set sail over the seven seas. As far as the eye could see, the proud hulls rode alongside the busy quays – Mediterranean carracks unloading spices whose strange, pungent aromas wafted over the water mingling with the ubiquitous tang of pitch; French and Dutch merchantmen bringing wine, cloth and glassware; low English coasters, and the massive, heavily armed vessels of the rich, friendless Hanse merchants. In midstream one of the Queen's galleys was making seawards on the gathering ebb tide, its varnished walls sparkling in sunlight thrown up from the dark, rich waters of the estuary. I paused briefly by one of the jetties to watch the ship's graceful lines, before completing my journey.

The Swan lay in a narrow sidestreet running at right angles to the quay. It was a low, mean building reeking of old ale, and not much frequented, to judge by the general air of disuse. I was glad when the landlord said gruffly that I would find Master Baker upstairs – nothing could be as bad as the stifling dinginess of the lower room. I took the stairs two at a time and bounded across the threshold.

The door was wrenched from my grasp and bolted behind me. I was taken completely by surprise but I must have drawn instinctively for the next thing I recall is crouching in a corner of the room, rapier in hand. By the light from the dingy window I could see my assailants – two men, a tall, ungainly fellow with a strange, crooked smile, pointing a short, wide sword in my direction, and a small, wiry man still standing by the closed door. His weapon was a very narrow left-hand dagger which glinted against his coarse brown doublet. Both of them moved forward and my future prospects seemed distinctly limited. Frightened I certainly was, but also strangely exhilarated and my mind was very clear. There was a table close at hand and a couple of quick paces put this obstacle between me and my attackers. The two men only glanced at each other and kept moving forward.

There was little I could do. My only advantage lay in the longer reach of my rapier. I would have to engage the bigger of the two and somehow try to parry the rush of the man with the dagger. I wedged one end of the table close to the wall, making it impossible for them to work their way round from that side. Now I could only wait for them to take the initiative.

The man with the sword made one or two sweeping passes in the air, trying to pin me back against the wall. I riposted, and nearly pricked his arm at the first attempt. He took a step or two back and crouched lower. His companion remained behind him and to one side, biding his time. The big man lunged forward suddenly, his sword aimed at my midriff. I parried the blow easily and this time my riposte did draw blood. It did not stop him. He went on making lunges and passes, all the time smiling his ugly smile. I fended off his blows and tried to keep half an eye on his companion. My vigilance was not equal to the task. The shorter man found an opportunity to dart forward and wrench the table away. At the same time he plunged the dagger into my left shoulder and I felt its point grind on the bone. He sprang back and I was sure my last moment had come.

Then the attack stopped. The assassins stood, weighing their weapons and savouring their power.

'Frightened, ain't he?' The tall fellow with the crooked smile laughed.

His companion sniggered.

'Reckon he thinks his last moment has come.'

'What do you want with me?' I tried to sound calm and dignified. I did not succeed.

' "What do you want with me?" ' the tall man mimicked and seemed to find his joke very funny. 'Ah, yes, that's the question, ain't it? Now it might be that fat purse hanging at your belt.'

'Or that nice velvet cape,' his friend added.

'Yes, or again it might be those pretty rings.'

He sighed and shook his head.

'Yet I fear if we took those things, Master Dudley would believe we were only common thieves.'

'And are you not?'

His rodent-like companion lifted his nose in mock disdain.

'Oh, Master Dudley, how could you suggest such a thing. We are honest messengers.'

The other interposed.

'Ah, what you *should* say, Tom, is that *today* we are honest messengers. But tomorrow we might be something very different.'

I was sweating heavily and the pain in my arm was getting bad. I was determined not to give these ruffians the pleasure of playing cat and mouse with me.

'Stop these riddles. If you want to kill me just come and try.'

'Oh, I *am* sorry if our riddles puzzle you. I thought an educated young gentleman like you would take our meaning. I see we shall have to put it very simply, like the catechism.'

The tall man assumed the piping voice of an ageing parson and intoned.

'What is your name?'

My mouth remained tight shut until a sharp jab from the 'parson's' sword and gruff 'Answer the question!' persuaded me that I had better play this macabre game.

'Robert Dudley.'

'And, Robert Dudley, are you planning a maritime venture?'

'Yes.'

'Do you wish to see my friend and I ever again?'

'Only on a gallows!'

'Then you must abandon your plans.'

'Never! If you think...'

'Listen, my fine gallant.' The clerical pose was dropped. 'This is a warning. Sell your ships. Don't start recruiting crews. Otherwise you will meet my friend and me again and then we shall have changed our employment. We won't be messengers, we...'

There was a sudden noise of steps on the stairs, then a rattling and banging at the door. For a second the big man took his eyes off me. It was all I needed. With all my strength I had left I ran my rapier into his stomach, and drew it back, to face the other assassin. Hands clutched to his belly, the big man collapsed to the floor: his face still wore that crooked smile, now parodied by pain. The other panicked. Sparing only a fearful glance for his companion he rushed to the window, wrenched it open and pulled himself through. I doubt whether his judgement was sound; I was trembling violently and my wound was sending spasms of pain over my whole body. If he had stayed to finish the job he might well have succeeded.

The noise at the door continued. I went across and fumbled one-handed with the bolt. It was Robin. He took in the situation at a glance, then caught sight of the blood on my doublet. With scarcely a word, he made me sit on the table while he opened my clothing to examine the wound. He bound it with strips torn from my shirt and made a makeshift sling from his silk sash.

'Follow me closely down the stairs, in case there are more ruffians about.'

But the room below was deserted, and soon we had put a safe distance between ourselves and the Swan. As we went along I told Robin what had happened, but he merely nodded, and did not break his silence until we had found and boarded a barge at the Bridge and were heading downstream back to Greenwich. Then he settled on the cushions in the bow and stared at me hard and long.

'I know,' I said, 'I should have listened to your warning. But I came in good faith. The message was from Matthew Baker, you saw it yourself.'

'How do you know the message came from him?' Robin gave me a withering look. 'You talk of sailing round the world, yet you cannot even conduct yourself safely round London.'

'How could I know that someone was after my blood.'

'And who is that someone?'

'I cannot imagine. No one I know would want to stop my voyage.'

Robin looked thoughtful. 'What exactly did they say?'

I told Robin as much as I could remember and at the recollection I started shivering uncontrollably.

'We must try to think of a man who desperately wants to put an end to your plans and thinks you can be frightened into abandoning them.'

'But why? Only a madman ...'

'Oh no, Bear cub, there are strong enough motives – jealousy, pride, fear.'

'You sound as if you know the man.'

'Raleigh.'

I laughed.

'Oh, come, Robin. I know he is your enemy but you need not suspect him of every crime committed in London.'

But Robin did not smile.

'No, I'm sure I'm right. The man who brought the message to your room is not one of Raleigh's servants but I am sure he is sometimes used by him. Think, Bear cub. Where is Raleigh now?'

'As far as I know at his Dorset manor where he has been ever since he was released from the Tower.'

'Yes. He has been there more than a year. And that exile from court he finds intolerable. Why is the moth away from the candle? Because the Queen has never forgiven him for marrying Bess Throckmorton. So he skulks at Sherborne and contrives any means that he can find to wriggle back into favour.'

'What has any of this to do with me?'

'Everything. Just think – how can Sir Walter commend himself to the Queen? Only by making a great voyage, and coming back laden with spoils. He knows as well as any of us that her Majesty keeps her heart in her strong box.'

'So, Raleigh plans an expedition. What then? The seas are wide enough for the two of us.'

'Not in Sir Walter's thinking. He needs money badly and cannot get ships and crews together quickly. If you should come home first and lay out your marvels before the Queen you will be her new darling, the reincarnation of her beloved Leicester. What would then become of Raleigh? His eclipse could well be total and permanent. Make no mistake, Bear cub, you are a real threat to Sir Walter.'

'But you are forgetting something. The Queen has not given her permission for an expedition yet. If Raleigh is planning a voyage there is nothing to stop him getting away first.'

'Oh, but there is a very real obstacle; he has no money. Once you have the Queen's charter, you can beat Raleigh by several months.'

I jumped eagerly at something he had just said.

'Once I have the Queen's charter? Do you think she will agree Robin?'

'I know her Majesty so well that I know I can never guess what she is going to say or do. I have mentioned your name whenever I have had a chance and, as you reminded me earlier, you are nearly twenty and quite able to look after yourself.'

'Must you rub salt into the wound, Robin? But seriously, do you think . . . ?'

'In another year you will be of age. Can you not wait until then?'

I thought for a moment.

'Yes, I can wait. On the other hand, if Raleigh is planning an expedition . . .'

Though it made my shoulder throb it was a relief to join in Robin's laughter.

'There is no better reason for sailing round the world than to score over Sir Walter Raleigh.'

'Will you persuade the Queen to let me go, then?'

'I will do my best.'

Robin was as good as his word. During the next few days he cautiously and subtly broached the subject of my voyage to her Majesty and reported back to me the progress of his suit. At last he told me that she had agreed; a charter was being prepared setting out the prescribed scope of my expedition. The next thing that happened was that I received a summons to be present in the royal audience chamber on a certain morning.

I remember I slept little the night before the audience and I was in my place long before the appointed time. Not however, before another suitor. I noticed him as soon as I entered the lofty room with its rich hangings, its hay-strewn floor and moulded ceiling. He was standing alone beside the crimson-draped dais and he actually had one foot on the lower step. Had the room been already crowded Sir Walter Raleigh would have stood out. Though well into his forties he was dressed with the ostentatious attention to fashion of a man half his age. Everything about his costume was designed to impress. The doublet with its enormous sleeves was of brilliant white encrusted with jewels and gold thread. The ballooned upper hose was of the same material slashed with purple, the colour of his stockings. His ruff was very high and framed a thin face with a high, creased forehead and dark, darting eyes.

Since we were almost the only occupants of the vast chamber I could not ignore him, not that I had any cause to do so. I swept him a courteous bow from the centre of the room. For a moment he made no response, then he sauntered forward, a light smile on his lips. A few paces away he spoke.

'Good morning, Sir Peter.'

He brushed past me without a glance to greet a young man just entering the room. In my anger I must have turned the colour of the royal dais itself and was only thankful that there were so few people there to witness my humiliation.

Slowly the room filled and soon I was being greeted and congratulated by friends and by opportunists who had shrewdly decided that I was worth cultivating. There were even a few who came to ask for a place in my forthcoming voyage. Then there was a fanfare and the royal procession entered. First came the Queen's gentlemen and household officers. Robin as Master of the Horse was prominently placed and he winked broadly as he passed. Then followed the Lord Chancellor bearing the royal seals in a red silk purse on a cushion. He was flanked by other officers carrying the sceptre and the sword of state. Then came the maids of honour and finally the Queen, over sixty years of age but erect and carrying with seeming ease a great weight of padded clothing and jewels. I have been in many courts where things are done more sumptuously and seen monarchs attended by more pomp and ceremony, but never, I think, have I encountered a better combination of display and dignity, splendour and simplicity than graced the court of Elizabeth of England.

The procession made its way through the crowded presence chamber and her Majesty took her place in the chair of state, with Robin standing on her left and the great Lord Burghley on her right. I waited with impatience and mounting excitement as those more important than I were presented – ambassadors, nobles and Sir Walter Raleigh, who now received permission for his absurd treasure hunt. At last my name was called and I knelt before the Queen. Taking a scroll of parchment from a cushion held by a servant she handed it to me, at the same time bidding me rise.

'Master Dudley, you have persuasive friends,' she said, smiling at Robin. 'What do you think, my lord of Essex, have we the makings of a great mariner here?'

For me the Gloriana magic had long since faded. At close quarters the Queen's age was obvious. Indeed, it was more noticeable for her attempts to hide it. Layers of paint could not conceal the wrinkled skin nor vermilioned lips distract attention from the black teeth. The sparkle of jewels braided into her auburn wig was no substitute for the lustre of real hair. As she and Robin laughed together, exchanging caresses and glances, I wondered how he could devote his energies to flattering an ugly old woman. More than ever I was glad to have made my escape.

Robin assured the Queen that no man knew more of ships and navigation than I and that I lacked only experience to add lustre to her reign. Elizabeth made some pleasant remarks to which I responded, I suppose, with suitable gallantry and modesty. Then she took my hand in her own bony, ring-laden claw.

'Go, then, with our blessing – sweet Robert Dudley. Take care you return to us safely and bring us proof of your valour and enterprise.'

I backed away, bowing and returned to my place. I longed to examine my charter but I could not do so until the audience was over and I had returned to my own privy chamber. Then I excitedly unrolled the document that I fondly believed was to launch another Francis Drake upon the world. As I scanned the seemingly neutral legal phrases I was suddenly aware of sinister implications behind them. My thoughts went back to the Swan at Queenhythe. Mindful, the document read, of my youth and inexperience her Majesty had resolved that my expedition should venture no further than the Americas and that I should be accompanied by a more seasoned mariner. Therefore I was empowered to undertake a journey in search of El Dorado – in the company of Sir Walter Raleigh.

7

In the royal menagerie at the Tower of London they used to have an African lion, an aged shaggy beast, called Edward VI, because he had come there as cub in the reign of the boy king. He lived in a large vault with an iron grill set in the wall so that people could look at him. He was shut in, enclosed; there was nowhere he could go, no way he could escape. Yet all the time he prowled round and round his cell. Every day he walked miles, circular miles on a journey with no destination.

For months after I received my charter I behaved like that lion. I was imprisoned as surely as he was, in a cage of my own ambition. I had wanted to go on a voyage, had pestered to be allowed to fit out my own expedition. Now permission had been granted and I could not escape. I was angry, resentful, humiliated, and I felt completely helpless. But I did not give way to passive melancholy. On the contrary, like that restless lion I lived in a perpetual frenzy of plans and preparations. I haggled with chandlers and harried shipwrights as though nothing else in life mattered, as though I really were about to embark on some grand voyage instead of dancing attendance on a foolish, middle-aged exotic with mad dreams of El Dorado.

During those winter months I was scarcely ever in one place for more than a few days at a time. I visited Deptford frequently to keep an eye on the fitting out of my supply ships and to continue my lessons in practical seacraft. But my presence was increasingly needed in Southampton where the *Bear* and *Bear's Whelp* were a-building. I soon discovered that I could not leave the shipwrights to follow my detailed plans and instructions; they were too set in their traditional ways. If I ordered a 68 foot mainmast with a main top of 31 feet I would arrive in the yard to discover that the carpenters had made a mast with an overall length 78 feet because 'master says she's too narrow in the beam for anything taller'. 'Master' had to be made to realise that he was not dealing with an empty-headed young gentleman who could not tell a rib from a spar. He was convinced eventually and I had the thrill of seeing the two vessels grow to my exact specifications – trim, lithe ships capable of out-distancing anything else afloat. But it took a great deal of hard talking and far too much time. I found myself riding the London to Southampton road in all weathers.

Nor could I completely neglect my estates. Indeed, if I were to set out on a long and hazardous sea voyage I had to ensure that everything was in order before I left. As soon as they knew that I was in more or less complete control of the Dudley lands my bailiffs and tenants began to bombard me with complaints, appeals and demands for urgent action. The tedious Brindley kept insisting that I should deal with many of these matters personally and I began to realise that there was some sense in what he said. I did begin to take an interest in my inheritance but I also simplified the administration by some bold strokes of which Brindley certainly did not approve. For a start I sold most of my outlying lands, those which could not be conveniently supervised from Kenilworth. Most of the proceeds went on equipping my expedition. Then I dismissed my Kenilworth bailiff and installed John Sturdy, a brilliant young man and a friend from my Oxford days. That set many Warwickshire tongues wagging but I knew that John had the energy and the clear head necessary to run efficiently all my Midlands estates. I arranged to put in a personal appearance at Kenilworth every two months to discuss problems with John, preside over manorial courts and meet under-bailiffs and tenants who felt that their affairs needed my personal attention. In this way most of my people were kept reasonably happy and I was able to devote the greater part of my time to maritime matters.

The biggest problem was finding the right men. I employed two muster masters, to scour the docks of London and Southampton for experienced and reliable crew. One of them spent the money I gave him on drink and then disappeared. The other hired several of his friends at exorbitant rates – ruffians from the slums of Shadwell and Ratcliff, whose experience came wholly from the coastal sea-coal trade and who knew nothing of deep sea navigation.

The problem was solved for me very suddenly one day in February. I was at Bedford House recovering from a chill which I had caught riding most of the way from Southampton in a snowstorm. Fussing servants and physicians had tried to confine me to bed but I had only allowed myself to be propped on a couch before the parlour fire. There I could work at the charts, notebooks, lists and bills spread on a table beside me in only moderate discomfort. On that particular morning I sat half-choking in the stuffy atmosphere of the tight-shuttered parlour. The smouldering tobacco leaves in the hearth and sickly odour from the herbs in the perfuming pan may have kept the air free of contagion but they had given me a headache. The disgusting taste of the physician's lungwort clung like soot to my palate. And every time I checked the sailmaker's account I arrived at a different figure.

Suddenly I was aware of raised voices. Someone was in the great hall shouting. His roar shook the parlour door and reverberated through my throbbing head.

'Out of my way, pretty boy!'

There was no mistaking that voice. The shock of memory brought the sweat to my brow.

An instant later the door was flung open and Abraham Kendall stood, staring at me with his good eye. He was an intruder in a gentleman's house. The gentleman's servants stood behind him twittering their apologies. I was that gentleman but I was powerless to assert my authority. I felt like a wretched ship's boy caught out in some misdemeanour.

'Lad, lad, what have they done to you?'

He strode straight to the windows and threw them wide.

'This place smells worse than a poxy bilge.'

A minute later he had expelled my attendants, fastened the

latch against them and seated himself in an armchair beside the fire.

'Now, lad, about this expedition of yours.'

I had apparently hired a master for the *Bear* and a pilot-general all in one. Kendall explained that he had just returned from a voyage and heard on the London waterfront that the ship's boy of the *Swiftsure* venture was grown into an admiral able to commission his own men and vessels. He had complete confidence in me as a navigator, he said. After all, had he not taught me himself during the homeward voyage from Cadiz? But he was equally certain that I knew nothing about seamen. Therefore, he had undertaken to recruit my crews. As I recall, my approval of this arrangement was neither desired nor sought.

Spring came and with it the launching of the *Bear* and the *Bear's Whelp*. A few weeks later, when the fitting out was completed, I took Kendall down to Southampton with me for my ships' sea trials. On a glittering morning in early June we stood on the quayside gazing for the first time on the completed flagship. Bacon tells us that true beauty consists in inner virtue and is not obvious at first sight but when I saw the *Bear* that soft, summer morning I knew she was the most beautiful thing that had ever entered my life. She rode easily at anchor resplendent in her green and gold livery, her fresh creamy sails furled, the bear and ragged staff gleaming on her painted stern.

'A trim looking ship, Master Dudley. A mite too tall, perhaps, in the main and foretops but that can soon be set to rights.'

'No, Abraham, she's tall on purpose, for greater speed.'

As we were rowed out to the *Bear* I explained to Kendall how the dimensions of both ships had been mathematically calculated. He smiled and nodded but I knew that he was reserving judgement. So was the *Bear*'s captain, Benjamin Wood, who met us as we climbed aboard. Wood was one of Kendall's best finds. A Suffolk Puritan of simple ways and transparent honesty, he was also one of the finest captains of the day. He had sailed with Drake and even assayed his own voyage of circumnavigation. Now, at about forty, he was in his prime. Thin, already grey, but bright of eye, he was universally respected by his men, even by those who found his constant bible-quoting rather tedious.

'She looks very grand, Master Dudley, but I know you'll want me to speak my mind.'

We had toured the decks and now stood together on the poop watching the small crew weigh anchor and let out the mainsail.

'Ay, Mr Wood, speak your mind by all means.'

'Then, sir, I think she's a young man's fancy. She's a proud looking ship with her tall masts and her pennants and her gay colours. But pride goes before destruction, as Solomon says. With full sail and a gusty wind she'll yaw. And if some of the gunports are open...'

He looked at me severely and Kendall nodded silently. Clearly it was not only the *Bear* that was on trial.

'Then we must put her through her paces, Mr Wood.'

We were now slipping rapidly down Southampton Water before a freshening offshore breeze. In little more than an hour we had cleared the sandbar off Calshot. As soon as we had a leadline reading of fifty fathoms I ordered full canvas. Men swarmed aloft to free the furled sails. With a crack they bellied out. Sheets and tackle groaned as they took up the strain. And the *Bear* hurled herself through the water.

Kendall and Wood looked anxiously aloft, scanning spars and braces for any sign of weakness. Then they hurried away to check mast wedges, convinced, doubtless, that with such a sail area the masts must be pulled clean out of their seating. They might doubt but I knew. I knew that this living organism, conceived in my own brain and now drawing life from wind and sea, was beautiful and perfect, that she would do all and more than was required of her. I leaned against the rail and gazed down at the surging, curdling wake swirling along the ship's side and stretching out behind in a white, pike-straight line. No sign of yawing and the helmsman was obviously finding the *Bear* easy to handle.

Her sheer speed was exhilarating. Already Brown Down Point was coming into view and the Isle of Wight's coastal fortifications could be clearly seen to starboard. My page, Will Bradshaw, was standing close by, his long hair tousled by the wind, a look of complete rapture on his face. He was about the same age that I had been when I first went to sea and I knew exactly how he felt. But there was work to be done.

'Will!'

'Sir!'

'Fetch the log and line from my chest. We must take a reading.'

By the time Will returned, Kendall and Wood were back on the poop deck. They looked curiously at the large coil of thin cord and the wooden triangle which the lad brought to the rail. I beckoned them over.

'Are you familiar with the log and line, gentlemen?'

Kendall grunted and Wood made some remark to the effect that, in his experience, the log and line was too inaccurate to be of any use. What they were both thinking but would not say was that this was another of Master Dudley's new fangled ideas and that they did not trust it.

'Let me show you how it works then. Will, be good enough to hand Captain Wood the minute-glass. Now, then, Captain if you will kindly turn the glass when I say "Now".'

I took the log and threw it with all my might so that it would land well clear of the ship's wake and hold its place steady in the water. Will, whom I had already instructed in the art, let the fifteen fathoms of 'stray line' run out. As the small piece of red bunting passed through his fingers 1 called out, 'Now, Master Wood.' The Captain turned the glass and the sand trickled steadily through.

'Master Wood, as soon as the last sand has passed through please be so good as to call out "Stop!" '

All eyes were fixed on the glass in Captain Wood's hand, so that he had scarcely any need to signal the end of the minute. As soon as he did so, Will stopped the line and tied another piece of cloth around it.

'There, gentlemen, now all we have to do is haul the line inboard and measure the distance between the two markers. That will tell us how far the ship has travelled in one minute. Then we convert that into leagues to the hour.'

Kendall was unconvinced.

'That's all very well, lad, as long as the wind stays constant —

which it don't.'

'We take a fresh reading at every major change in wind speed or direction.'

Kendall grunted. Wood's brow was still wrinkled in a sceptical frown.

'Even if this reading is accurate, Master Dudley, what use is your instrument in rough weather?'

I laughed.

'Master Wood, you remind me of the man who vowed he would never have a sundial because it would not tell the time at night.'

At that point Will came up to report that the *Bear* had made sixty-three fathoms in a measured minute.

'There, gentlemen, sixty-three fathoms in a minute. That means . . . let me see . . . 3780 fathoms in an hour. Allowing 2500 fathoms to the league we have a speed of one league, 1280 fathoms – just over one and a half leagues to the hour. A good pace, gentlemen . . .'

It was then I noticed that the Master and Captain were staring at me with comical expressions of astonishment on their faces. I had not meant to show off my natural talent for figures but clearly I had put on an unwitting display of mathematical ability which left them breathless. By the end of that morning's sailing both the ship and the admiral had made a favourable impression on two seasoned mariners.

The trial went well in every way. Except for a few minor details, the *Bear* proved as fine a ship in reality as I had known her to be on paper. Kendall, Wood and the *Bear*'s builders were unstinting in their praise of her designs. I should have been elated but as we sat at dinner in a Southampton inn my excitement and enthusiasm drained away. The talk was all of the forthcoming expedition and Kendall was telling how he had recruited some senior mariners in Plymouth.

' "But," says they, "we're committed to Sir Walter Raleigh. He's hired us for his ships on the self-same venture." "Oh," says I, "and what has Sir Walter agreed to pay you?" "Eightpence a day and a share of the booty." I laughed real hearty at that. "And what sailor ever came back from one of Sir Walter's voyages with any booty? No lads," I said, "best join a fine new ship under an admiral who's forgotten more about navigation than Raleigh ever knew despite his youth. Master Dudley only takes the best men," says I. "He pays them tenpence a day and offers a far better chance of booty than Raleigh." '

I should have been amused and flattered at Kendall's silly prattle but it only served to remind me that I could no longer put off dealing directly with Sir Walter Raleigh. I need hardly say that the leader of the forthcoming expedition had made no attempt to communicate with me. He was obviously waiting for me to go cap in hand to him for my 'orders'. Now I had no option but to do just that. No longer could I take refuge in the assembly and preparation of my own ships and men. All my plans were well forward. It was a slight consolation to learn that Raleigh was not faring nearly so well. He was having to borrow ships from Lord Admiral Howard and anyone else who would lend and he had precious little money to spend on men and supplies. Yet I had to go and deal with the man; had to be pleasant to him, swallow his insults and steel myself to serving under him for six months or more. The following day I set out for Sherborne Castle with only my page for company, leaving some servants to follow with the pack animals.

I must confess to a certain curiosity as to what I would find at Sherborne. Rumours were rife of Raleigh's ambitious building works there. At court men told each other in shocked whispers that the ex-favourite used his country retreat as a sanctum where he could secretly consort with atheists, magicians and necro-mancers. Certainly the castle looked forbidding – grey and grimly defensive against a sky of swirling clouds that threatened thunder – as we climbed towards it past a straggle of mean houses connecting it with the town. Sherborne Castle was a Norman fortress, turned into a palace in more peaceful times, yet unable to rid itself of the atmosphere of fear and oppression in which it had been conceived. It was similar in many ways to my own Kenilworth. Indeed, it was widely believed that Raleigh planned to imitate and hoped to excel my father's magnificent building.

New stone gleamed from the upper storeys of the main gate as we approached the bridge over the empty moat, giving some promise of the splendours awaiting within. However, before we could cross the impressive threshold we had to rein in our horses and pull to one side of the road. Out from the castle came lumbering a large waggon pulled by two horses. It was the first of seven or eight such creaking vehicles, each piled high with chairs, tables, boxes, chests, bales and a miscellany of household goods roped securely to the cart frame. Around and among the cavalcade ran scores of servants, some carrying small bundles, others shouting instructions and warnings to the drivers of the lurching waggons. The scene resembled nothing so much as the start of a royal progress and I could not imagine what it signified. At last I attracted the attention of one of the servants whose aloof bearing, staff of office and lack of any kind of burden marked him as a man of consequence. On learning that I had business with his master, the major-domo bowed respectfully.

'You'll have to come down to the new castle, sir.'

'New castle?'

'Yes, sir. If you'll be so kind as to come a few paces this way.'

He advanced towards a vantage point on the edge of the moat mound and pointed across the park to the south. Beyond the river stood a new, small, square house with corner towers and a crop of spiralling chimneys. It looked pleasant and homely, the sort of manor house suitable for a country gentleman of modest means. This, it appeared, was the great courtier's much vaunted 'castle'.

We made our way down to the new residence, avoiding as best we could the clutter of unpacked desiderata and the scurry of servants hurrying in and out of doors. At last we found someone to take our horses and convey us to where the originator of all this confusion stood. He was on the river bank, overseeing an army of sweating workmen who, with picks and spades were bent on converting a water meadow into a garden. He was giving orders to his head gardener as I approached, bowed and apologised for calling at such an inconvenient time. Sir Walter smiled affably and grasped my hand.

'My dear young man, not at all, not at all. In fact, your arrival is most timely.'

He was dressed now not in ornate court clothes, but in what was, I imagine, the simple garb he considered appropriate to a working landlord. The overall impression was immaculate. No speck of mud soiled his long boots. The half unlaced jerkin of white buckskin gleamed. The ruff was crisp and newly pressed. The scarlet lining of his cloak matched the small visible expanse of hose. The beaver hat looked as though it had been polished. And the short cane, topped only with modest silver, completed the appearance of careless elegance.

'Yes most timely.' He took me by the arm and steered me at a saunter towards the excavations.

'It is so difficult for a rural clod, like myself, to keep abreast of fashion and here you are, fresh from the court, brimming with all the newest ideas. Tell me, now, how should I plan my garden. I had thought of something in the Italian taste. Is that still in vogue?'

He chatted on in the same vein, charming with an undercurrent of sarcasm, while we toured the nascent gardens. Then he insisted on showing me all over the house, apologising all the time for its modesty, lamenting that it could not compare with the great Dudley houses, explaining that it must 'serve' for one upon whom 'fortune no longer smiles'. It was a performance at once nauseating and disarming. Raleigh gave every appearance of being an embittered ex-favourite accepting his reduced circumstances with a bad grace. It was impossible to see in this rather sorry figure a dark intriguer capable of violence or even murder.

Several times I tried to bring the conversation round to the forthcoming expedition but my host refused to be drawn. Not until I had been accommodated in a hastily-prepared chamber (more apologies), dined sumptuously on what Raleigh insisted was but 'simple country fare', taken for an afternoon's hawking in the castle park, supped (again in princely fashion) and settled by a peat fire in Raleigh's cosy parlour – only then did Sir Walter permit discussion of naval matters. Lady Raleigh and other members of the household had withdrawn to the other end of the room and were clustered around the virginals, playing and singing. Sir Walter sat in an upholstered chair, stretched his legs before him, set taper to a pipe of tobacco (an abhorrence of this pernicious habit was, I think, the only opinion I shared in later days with King James) and gazed into the fire.

'Your preparations are well in hand, I hear. Your two capital ships lie ready in Southampton and your supply vessels – the *Mermaid*, the *Earwig* and the *Frisking* are their names I believe – are fitting out at Deptford.' He smiled and a curl of smoke twisted from the corner of his mouth.

'You are very well informed.'

'This is a very important venture, Master Dudley. I must make sure that all my ships and men are as well found as possible.'

'I had hoped, Sir Walter, that you would have communicated with me before now to discuss the purpose of the expedition.'

Raleigh turned his head towards the group clustered round the virginals, and hummed the air of a galliard his brother, Carew, had just struck up on the lute. He stopped and allowed the familiar, aloof, patronising smile to rise to the surface of his face.

'Master Dudley, I applaud your enthusiasm and the great expense you have been to in fitting out ships for her Majesty's service. England needs young men of your spirit and . . .' He hesitated just long enough to make his point. '. . . and breeding. One day you will I am sure venture great things for the honour of Dudley and England. For the moment, you must be content to leave the planning of great enterprises to those of us who are experienced in these matters. Real navigation cannot be learned from books nor fair weather bought with gold.'

I knew by the tingling that the rebuff had brought hot colour to my cheeks but I was determined not to react. I was equally determined to discover to what enterprise I was committing my money and effort.

'I hope our great enterprise will not turn out to be a wild goose chase, Sir Walter.'

Raleigh took the pipe from his lips and leaned forward.

'Your meaning, Master Dudley?' The voice was emotionless but the feeble shaft had obviously struck home.

'I would be reluctant to venture my reputation on a quest for the mythical man of gold.'

I had quite expected my taunt to provoke one of the sudden flashes of anger for which Raleigh was noted. Yet the look which came over his face was not one of fury. He sat back in his chair and gazed at the ceiling, but he was not looking at the Raleigh lozenges embossed in plaster.

'El Dorado – a myth? I wonder. I wonder.'

That dreamy, distant stare: it was, I realised with a shock, the same expression that I had seen on the face of Thomas Cavendish when he spoke of Cathay and the Spice Islands.

Suddenly, Raleigh was on his feet. With a curt 'Come with me', he strode the length of the room. I followed him across the hall, up the main staircase and into a first floor chamber which the owner had clearly designed as his library. By the light of wall torches which the servants quickly lit I saw open chests and boxes full of books and papers, glazed doors standing open to reveal shelves as yet largely empty. But there was one bookcase, against the far wall, which was not vacant. Behind its latticed panes the leather and vellum volumes stood in ordered rows. It was to this that Raleigh marched, his cane tapping the bare boards and striking echoes from the as yet un-tapestried walls. He opened the case with a key which hung from his belt.

'Look well, Master Dudley. Here is every book, every pamphlet ever written about the Americas.'

His fingers ran lovingly over the softly glowing spines.

'See, Gamboa's *History of the Incas*. You do not, I think, read Spanish? No? A pity; most books about the New World are written by Spaniards. Here is Cieza and Gomrara's account of the conquest of Mexico. And here, André Thevet's book on Brazil. Over here,' He moved to a low table piled with papers, 'maps and charts, some of them very recent. Look at this one, drawn only a few months ago by a Spanish prisoner taken by Captain Popham. See, it locates for the first time the land of the Amazons, the fierce, female warriors. Around this lake live a people whose heads are shrunk into their shoulders. And here is the mountain Kingdom of Guiana. This is where the lake of Gran Manoa is situated. The floor of that lake is carpeted with gold. Every year at their major festival the king of Guiana is covered from head to toe in oil and gold dust. He plunges into the lake and all the people throw in their offerings – gold rings and bracelets, brooches, ornaments, bells and charms. Think of it: a fortune thrown into the waters of that lake once every year for centuries.'

'But surely . . .'

'I know, you are going to say these are only travellers' tales. If that is the case, why is Spain about to colonise Guiana and the Orinoco basin?'

'You know that for certain?'

He did not answer immediately, but walked back to the book-case and from it took a small inlaid walnut box of Italian design. He set it upon the table, unlocked it and drew out a sheaf of written papers.

'I said that my Captain, George Popham, had captured a Spanish ship and taken from it a gentleman who knew the Orinoco basin. That gentleman was none other than an agent sent by Antonio de Berrio with letters and a report for King Philip.'

'Berrio, is he not the governor of Trinidad?'

'Not only is he the governor of Trinidad; he has also spent twenty years and more exploring the Orinoco basin, searching for the kingdom of El Dorado. And now,' he prodded the letters with the gold handle of his cane, 'now he has found it. One of his men, Domingo de Vera, has travelled to the very edge of El Dorado's mountain fortress. So Berrio writes to his king for men and horses to mount a great expedition and claim yet another source of great wealth for Spain.'

'But who is to say that Berrio is not mistaken. His man, Vera, has not been into Guiana. What proof has he that its people are not just simple savages like their neighbours?'

Raleigh reached again into the walnut casket. Whatever he took out was so small as to be completely concealed within his closed fingers. He took my hand and laid the contents of his own upon the palm. It was the figure of a man no more than two inches long. He was naked. Every feature of his body was perfectly fashioned. Fashioned in solid gold. Raleigh smiled at my obvious amazement.

'Well, my sceptical friend, is El Dorado a myth, or are you now gazing upon his image?'

'This was sent by Berrio?'

'To convince King Philip. But by the greatest good fortune it fell into my hands together with all de Berrio's maps and papers. That means that we have a unique chance to forestall the Spaniards and claim Guiana in the name of her Majesty. Would we be loyal subjects if we passed up that chance?'

My mind was in a whirl that night. No wonder my sleep was disturbed by dreams in which Queen Elizabeth jumped into a lake and was rescued by Sir Walter Raleigh whose superior, smiling features were fixed in immobile gold.

8

A few days later I was back at court to take my formal leave of the Queen. It had been agreed that I should gather my fleet immediately at Southampton and there await Raleigh's summons to rendezvous with him in Plymouth. I knew full well why he did not want me in Plymouth; he did not wish me to see for myself how far his ships were from being ready. I, therefore, steeled myself to several weeks' delay, ordered Kendall to man my vessels with skeleton crews in the interim and delay taking on board fresh provisions as long as possible. I do not know whether the calmness I affected as I took leave of friends and set my affairs in order deceived anyone. I expect it was obvious to all who knew me well that I was in a turmoil of suppressed excitement. Soon I would be at sea, the youngest gentleman adventurer ever to share command of a fleet in the Queen's name.

But that was not the only cause which set demons within my bosom, disturbing sleep and playing havoc with appetite; my waking thoughts and turbulent dreams were dominated by the golden man. I could not rid my mind of the crude outline, the sullen gleam and the enigmatic smile which half-beckoned, half dared me to seek his master. My better judgement still told me that Raleigh's land of El Dorado was a myth but my imagination manufactured an arsenal of counter arguments: Just supposing it were true; was the wealth of the Incas not considered a myth before Pizarro found the hoarded riches of the sun-king?; Had not Dr Dee proved mathematically that precious metal abounds in the unexplored regions of the world?

I say that my excitement must have been obvious to many at

Windsor and Nonesuch that late summer and autumn but I flatter myself. The court was, as always, preoccupied with its own scandals and sensations. Of course I sought out Robin as soon as I returned, in order to tell him my latest news and discuss all that I had seen and heard at Sherborne. He was not in a mood to listen. He had had one of his periodic arguments with the Queen and was more interested in impressing me, or anyone else who would listen, with the justification for his sense of grievance. He poured out his complaints one showery morning as we rode in Windsor Great Park.

'Just like '89! It is just like '89 all over again!' Robin's shouted indignation set the rooks spiralling into the air with their own shrieks of raucous anger.

It was all I could do to keep up with him as he spurred his grey mare through the dripping woods.

'She refuses to let me lead an expedition to Brest. The Spaniards seize the harbour. They build up a new invasion fleet there. But I must not go and force them out. I could fit out twenty sail immediately. Others would join me. But no, nothing is done. Nothing!'

He reined in suddenly where the path forked beneath a wide, broad-limbed oak. I drew up beside him and let my sweating bay crop the grass.

'Calm yourself, Robin. The Queen is only concerned for your safety. Many men would be flattered . . .'

'It is easy for you to say such things. You have your leave of absence. Soon you will be a thousand miles away. God, how I envy you!'

I laughed.

'You, envy me, Robin? It would suit you not at all to be away from the Queen, away from the fount of power and authority.'

His eyes widened in mock incredulity.

'The fount of power and authority? Have you learned nothing, Bear cub? The fount has long since run dry. There is no power, no authority.'

'Robin, this is stupid talk.'

I turned the bay's head towards the left-hand fork and legged him into motion. Robin's hand flashed out and grasped the bridle.

'No, Bear cub, you must listen. Do you know what rules this nation? Not the Queen. Not the Council. I used to think it was the Council. Now I know that Cecil and the others are as impotent as I am. And certainly it is not parliament, though God knows those curs try hard enough to rule. No, it is nothing but a painting...'

'What nonsense! Robin...'

'A very beautiful painting – glowing with the colour of a Hilliard, the face created by Gheeraerts, perhaps, aloof yet serene and gracious. Gloriana, a madonna to be worshipped, beautiful, young, radiant – and mute.'

I tried unsuccessfully to shake the reins free.

'And what is behind the painting? A petulant, senile old woman.'

'Robin, you must not talk like this. It could be dangerous for you.'

'Dangerous! God's blood, Bear cub, can you not see how dangerous it is to keep silent. Elizabeth Tudor is sixty – nearly sixty-one. She can no longer govern but she will let no one make decisions, so government goes by default. Scarce a month goes past without some plot against her being discovered. Only a few weeks ago Lopez, her own physician, was despatched at Tyburn for trying to poison her. Yet this stupid woman will not name her successor. So we have no rule, no security, no heir. Yet nobody realises it. Everyone is dazzled by the beautiful picture. One day soon that canvas will be slashed from top to bottom, side to side. For the first time Englishmen will look behind the portrait and they will see that the Queen is dead.'

Essex's grey pawed the ground, impatient to be back in his dry stable.

'And what else will her Majesty's loyal subjects see besides the corpse? Nothing! Nothing, but a black, frightening void. And from that void the growing din of anarchy and the roar of Spanish guns.'

It was useless to remonstrate. One had to enter Robin's world of black melancholy to lead him out of it.

'What is the remedy, then?'

Robin released my reins. Side by side we rode forward along the path. Water from the saturated canopy of leaves dripped around and on us.

'The Council must take more decisions in the sovereign's name, stand up to Spain, nominate an heir. We must show our enemies that nothing would be gained by the Queen's death.'

'And if the Council's decisions do not meet with the approval of my lord of Essex?'

He turned his still boyish smile upon me.

'What a solemn fellow you are, Bear cub. You look very little like a young man just off on his first great adventure. Perhaps a race will put some colour into those grey cheeks. A hundred pounds if you come first to the postern!'

And once again I was spattered with mud thrown up by his horse's hooves.

The court returned to Westminster in October and one of the first functions was a banquet in honour of the new French ambassador. I had expected to be away long since but my increasingly frequent letters to Raleigh were answered by vague references to delays he was experiencing because of bad weather and dishonest chandlers. Every message from Sherborne (for Raleigh would not lower himself to deal personally with the merchants and carpenters at Plymouth) urged the necessity for patience and careful preparation and informed me that the admiral would be ready to sail 'in a few days'. So it was that I took my part in the feasting and dancing in the great banqueting hall as the most reluctant of all the revellers present.

I danced with many of the ladies of the court and drank a little too much with my friends. Many people wanted to pledge my health and wish me well for the voyage. It was all very pleasant and I really began to feel like an intrepid adventurer about to launch out on a great enterprise. The wine and the congenial company made me forget my frustrations for a while. Only one thing vexed me; Margaret would not dance with me. Every time I approached her she seemed preoccupied with a fat, gaudily dressed, middle-aged man whom I had never seen before. I discovered from friends that his name was Sir Anthony Wingfield, a hanger-on at court. Whoever he was, he obviously found the attentions of a young girl very flattering. Nor did Margaret apparently consider his company displeasing. Through the wavering forms of the dancers I watched the two of them with growing disgust. They laughed together. Margaret fed her 'beau' with sweetmeats. Wingfield ran podgy fingers through her hair, along the nape of her neck and the line of her chin.

At last I could watch no longer. I elbowed my way unsteadily through the dancers and went right up to Margaret and her companion. I bowed and asked her to dance with me. Without waiting for a reply I half led, half dragged her to the floor. The musicians in the gallery were playing a pavane. Margaret and I took up our places in the line of performers treading the slow, stately steps. The thin powdering of chalk did not conceal the angry, embarrassed glow on her cheeks.

'Robert, what do you think you are doing?' The words were whispered through lips that wore a static, polite smile.

'I am rescuing you from a tiresome old fellow who seems to think he owns you.'

We had paraded the length of the hall before Margaret spoke again. She was curtseying and her eyes were cast towards the floor so that I could not see her expression.

'He does own me.'

'What do you mean?'

'I am to be married to Sir Anthony Wingfield.'

I stopped and the next man bumped into me. With a mumbled apology I slipped mechanically back into the routine of the dance. The disjointed fragments of our whispered conversation were interspersed between the sedate courtesies of the pavane.

'You cannot!'

'I can. I have no need to seek your permission.'

'You do not love that fat old fool.'

'What has love to do with marriage?'

'But, you cannot want to . . .'

'It has been arranged by my father. Sir Anthony is a wealthy

113

neighbour.'

'And you have agreed.'

'Of course.' She looked defiant, and still angry. 'Besides, it is no concern of yours.'

'Yes it is.'

'Oh, indeed? Do you suppose you can ignore me for months and then come and tell me who I may or may not marry?'

'Yes. I want to marry you!'

I must have shouted the words for our neighbours in the dance turned amused glances towards us and the ladies giggled. Margaret looked furious.

'Master Dudley, the wine has made you forget yourself.'

She bobbed a quick curtsey and hurried from the floor.

I stumbled out of the hall with mocking laughter ringing in my ears. In my own outer chamber Will Bradshaw sat up yawning in his truckle bed as I entered.

'Go back to sleep, Will. I shall undress myself tonight.'

A good fire was burning in the bedchamber and enough of the candles were lit to give the room a warm half light. I fell onto the bed and tried to still my swirling thoughts. What had I said to Margaret – 'I want to marry you?' Was I drunk? Was it not rather that Pliny's dictum was right: 'Truth is said to be in wine'. But if it were true why had I never told her before? Was it that I was too busy with the plans for my voyage? Partly that, of course, but more important was the fact that I had never thought about setting up home and taking a wife. I had had no one to urge such considerations upon me or indulge in matrimonial bargaining on my behalf. As for Margaret, I suppose I had assumed that she would always be there. Now I knew that I had been wrong and the shock and pain were far worse than I could ever have imagined.

I lay still, staring up at the bed's heavy drapes, silky and soot-black in the dim light. And I remembered. Sunlit hours in the garden at Chelsea, hasty kisses in Greenwich's quiet arbours, assignations in Windsor park. The memories took on the grotesquerie of dreams and I slept.

'Robert! Robert!'

Margaret's voice so filled my slumbering fantasies that it was only with difficulty that I extricated myself from the dream world and realised that it was really she who was whispering my name and shaking me gently. I sat up quickly. I must have been asleep for an hour or more; the fire had subsided to a dull glow and only two stubs of sputtering candle remained alight. Her face glowed pale in the darkness and a tear sparkled on her cheek. I pulled her down beside me and held her tight.

'There, my sweet, what is it? Why are you crying?'

'Oh Robert, I do want to marry you. I do, I do!' Her sobs shuddered through both our bodies.

I stroked her hair and kissed her forehead.

'Darling, I want that too – truly I do. I am a fool not to have asked you before.'

'Now it is too late. I have to marry that horrid, fat, old man.'

I propped myself on one elbow and looked down at her.

'But why? You do not love him. Surely your father...'

'My father says I am nineteen and if I cannot find a husband of my choosing I must marry one of his.'

'Curse your father for a callous fool.'

'No, Robert, you must not say that. He gave me time to seek a husband I could love.'

'Sweetheart, you should have told me.'

'*I*, told you?' A trace of anger tinged her voice. 'Is it for the woman to ask the man? Besides you have had little time for me lately. And now you are going away. Perhaps you will never come back. There are so many storms and Spanish ships and sea monsters...' She began to cry again.

'Darling, sea monsters only live in mariner's tales.'

'How do you know?'

'I know.' I stooped to kiss her chin, her neck, the swell of her breasts above the low-cut dress. 'As for Spaniards and storms do you think I am not man enough to face them. I will come back and then I will marry you.'

'Oh Robert, my darling, it is too late. I have given my word and the date is fixed. My father would never cancel everything; it would make him look foolish to all our neighbours.'

115

'And no doubt the dowry has been fixed to the satisfaction of your fat lover.'

'Robert, please do not be bitter. If I can accept it you must, too.' Her hands loosened the bodice of her dress and freed the breasts from their confinement. She pulled my head down to them. 'We belong to each other in spirit and my body is yours now if you want it. Let that be enough.'

Dear, sweet Margaret. Never before had she made any unchaste suggestion. I knew then, beyond a shadow of doubt, that I could not condemn her to nights of mauling and pummelling by Sir Anthony Wingfield. I kissed her lips long and softly then drew back.

'What, shall I make court scandal of you like Bess Throckmorton and all the others. When I bed you, and bed you I shall, it will be as your husband.'

'But, Robert that cannot . . .'

'That can be, my sweet, and shall be. And now you had better return to your own chamber or there will be gossip. It would be a shame to suffer the taunts of wagging tongues without having first enjoyed ourselves in sinful pleasure.'

But only after repeated kisses and assurances that all would be well did Margaret tiptoe past my sleeping page and disappear into the darkness.

From London to the Cavendish manor of Hornsey, where Margaret's father was staying, was only a morning's ride. The following noon found me seated beside Richard Cavendish in a walled corner of a neat garden which radiated the drowsy warmth of a belated summer. He was spare, old, of acerbic wit and well set in his ways, as are many widowers and bachelors. I found it difficult to realise that this was the father of whom Margaret spoke so affectionately. He made it quite clear to me that I had intruded upon that period of his day habitually devoted to reading and reflection. Having long attained the seniority which does not have to mask its feelings with civility, he brusquely demanded the reason for this disturbance.

It was only then that I realised I had no good reason. On the journey down I had, of course, rehearsed a score of excellent arguments why Margaret should marry me rather than Wingfield. Now, for the first time the enormity of what I was asking Richard Cavendish to do occurred to me. He had made an amicable and mutually satisfactory arrangement with an old friend and neighbour about the marriage of his younger daughter. No sane person would question his right to do so, nor assert that love had a stronger claim than wealth to Margaret's hand. Cavendish had provided satisfactorily for Margaret's future. She would have a comfortable home and an assured social standing. The Wingfields were known at court, so that, in the intervals of producing children, Margaret could keep up her fashionable friends and interests. Above all, the Queen's blessing on the match had been sought and obtained. This had involved months of hard negotiating for Cavendish. And I was about to suggest that he should set all this aside in favour of a young courtier who still had to prove himself. I suddenly wished myself as insignificant and capable of immediate flight as a drowsy wasp which was visiting the last of Cavendish's roses.

'You have not ridden all the way from London to gaze at the flowers, have you?' My reluctant host took no trouble to conceal his impatience.

'No, sir, I . . . I have come to talk to you about your daughter, Margaret.'

Ostentatiously he opened the large book which lay on his lap and held it close to his eyes. When he spoke again it was without looking up.

'Well, what about Margaret? Is she ill?'

'No, sir, she . . .'

'Hm! Not ill. Then, I suppose you want to marry her.'

Noisily he turned a page and ran his finger along the top line of print.

'Yes, sir, I do.' I tried to make the words sound forthright, determined, but the effect was blunted by his seeming indifference.

After half a page of silent reading he did me the honour of a sideways glance.

'Leicester's bastard, are you not?'

'Yes, or rather . . .'

'Knew your father well. He was an empty-headed braggart. Are you cut from the same cloth?'

The insult prodded my lightly slumbering anger.

'Sir, I must ask you to be careful how you speak of my father.'

Cavendish chuckled quietly, as though sharing some private joke with the large volume before him.

'My choice for Margaret does not meet with your approval?'

'I do not believe that she loves Sir Anthony.'

'Why should she not?'

'He is old enough to be her father.'

'And does Margaret not love her father?'

'Sir, you twist my words.'

'Sir, you choose your words badly.' Cavendish still addressed himself to the printed page. 'Margaret loves me and she will do as I ask her.'

He snapped the book shut, placed it on a low table, and raised himself slowly from the chair. Leaning on a cane he began to walk along a grassy path between the roses. It was obvious that I would wait in vain for an invitation to accompany him so I took my place at his side unbidden.

'Certainly Margaret loves you, sir, and certainly she will obey you. She would let her heart be broken rather than hurt your feelings. Perhaps that is a good reason for considering her wishes very carefully?'

Cavendish paused to gouge a weed from the flower bed with the end of his cane.

'And do you think a girl of nineteen is the best judge of her own future happiness?'

Before I could reply he turned to face me. For the first time in our conversation he talked to me instead of at me, emphasising his words by tapping my chest with the ivory handle of his stick.

'Margaret fancies herself in love with you and no doubt you dote on her. Well, Master Dudley, if I thought you worthy of her, you should have her.'

I raised my voice to protest but he frowned angrily.

'Do not interrupt. I know a great deal about you – more than you think. Margaret talks of little else. You are rich enough. You are well bred, for all that your father was a fool. But you have caught a deadly disease – one that seemingly afflicts half the young men in England.'

'Sir, who has been spreading lies about me? If they have told you I have the French pox . . .'

Cavendish thought this very funny. His thin laughter brought on a fit of coughing, so that it was some while before he could explain.

'No, lad, not the pox – though for all I know your whoring in London has left its mark. No, I was talking of sea fever. It is virulent and it kills.'

He plucked a crimson rose and held it to his nose between long, bony fingers.

'I had a nephew once, my elder brother's only son – the only son either of us ever had. A fine boy, a brave boy. I think you met him.'

With a shock, I realised he was talking about my late friend and hero, Thomas Cavendish.

'He caught sea fever. He sailed the world around, but that did not cure him. And now . . .' The vivid petals fluttered to the grass as he unclenched his hand. 'Would you marry my Meg and leave her a broken hearted widow within months, Master Dudley?'

There was no answer. We walked in silence for several minutes. The old man pointed to a maze which he had planted three years before, and a sprinkling of young cedars fringing a wide lawn.

'For posterity, Master Dudley. I shall never sit in the shade of these trees, nor will my grandson when he inherits. But please God there will still be Cavendishes here when these cedars tower aloft.'

We crossed the lawn towards the sprawling, red-brick manor. We had reached the centre when Cavendish stopped and looked at me again.

'This voyage of yours – is it very important to you?'

'Very important, sir. It is something I have dreamed of for years.'

'Hm! And Meg? How important is she to you? If I said you

could marry her on condition that you gave up your expedition what would your answer be?'

'Well, sir...I...'

'Aha, as I thought.'

He turned and stamped towards the house. Despite a slight limp he moved with surprising speed and agility. I found myself almost running beside him.

'Sir, your decision is a hard one.'

'My decision? Oh, no, it is you who have made the decision, not I. You have decided that your love of the sea is greater than your love for my daughter.'

I argued, protested, as I hustled along beside Cavendish at an undignified trot. It was useless. The subject was closed as far as my host was concerned. Without a word he preceded me into the courtyard and ordered my horse to be brought. He stood impassively, leaning slightly on his stick as I mounted. I thought he was not even going to offer me a civil farewell. But he did speak, head on one side, eyes shielded against the low, autumn sunlight. And for the first time there was a different timbre, almost one of tenderness in his voice.

'You sit your horse very much like him.'

I said farewell and gathered up the reins. He stepped forward and put a hand to my bridle.

'Take care, lad. Come back safe. If your voyage cures you of sea fever, we will talk again of Margaret.'

'But...Sir Anthony Wingfield...?'

'Leave Sir Anthony to me. He is, after all, old enough to be her father.'

He turned and walked into the house.

Pure joy overtook me on that ride back to London. I galloped up Hampstead Hill and across the heath to Highgate shouting and whooping with sheer exultation in the warm, soft, autumn sunlight. A few hours before I had known only frustration and despair. Now I had found a love and a purpose. Everything in the world seemed right. Raleigh and his procrastinations were mere petty annoyances. Life, which for as long as I could remember had possessed little meaning, was now falling into a pattern, a pattern which included adventure and Margaret.

My news and joy had to be shared with my betrothed (for so I now regarded her) without delay. But just when it was vital that I spend a few moments alone with her fate seemed to deny us any opportunity to meet. The Queen took to her bed with a chill and demanded the constant presence of her maids of honour. At the very time that Margaret was released for a few hours' rest I was closeted in a London tavern with three young gentlemen who were trying to persuade me to take them on my voyage. Two days passed without my catching so much as a glimpse of Margaret. The delay would have mattered less at almost any other time of year; the worst sailing weather now lay immediately ahead. I had resolved to wait no longer. I was determined to assemble my crews, load water and victuals and take my fleet from Southampton to Plymouth, whether Raleigh ordered it or not. But I could not leave without seeing Margaret. Eventually I was reduced to loitering in the Presence Chamber in the hope of catching her as she left the Queen's private rooms. I smuggled a note into her by one of the other maids.

An hour later the door opened and a little procession came out. Three women, flustered and fussing, preceded two of the Queen's guards. Between them the two men were carrying a pallet and on it lay Margaret, eyes closed and limp. I rushed up.

'What is the matter? What has happened to her? Is she ill?'

I was 'shushed' by the senior of the ladies, a hard featured matron of some forty years.

'She has fainted. It is stuffy in there and the herbs are overpowering. You men, set her down there.'

The soldiers lowered the simple bed to the floor. Margaret lay pale as death, making no sound or movement.

'Very well, you may return to your post, now.'

The guards withdrew while the ladies gathered round their patient, fanning her and loosening her clothes. Then the matron clapped her hands.

'Come ladies, what Mistress Cavendish most needs is rest and quiet. We will leave her for a while. Come along, come along.'

She shooed her companions back into the inner chamber and as she turned to close the door behind her she smiled at me and winked.

No sooner were we alone than Margaret jumped up and ran into my arms.

'Oh, Robert, Robert, did I worry you? Forgive me, but it was the only way I could think of to escape. Now, quickly, tell me what happened when you saw my father.'

We went to my rooms and I described my interview with Richard Cavendish. It was a joy to see the relief and pleasure in Margaret's face when she knew that she was free of Sir Anthony Wingfield and that her father had held out at least the possibility of our marriage.

'You see, Robert, I told you he loves me and wants me to be happy.'

'That is why he is not sure of me. He thinks I may spend too much time at sea and leave you alone, perhaps one day even widowed.'

Margaret leaned on the casement sill and gazed wistfully down into the sunlit courtyard.

'I know you must go on this voyage and I would not try to stop you. Part of me wants you to go and to return with strange stories and quantities of treasure. The other part of me is full of fear. I suppose it will always be so. When we are married I shall feel the same every time you go away – even if it is just for a short journey. If one day you should fail to return I think I could bear it, as long as we had had a few years of happiness together.'

I went across and put my arms round her.

'This is no time for mournful thoughts of death. I must leave tomorrow; I cannot go if you are in this sombre mood.'

Margaret frowned.

'Tomorrow? So soon?'

'The sooner I go, the sooner I shall return, and the sooner we can be wed. Now, how shall we pass the time that remains?'

'I should return to the Queen...'

'That you should not; you are without doubt too sick. Now, shall we have a song?'

We had many songs – ballads of love and nonsensical ditties but it was Margaret's favourite with its strain of melancholy that we came to in the end, joining our voices as I played the lute.

My sweetest Lesbia, let us live and love
And, though the sager sort our deeds reprove,
    Let us not weigh them. Heaven's great lamps do dive
Into their west and straight again revive.
But soon as once set is our little light,
Then must we sleep one ever during night,
        Ever during night.

When timely death my life and fortune ends
Let not my hearse be vexed with mourning friends.
    But let all lovers rich in triumph come
And with sweet pastimes grace my happy tomb.
And Lesbia close thou up my little light
And crown with love my ever during night,
        Ever during night.

When I reached Southampton I found everything at the harbour under Kendall's rigid control. Within two days of my arrival he had assembled the full complement of nearly three hundred men and had loaded most of our supplies. From the admiral's cabin on the *Bear* I could see the line of ships – my ships – along the quay, alive with activity as sailors, soldiers and dock workers hurried about their duties.

My quarters were luxurious. They lacked, perhaps, the opulence with which Francis Drake surrounded himself but they were extremely comfortable. The table, specially made to my own design, had a long drawer for my charts and rutters. The massive chair was well provided with cushions. There was a carved, inlaid chest for my clothes and a stouter, iron-bound coffer for my plate, books and precious navigational instruments. A Molyneux globe stood beside the table. The Bruges tapestries fixed to the wall were a present from Robin. Margaret had made the brocade hangings for my box bed and the coverlet embroidered with the bear and ragged staff. Often as I watched my page, young Will Bradshaw, tidying the cabin as I had done for Robin five years before, I reflected that few men could boast they were ship's boys on their first voyage and admirals on their second.

November 3 was a Sunday and I led the whole company to church where we received the body and blood of Christ together and were blessed by the local parson. Afterwards I dined the captains, masters and commanders in one of the city inns. They were a good company – senior mariners and soldiers – all with a taste for adventure and not afraid of the unknown. As well as Kendall and Wood there were Thomas Jobson and Nicholas Wyatt who commanded the land forces, Richard Monk, captain of the *Bear's Whelp*, John Wentworth of the *Mermaid*, captains Vincent and Lister of the supply vessels and half a dozen others whose names I have forgotten. We feasted merrily on pasties, boiled mutton and roasted fowl which we relished all the more because we knew we would not taste the like once we had put to sea.

As I gazed along the table at their weatherbeaten faces and listened to them talking of journeys past and old perils I could scarcely believe that they were assembled to serve me, that these men who between them had travelled the seven seas accepted among their brotherhood one whose navigation had been over paper oceans and along inked coastlines. Yet here they were pledging their loyalty and toasting my success with genuine enthusiasm. It was a warm and invigorating camaraderie. I could not match their tales of adventure and strange foreign lands but I could discuss with them the latest methods of direction and position finding I had learned and was longing to practise. After the meal had been cleared they clustered around, fascinated, as with my poniard I inscribed globes and segments on the oak board and tried to explain the principles of great circle navigation.

If our heads had not been together over the table we would probably have seen the disaster for ourselves. In fact, we knew nothing of it until we were interrupted by a hammering on the door of our private room. A breathless sailor tumbled in.

'Masters! The *Mermaid*! Look!'

We turned to the window in the direction of his pointing finger. It was an overcast day and at first there was nothing to be seen. Then we realised that there was a smudge of darker grey against the pewter sky, that it was drifting up from the quay where a crowd of excited people were already gathering.

' 'Tis the *Mermaid* afire!'

Kendall flung himself from the room followed by the rest of us. On the quayside some enterprising sailors had already formed a human chain up the *Mermaid*'s gangplank and were passing buckets from hand to hand. Ignoring warning shouts from behind, I forced my way past them. Black smoke poured from the main hatchway unstanched by the water emptied in by half-choked sweating seamen. I shouted at one of them through the swirling cloud.

'Where did it start?'

'Main hold, sir, in the canvas and spare tackle.'

'Near the powder kegs?'

'Farther forard, sir, but it's spreading. We shan't stop it.'

'No, she's got a good hold.' It was Kendall who spoke. As if to confirm his words there was a sudden roar. A sheaf of flame like an outstretched, groping hand thrust through the smoke and sent us rushing back to the gunwale. Kendall grabbed my arm.

'Come ashore. There's no saving her. She'll go up any minute.'

He pushed me ahead down the gangplank. On the quayside I turned to him.

'Master Kendall, fix me a towing line and cut her free.'

Without waiting for his reply I ran along the dock.

Two sailors were lounging against bales, watching.

'You two, come with me!'

Looking down over the slimy wall as I went, I soon saw what I wanted. We dropped into the boat and cast off. I set the sailors to the oars and grabbed up the rudder line.

'Now row for all you're worth!'

I steered straight for the *Mermaid*'s bow. Kendall, I could see, had done his work. She was free of the quay. A gang of men with long poles was fending her out towards the channel. But I could also see flame spurting from a dozen places on the main deck. I was taking a terrible gamble. The *Mermaid* was now far enough from the harbour buildings to do little damage ashore when she blew up but she was drawing closer to my other ships.

With fifty yards of open water between us and the *Mermaid* the boat suddenly veered to starboard. One of the seamen, a short, thin fellow had stopped rowing. He looked at me with terror in his eyes.

'It's madness, sir. She'll explode any second. We'll be killed . . .

'Stop whining and pull on that oar. Otherwise you certainly will be killed.'

I half drew my sword. It was enough. With short, clutching strokes, the coward threw himself into his work.

As we drew close the searing heat was almost intolerable. Fragments of burning timber fell all around us. At last we were under the bow. I made fast the trailing rope to a ring at the boat's stern. Then my men were desperately straining at the oars. The *Mermaid* was already making way but we seemed to make no impression on her progress. The doomed ship was drifting in towards the *Bear*. Only a few paces away I could see Captain Wood on her main deck organising groups of men to fend off the *Mermaid* if she came too close. And every second she moved closer.

I lashed the rudder and sat between the rowers. With a hand on each oar I lent my weight to theirs. Slowly, too slowly, the *Mermaid*'s bow came round. Arms aching, bodies sweating with heat and exertion, we saw the burning ship respond to our efforts. Like a water beetle dragging its prey we forced our way across the sluggish Itchen.

'That's far enough, sir!'

I agreed with the anxious plea on my left. Standing up, I drew my sword and sliced through the rope. Suddenly freed of its burden, the boat leaped forward. I overbalanced and fell heavily on my companions. There was a moment of scrambling confusion, then our little vessel heeled right over and we found ourselves in the water. The next instant is one of the most vivid and bizarre of my memories. I was below the water, sinking – or perhaps rising – face upwards, fighting for the translucent surface, when suddenly that surface was suffused a vivid pink. At the same moment the roar of the explosion reached my ears, muffled and muted but unmistakable. When my head emerged the *Mermaid* had disappeared but bits of her were splashing all around.

I gulped acrid air and looked about for my companions. One of them was a few yards away clinging to the upturned boat. I swam over and asked if he had seen his fellow – the little man who had wanted to turn back. He had not. We scanned the debris-strewn water without much hope. Then the sailor pointed. Together we dragged the limp form over to the boat and managed to get him lying across it. Whether he was dead or unconscious I did not know but there was nothing we could do for him until help arrived.

We did not have to wait long. Within minutes Captain Wood and a boatload of men from the *Bear* drew alongside. Soon I was in dry clothes and seated in my cabin. Wood stood morosely by the stern window. Kendall was pacing to and fro.

'Deliberate, lad, it must have been deliberate.'

'No, Abraham, it was more likely some careless sailor knocking over a lamp.'

'We finished loading the *Mermaid*, yesterday morning. I checked her myself and saw the hatch fastened down. No one had any business in the cargo hold today.'

Wood turned away from the window.

'Captain Wentworth says the hatch cover was secure before church. The crew went dining and drinking after the service. When the first men arrived back on board the hatch was open and the fire already started. It was no acident, Master Dudley.'

'You've no idea, who . . . ?'

Wood shook his head.

'I don't know who or why.'

Kendall snorted.

'There's no puzzle about why. Someone wants to delay us.'

'Raleigh?'

'Aye. He's not ready to start. You are. That makes him look very silly. Now he has a breathing space. He knows it will take several days for you to find and equip another ship.'

'You may be right. If only I could be sure . . .'

At that moment there was a knock at the door. Will Bradshaw came in to report that the wounded sailor was dead.

'Thank you, Will. Where have they put him?'

'On the foredeck, sir.'

'I will come right away.'

Wood and Kendall accompanied me across the maindeck and up the gangway. A small cluster of sailors stood around the pale figure lying in a pool of water. Were they feeling what I felt – one man dead, one ship lost before we had even left port. It was not a good omen. I looked down at the pathetic figure. And then I had a shock.

'Master Kendall, what was this man's name?'

'Thomas Machin, Master Dudley.'

'How did you find him?'

'He came from Plymouth with three or four others. They were hired by Raleigh but came on here when they saw that Raleigh's fleet was not ready.'

'Get rid of all the men who came from Plymouth.'

'But, Master Dudley, we have to find a new ship. We shall need men to man her.'

'I have no intention of replacing the *Mermaid*. We will sail with four ships and they will be manned with men I can trust. You were right, Abraham. Come, we have much to discuss. I wish to sail on the first available tide.'

Back in my cabin I was confronted by a puzzled Kendall and Wood. My pilot-general rested his hands on the table and scrutinised me with his good eye.

'Now, lad, what's all this about me being right. I know you're upset about losing the *Mermaid* but that's no reason for hasty action . . .'

'Abraham, I now know that you were right about Raleigh. He wants to delay me by any means at his disposal.'

Wood seated himself on a joint stool and stretched his long legs before him.

'A few minutes ago we were trying to convince you of that.'

'That was before I made the acquaintance of Thomas Machin.'

Kendall shook his head.

'You talk in riddles, lad.'

'When we were in the boat together I thought there was something vaguely familiar about him but there was no time to think about it then. It was only when I saw him laid out on the foredeck just now that I was able to place him. He has grown a beard since we last met but without his sea cap I knew him well enough.'

'Who was he?'

'He was one of two ruffians who attacked me at Queenhythe not twelve months ago.'

'You're sure?'

'Do you think I would make a mistake about such a matter. I have dreamed of seeing that fellow on a gallows or at the other end of my sword. Now I am sorry he is dead, for, by God, if he were alive he should talk. Since he cannot I have a sudden desire for another meeting with Sir Walter Raleigh.'

'Nay, lad, he would deny it, and we've no proof. Let me question some of Machin's cronies and see what they know.'

But when Kendall sought out the dead seaman's closest friends, he discovered that they had vanished. It was now obvious to all my colleagues that we must weigh anchor as soon as possible. It took three days to replace the essential supplies the *Mermaid* had been carrying, choose crews for the remaining vessels and pay off the residue.

On the afternoon of Wednesday 6 November the *Bear* slipped out of Southampton before a freshening breeze followed by the three smaller vessels. It was a moment I had imagined often – the beginning of my great adventure. Inevitably, perhaps, the reality could not match the dream. The ships were trim and freshly painted. The sails glowed golden in the rays of the declining sun. The flags and pennants made a brave show. The crews gave the customary three cheers for her Majesty as we left the harbour. But I felt none of the elation that I had always thought I would experience; only a dull sense of foreboding which was not entirely due to the burden of responsibility I had shouldered.

9

Save for the odious smell of tobacco from the pipes of Sir Walter Raleigh and two or three members of his entourage who flattered him by emulation, the atmosphere was very congenial. With twenty or so captains, lieutenants and masters seated around the table, the *Bear*'s great cabin was rather cramped. Yet everyone seemed to be enjoying himself, except, perhaps, Abraham Kendall, who kept running a finger round the inside of the ruff I had ordered him to wear, and scowling at me over the dishes and flagons. Sir Walter, seated on my right, was at his wittiest and most charming. As I listened to the fluent succession of bawdy jokes, some of which would have shocked even our virgin queen, I realised what a brilliant actor the man was, able to judge the mood of an audience and nicely adjust his conversation accordingly. The excellent food and wine I had gone to great expense to provide also contributed to the general conviviality.

We had been in Plymouth almost a week. My first task had, of course, been to inform Raleigh of our arrival and invite him to inspect our ships. He made many excuses for not immediately responding to my overtures and delayed doing so as long as he decently could. During those few days my interviews with him were always brief and inconclusive. He concealed well his own annoyance that I had brought my fleet to Plymouth and was careful to give me no opportunity to voice my anger and suspicions. For my part I determined to have the *Mermaid* incident out with him but in the meantime to yield no point to him in courtesy and civility. It was certainly not my plan to argue with the expedition's leader in public but, Raleigh, it seems, did not share my reticence.

There was a lull in the conversation and for a moment we could clearly hear the lively south-westerly strumming the ship's rigging. Then Raleigh half turned and put an arm round my shoulder.

'Masters, I give you a toast. The youngest member of our company. You must not let his damask cheek and want of experience deceive you. Here is a man who is placing his youth, his zeal and his considerable fortune at his sovereign's disposal in this brave venture of ours. Gentlemen, please raise your goblets to salute Robert Dudley, for in him you salute the next generation of English adventurers, who will take up the standard when we are obliged to lay it down.'

Raleigh's men responded warmly to this attempt to put Master Dudley in his place. Several of my own, to their credit, were less enthusiastic. I rose to make my reply.

'Sir Walter, you are very kind. It is a great encouragement to know that the years I have spent in study and preparation for this voyage are appreciated by a mariner whose exploits have won wide acclaim. Gentlemen, in proposing the toast of our admiral I ask you not to be deceived by the unfortunate lack of permanent achievement which has dogged his earlier voyages, nor his rumoured dislike of the sea and his proneness to *mal de mer*. I ask you to drink to a commander who has staked his reputation on the success of our expedition and to drink also to the speedy beginning of that venture.'

Kendall led the boisterous applause for my little speech.

'Well said, lad. Aye, let's be getting under way.'

There was a chorus of agreement but Raleigh shook his head, slowly, solemnly.

'Alas, gentlemen, I share your enthusiasm to be gone but Providence apparently does not.'

'Your meaning, Sir Walter?'

'Ah, young man, if you knew our Devon coast you would not ask. These south-westerlies at this time of year bode storms. There can be no setting forth until we see a break in the weather. I will not hazard my ships by a too hasty start . . .'

'What ships?'

Head down, Kendall was staring morosely into his goblet but there was no mistaking his gruff voice and heavy Devon accent. Raleigh ignored the interruption.

'The first lesson a mariner must learn, Master Dudley, is patience.'

'Sir Walter, I have been patient enough this last two months. My ships and men have been awaiting your summons since early September. All my preparations have been carefully made.'

'Carefully, Master Dudley?' Raleigh looked around the table with a look of amused tolerance. 'We hear that one of your ships was so carefully loaded that she blew up in the middle of Southampton harbour.'

Raleigh's men laughed.

The vivid memory of the *Mermaid*'s end and the destruction which had so nearly visited all my ships obliterated my self control.

'It is true I lost a fine ship but the cause of the fire I think you know better than I, Sir Walter.'

His scornful laugh was deliberately provocative.

'What should I know of your mismanagement, young man?'

'I imagine you would rather I answered that question in private.'

'On the contrary, if you have wild allegations to make it is only proper that you should make them in front of all our colleagues. If our expedition is to carry a malcontent and a potential mutineer we should all know of it.'

Kendall shook his head violently at me. Captain Monk laid a restraining hand on my left arm. Twenty faces were turned towards me, some hostile, some anxious, all tense, expectant. I knew the trap that had been so cleverly set but my fury would not be restrained. In a breathless tirade I poured out my accusations and suspicions. The Queenhythe incident, the mysterious hindrances over supplies, the *Mermaid* fire, my recognition of Thomas Machin – I omitted nothing.

When I finished there was uproar. Some men were on their feet. There were shouts and countershouts. Peter Carew, a relative and henchman of Raleigh, drew his sword and brandished it in my direction.

'Sir Walter, let me teach this insolent fellow some respect for his betters!'

Immediately, young John Wentworth took up the challenge. With an oath he leaped to his feet, the stool clattering to the floor behind him. In a quick movement he had the point of his rapier pressing Carew's throat.

'Gentlemen, put up your swords.'

Raleigh's crisp command froze the action. Slowly and with exaggerated calm he rose to his feet.

'We will take our leave of you, Master Dudley. Tomorrow, when wiser counsels have prevailed with you, I shall expect your apology for the absurd accusations you have made.'

Raleigh made a dignified departure from the *Bear*, followed by his officers like ducklings in line astern. We gave each other a civil farewell at the head of the gangplank so that our men should not be aware of any rift. My own officers then went about their duties and I returned, still seething, to the main cabin. To my surprise it was not empty. I recognised the swarthy, grey-haired man who stood staring out at one of the ports as George Popham. I dropped into a chair.

'Your sun has gone. You should be circling it like the other attendant planets.'

He turned and walked over to stand in front of me – a man in his mid fifties, face scoured by the wind and sun of a score of voyages.

'I stayed to tell you that you are right about Raleigh. He does mean you harm. As long as you stay here you are in danger.'

'Why are you telling me this? Is it the prelude to some further trick?'

He pulled up a stool and sat facing me.

'I have no cause to love Sir Walter Raleigh and I certainly have no part in any of his dishonourable schemes.'

'You are one of his captains. Why, you are the very man who brought back the news of El Dorado which is the reason for this voyage.'

Popham let out a long sigh.

'Master Dudley, I am a privateer. Have been for thirty years.

I make no apology for it. I've brought a great deal of gold, silver and spices into England and caused King Philip many headaches. I'm getting old for the life now but it's the only life I know and, please God, I shall die on the Main as I've lived there.'

The door behind me opened and Kendall shambled in.

'Ah, George, I hoped you'd stay. Trust this man, Master Dudley, he's one of the finest seamen and the honestest rogue afloat.'

He seated himself on the edge of the table.

Popham chuckled.

'That sounds more like a description of Abraham Kendall to me. No one but a brazen-faced rogue could have cheated the governor of Santa Marta the way you did in '87.'

The two old sea dogs were immediately launched on a string of outrageous reminiscences and seemed oblivious of my presence. At length I had to interrupt.

'Captain Popham thinks I am in danger here.'

'How so, George?'

'Best let me tell it my way, Abraham. I'm a long-winded old fool when it comes to words. That's what comes of talking to yourself for hours on end. It can be a lonely life at sea, as you well know. Well now, I was explaining to your young admiral how I got tangled up with Sir Walter Raleigh.'

Popham explained how, about ten years before, he had had a run of bad luck and how he had had to forsake his complete independence and hire himself and his ship to Raleigh. Sir Walter had used him in setting up his Roanoke colony. The narrator spoke bitterly of that ill-fated experiment.

'Men, women and children vanished without trace before we could get supplies and reinforcements to them. I saw the broken stockades, the miserable wooden huts. I saw candles and old shoes with teeth marks in them. I saw the rows of graves. *I* saw them, Raleigh did not. He never visited his fair land of Virginia. Never saw the misery that men call a colony.'

'Do you condemn all colonies?'

'That I do.'

'But the Spanish, New World colonies ...'

'Are not worth the blood and gold it costs to keep them, as you'd know if you'd seen them. What is the typical Spanish settlement? A huddle of houses by the shore or the river. A handful of anxious white men sweating in the tropical sun, mistrustful of their native servants, always on the watch for an Indian attack. They depend on the crops culled from a meagre earth and supplies from Europe.'

'But the colonies bring wealth to Spain.'

'Do they? Do you know how many bullion ships are lost to pirates and storms every year? Do you know how much Philip's Council of the Indies spends in ships, arms and men to defend the New World settlements? No, Master Dudley, colonies would be all very well if they could be properly established and regularly supplied by fleets from home. But no nation can afford that; certainly England cannot.'

He paused to moisten his throat with a draught of wine. I wondered if he would ever get to the point or if there was, in fact, a point to get to.

'Captain Popham, this is all very interesting but how does it affect our present voyage?'

'I'm coming to that, Master Dudley. Raleigh's Roanoke colony failed and it was a great blow to his pride for he was possessed with the thought of founding colonies to rival Spain. And still is. Now he desperately needs to recover royal favour and a successful colonial venture is more important to him than ever.

'Eight months ago I captured a ship of the Spanish royal fleet off Trinidad. There wasn't much of value aboard but there was an official carrying messages for the King and I brought him back to Raleigh. I went off to the Azores immediately and thought little more about it. When I returned to England I found Raleigh getting together this expedition to colonise Guiana, and all because of the letters I'd captured for him.'

'But Raleigh was planning this voyage a year ago, long before you brought him the Spanish reports about El Dorado.'

'No, Master Dudley. He was planning a voyage of exploration, a journey up the Orinoco to see if there was such a place as the kingdom of El Dorado. Now he's convinced that kingdom exists.'

'And does it?'

'Oh yes, Master Dudley, there's a rich Indian city somewhere in the mountains of Guiana, though you mustn't believe many of the wonderful stories told by men who haven't been within a thousand miles of it. I've seen gold objects brought down the Orinoco and talked with Indians who live on its banks. There's a kingdom there, right enough, one to rival the land of the Incas for wealth.'

'Then, surely, Raleigh is right...'

'To plan a voyage of exploration? Yes. To take several boatloads of men up the Orinoco for a quick raid on El Dorado's kingdom? Yes. To make one expedition and hope for a good profit in plunder? Yes. But to set up colonies, to try to rule Guiana from London? No, that's madness and dangerous madness. The Orinoco basin is a maze of treacherous rivers running through dense forests. A boatful of men could wander it for months and never find its way out. And somewhere – who knows how far – up river are the mountains where El Dorado reigns. To reach that kingdom, conquer it, hold it and rule it in the name of the Queen would take an army of several thousand and a fleet bigger than Spain's.'

'Raleigh must know that.'

'Raleigh knows what Raleigh wishes to know. Why, he has already drawn up a map of Guiana, a land which no European has ever seen. He showed it to me not three days since – rivers and mountains, the great lake of Gran Manoa and with El Dorado's walled city standing on its shore. It does not matter to Sir Walter whether these places exist or not. They exist in his mind and that is enough. He will squander the lives of a hundred Englishmen to reach his golden land and he will destroy anyone he sees as a threat to his ambition.'

Popham raised the goblet to his lips and set it quietly back on the table. For a long time no one spoke. Outside, heavy clouds rolling in from the sea had brought in a premature dusk. A growing darkness had filled the cabin while the captain told his story and I called for Will to come and light the lamps. When the page had withdrawn it was Kendall who spoke first.

'So, George, you think we should go without Raleigh?'

'You'll waste a great deal of money if you wait for him to be ready and he will stop at nothing to keep you and your ships here.'

'But how shall we find Guiana without him? He has all the captured maps, charts and accounts of the region.'

'I'll be your guide. Few Englishmen know that coast better than I, and I have friends among the Caribs.'

I walked across to one of the ports. The horizon was lost in a dark grey sheet of sea and sky. Across the anchorage rain pimpled the water.

'Raleigh seems to be right about one thing. This is no sailing weather.'

Kendall snorted.

'I've been in and out of Plymouth more times than Raleigh's had whores. We only need the wind to veer a few points and we can clear the harbour on the ebb. If we have to we can always put in at Falmouth or Fowey.'

That was eventually what we agreed to do. All my captains were to hold themselves in readiness and keep watches posted so that they could hoist sail and let go anchor on a signal from the *Bear*. Popham's *Fury* would follow and we would all be well out into the Cattewater before Raleigh could get any of his ships away in pursuit. There was a rumour of some contagion in the town so I was able to order all crews to stay aboard without arousing suspicion. After our conference George Popham was rowed across to his ship under cover of darkness and there was no more contact between us before we left Plymouth.

I was not altogether happy about Popham and the story he had told us. Somehow the pose of the honest, bluff mariner was too good to be true. There were deeper undercurrents in the man and I wondered whether he might not have been sent by Raleigh to panic us into setting out in bad weather in the hope that we might come to grief on some craggy Cornish outcrop. When I mentioned my doubts to Kendall he laughed them away.

'No, lad, George Popham can be as cunning as Old Nick himself, but not with his friends – and he and I have been friends for years. I've told him all about you and he knows he's better off

137

following you than Raleigh. Otherwise he wouldn't be coming with us.'

'I suppose you are right.' But I was not completely convinced.

The weather remained squally for three days. Blustering winds rocked the ships at anchor and shook showers from the sodden yards onto the grumbling, confined crews. They resented being cooped up when they could have been making the most of their last few days in England – the last that some of them would ever spend in England. I resented not being able to explain to them. It was not the kind of relationship I wanted with the men under my command. I had always imagined myself as the sort of commander who would inspire confidence, loyalty, admiration, who would share dangers and triumphs equally, rule by example and not fiat. Now, even before we were at sea I was making unreasonable demands, depriving the men of liberty for secret reasons of my own. More than once I overheard – and was, perhaps, meant to overhear – whispered complaints about the beardless, inexperienced youth who knew nothing about ships and could not handle men.

Fortunately for all of us, the wind dropped before dawn on the fourth day. I was awakened in the middle of the second watch and arrived on deck to find the sky clearing from the east and a light, offshore breeze whispering in the rigging. I asked the pilot the state of the tide.

'On the turn in about an hour, sir.'

I was joined by Kendall and Wood. We decided to allow three hours, until the ebb was running strongly.

When the first rays of the sun touched the masthead, I gave orders for the men to be roused and the pre-arranged lantern signal given to the rest of the fleet. There was no question of getting under way quietly. I concentrated on speed. The master shouted his commands. The windlass creaked. The mainsail unrolled itself with a rattle and cracked as it stretched before the wind.

Then we were moving. Save for a group of startled fishermen on the quayside no one saw our departure. As the *Bear* slipped across Sutton Harbour I looked astern and saw my other ships all crowding canvas and leaving their berths. Through the harbour's narrow entrance and on past the citadel we went, while Plymouth – and Sir Walter Raleigh – slept. Out into the Sound under half sail, keeping to the centre of the channel. Within the hour we were off Rame Head. There I gave order to furl the flagship's sails and wait while the other vessels came up with us. The *Bear's Whelp*, the *Earwig* and the tiny *Frisking* were soon riding at a few cables' length. With Kendall at my side I leaned over the stern rail, scanning the stretch of water we had just crossed. Neither of us spoke a word but we were both thinking the same thought. There was no sign of Popham and the *Fury*.

I steered a south-westerly course for the Eddystone Rock and, passing that safely to larboard, made for Ushant. The *Bear* alone would, I am sure, have cleared the Channel. Perhaps the *Bear's Whelp* would, too. Unfortunately, the larger ships had no chance to hoist full sail: we had to wait for the pinnaces which, being lighter and carrying less canvas, made slow progress through a choppy sea. And so the change of wind caught us. It swung round during the afternoon first to the west and then south-west. Storm clouds rolled quickly in from the horizon. With sails close furled the *Bear* dipped into the swell, sending showers of spray as high as the masthead.

It found its way inside the collar of my leather sea-jacket as I stood disconsolately at the stern rail watching the *Earwig* and the *Frisking* fall farther behind. I ordered the ship's master to take in more sail.

'If I take in any more I shan't be able to hold her into the wind,' he shouted above the gale.

Captain Wood came across the deck and stopped to speak in my ear.

'We must make for harbour before nightfall, or we'll lose sight of the others.'

Water dripped from his nose and beard as he waited for my reply. I hated to admit it but I knew he was right.

'Falmouth is nearest?'

'Ay, sir, due north.'

'Then, we will go in there. Have the master make course for Falmouth.'

Soon the *Bear* was running swiftly northwards and the rest of the fleet followed our lead. But the gale increased its fury by the minute. The other ships were only visible intermittently through the veil of rain and spray. All masters lit their signal lamps and this helped the fleet to stay together. But the mariners had little time to worry about the fate of the other ships: they were too busy hurrying about their own jobs and keeping their footing on the bucking, slippery decks.

I went to my cabin so as to be out of the way. Will had put out dry clothes for me. I changed with difficulty and threw myself down on the bed. Was nothing going to go right? First Raleigh and now the elements were against me. I could have wept with frustration.

There was a knock at the door and Captain Wood entered. He stood in the middle of the room, legs apart, swaying to the motion of the ship. 'God willing, we shall reach Falmouth within the hour, Master Dudley.'

'Shall we make the tide?'

'Well enough, I think.'

'Can you still see the others?'

'No, Master Dudley, nor shall we.'

He shook his head gloomily.

'The wind's still increasing and the pinnaces will have to run before it.'

I swung my legs over the edge of the bed.

'They are in great danger, then?'

'They're in God's hands, Master Dudley, but Vincent and Lister know this coast well. If they clear Dodman Point safely before dark they'll run for Fowey or Plymouth.'

'Plymouth!'

'Ay, 'tis the widest entrance and the safest anchorage in this weather.'

'And Raleigh waiting to welcome them back with open arms.'

'We must just pray they come safe to haven, Master Dudley. That's the important thing.'

I nodded and thought how irritating it is to have one's nose rubbed in the truth.

With the last of the light we ran in between the twin castles of Pendennis and St Mawes and thankfully reached the calm water beyond.

Next morning I was on deck early but not as early as Abraham Kendall. He shook his head as I anxiously scanned the anchorage.

'No, lad, not one.'

'Not even the *Whelp*? What's to be done Abraham?'

'Send a messenger by road along the coast to find the others. They'll be somewhere between here and Plymouth. Give orders for them to join us here.'

'That will take a week or more. Besides, when Raleigh knows where we are he will order us back to Plymouth. No, that I will not do. Come to the cabin.'

We leant over the table where I had spread out the North Atlantic chart. With the dividers I traced out our proposed route.

'Ushant, the Canaries, Cape Blanco on the African coast, then the Cape Verde Islands. Now, Abraham, where is the best rendezvous point?'

Without hesitation, Kendall jabbed a finger at a point amidst the web of rhumb lines criss-crossing the ocean.

'Here, in 29° due north of Tenerife. There's water to be had on most of the Canary Islands. The Spanish colonists don't have many ships and what they do have are mostly ill-armed merchantmen. But you can't set sail without the others and hope that they'll meet you at Tenerife. What if they don't arrive? You can't look for Guiana with one shipload of men.'

I searched the worried face, with its glazed right eye, its bushy brows drawn close together, its wrinkled forehead. This man had done so much for me, was genuinely concerned for me, but now that very concern threatened to smother me. I wanted to grasp Kendall by the shoulders and shout at him, 'Can you not see what this voyage means to me? Surely you realise I must go.

Even if it means going with only one ship. I cannot turn back now.' Instead, I said, bitterly.

'You were wrong about Popham, and you are wrong now.'

I left him. I left the *Bear* and had myself rowed across to the harbour steps. Striding quickly through the town, I soon gained the beach – and solitude. There was no one in sight save a few fishermen, prodding for dab in the sand near the distant low-tide line. Watching them I recalled my first encounter with fisherfolk, recalled also the simplicity of childhood. 'Take me out in your boat,' I had ordered, knowing only that boats went on the sea and the sea was the highway to adventure. How easy it had all seemed.

But how hard it was in practice. I thought of all the people who for love or hate, jealousy, concern or some other motive had tried to stop or dissuade me from my enterprise – Essex and Raleigh, Margaret and her father, and now Kendall. Then I thought of all that had gone wrong during the last few days and wondered if God, too, were not against me. Perhaps all of them were right. Perhaps I was a deluded young fool afflicted by the sea fever which Richard Cavendish so much dreaded. Perhaps I should seek some other outlet for my energy and talents.

'Well, God,' I demanded aloud, 'is that what I must do? Sell my ships, stay safely at home and play the country squire?'

The only reply was the screech of gulls as they hung in the air, bright flecks against the greyness of Rosemullion Head, then swooped to where the stooping fishermen worked. But I had already answered my own question. To give up all thoughts of maritime adventure would, I knew, be a monstrous act of self-betrayal. I must at least try my fortune at sea or live ever after with a millstone of regret hanging round my neck.

But could I venture forth with only one ship? Was Kendall right? I did not know. I could not know. I had no experience. There and then I knelt in the sand and prayed God for some sign that would make everything clear.

As I turned back towards the town I saw a figure running towards me along the beach. When he stopped and stood panting before me, I recognised him as one of the *Bear*'s young foretop-men.

'Well, Dick, what is it?'

'It's the *Frisking*, sir. She's just come into harbour.'

10

I left Falmouth on Sunday 1 December with the *Bear* and the *Frisking*. The pinnace had taken a battering before Captain Vincent, with great skill and courage, had got her into Mevagissey, so we had had to beach her for recaulking and this lost us more time. However, when at last we did set sail, we made good time for several days, heading directly for Finistere, coasting Portugal and then setting course for the Canaries.

I cruised around some of the islands in the pinnace, noting those that were inhabited and those that were not, locating the principal harbours and making a rough assessment of Spanish maritime strength. I steered away from other vessels whenever we saw them. I had determined to wait until my fleet was up to full strength before giving the Spaniards a demonstration of my fire-power. The weather was warm, the work congenial and the men content. When they were off duty the sailors spent their time fishing or lying in the sunshine to mend their clothes, read or play dice. I recorded the coastline and the lead and line soundings on the new charts I was making. Kendall helped me in this work and young Will Bradshaw was invaluable. He proved to have a hitherto undiscovered talent as an artist. He would sit for hours on the afterdeck making sketches of the islands, of seabirds and fish which he copied into my log and then coloured with painstaking care. In the evenings he worked at the chart by the light of the cabin lamp, adding cartouches, decorative features and writing in the names in a neat hand.

On Christmas Day I gave a feast. The ships were anchored in a shallow bay on the sparsely-inhabited western side of Tenerife.

The only Spanish settlement was twenty miles away across the mountains, so I considered it quite safe to allow the whole crew ashore. After divine service aboard the *Bear* we rowed across to the beach where we soon had a fire going and were roasting three sheep and some chickens. Before dinner there were races, a tug o' war and other contests between the crews of the two ships. Afterwards, when we had eaten and drunk our fill, most of us were content to laze on the sand or swim in the cool, clear water. As usual, Will Bradshaw's tousled fair hair was bent over pen and paper. He sat with his back against a rock, face set in a mask of concentration. I came up behind the artist and saw that it was the stately peak of Teide which had caught his attention. To the south the snow-capped cone stood above the cloud like a floating island in the sky. I perched on Will's rock.

'The last landmark.'

'Sir?'

'That was what men called Teide in ancient times, Will. They believed it stood at the edge of the world.'

With delicate strokes the boy touched in a suggestion of cloud. A group of sailors nearby had broken into raucous song but Will was obviously oblivious to them.

'Strange how little they knew about the world, sir.'

'How, strange, Will?'

'Well, the Greeks were such clever people. They taught us most that we still know about astronomy and mathematics and medicine. That's right, isn't it, sir?'

'Yes, Will.'

'Yet to them the world meant, the Mediterranean, Europe, the Levant and a little bit of Asia.'

He laid aside the board to which his paper was pinned.

'Just think how Ptolemy would have been amazed if someone had told him that one day ships would sail right round the world. And yet, we will soon know about all the lands and all the peoples of the earth.'

Will's faith in progress was touching, though in need of some modification. I started to explain to him that there were still enormous problems to be faced and discoveries to be made before we could really claim to know our planet. The lad turned to face me and for some minutes paid polite attention to his master's lecture. Then, without warning, he jumped to his feet, shouting and pointing out to sea.

I spun round. Coming from behind the headland to our right was a Spanish warship under full sail. She bore down rapidly on the spot where our vessels were anchored. Angrily, I looked up towards the high ground where I had posted sentries. There was no sign of them. Others had now seen the danger and from all directions men were running down the beach.

The sound of gunfire began before the first boat pushed off. Roar after roar echoed round the bay as we crossed the water with frenzied strokes. Standing in the prow of one of the boats, I saw the *Frisking*'s mainmast topple overboard, dragging a tangle of rigging and tackle. The pinnace, being further offshore, bore the brunt of the attack but a few balls were striking the *Bear*.

As I scrambled aboard, Captain Wood and the master were already shouting orders to the scurrying crew who were leaping up the rigging, running out cannons and manning the windlass. Splinters of wood and broken spars lay around the deck but there seemed to be no serious damage. It was not so with the *Frisking*. Battered and mastless, the defenceless little ship was already settling in the water.

The cowardly Spaniards were content with this easy success and had no stomach for a fight. Even as the *Bear* got slowly under way, the galleon showed us her high stern and moved away to the north-east. by the time we had come round and started to give chase she had a clear league start on us. Kendall and Wood joined me on the foredeck as I strained my eyes to make out all I could of the enemy.

'Best give it up, lad, we'll find her again tomorrow.'

'Thank you for your advice, Master Kendall, Captain Wood, we'll have every inch of canvas we can carry.' Anger had made me cold, calm and clear-headed. Without question, Wood went away to give the order.

'She carries half as much sail again as us.'

'She is three times our size and the *Bear* is built for speed.'

'We've only half our complement aboard. If it comes to a fight...'

'Master Kendall, you will permit me to run my own ship.' Right or wrong, I had to make my own decisions.

For an hour we tailed the galleon along the barren coastline, gaining steadily on her. She was no wallowing merchantman with guns added to make a show of ferocity but a vessel of some six or seven hundred tons and one of Spain's principal ships of war. It was probably sheer chance that had brought her to the Canaries at the same time as us. It was obvious that if it came to a fight the *Bear* would need all her speed and manoeuvrability to keep out of range of the Spaniard's massive broadside. As the distance between the two ships shortened I planned my tactics.

Then, suddenly, we were no longer gaining on our foe. I called Wood to the poop deck.

'Captain, why are we losing way?'

Wood pointed to the steeply-canted mainsail.

'We've come several points to starboard and close to the wind, Master Dudley.'

I pointed to the galleon, whose sails were still bulging.

'The Spaniard is not slowing down.'

'Her captain knows the winds and tides around these islands. He's standing well out and probably finding a current.'

'He will be making for Santa Cruz?'

'Without a doubt.'

We were approaching the north-easterly tip of Tenerife. Santa Cruz lay around that point and some twenty miles along the coast, facing south-east.

'There must be some way of catching him first. Come below; we will look at the chart.'

In the great cabin I traced the course the enemy was following.

'He is standing out well to the north of us. Soon he will have to turn and run before the wind to Santa Cruz. That will bring him across our bows.'

'Not so, Master Dudley. We must likewise steer northwards before we reach the point.'

'Why?'

'Lest we are caught on a lee shore, Master Dudley. Running into the north-easterly as we round the point we dare not be too close to the land.'

'But if we stand out northward now, we must lose her.'

'If we do not, we are like to be lost ourselves.'

I stared at the chart. Everything Wood said made sense and yet I could not bear the thought of our cowardly foe escaping us.

'That is a risk we must take, Master Wood. Hold the ship on her present course, if you please, and do your best to intercept the galleon when she turns into the wind.'

As Wood stooped to go through the doorway I heard him mutter to himself 'Vengeance is mine; I will repay saith the Lord' but I knew he would carry out my orders however foolhardy he thought them to be.

Slowly the rocky foreshore slipped past to starboard. The sails flapped occasionally, and Kendall kept up a stream of shouted orders in his efforts to catch every breath of wind. On the poop deck all ears strained to the regular calls of the leadsman – 'Fifteen fathoms, sand ... seventeen fathoms, sand ... thirteen fathoms, sand and gravel ... seven fathoms, rock ...' We peered anxiously over the side at the smooth, grey boulders with waving weed. Before Wood could ask, I ordered a change of course two points to larboard. The *Bear* drifted into deeper water.

We were now approaching the northern tip of the island. Ahead of us the galleon had already changed direction and was now running south by south east on a course which would take her directly to Santa Cruz. Could we cross that course or, at least, come close enough to frighten the Spanish captain into turning away from the harbour? Could we, one way or another, force him to fight?

We sailed clear of the point and immediately encountered the combined force of wind and current forcing us round the foreland. Only a hundred yards away waves crashed in a white frenzy against the island's jagged extremity. Too late I saw the line of creamy foam running straight out to sea beyond the headland. The row of submerged rocks lay right across our path and there was no way we could avoid it.

'Take in sail!'

As the canvas was furled the *Bear* slowed but continued to drift towards the rocks. I ran forard and strained my eyes towards the breakers ahead. Was that clear patch a delusion? I sent Will to the foretop. He called down that there did seem to be a narrow gap in the barrier.

'Take her through there, Master Wood.'

The order may have sounded calm and confident. I certainly hoped my voice was not trembling as much as my limbs. For I knew that what I was asking was almost impossible – to take a ship through a problematical gap some thirty feet wide in vicious rocks, on a lee shore, into the wind.

The master and captain stood in the prow. Beside them were ship's boys ready to relay orders to the teams of men who manned the ropes and fending poles. As we drew closer to the rocks the sound of crashing breakers drowned the shouting and the drubbing of bare feet on the deck. Slowly now the *Bear*'s keel cut through the foam. To starboard the sea-smoothed rocks stood as high as the deck, every dark cleft and shining crag clearly visible. The swirling water tried to throw us against that wall, and the whip-staff men had to put all their weight into holding the *Bear* on course. In the ship's waist the fending poles were run out. To larboard we seemed well clear. If we could stop the stern swinging, I thought, we would be through and on an excellent interception course with the Spaniard. Then, like a rearing horse, the bow leaped into the air and immediately plunged down again. I was sent sprawling on the deck. It was some moments before I could gather my wits and realise what was happening. Just clear of the main barrier the *Bear* had found a submerged rock on the larboard bow. She had ridden over and fallen back into deep water. I could still hear the rock scraping along the keel as the *Bear* escaped into deep water. Now shipboard sounds began to reassert themselves over the thunder of the surf.

'Twelve fathoms, sand.'

The leadsman's cry was reassuring. But pray heaven we were not holed. Men were already scurrying below decks to search for damage. Captain Wood ordered the *Bear* hove to until they had finished their search. Minutes later he reported to me on the poop deck.

'She's shipping some water through strained joints on the water line, Master Dudley, but nothing that the pumps can't cope with. No other damage.'

'Thank God for our double sheathing, Master Wood. Resume pursuit, if you please.'

The galleon was now some three miles distant but bearing obliquely towards us as she ran before the north-easterly wind. We now came onto a south-easterly course and I estimated that, under full sail, we could match the speed of the larger ship, even though we had the wind on our beam. If I could close the range to less than a mile and get on a parallel course I could open fire with my culverin. That would slow the Spaniard down and force him either to close the range or abandon the idea of reaching Santa Cruz.

Slowly our paths converged. I had the cannon run out and managed to man most of them. The master gunner was, unfortunately, among those left behind but the deputy I appointed seemed to know what was needed. He was helped by the men who were anxious for a fight and who made up in spirit what they lacked in experience.

At a mile and a half I decided to let the Spanish captain know my intentions. I opened fire with a bow-mounted saker. Only a few of the five pound shot found their mark but they drew a response from the enemy.

'Clever bastard,' Kendall muttered. 'He's changing course. Turning towards us.'

'He wants to bring his cannon to bear.'

'No, lad, he wants to cut across our bows.'

Kendall was right. The galleon still had enough lead to swing across our path and get to leeward of us. If she was successful we could no longer block her entry to Santa Cruz.

'Master Wood, alter course, too.'

'We haven't much room, Master Dudley. If we go too hard a'starboard we'll find ourselves on a lee shore.'

Kendall swore.

'As that captain knows full well.'

I could have wept with frustration. To have come through so much and to be cheated of my prey at the last moment. It was intolerable.

'Gentlemen, what are we to do?'

Wood gave Kendall a glance which said 'The young admiral has come to his senses at last.'

'Our only chance of making her fight is to overtake her. On her present course she must lose speed. If we keep the wind behind us we may be able to draw alongside, cripple her, even board her, before she can make harbour. If the Lord has delivered her into our hands that is the way we must take her. If not . . .' He turned his eyes heavenwards as if to say, 'who are we to question the inscrutable ways of Providence.'

The galleon crossed our path about half a mile ahead, under a vigorous fire from the saker. As she came back onto a direct course for Santa Cruz her mainsail was holed and men were swarming up to the foretop to replace a shattered spar. Apart from one or two desultory shots, her crew wasted little energy returning our fire. All their efforts were chanelled into the race for haven and safety.

The *Bear's* canvas and timber strained to deny the foe his refuge, and seventy Englishmen willed their ship through the water. We kept up an incessant attack with the saker and loosed off some of the cannon long before we were level with the enemy, just to frighten them. And then we were level and I ordered the starboard gun crews to fire at will. The *Bear* rocked as the massive bronze guns embossed with the bear and ragged staff, roared their message of hate. As the range closed our fire became more accurate. At six hundred yards I saw, through the drifting smoke, the Spanish mizzen topple over the stern. A cheer went up from the English decks as the Spanish sailors worked feverishly with axes and knives to cut loose the dragging mast and tackle.

In the *Bear's* waist Master Jobson had assembled the soldiers and distributed arms. They stood in their silent ranks, helmets and breastplates gleaming, pikes at the port. Will had brought my armour to the poop deck long ago but I had been too busy to put it on. Now I did so, at the same time giving the order to close with the enemy and throw out grappling irons as soon as possible. I could clearly see confusion on the galleon's main deck as the dead and wounded were dragged unceremoniously clear and their places taken by comrades. Her superstructure was gashed in many places and her main to'gallant was in shreds but she was still making good way. We had our share of dead and injured. Two cannon had been put out of action. It took several minutes to lift one of the heavy bronze pieces off the broken body of one of the gunners, a lad of about my own age. Others lay screaming and groaning about the deck until they could be got below. For their sakes there was no turning back now; I had to press home the attack and bring it to a successful conclusion. The two ships were now less than a hundred yards apart and hammering each other with heavy shot. Again and again the *Bear* shook as the fifty pound balls thudded into her planking. But still she drew closer to the foe and along the rigging men were poised with ropes and grappling irons.

There was scarcely fifty yards between the two vessels when the Spaniard changed course. At first, I thought she was swinging round to bring her other broadside to bear but she showed us only her stern and ran directly towards the land. Kendall laid a hand on my shoulder and pointed beyond the galleon. There lay the welcoming stone arms of Santa Cruz harbour. Even as we watched there was a shrill whining overhead and a loud splash in the sea behind us. The shore garrison had opened fire and we were well within range. Our cannon fell silent and the sound of shouts and jeers came clearly from the Spanish ship. Her afterdeck was lined with jubilant, gesturing sailors. I went to my cabin and left Captain Wood to turn the *Bear* around and sail her back to the bay where the rest of our men were waiting.

I felt deeply humiliated by the failure of my first naval action. I had allowed myself to be surprised by an enemy. I had lost a ship and a dozen or so men. In my attempt to come to grips with the Spaniard I had almost destroyed my flagship. And in the moment of victory I had been cheated of success. Abraham tried to cheer me up, reminding me that no admiral ever won all his battles. But a leader's first battle is as important to him as a man's first mistress. He needs the confidence which only success can give. But despair quickly gave way to resolve. I had failed to capture the galleon but in one way or another I would be revenged on the colonists of Tenerife.

There were also practical reasons for positive action. The *Bear* now had to carry a hundred and forty men as well as all the cargo and equipment that Captain Vincent had salvaged from the *Frisking*. The overcrowding was intolerable and there could be no question of making a long Atlantic crossing until I had replaced my lost ship. That necessity helped to form my plan. The Spaniards had destroyed my pinnace. Very well then, they should provide a substitute. I called a full council of all officers in the great cabin the following morning and put my plan to them.

'Gentlemen, the Spaniards probably think they have frightened us off. Is there any sign that they are keeping a watch on us?'

Thomas Jobson, a red-faced, balding man with a thick grey beard, nodded.

'We've seen one or two horsemen on the ridge above the bay.'

'The Spaniards' look-out system seems to be better than ours.'

'Our sentries have been punished, Master Dudley. They're lying below in irons, even now.'

'Good. 'Tis no bad thing that the enemy is keeping an eye on us. They will be expecting to see us sit here for a few days licking our wounds and then slink away. So we will let them see exactly that. Captain Wood, how long will it take to repair our damage?'

'Two days, at most.'

'Well, make as much show of it as possible – lots of men running about with buckets of pitch, planks and ropes, sailors all over the rigging working on sheets and spars. Any spare men can feign injuries. I want them laid out on the beach or the deck as though resting and having their wounds tended.'

As I looked at the puzzled faces round the table I could scarcely suppress a laugh.

'Don't be amazed, gentlemen. Have you never had a secret desire to be actors? Well, here is your chance. We are to act a play, or, rather, a mime, for the benefit of our hosts. We shall present the spectacle of a badly mauled ship and a dispirited English crew. Any Spaniards who care to watch our performance will see us making frantic efforts to repair our ship and nurse our decimated company back to health. Three days hence they will observe us limp away in the direction of the setting sun, never to trouble them again.'

Young Nick Wyatt was the first to see the point of my ruse.

'And when they think we've gone away we shall attack them and take them completely by surprise.'

'Exactly. Tonight I shall lead a handful of men over the ridge. By midday tomorrow we shall be at Santa Cruz. We will work out our plan of attack and return under cover of darkness. The next evening, Saturday, we will land the men we need for our assault and make our way towards the town. On Sunday morning Captain Wood will weigh anchor and the *Bear* will sail away. And the following day she will rendezvous with a new addition to our fleet laden with whatever victuals and treasures the citizens of Santa Cruz can be persuaded to donate.'

As the last light faded from the sky I was rowed ashore with Jobson, Wyatt and three soldiers. We were lightly clad and we carried few arms. Anyone who saw us in the hills or on the road near Santa Cruz would, we hoped, take us for a group of peasant farmers on our way to buy provisions. We began to climb the steep hillside. With the aid of a half moon we scrambled upwards over jagged boulders and treacherous scree. It was painful and exhausting work. Time and again we cracked our shins and tore our hands. Frequently we had to wait for one of our number who lost his footing and slithered back down the slope. But at last we reached scrubland and then the forest belt. Now the going was easier underfoot but we had to contend with creepers and low branches that twined themselves around our legs and plucked at our clothing. We forced ourselves onwards and upwards. Each step was an agony but we could not stop until we had reached the summit of the ridge. Dawnlight was filtering through the trees ahead of us before the gradient eased and we threw ourselves down on the moss and pine needles.

The eastward descent in daylight was altogether easier. By mid-morning we were looking down on a wide arid valley where only cacti grew. A road of yellow-grey dust wound through a landscape of yellow-grey dust and rock. At its end sprawled the shamble of buildings which was Santa Cruz. We watched the road carefully to see who and what passed along it – an old woman with a donkey; a group of native Guanches, striking figures with their dark skins, fair hair and tunics of leather and plaited rushes; several peasant farmers bringing cartloads of wine down from their vineyards in the hills. When we saw a string of men and laden donkeys ambling towards the town we decided to move. Two of our number stayed in a hiding place among the rocks with orders to make their own way back if the rest of us had not returned by the time the sun moved behind Teide. Wyatt and one of the soldiers strolled casually towards the roadside before the little caravan arrived and walked slowly just ahead of it. Jobson and I shuffled along a few yards behind the last donkey.

Santa Cruz was little more than a large village. The houses, some of timber and some of stone, were strung in no visible order around the wide harbour. We noted carefully the position of the warehouses in which barrels of wine and other produce were stored prior to shipment. The church was, inevitably, the most impressive building in the town and, according to Wyatt, who went inside to assess its looting potential, it was well stocked with plate and ornaments of gold and silver. I was more concerned to explore the harbour's defences. The two well-built stone moles enclosed a deep-water haven where a score of ships could easily have berthed. In fact, the only major vessels in port were two caravels. They were riding high in the water and had obviously not yet begun to take on cargo. The galleon, I was gratified to see, had been beached and her carpenters were busy repairing several holes near the water-line. The garrison was situated on rising ground immediately to the north of the harbour. Two large cannon gazed seaward from on top of the strong, stone building. My companion and I loitered near the citadel, ostensibly engrossed in watching fishermen mend their nets. Between us we counted a dozen Spanish soldiers and a handful of

Guanche auxiliaries.

It was a considerable effort to appear completely casual as though we had every right to be in Santa Cruz while at the same time not giving ourselves away by speaking in English or appearing too inquisitive. However, no one took any notice of us and we were able to see most of what we wanted. The sun was still high in the sky when we left Santa Cruz to its siesta slumbers and shambled back along the dusty road to rejoin our colleagues. On the way back to our ship Jobson, Wyatt and I compared notes. Our plans were complete long before we scrambled over the last few rocks onto the sand of Bear Bay (as it was now named on my chart).

'Now, gentlemen, this is Santa Cruz.'

All the officers had dined with me in the great cabin and, as soon as the dishes were cleared, I spread out my rough drawing of the town on the table.

'We shall be in three parties. Master Wyatt will go straight to the harbour and board the caravel which is moored here, at the seaward end of the mole. She's called the *Santa Anna*. She must be made ready to sail immediately. Master Jobson's group will go straight to the end of the mole. There's a chain across the harbour mouth and the mechanism operating it is here. You will lower that chain. Both groups will then remain exactly where they are and do nothing until they hear my signal.'

'Where will you be, sir?'

'I shall take a dozen men to the garrison. When we have disposed of the guards we will fire one of the cannon. That will be your signal to attack the town.'

Several of the officers smiled and exchanged glances. My next words were slow and deliberate.

'You will have exactly one hour to take all that we need.'

That set the tongues wagging.

'One hour?'

'What can we do in one hour?'

'You have told us there are more than two hundred houses and buildings there. If we are to search them properly and bring away everything of value . . .'

I cut across their protests.

'We are not going to ransack every house. This is not to be a disorganised orgy of looting. You are to make that quite clear to every man under your command. I will not have drunken sailors staggering down to the harbour with loads of trash after a night of drinking and rape. Master Jobson, you will have the largest party. You will open up the warehouses and bring out wine, canvas, timber, anything else that can be useful to us. Master Wyatt, you will attack the larger houses and shops along the seafront, here. Take food, money, plate, but nothing too cumbersome.'

'Aye, sir. But what will you be doing?'

'I have a score to settle, Nick.'

We discussed every aspect of the raid in careful detail. I told the captains that after one hour I would fire the garrison's second gun. That was to be the signal for everyone to fall back to the caravel in an orderly fashion with their loot and with the wounded. Everything was to be carefully stowed away on board and the crew was to await my order to weigh anchor, and, if anything had happened to me, Master Kendall was to be in command. My repeated insistence that everything must go according to the pre-arranged plan called forth knowing glances and shaking of heads among the older officers, but no one challenged my orders.

There was one change to my original timetable: because the ascent of the ridge was so exhausting we decided to rest in the woods for most of the next day. Next morning, as the church bell of Santa Cruz summoned the unsuspecting citizens to mass, a hundred Englishmen lay not ten miles away, some still rolled in their cloaks asleep, others already sharpening swords and checking harness. At dusk we divided into our three parties and made our descent along a dried watercourse. By nightfall we had reached the road. We waited an hour or so, to give the town time to settle into slumber. Then Jobson and Wyatt set off with their groups.

I carried in my purse a watch, set in gold and mounted with

jewels. Such instruments were a great novelty in those days, though now we almost take them for granted. I am not sure the change is all for the better. At one time gentlemen used to meet for business 'in the forenoon' or 'after dinner'. Now that every man of substance carries the time in his poke everyone is in a hurry: 'I must be with Lord This at 10.0 and with Sir John That at 11.15 sharp'. The pace of life has become altogether too fast, for my liking. For all that, I must admit that I was often glad of that first watch of mine.

Consulting it just outside the town by the light of a close lamp, I discovered that it wanted only a few minutes to midnight. Since there was no commotion from the harbour it was obvious that all was going well for Jobson and Wyatt. My party consisted of Kendall and a dozen seamen. We made no sound as we moved along the waterfront, our boots muffled with strips of cloth. The garrison was easy to locate for it was the only building showing any light. There were two doors, one to the soldiers' sleeping quarters, the other to the guardroom. The single sentry stood on the edge of the mole a few paces away. If he had not been stamping his feet to keep warm and talking to himself he might have heard the assailant creeping up behind him. He did not. His body, lowered carefully down the wall, made the gentlest of splashes in the lapping tide.

Kendall crept into the sleeping quarters with six men. With the others I burst into the guardroom. It was over very quickly. The three Spaniards who sat at the table playing dice scarcely had time to get to their feet. By my instructions there was as little killing as possible. One of the soldiers started shouting and was run through by the *Bear*'s boatswain almost as a reflex action. The rest we soon had trussed, gagged and lying face downwards in the adjoining, lampless room.

Kendall sheathed his sword. The grin on his lop-sided face made him look almost evil.

' 'Tis all plain sailing now, lad. Shall I fire the cannon?'

'Not for a few minutes, Abraham. Something else must be done first. Come with me all of you!'

We ran out onto the mole. A few yards away the galleon rode

quietly at her moorings, her spars and halyards silvered by moonlight. A large gilded figure of St Catherine glowed on her sterncastle.

'I thought that was what you had in mind,' Kendall whispered. 'She'll make a fine prize.'

'No, Abraham, we cannot take her. She is too damaged.' I pointed to the shattered stump of the mizzen mast and a jagged black hole under her stern. 'She would slow us down. We will just finish the job we began on Christmas Day.'

Kendall chuckled.

'They don't seem to have posted any guards.'

'Why should they? They are in a friendly port and, as we all know, the only enemy ship in the islands sailed away this morning. Come on!'

Kendall took most of the men forard to the crew's quarters while I went aft with the boatswain and two sailors to see what officers were aboard. The captain woke suddenly with his mistress screaming in his ear and my sword point at his throat.

'Master Robert Dudley at your service.' I bowed. 'My apologies to you and your lady for calling at this inconvenient hour. However, if you can incommode yourself sufficiently to arise and accompany me to your great cabin there are one or two tedious formalities I am afraid we must discuss.'

His English was as fragmentary as my Spanish but he got the gist of my instructions and struggled out of bed muttering all manner of threats and maledictions. In the great cabin the other prisoners of rank had already been assembled – three gentlemen of impressive lineage, trying to look dignified in their nightshirts, and two pages. Kendall came in to report that the few crewmen aboard were safely locked in a fore cabin with a guard at the door.

'Master boatswain, I think we will have that cannon fired now, if you please.'

The mariner hurried away on his errand and I turned to the prisoners.

'Your keys, gentlemen, if you will be so kind.'

By means of signs I made them understand that I wanted the

keys to the ship's chest and their personal coffers. Equipped with these, my men were soon piling an assortment of items on the cabin floor – bags of gold excelentes and silver reals, embroidered doublets, silk shirts, a jewel-hilted rapier, a crucifix brilliant with coloured enamels, an ornate rosary, cups and dishes of silver, books, pictures, jewellery and assortment of personal trifles. What interested me more was the captain's navigational aids – charts and rutters for the Atlantic, Azores, Canaries, and the coast and islands of the New World, a magnificent armillery sphere, astrolabes, cross-staffs, nocturnals and an ivory quadrant of superb workmanship. Everything we wanted was soon packed into two of the chests. I sent four of the soldiers to carry them around the harbour to the caravel, then addressed myself once more to the Spanish captain.

'Señor, you have robbed me of a fine ship. I am come to repay the compliment.'

To judge by his fresh outpouring of imprecations, he took my meaning.

'Master Kendall, see that the officers are quartered somewhere comfortable but secure. The rest of you, go and lay your hands on whatever axes and marlinspikes you can find.'

I went back on deck and noted that the nocturnal peace of Santa Cruz had been decisively broken. Shouts and cries, clashing steel, smashing timber, shattering glass – all the sounds of violence filled the air. More were soon added as my avenging demons, deep in the galleon's hold, hacked holes in her side below the water-line. The devastation took a long time for the ship was stoutly built. Frequently, anxiously, I looked at my watch. Just as I had decided to call them back on deck, the soaking sailors clambered up through the centre hatch to report that their work was done. I freed the prisoners (having first taken the precaution of locating and removing their small arms), ordered my men ashore, cut the galleon's mooring ropes, and led my party, running, around the harbour. I sent my boatswain, with two companions, to fire the second cannon and its roar echoed across the water just as I reached the *Santa Anna*.

I made my way to the afterdeck through a crowd of jostling

men, humping bales, barrels, boxes and bundles of every size and shape. By the light of lamps they were stowing their booty below. They were in jubilant mood, finding time amid their bustling activity to make jokes and clap each other on the back. One of them even grabbed my hand and called 'Three cheers for the admiral!' before I reminded him that there would be time enough for that when we were safely away from Santa Cruz.

I found Nick Wyatt on the afterdeck and asked if everything was going according to plan. He certainly looked well pleased with himself.

'Tom Jobson ran into some trouble at the warehouses and I sent some men to help him. Apart from that, everything's worked out just as you said. Santa Cruz will remember this night for many a long year.'

At that moment Jobson, himself, came up the companionway. Blood was trickling from a cut on one cheek but he was smiling.

'Well done, Master Dudley, our voyage is made at the first throw of the dice.'

'It is you who have done well, Tom. You had some trouble?'

'The *audiencia* turned up unexpectedly with a dozen armed men: I was glad of it. It would have seemed almost a sin to take all this fine canary wine without some sort of fight.'

'Are all your men aboard?'

'I left a few of them to search the smallest warehouse. We had no time to look in there before.'

'Then please recall them. I intend to sail immediately.'

Jobson sent a man to hasten his laggards but after ten minutes there was still no sign of them. Further down the harbour a large crowd of angry Spaniards was growing and someone had had the inspiration, somewhat belatedly, to ring the church bell. We had achieved surprise and made a successful raid. Now it was vital to get away before the colonists recovered from their shock.

'Master Wyatt, hoist mainsail and prepare to cast off.'

'But, sir, there are still twenty or more of our men ...'

'They knew my orders. I will not hazard the success of this venture for a few greedy fools who have not learned the meaning of obedience.'

I looked along the mole towards the dark huddle of warehouses. There was no sign of the missing men.

'Cast off, Master Wyatt.'

The *Santa Anna* slipped away from the harbour wall. The sheet of black water widened, streaked by the light reflected from lamps among the agitated crowd. Soon even these disappeared as we rounded a headland and made for the open ocean.

The officers and I crowded into the small cabin below the afterdeck. We sat on stools, chests and bales, victorious brothers in arms, relaxing after battle.

'With your permission, Admiral, we'll sample the vintage.'

With the point of his sword, Kendall drew the bung from a barrel. We filled goblets, helmets, and any other recepticals we could find to toast our success.

We were still drinking when the first rays of the sun penetrated the cabin. Suddenly the sound of cheering came from on deck. At first we thought it was just the sailors celebrating in their way but the shouting was so prolonged that eventually we all staggered to our feet and went out of the cabin. Sailors and soldiers lined the starboard rail. I elbowed my way through the ranks and looked towards the sunrise. Less than a mile away there was another sail. It was the second caravel from Santa Cruz. From the masthead flew an improvised cross of St George and its rail, like our own was lined with cheering Englishmen.

11

And so I became a pirate or, to use the term preferred by the government and the Navy Board, a privateer. I had two vessels which more than compensated for the loss of the *Frisking*, a re-stocked larder and enough wine to last the whole voyage. After I had allocated to the crew an eighth share of the spoils there was sufficient left to make up for the *Mermaid*. Jobson was right; our enterprise was indeed, 'made' at the first throw of the dice. His metaphor was apt; I was just like a gambler whom success spurs to further folly. A prudent captain would probably have been content with his winnings and would have set course for home. I was staking all my gains on the next throw of the dice. Ships, prize vessels, men, booty – all were now invested in the long Atlantic crossing, the chance of further gains on the Main and the gambler's dream of El Dorado.

For almost a week we cruised to and fro along the twenty-ninth parallel of latitude waiting and hoping for the *Bear's Whelp* and the *Earwig*. They were lazy days of calm weather and warm sunshine. Apart from cleaning, repairs, pike drill and whatever other diversions the officers could devise, the men had nothing to do but trail their lines overboard for tunny fish and mackerel, sing bawdy ballads and songs of home, and gossip. A ship is a small place: secrets, personal animosities and discontent find few secure hiding holes. Grumbles soon become common property, particularly when there is little action to occupy men's minds. There were grumbles in plenty aboard my little fleet.

I well recall a conversation I overheard one night between two members of the second watch. The boatswain's mate, in charge

163

of the watch, had gone forward leaving the helmsman and the watch boy by the whip-staff. I went onto the poop deck for some fresh air before retiring for the night and so was above the two mariners and out of sight. The older man had a throaty, catarrhal voice, one I certainly would not have troubled to listen to if I had not heard my name mentioned.

'It's all very well for Master Dudley with his fine houses and his servants and his lands. One bit of gold more or less don't make no difference to him. But what about us poor seamen? What have we come on this trip for? What are we risking our lives for? Loot and prize money. There's not a man aboard who'd sign on for another voyage if he had enough gold to set himself up ashore in a farm or an alehouse.'

'You had your share of the Santa Cruz loot.' The boy obviously had a mind of his own.

'Tah!' His companion spat noisily. 'A little silver dish and three pieces of eight, what good are they?'

'They might have been some good to you if you hadn't diced half of them away this morning.'

That riled the older man.

'Listen, you ignorant brothel accident. Listen, and you might learn something.'

'Let go! You're hurting my arm.'

'I'll let go as soon as I've talked some sense into you. Now at Santa Cruz we could have had gold and silver enough for every man if we'd gone through all the houses. And if that galleon wasn't worth a thousand pound I'm a Dutchman. But we weren't allowed to ransack the town and we didn't put a prize crew aboard the galleon. Oh no, our precious admiral says, "Only one hour of looting in the town lads," and "We can't take the galleon with us, my fine fellows." And why not? That's what I want to know and you want to know, too, don't you?'

The boy squealed in the darkness.

'Ouch, yes all right.'

'Ask me then. Ask me why Master Dudley didn't let us make our fortunes in Santa Cruz.'

'Ow! All right, all right. Why didn't he?'

'Because he knows we wouldn't have sailed his ship to America. We'd have taken this tub and the prizes straight back to England. Right, lad, you can go now and turn that hour-glass. I don't want to stay out here any longer than I have to.'

The lad scrambled away and a moment later his clear voice intoned the hourly chant.

'Second glass gone and the third flows!'

I went to my bed to ponder on why men were born some rich some poor and whether 'adventure', 'honour', 'pride of achievement' were luxuries only the wealthy could afford. Once, I had thought of mariners as a brave breed of men inspired by the challenge of the unknown. I had long since discovered that most of them were reluctant sailors who were driven to face the appalling discomforts and dangers of deep-sea voyaging by the greater discomfort and danger of their own miserable lives ashore. The master's lash and the storm's fury were more tolerable than an empty belly, vagrancy, and the threat of the gallows if a man stole to feed his family. Everyone who went to sea had but one dream, that of coming back wealthy with a share in some great prize or treasure. For a few, a very few, that dream came true. The most popular captains were the ones who were the most successful pirates. Such captains pleased their men, their backers and their Queen, if their exploits were at the expense of Spanish Philip. Leaders who had other objectives – exploration, discovery, colonisation – who were more interested in adding to the treasury of knowledge, than to the coffers of the realm, were frequently misunderstood, mistrusted and abused. My mutinously-inclined helmsman was right about the power of a crew to force a captain to sail where they wished. Many expeditions had come to grief because of divided objectives, when leaders and led could not agree on whether they were pursuing loot or some higher goal.

I knew, therefore, that I could not afford to delay any longer in the slender hope of meeting up with my missing ships. On 4 January we took on water at one of the uninhabited islands and made sail southwards for the brazen, burning strand of Africa. It was thrilling to see the strange sights other travellers had written of and to know I was in the company of men who had explored the fringes of human experience. Here were the distant snow-tipped peaks of the High Atlas, the undwelt Sahara with its shifting sculptures of yellow sand, the spiny flying fish which hurled themselves through the air and sometimes fell on our decks, and the cavorting porpoises which pursued them.

But more exhilarating was the navigation of my own ship over the wide Atlantic. I was the first captain to rely on great circle navigation for a voyage across the ocean, and when I took readings the *Bear*'s great cabin resembled nothing so much as a schoolroom. Three or four times a day the senior mariners gathered around the Molyneux globe as I fixed the ship's latitude and longitude, spun the varnished sphere and, when rectified, moved the quarter circle across its surface to indicate the new course. They gazed fascinated yet cautious, those seasoned men of the sea, reserving their judgement, like farmers looking over lush green fields in June. They were not fully convinced by my calculations, not altogether happy about my use of log and line to assess the convoy's speed, were sagely sceptical of my confident prediction that we would make a landfall at Trinidad on the last day of January. I am not altogether sure that I fully believed my own prophecy, so it was a considerable relief when, on the night of 30 January, the watchman reported a pale stretch of water ahead and we found ourselves in fifteen fathoms. At daylight we made out the coast of Brazil in eight degrees and altering our course a few points to the north we soon came up with Cape Carao, the south-east tip of Trinidad.

'There it is, Will. Just as Colombus saw it nearly a hundred years ago.'

It was mid-morning and already the island's wooded slopes wavered in the dry equatorial heat. From the *Bear*'s poop deck young Bradshaw and I watched the caravels – now renamed the *Regard* and the *Intent* – work their way along the shore, gathering information about possible native and Spanish habitation. Will, busy as usual with pen and paper, paused in his work.

'If Columbus discovered Trinidad a hundred years ago why have the Spaniards never colonised it?'

'A good question, Will. Perhaps we shall learn the answer in

166

the next few days. It may simply be that they lack the men and ships to control the island. On the other hand, perhaps there is nothing there worth possessing – no gold, no silver, no pearl beds. That we must find out for ourselves.'

'Do you think Raleigh is here with the rest of the ships?'

The possibility had occurred to me often. It was, I thought, unlikely but there was just a chance that the main body of ships could have left England shortly after the *Bear* and the *Frisking* and, by taking a more direct route, have reached Trinidad ahead of us. I profoundly hoped not; I had no stomach for another confrontation just when the expedition's principal task was beginning and should not be satisfied until our initial exploration of the coastline was completed.

We turned the south-west corner of the island and anchored in a harbour which, because of its clamorous population of large ungainly birds went down on our chart as 'Pelican Bay'. That evening I called a captain's council. We sat around a trestle table on the *Bear*'s poop enjoying the cool onshore breeze and planning our next move. Nick Wyatt reported first on the caravels' reconnaissance.

'There are only a few native villages along this coast. Some of the people came down to stare at us from the rocks but when we landed in the boats to try and speak to them they ran into the woods.'

Benjamin Wood brushed a fly from his forehead.

'Doubtless they have good reason to be afraid. The only other men to approach them by sea have been Spaniards come to convert them with swords and crucifixes.'

'There was no sign of Spanish settlements, Nick?'

'None, Master Dudley.'

'That bears out what we know about the island.' Kendall leaned forward over the map on the table, using as a pointer the poniard with which he had been carving his salt pork. 'They've got a garrison here in the north but they don't seem to control the rest of the island.'

Jobson disagreed.

'You're forgetting what happened to James Lancaster and Jacob

Whiddon. About two years ago Lancaster tried to land along here.' He indicated a point slightly to the north of our present position. 'He was seen off by Spanish soldiers. And what happened when Whiddon called only a few months back? Eight of his men going ashore were ambushed and killed near Paracoa.'

'Well the fact remains they've shown no interest in us.' Nick Wyatt wiped his knife on his sleeve and thrust it back into his belt.

Jobson frowned.

'Don't you be so cocksure. Just because we can't see them doesn't mean they're not looking at us. They may be waiting for us to go away or they may be hoping we'll get careless and lay ourselves open to attack. I say we must keep a double guard, Master Dudley.'

'You are right, Tom. It would be foolish to let ourselves be taken unawares. Yet I suspect there may be another reason why the Spaniards are not very interested in us . . . The Golden Man.'

Seven pairs of puzzled eyes turned towards me.

'You see, gentlemen, the governor here is Antonio de Berrio, an old man, turned seventy. And he is ruled by one obsession, to conquer the kingdom of El Dorado before he dies and make himself and his heirs its masters. Even now he is awaiting the arrival of several galleons from Spain bringing an army for the ascent of the Orinoco. So he is not very worried by three little English ships.'

Nick laughed.

'He'll get a surprise when Raleigh comes with the rest of the fleet.'

'If Raleigh comes.'

'He will come, Abraham. He is as obsessed with El Dorado as is de Berrio.'

I pointed to the vast delta of the Orinoco which poured itself into the ocean in a myriad rivulets. On the map the conjectural network of rivers resembled an open hand stretched out to grasp the tiny island of Trinidad.

'Somewhere beyond that delta and up the main river lies the wealthiest country in the world – or so they both believe. Trinidad is only important as a base from which men and supplies can be shipped across to the mainland.'

We gazed westwards across the stretch of water known as the Serpent's Mouth. South America was a thin, dark line against the sunset sky. It was Nick Wyatt who spoke the question in all our minds.

'Is it really there?'

'Who knows, Nick? Many men have died looking for it.'

'And are we to join them?' It was the lugubrious Captain Wood who spoke, but they all looked to me for an answer – an answer I had not yet given myself.

'That is a decision I cannot make for any one of you. When and if I go to explore the Orinoco I will only take officers who have volunteered.'

The silence that followed was broken only by the screech of a tropical bird hidden somewhere in the forest. Now that the searing heat had worn off the day the mingled scents of the land wafted towards us over the cool water – sweet odours of fruit and flowers, the muted stench of mangrove swamps, the indefinable smells of unknown origin. At last Abraham Kendall laughed his deep bellow of a laugh.

'Well, I'll seek him out if he's there. Meanwhile I'll drink to him. Come on lads, raise your cups and let's have a toast – to the Golden Man, whether he be a heathen emperor or a ghost.'

We all joined in the toast heartily enough but I think I was not the only one who sensed another presence, as though the continent itself was watching us and waiting for us.

There was no question of an immediate assault on the Orinoco. We had quite enough to do in Trinidad for several days. Shore parties brought back fresh water and killed an abundance of wildfowl. But the one commodity we wanted most urgently proved the most elusive. That was information – about the island, the Spanish garrison, the mainland. We caught many glimpses of the naked Indians and discovered some of their simple villages but as soon as we approached, their painted bodies disappeared into the deep shadow of the trees or dissolved into the landscape. There was nothing for it but to establish a shore base and organise a full scale expedition to explore the island.

We built a stockade on the beach of Pelican Bay and established most of our men there in wooden cabins. At dawn on our third day I led a force of fifty soldiers eastwards along the beach. Our scouts had located a large Arawak village a mile or so inland and this was the objective of our 'attack'. We proposed to let the inevitable watchers see us march away. We would enter the forest then split into detachments in order to encircle the village. At that point I would enter the settlement with a small escort and try to talk with the elders. I explained this plan to all the men before we left the stockade and gave strict instructions that under no circumstances were any of the natives to be harmed. I would rather, I told them, that every painted savage slipped through our fingers than that a single man should be detained by violence. We had to show these people that we were not Spaniards.

The first part of our scheme went according to plan. We trudged through the dragging sand until we were well out of sight of our ships and our camp. Then we were confronted by a small estuary plaited with the grotesque roots and branches of mangrove trees. The sun was now above the rim of the low hills and slanting into our eyes as we circuited the swamp. Already we were sweating with the effort of wading through sand under the weight of weapons and part armour. When we found a point at which the river could be forded I called a halt and let the men drink of the turgidly-flowing but clear water. While we refreshed ourselves and emptied the irritating grains from our boots I sent a small party up river to see whether it was safe to enter the forest by that route. They were gone almost an hour. Then, just as I was beginning to think they must have been ambushed, the sound of crashing in the undergrowth and shouted curses announced their return.

They stumbled into view pushing before them two young Indians whose arms were tied behind them. The captives were trembling and terrified. At the sight of another forty armed white men they stopped and drew closer together until a hand from behind sent them staggering onward. When they reached me they fell to their knees and touched the ground with their foreheads all the time uttering a strange sound between a mutter and a puppy-like whimper.

I drew them to their feet and ordered their thongs to be untied. Now I saw, with something of a shock, that they were scarcely more than boys. Though they were tall and the broad bands of red paint across their chests and faces gave them an air of primitive ferocity, they could not be above fifteen years. I smiled reassuringly but they would not meet my eyes. I held out to them water and some fruit we had picked in the mangrove swamp. They were too frightened to take it. There was obviously nothing to be gained from the natives until they had overcome their fear. I turned to the leader of the scouting party, a red-haired young man called Hob, and let loose my anger.

'Who gave you orders to take prisoners?'

'We had to, sir. Honestly, I can explain how it was.'

He seemed genuinely worried but there was something about the way he steadily returned my gaze which seemed too good to be true.

'Your explanation had better be convincing.'

'Well, sir, it was like this. We split into two parties. The other lot worked through the wood. Jake Smith, Will Crozier and me went carefully along the bank. Suddenly, round a bend in the river comes this boat . . .'

'Boat?'

'Well, sir, a sort of boat made out of a tree trunk.'

'You mean a canoe?'

'Very likely, sir. I don't speak the language. Well, there was these three savages in the boat and they saw us and shouted out and began to turn their boat round. Well, sir, what could we do? We knew they would go back and warn their village. We had to stop them.'

'Get on with it, man. What did you do?'

'Well, the river was narrow just there and flowing pretty fast. They had a job turning their boat round. We ran along the bank and we began to throw rocks at them – not to capsize them, of course, sir, just to fluster them as you might say. Well it worked. One of them lost a paddle and the boat swung round and hit the bank and we grabbed them and brought them back.'

'You said there were three of them.'

'Ah, well, sir, there were but we . . . er . . . had a spot of bother and while we were sorting it out one of them slipped away.

'What sort of bother?'

'One of them – that vicious looking one with the squint, sir – he sat down in the path and refused to move.'

I looked at the prisoners who had, once more, thrown themselves down to the ground and were hiding their faces. For the first time I noticed the weals across one of their backs. I turned back to the truculent, over-confident Hob.

'Did you beat this lad to make him go with you?'

'If I hadn't, sir, we'd have been there still and the other savage fetching some of his cannibal friends to attack us, like as not.'

'What did you beat him with?'

'Just a small stick cut from a tree, sir.'

'That tells me very little. Go and cut another similar stick and show me.'

While Hob went off I tried again to talk with the Indians but with no more success than before. I examined the marks made by Hob's 'little stick'. They were thin lines and from the way they had bitten into the skin it was obvious that the blows had been laid on with relish. I called the surgeon over and he produced a jar of ointment but when he tried to apply it the wounded boy went almost wild with fear. He clawed at the unguent with his hands. Then he lay down and rubbed his back on the stony ground to scrape off the unwanted medicine.

At this point Hob returned stripping the leaves from a thin, whispy lash of a branch with his knife. I took it from him and tested its strength and suppleness.

'Now take off your armour and your shirt.'

'But, sir, it's only a savage.'

At those words I came close to fouling my own hands with the insubordinate and hot-tempered soldier. Instead I turned my anger into words.

'Savage or not he belongs to this island and we need the friendship of its people. You beat this man, and one of his friends, or perhaps a brother, saw you do it. Now he has gone back to tell

172

his people. Perhaps they will come and attack us out of revenge. Certainly they will have no reason to help us. You have put our whole expedition at risk – and all because you cannot obey orders. Now strip, or Master Kendall shall strip you.'

Sullenly, Hob fumbled the buckles of his harness undone, then peeled off the sweat-soaked shirt.

'Now spread yourself against that tall rock.'

He moved across to where a pillar of stone stood by itself as though plunged into the ground by a giant hand. Instinctively the rest of the men gathered round to witness the flogging. The boatswain stepped forward to take the lash from me but I waved him aside. I beckoned to the injured Indian. He came slowly, cautiously. There was a gasp from the watchers as I put the stick into his hand. Kendall opened his mouth to protest but I waived him to silence. We all stood motionless, our eyes fixed on the young Arawak.

For some moments he stared uncertainly at the whip. He looked from it to the bare brown back of his attacker and then at me. I nodded. I could almost see the realisation sweeping over him that his dignity was being restored. He stood up straight with all the pride of a young warrior and walked slowly, sedately forward. When he reached the rock he stopped. Twice he raised the branch in the air and brought it swishing down, testing it. Then he aimed it across Hob's shoulders, drew his arm fully back and brought the lash whistling down on the bare flesh. I expected a hail of furious blows to follow and was already calculating how many I would allow before I moved to stop him. But the young man stepped gracefully back, turned, walked up to me, returned the whip and help up a hand in salute. I returned the gesture. Whereupon the Arawak nodded gravely and walked back to his companion. They exchanged a few words in their own language then walked away together towards the forest.

'Do you think that was wise, lad?' Abraham Kendall spoke quietly so that none of the men could hear.

'Perhaps, Abraham, perhaps not. We have to win their confidence somehow.'

'What do we do now, return to camp?'

'We go on as planned.'

'But they'll have been warned. The village will be empty. They may even lay an ambush for us.'

'In that case, Abraham, you can have the pleasure of telling me I was wrong.'

'I shan't have much chance to gloat when I'm in some savage's stewpot.'

'Oh you need not fear on that score, Abraham. They would never get their teeth into your brine-soaked hide. Now, muster the men. We march immediately.'

'Very well, Master Dudley. What about young Hob.'

'He has suffered enough. His own shipmates are unlikely to let him forget the day he was beaten by a mere "savage".'

We resumed our march, divided, as arranged into separate contingents and were in position close to the village by mid-afternoon. Below the sparsely foliated trees the air was still and sultry for the 'forest' was more a tract of open woodland with many clearings and the shade was intermittent. The clearings in the immediate vicinity of the settlement were planted with crops and from our hiding place we could hear Arawak women chattering as they prodded among the green stems with their simple tools.

I had decided that Tom Jobson and Nick Wyatt should accompany me into the village together with four soldiers, one of whom spoke fluent Spanish. (It was Wood's conviction that there were sure to be a few natives who had spent some time as captives of the 'papist dogs' and who would, therefore, speak a few words of their language.) We worked our way under cover of the sparse undergrowth until we were within a hundred yards or so of the circle of thatched, wooden huts. We could clearly see people going about their normal tasks. Two men were stretching an animal skin on a frame. In the shade of a large tree a potter was working, two boys keeping him well supplied with water from the river. A group of younger children were crouched on the ground engrossed in a game which seemed to involve the throwing of stones into a square marked in the dust.

'I don't like the look of it, Master Dudley. They must know we're here. It's obviously a trap. I still think...'

I knew very well what Abraham Kendall thought. He had insisted three or four times that I should let him go instead of me.

'For the last time, no, Abraham. Someone has to show some trust if we are to establish a relationship with these people.'

'Yes, but if you get killed...'

He stopped, abruptly and pointed.

'Look!'

The open space in the centre of the village had suddenly filled with people; not the casual throng of natives going about their own affairs, but a large crowd organised into a single purpose. The focal point of the assembly was a tall man with an animal skin thrown round his shoulders and an elaborate headdress of dyed cloth and feathers. He was flanked by painted warriors carrying bows and arrows. Behind him, excited but silent, stood the rest of his people.

Slowly, regally, the chief and his retinue walked towards the spot where we thought we were concealed. Mustering what dignity I could, I moved forward from the screen of trees and my own little entourage gathered around me. The two parties met on the edge of the village. The chief, a tall, wrinkle-faced man of middle years held up a hand.

'Babage!'

I repeated the greeting. Close to the chief's right elbow I saw the lad Hob had beaten. He returned my gaze with the faintest of smiles and I knew that all was well. The chief was speaking again. I stood, deferentially listening to the stream of strange sounds, and wondering how I was going to reply. Then another young Arawak stepped forward and began translating his master's words into Spanish. I summoned our interpreter and in the following, laborious conversation managed to convince the chief (whose name was Mointiman) that we were enemies of de Berrio's men and that our Queen offered friendship and peace to the people of Trinidad. I backed up my statement with gifts. From a coffer set before me on the turf I took rolls of coloured cloth, beads, knives, fish hooks and a sword. Montiman called an order. Two of his men stepped forward, lifted the chest and disappeared with it into one of the huts. Another command and a gaggle of maidens appeared through the crowd bearing baskets of fruit, nuts, meat and some strange root vegetables.

The situation seemed safe. I turned to Kendall.

'Order the rest of the men to come into the village.'

Abraham frowned and opened his mouth to remonstrate but I cut across his protest.

'Now, if you please, Master Kendall.'

Warily our sailors and soldiers stepped forward, looking all around them and keeping tight hold on their weapons. Mointiman shouted another command and some of the women went over with offerings of food. The result was predictable and immediate: the men had not been close to members of the opposite sex for weeks; now they were confronted by girls and young women whose dark bodies were almost completely uncovered. The Indian ideal of beauty was a long way from the European but these creatures were female and that was all that mattered to the seamen. Within seconds they were reclining on the ground beside their discarded weapons allowing themselves to be fed by their hostesses.

After these lengthy preliminaries, the chief led the officers and myself to one of the buildings. Inside it was dark and the air heavy with smoke from a central fire, very much like an English peasant's cottage. Mointiman sat cross-legged on a woven mat, his warriors standing around him. I was motioned to another mat. Then food and drink were set before us. For an hour or more the unsmiling chief plied me with questions about my country, my Queen, my ships, the number of men I had brought and why I had come. When I tried to counter with inquiries of my own I was politely but firmly silenced. The etiquette in that remote, primitive hut seemed to be as well-defined as that which ruled the presence chamber at Westminster. In one way I was glad of the interrogation for it gave me a good excuse for not consuming too much of the burnt meat and foul-smelling liquor which formed the basis of the feast.

Then, suddenly, the audience was over. Mointiman rose, raised his hand in salute and strode through the narrow doorway followed by his silent attendants. I and my party stumbled out into the dazzling sunlight. Our men were still enjoying themselves: some were walking about the village laughing and talking in sign language with the women; others were playing with the children, giving pick-a-back rides and showing them their knives and guns. But the chief was nowhere to be seen and so there was nothing to be done but to return to camp and hope that further contact with these people would provide us with some of the information we so badly needed.

We had almost reached the edge of the forest when I was aware of an Arawak man walking by my side. No rustling of the bushes had signalled his approach. No one had seen him come. He was just suddenly there matching my stride and gait with good-natured mimicry. I recognised him as Mointiman's interpreter. He explained in Spanish that he had been ordered to go with us, to tell us all we wanted to know, to give any help he could and to stay as long as we needed him. He looked at me with the wide self-confident smile I was to come to know so well and I can honestly say that at that moment an angel from heaven could not have been more welcome.

During the next few days the stocky, little Indian showed me and told me about many of Trinidad's mysteries. He was himself not the least of those mysteries. For a start, there was something very unusual about his name – Balthasar. He told me how he had come by it. He was brought up in a village in the north of the island. Some five years before, the Spaniards had attacked it, killed the chief and taken most of the people prisoner. The men were forced to build de Berrio's capital of San José de Oruña. The women became concubines and menials. Balthasar saw his own wife become the plaything of some of the Spanish officers and die in childbirth within the year. But he was marked out by the invaders for more favoured treatment. He was taken into the governor's household, taught to speak and read Spanish, instructed in the Catholic faith and baptised. The priest who gave him his new name thought that 'Balthasar' was a great joke. I could see nothing amusing in it until the Bible-loving Wood explained.

' 'Tis out of the book of the Prophet Daniel, Master Dudley. When the prophet and his people were made captives by

Nebuchadnezzar, King of Babylon, Daniel was taken into the king's palace. He was given a new name, the mark of his slavery and degradation. That name was Balthasar.'

Balthasar hated his captors but he was careful never to show it. Watching him move about the camp with a flashing smile for everyone he met, I could understand how easily he had fooled the Spaniards into believing that he was their friend. Through my Spanish interpreter he told me how he had used his privileged position to help his people whenever possible and though he had had to guide the conquerors around the island, showing them where food and water were to be found, he had kept from them what they most wanted to know about – the gold mines of Trinidad. At last he had made his escape and taken refuge with Mointiman's people at the southern end of the island.

'You have gold mines on Trinidad – gold like this?' I took a ring from my finger and put it in his hand, trying not to sound too excited.

Balthasar nodded cheerfully.

'Yes, yes, we have this too, this gleaming *calcouri*, what you call gold.'

'Will you show us where your *calcouri* comes from?' I tried to sound casual.

The Indian's perfect teeth showed dazzling white against his dusky skin but he made no reply.

'My Queen is the enemy of the Spaniards. I am pledged to fight against them in her name. We, too, live on an island and the King of Spain tried to conquer us. We drove him and his soldiers away. We can also help your people.'

'Then I will show you whatever you want to see.'

My promise to Balthasar had been deliberately vague but I had not intended to deceive him. The Indian's story had certainly raised my hatred of Spain to a new pitch and there was nothing I would have liked more than to drive the invaders out of Trinidad. If there really was gold in this island it could only be a matter of time before de Berrio or his successor found it. Unless England intervened. If we could throw the Spaniards out might this not be an excellent site for the first English New World colony? The people were friendly. There was an abundance of food, fertile soil and excellent harbours. From such a base the Queen's ships could sally forth to explore and possess the mainland. But did I have the necessary manpower to storm de Berrio's garrison and how many men did the governor have at his command? Not for the first time I cursed the loss of my other ships and the man who was responsible for that loss.

Since I could make no decision without seeing San José de Oruña for myself, I mustered a reconnaissance party two days later. I left Kendall in charge of the Pelican Bay encampment with orders that the *Bear* and the *Intent* were to be careened. I set sail northwards in the *Regard* with Nick Wyatt, Tom Jobson and twenty soldiers in addition to the caravel's crew.

We sailed some forty miles up the coast until we reached an area where land and sea overlapped in tangled, greasy swamp. Balthasar pointed to a channel amid the reeds and mangrove trees. We struck sail and ran out the four long oars or 'sweeps'. The sweating, grumbling sweepmen bent their backs to the task and the *Regard* moved slowly inshore. The stinking vegetation closed around us and I expected the shallow drafted caravel to ground at any moment. But the leadsman found a constant two fathoms and a sandy bottom. Evidently we were in the outlet of a small river. We anchored eventually when the channel became too narrow for further progress. We waded ashore and, following Balthasar in careful single file, we groped our way through the swamp. Without our guide to show us the causeways we would never have gone fifty yards. There was no doubt that, without similar help, a whole army of Spaniards could never have found our ship, which was, therefore, perfectly safe until our return.

We reached the wooded ridge beyond the swamp and followed it northwards, keeping well within the cover of the undergrowth and eschewing all paths. Suddenly, without warning, Balthasar disappeared from my side. Startled, I looked to right and left, my sword half drawn. Then I saw the Indian's perpetual grin framed by broad leaves two feet above my head. He crouched on the lowest bough of a gigantic tree and beckoned to me. I shook my head. This was no time for playing games. But he was insistent and held out a hand to pull me up. I was well aware of the laughter of my men (quickly silenced by Jobson) at the sight of their admiral scrambling up a tree like a thieving schoolboy.

It was a long climb, though not a difficult one. That Methuselah of a tree sprouted a thousand stout branches before thrusting its head high above its fellows. Perched in its topmost fork I could see the landscape spread before me like a map. To the west the wide Gulf of Paria with the dark mainland marking its limit. To the north the wooded slopes of Trinidad's farthest range of hills. Here and there a white ribbon of water fell among the trees down to the Caroni river. And on the far bank of that river, due northwest from my present position, the garrison town of San José de Oruña.

It was grey and ugly, like a piece of jagged rock thrown down on green velvet. And it was formidable. Even from a distance I could see how hard Balthasar's people had had to work building it. The town was walled on all sides and there were towers at the angles and the gateways. Most of the buildings seemed to be of wood, though a few – doubtless the church and de Berrio's residence and the court house – were more substantial. The main gateway faced the river where many boats were tied to a long wooden jetty. The river was de Berrio's lifeline: six miles down river lay his harbour – Port of Spain – and beyond that Madrid. The river was also his highway to the interior. Along it flowed the tribute of maize, fowls, eggs, fruit, skins and pots extracted from the Indians. No wonder he chose to ignore me and my little contingent of Englishmen. His fortress was impregnable to such a small force.

I stayed in my lofty eyrie till I had crammed every detail of the terrain into my head and until my cramped legs went numb. Then I descended and ordered the return to the ship. There was nothing else to be done. Balthasar dared not approach any closer to San José and there was no way that any of my men could have got into the town to gather information about the enemy's strength.

Throughout the journey back to Pelican Bay I turned the problem over in my mind. The Spaniards were secure in San José and could laugh at any attack I might launch. But supposing they had a full scale native rebellion on their hands? Mointiman and his people had become regular visitors to our camp and I had developed a great liking for them. I wanted to help them. But would they help themselves? Would enough of the villages unite under my leadership in full scale attack on de Berrio's stronghold? Could I justify such action first to my captains and later to the Queen? Certainly, if Trinidad really boasted the gold mine of which Balthasar spoke.

The brief equatorial twilight lay shimmering on the water as the *Regard* rounded the headland of Pelican Bay. Etched against it was the black outline of a ship with furled sails. At first I thought my orders had been disobeyed and that the *Bear* had not been beached for careening. Then I saw my two other ships hauled up on the sand, lashed down with ropes to expose their hulls and fires over which the pitch was being melted. It would appear we had a visitor. Could it be Richard Monk with the *Bear's Whelp*?

Ashore, I hurried to my pavilion. Will met me at the doorway but I brushed him aside. The lamp had been lit on the table and it fell full on the features of the stocky man who occupied my high-backed chair. He rose and came towards me, hand outstretched and an affable smile creasing his swarthy face.

'Well, Master Dudley, here I am as I said I would be. Captain George Popham at your service.'

12

For a moment I was bereft of speech.

George Popham certainly was not. I never knew him prolong a silence. Talking for him was almost an obsession.

'Thought I'd find you here, lad. Been here only a few days, I gather. We're well met, then. Having your ships careened, are you? That's good. Not that the *Bear* will be much use to us when we start up the Orinoco: too many shallows and sandbanks off the coast.'

He poured Canary wine from a flagon.

'Well met, Captain Popham, well met? There is no man in the world I less want to meet than you!'

My visitor was unabashed. He held out to me the brimming goblet.

'Now there's a nice welcome for a man that's come five thousand miles to help you. Here, lad, cool your temper in a drink.'

My throat was parched but I turned my back on the wine.

'You tricked me into running out of Plymouth into a howling gale. You cost me two good ships and nearly ruined my enterprise. Now, I suppose, you have come at Raleigh's behest to finish off the good work. In God's name, Popham, do you think me such a fool to be caught twice!'

'Lad, lad.' The old captain put a hand on my shoulder. 'You must learn who your real friends are. Ask Abraham Kendall, if ever I let a man down who put his trust in me.'

I shook him off.

'I can make up my own mind about friends and traitors.'

'And you put poor George Popham among the traitors.' A deep sigh expanded his large frame. 'Ah well, I can't say I blame you. It must have looked bad when I didn't follow you out of Plymouth.' He reseated himself in my chair. 'Would you like to know what stopped me?'

'Oh, doubtless you have concocted some excellent excuse in the last couple of months. Well you can save it for someone more gullible. I shall have you rowed back to your ship. And you can think yourself fortunate to be leaving uninjured.'

Popham tilted the chair back.

'Brave words, youngster, but they don't do you justice. Think, now; is it really likely I'd come all this way after you just to do you a mischief. And if I had come for that purpose wouldn't I have done my worst by now. I sailed into this harbour five hours ago to find two of your ships pulled up on the beach and all your men ashore. What could have stopped me running up a Spanish flag and then pounding your vessels to pieces?'

At that point Will came in with my supper. As the lad clattered the silver dishes and set another chair at the table I pondered on Popham's words. There were very few men who made me feel unsure of myself but Popham was one of them. I sat, and Will uncovered a dish of roasted wildfowl. There was a sauce made (as the page explained) of mangrove fruit and wild honey. The savoury fragrance awoke my giant slumbering appetite and I hacked greedily at the meat with my dagger. Between mouthfuls I muttered to Popham,

'Tell your story, then.'

As he spoke I gave every appearance of being more interested in my meal – an attitude not altogether contrived.

'When I got back to the *Fury* after our little conversation that night in Plymouth I found one of Raleigh's men waiting for me. Very civil he was. Brought an invitation from his master to take wine with him in his lodging. Well, naturally, I went ashore and followed the fellow to the house. Sir Walter welcomed me warmly and set me before the fire with a jug of mulled wine. Only there was more than spices and sugar in that wine. I woke up to find myself in a small locked room and with a head full of molten lead.'

'You mean Raleigh drugged you?' Despite myself Popham had succeeded in engaging my interest.

'Drugged me and very near poisoned me. I told you he'd stop at nothing to prevent you setting out. Of course, by the time I came to you were gone. Raleigh was furious. He sent men to "question" me and discover your plans.'

He held his left hand out to me across the table, palm uppermost. It was a featureless surface of lurid, translucent pink with pockets of pus at the edges.

'A candle flame is a very simple and efficient instrument of torture.'

'So you told them what they wanted to know?'

'No, lad. It takes more than a little pain to open my lips. Not that I wouldn't have given in eventually if they'd carried on. Fortunately for me the storm blew up and your *Bear's Whelp* came staggering back into harbour with news of your fleet scattered and the *Earwig* foundered.'

'The *Earwig*!'

'I'm afraid so, lad. Thrown on the rocks off Gribbin Head. There were no survivors.'

I pushed the half-empty platter away from me. The flickering light from the camp fires threw vivid shadows on the walls of the tent. I thought of young John Lister and his men who had paid so dearly and so quickly for signing on with Robert Dudley.

'And what of the *Whelp*?'

'Safe, and all in her. Doubtless she's even now at sea with Raleigh's fleet.'

'My ship and men – at sea with Raleigh? Is there no end to your catalogue of bad tidings? What does Monk think he is about?'

'You mustn't blame Captain Monk. Raleigh told him that you and your ships were engaged to serve with him on a voyage to find El Dorado. "Master Dudley has deserted me," he says, "and he'll pay dearly for that when the Queen hears of it. If you refuse to sail with me, Captain Monk, I'll send you up to London in chains."'

'So, Raleigh is spreading that story – that I deserted him?'

'And jeopardised his whole expedition.'

'Very clever. He seems to have made it impossible for me to return.'

'Oh, no lad, it's not as bad as that. The Queen's no fool. She'll take what Sir Walter says with a pinch of salt if we return successful.'

It was true. I knew Elizabeth of England well enough to realise that she assessed loyalty and service in strictly cash terms.

'When did Raleigh leave? And how do you come to be here before him?'

'He couldn't keep me locked up for long. He needed my ship and my men – and my men won't work for anyone but me, not after all the years we've been together. So I was set at liberty. I watched him scrabble together half a dozen ships and get stores and victuals from chandlers foolish enough to accept promises for payment. I had the *Fury* well stocked and my men aboard ready to slip our berth as soon as I gave the word. We got away on 14 January. I know Raleigh can't have started for at least another fortnight even supposing he had good weather. I came straight here by way of the Azores.'

Popham's face almost glowed in the full light of the lamp. Everything else in the tent was a blur. My eyes were fixed on his much as a cock is bewitched by the fox. Suddenly I realised that I had fallen under the spell of the captain's golden-tongued sorcery. Firmly I grasped again the charm of scepticism which alone could save me from this plausible man. I stood up, abruptly.

'Why, Popham? Why did you come in search of me? For all you knew I, too, had perished in the storm.'

'We heard that the *Bear* had been in and out of Falmouth. I guessed you would make for Guiana and I knew you would get there if you set your mind on it. You're a fine commander, you've an excellent ship and in Abraham Kendall you've got the best mariner afloat.'

'Very flattering, Captain, but you still have to answer my question. Why did you come?'

When, after a pause, he spoke again the genial warmth had gone out of his voice.

'Revenge, Master Dudley. Revenge against a man who bought my service and thought he'd bought my soul. A man who sends his servants to bully and torture. A man who murdered my daughter.'

'Murdered...'

'I told you how I got involved in Raleigh's Roanoke colony. How the settlers were left to the mercy of the Indians. How they all perished before we could get back to them with help and supplies.'

'Yes.'

'I didn't tell you that my daughter and son-in-law were among those settlers. I tried to talk them out of going but they were young and impressionable. They believed everything Raleigh told them about a wonderful land flowing with milk and honey. Peter, Margaret's husband, was a younger son with no inheritance. Virginia held out the promise of land and fortune. The last time I saw them they were standing hand-in-hand on the beach, happy and hopeful. I never discovered how they died. And now Raleigh's gambling everything on finding the kingdom of El Dorado. He thinks he'll found another benighted colony. We'll put a stop to that, won't we lad? We are here and Raleigh's hundreds of miles away at sea. By the time he reaches the mouth of the Orinoco we'll have found his golden kingdom and be on our way home loaded with treasure.'

At last I looked at George Popham with understanding eyes. I knew why I had never trusted someone wiser men found so amiable and honest. 'Good Old George' was a fraud, a pleasant, cheerful invention designed to conceal and protect the real man – a man lonely, sad and bitter. I hadn't the heart to tell him that my immediate plans did not include a journey up the Orinoco in search of El Dorado. The more I thought about it the more convinced I became that Trinidad was the key to English enterprise in the New World. Here was a land of friendly people, fruitful soil and gold. Here we could establish a garrison, perhaps a colony. From this secure base we could organise the exploration of the Orinoco basin and the mountain kingdom of Guiana. But we would have to act quickly and decisively. I wanted to make good my claim to the island before Raleigh arrived. Let him return to England with stories of El Dorado: I would lay at her Majesty's feet the real gold of her new kingdom of Trinidad. There was another reason for haste: Popham brought news of a large fleet already on its way from Spain, coming to the aid of de Berrio.

The first thing I had to do was talk with Balthasar about the support I could expect for an attack on San José. Such a talk would have to be in private; I was not prepared to discuss my plans with my officers until they were well formulated. I had been working hard to understand Spanish and could now hold a conversation with Balthasar which only occasionally needed to be augmented by sign language. Next morning I found the Indian on the beach watching the sweating seamen melting pitch over their fires and choking at the acrid fumes.

He seemed remarkably interested and when he saw me he pointed to the vats of bubbling pitch and then broke into an excited torrent of Spanish. He seemed to be saying that there was more pitch along the beach and I ruefully admitted to myself that my grasp of the language was not as secure as I had thought. Balthasar seemed determined to show me whatever it was he was talking about. He drew me towards the tide line where his canoe lay beached. Since I wanted a chance to talk with him alone I allowed myself to be settled in the unstable looking craft. Balthasar pushed the boat out, leaped aboard and began paddling.

After travelling parallel to the shore for about an hour, we landed and Balthasar led me up the beach. We scrambled up a dune sparsely sown with spiky grass. At the top my guide pointed and smiled his wide, all-purpose smile. And there was what looked like a lake of pitch. A vast solid, black shimmering surface of two hundred acres or more stretched before us. I stared incredulously and then walked down to the edge of this strange phenomenon. The surface was hard but sticky, just like pitch. I broke off a piece. As I rolled it in my fingers it slowly became soft and pliable. Balthasar was right; it was *pitch* or a substance very like it. Here, then, was further proof of the Trinidad's value to a sea-going nation. Was there no end to the bounty of this remarkable island?

We sat down beside the pitch lake and I asked Balthasar about his family, his village, his chief. He told me about the Arawak way of life. Their settlements, I gathered, were autonomous; no leader had ever arisen who had tried to forge them into a nation. Indeed, the idea struck Balthasar as very odd. Were none of the chiefs sufficiently well respected, I asked, to be able to unite all the villages? He thought for a long time, head in hands, eyes fixed on the sand.

'The elders tell stories of how it was in the old times when the Caribs used to attack from across the water. There was a great chief, Arkeabo, whom the gods chose to lead all the people of the island. He gave the people magic water to drink so that the Caribs could not kill them.'

'And would the people follow such a leader against the Spaniards? Would they follow Mointiman?'

The brown eyes sparkled. The smile was wider than ever.

'They will follow you.'

He threw himself down in the sand and rested his forehead on my boots.

'You will lead us, great lord, and we shall kill all the Spaniards. Our enemies and your enemies – we will chase them into the sea. You will lead us! You will lead us!'

Was it a statement or a desperate cry for help? I made him rise and sit beside me.

'Yes, Balthasar, we will free you from the Spaniards, and other servants of the great Queen will come to live here to stop your enemies ever coming back.'

He grasped my hand in both of his. His whole body trembled with emotion and there were tears in his eyes. He could not speak and for several minutes we sat embracing each other in silence. Then Balthasar jumped up and began pacing the dunes to and fro as though searching for something. He stooped and came back with a long white feather, shed, obviously, by one of the pelicans. From the top of his loin cloth he took a knife that I had given him. Slowly, carefully he split the quill from end to end. One half he gave to me. The other he pushed in and out of the loose fabric of his loincloth until it was securely fixed. He gestured to me to do the same. I pinned my token to my jerkin.

The next moment I thought the young Indian had been possessed by a demon. He threw his head back and laughed. He danced around me, screeching and whooping, like one of the inmates of Bedlam. But I knew why. I had promised to revenge all the indignities heaped on his people. And in his simple mind the vow was as good as the accomplishment. The great white lord had said he would do it. Therefore it would be done. There was something terrifying in the rapturous delight glowing in Balthasar's eyes.

What appeared so simple to the Indian was, of course, far from being so, as my senior officers soon let me know.

'It's madness, Master Dudley! Storm the Spanish fortress with a heathen rabble – it can't be done.'

Tom Jobson spoke as the expedition's military expert and his words drew a murmur of approval round the table. It was the evening of the same day and I had called a meeting in the great cabin of the refloated *Bear*.

'What other suggestions does anyone have? We must act quickly. Raleigh may be here in two or three weeks and a relief fleet from Spain may arrive at any time.'

'And the men are getting restless; they've heard talk of this gold mine. I say we find this mine, take all the gold we can load aboard and go.'

'And then leave the Spaniards to get control of it as soon as we have gone? No, Tom, there is no sense in that.'

'We don't know yet that there is any gold on Trinidad,' Nick Wyatt pointed out quietly. 'The natives talk about it but they haven't shown us any and they don't wear gold ornaments themselves. But we do know the tribes of the Guiana highlands have gold. Captain Popham has seen it and he has also explored the lower reaches of the Orinoco.'

I had deliberately excluded the captain of the *Fury* from the conference. That priest of the cult of El Dorado would only have obscured the real issue with his gilded visions of easy wealth.

'The search for the Kingdom of Guiana is too hazardous, Nick. You must not believe all George Popham tells you.'

The young captain blushed angrily.

'I never thought to hear Robert Dudley describe an adventure as too hazardous. Did we not come here to find El Dorado and to beat Raleigh to it if we could?'

I was about to reply in the same vein but Kendall intervened to play the peacemaker.

'No man here doubts the Admiral's courage. If he thought it best he would lead us up the Orinoco tomorrow and we would all follow – and perhaps half of us would come back. But he's also responsible for the safety and success of the expedition. If there is gold here then let's take it.'

'Aye, but we don't have to get ourselves killed storming San José.' Jobson was adamant. 'If the Spaniards won't come out and fight let them stay there, say I, while we take the gold from under their noses.'

The old soldier still seemed to have most of the others on his side, but Kendall was a powerful advocate and I let him plead my case.

'You can see no further than the end of your nose, Tom Jobson. Think, man. What'll happen when we get home with our holds loaded with Trinidad gold? Every fool who can hire a ship will be here to plunder the island. But if we oust the Spaniards and stake our claim we can all have shares in a new Trinidad colony. We'll all be rich men – rich for life, not just rich with the sudden spoils of a single raid. Tom, you'll be able to set up as a country gentleman. Young Nick, you'll be able to fit out your own fleet. All of you; you'll all be able to afford your heart's desire.'

That turned the tide of battle, though Jobson fought a spirited rearguard action.

'That's all very fine if there *is* gold on Trinidad. That's what we must find out first.'

I agreed.

'Yes, Tom. That must be our first priority. Tomorrow you can take a party in search of this mine. Some Indian guides will go with you. It should take you a couple of days to find it, assess the quantity of metal there and bring back some samples. Meanwhile, I shall persuade Mointiman to gather as many other chiefs as he can and I will talk to them.'

With that the meeting dispersed. I asked Kendall to stay behind.

'Thank you, for supporting me, Abraham. Without you I would have had to use force instead of persuasion.'

The old mariner growled.

'Make a good politician, wouldn't I: telling lies so convincingly?'

'Lies?'

'Of course lies, lad. You don't think I believed all that rubbish about Trinidad gold, do you?'

'Then why . . .'

'To hold the expedition together. I've seen too many ventures come to grief because the leaders have fallen out. You're young, but you've got this fleet together and you must do what you think right. All the mariners and soldiers sailing with you are older and more experienced. They think they know better than you. And they're right. That doesn't matter: right or wrong you've got to have your decisions obeyed. I've seen Drake flog an upstart officer from one end of a ship to the other because he opposed him. You must be prepared to do the same. Once lose control and the whole venture will collapse in faction and mutiny. Then we'll be lucky if any of us see home again.'

'But why are you so sure that I am wrong?'

He gazed intently at me across the table, his fixed and useless eye disconcertingly directed towards a point beyond my left shoulder.

'If there was gold here, lad, don't you think the Spaniards would have found it by now? If there was even a suspicion of precious metal de Berrio wouldn't let us wander all over the island as we have done.'

'But we know that de Berrio is obsessed with El Dorado.'

Kendall stood up.

'Look, lad, I know your real reason for wanting to raid San José and I respect you for it. But there's others who won't thank you for risking their lives because of a promise made to a heathen savage. They'll follow you and face every danger you lead them into as long as you can dangle before them the carrot of undreamed wealth. Take that away and you'll have a hard job to hold onto their loyalty. And now, Master Dudley, I must check the sentries.'

I walked out onto the main deck and stood alone in the warm, still night. The only breaches in the enveloping blackness were made by the dull embers of the cooking braziers, the sentries' lamps and the darting fireflies in the woods beyond. I thought of Thomas Cavendish, that gentle yet passionate man; dead, and many of his men with him, because he had failed to hold the trust and loyalty of his crew, because they would not follow him where he wished to go. How had the collapse of that expedition begun? Growing misgivings among officers and men; a commander too preoccupied with his own convictions to see the discontent spreading through his ship? Could not even the motive of self-preservation save him from his own desperate courage and intense vision? If not, he was a more dedicated explorer than I. I wanted to reach home safely. As the days passed I thought more and more of Margaret, longed for her, desired her, wished the whole voyage over so that we would be together and never again separated. I wanted to know that she was well. She had looked tired the last time we had met, weary from spending long hours nursing the sick Queen. What if she had succumbed to the same fever. Despite the warm air I shuddered, then went back to my cabin to spend several sleepless hours with my conflicting thoughts.

Jobson and his party set off early the following morning; and I organised native runners to go to all the nearby villages and fetch the chiefs to a meeting. I chose the site for the assembly with great care – a sparse hilltop overlooking Pelican Bay. There was just room on its summit for myself and a small entourage; everyone else would have to stand or sit on the slopes below looking up at the one who was proclaiming himself their saviour. On this peak I erected a stout wooden post which was to play a vital role in the ceremony I was planning.

They began to arrive next morning, the venerable heads of the tribes of Trinidad: fat, grey, lean, bald, short, tall, some naked, others swathed in the multi-coloured regalia of office. Some bore still the stamp of the fearless, barbaric warrior. A few were infirm and came to the rendezvous leaning on the shoulders of attendants or borne in hammocks slung on poles. Only age united them.

At noon the following day I surveyed the assembly from one of the stockade's guard towers. Several hundred men, elders and warriors, were seated beyond the camp, patient, expectant. Doubtless there were still others to arrive but I decided not to keep them waiting any longer. I gave the order for the men to muster and they formed up on the sand in four ranks. They made an impressive sight – gleaming helmets and breastplates, scarlet hose, an intimidating array of pikes and muskets, banners and flags fluttering in heraldic gaudy. All the gentlemen, like myself, were arrayed in their finest clothes and were resplendent in plumes, silks and damascened part-armour.

'Double your ranks by right line!'

In response to Jobson's bellowed order the troop formed into two open files.

'Advance your pikes!'

I walked slowly along the lines of sweating Englishmen, satisfying myself that they were fit to represent their Queen. When I had done Jobson resumed his staccato commands.

'Shoulder your pikes!'

'Advance to the right in line of march!'

With my standard bearer and officers I took up my position between the two ranks of men. The trumpeters blew a fanfare. The stockade gates were drawn back.

'March!'

To the steady beat of tabors we moved out of our camp, across the beach and up the incline towards the pre-arranged spot. Looking round, I could see the Indians following, some unable to resist falling in step with the beat of the drums. On the hilltop my men formed an open square so that I could be seen clearly by the jostling throng of natives below. Another fanfare sounded. Its final notes dissolved into a profound, tense silence. I motioned to my page. He stepped forward, carrying the brass plate he had been working on for the last couple of days. I took it from him and handed it to the *Bear*'s carpenter, who nailed it to the post. Its inscription was in Latin so that any educated European who ever saw it would understand it. I read it out in Spanish so that Balthasar could translate it into the language of his people.

'Robert Dudley, Englishman, son of the most illustrious Earl of Leicester, landed on this island the third day of February in the year of Our Lord 1595 with his army and claimed the same in the name of the Most High and Mighty Elizabeth, Queen of England, France and Ireland, Defender of the Faith, etc. To her now belong all rule and jurisdiction but the said Robert Dudley has authority to act on her behalf.'

In the silence that followed I gazed around at the green hills alive with parrots and brilliantly plumed birds, at the scarcely less brilliantly marked Arawak, then back to the fresh brass plaque flashing in the tropical sunlight. I had joined the ranks of the conquistadores. I was one of that select company of pioneers like Cortés, Pizarro, Drake, destined to bring the benefits of the old world to the new and the wealth of the new world to the old.

The natives had now fallen to eager discussion of my declaration. Another fanfare silenced them and restored the initiative to me.

'Men of Trinidad. You are now the subjects of Queen Elizabeth, as we all are. We are your friends, your fellow countrymen, your brothers. We have come to restore your freedom. The Spaniards came here to take your island, your women, your animals, your crops. They came to make you slaves. Will you, now, fight alongside us to throw the Spaniards out of Trinidad, so that your people and ours can live together here in freedom?'

I had, I suppose, hoped that my appeal would draw forth a spontaneous expression of support and solidarity. If so, I was to learn another lesson about these dignified, undemonstrative people. They considered my words in near silence for several

194

moments, the chiefs sitting with heads bowed or holding muttered conversations among themselves. Then Mointiman stood up and made a brief speech. After this they all withdrew. Seeing them shuffling away down the hillside I was at first afraid that they were politely rejecting my proposal but they congregated on the beach, the chiefs sitting crosslegged in a large circle, their followers standing or crouching around them. There was no reason for us to remain on the hilltop so I ordered the return march.

For an hour or more I waited, anxious and impatient, inside the stockade. I tried unsuccessfully to concentrate on writing up my log. I spent some minutes checking Will's latest maps. I toured the camp and inspected the men's living quarters. I set some soldiers to digging new latrines. Frequently I climbed to one of the watch towers to see if the chiefs were still in conclave. Always they were.

I had returned to my tent and was talking with Nick Wyatt when a sentry entered to tell me that a deputation of chiefs had arrived and was waiting to see me. Quickly I summoned the officers and my standard bearer. My great chair was placed outside the tent. Seated in this and flanked by my attendants I received the Arawak leaders.

There were six of them, Mointiman and five others, together with Balthasar and an escort of warriors aglow with smears and circles of red and blue paint. Mointiman was their spokesman and what he had to say was relayed to me through the young interpreter who all the time fingered the half feather still threaded into his loincloth. The burden of their message was that they would provide five hundred fighting men for a raid on San José de Oruña as long as the contingent was under the command of one of their own number and as long as it was understood that the commitment did not extend beyond this single expedition.

I tried to haggle over this second condition but Mointiman pointed out that some of his colleagues did not share his trust in the Englishman. They would join with me in a raid on the Spanish capital. Any further military action which might still be necessary would be the subject of subsequent negotiations. I accepted their terms and it was agreed that the native levies would assemble at Pelican Bay in five days' time. I stood up to bid the chiefs farewell.

At that moment a volley of musket fire cracked out close at hand. I ran across the sand and climbed the ladder to the guard post. I shouted orders as I went. Our Arawak friends must be brought in to safety. The gates must be closed. I need not have worried. From the top of the stockade I saw, not a troop of Spanish infantry, but Jobson and his men waving excitedly from the edge of the forest.

Next moment they were running over the rocks and floundering heavily through the loose sand. I knew at once that the strict Jobson must be in relaxed and jubilant mood to permit this disorderly return to camp. The shouting, laughing soldiers were met by their comrades and stood around in chattering groups. There was no need to ask whether their expedition had been successful. The commander brought up the rear accompanying three pairs of men who were carrying wicker baskets slung from sagging poles over their shoulders. I welcomed Jobson warmly and took him to my pavilion. The heavy burdens were set down in the middle of the tent. All my officers crowded in at the doorway to see the trophies. Will brought my chair in. I seated Jobson in it and gave him a brimming goblet of wine. He drew off his helmet and let it clatter to the ground beside him.

'Well, Master Dudley, it's there sure enough, any amount of it. Take a look for yourself.'

I undid the fastening on one of the wicker baskets and picked up a fist-sized chunk of rock. It was greyish black but through it ran thin, glistening, yellow veins. The others dipped their hands excitedly into the bundle to examine the Trinidad gold. It was Jobson's moment of triumph and we all listened as he described the discovery of the mine.

'It lies about fifteen miles inland surrounded by hills. The local people there dig the rock from the hillside and smelt the gold. Not that they've much use for it. It doesn't seem to interest them greatly.'

'Then they show more wisdom than you, Master Jobson.'

The voice was George Popham's and we all turned to look at the frowning mariner. He held a piece of rock in his hand and had been examining it with Abraham Kendall, who stood beside him.

'What do you mean?'

'I mean, Master Dudley, that this isn't gold.'

Jobson jumped to his feet.

'Curse you for a jealous knave, Popham. Of course it's gold. Use your eyes.'

'All is not gold that glisters. I don't blame you: it's an easy enough mistake. Frobisher brought back a shipload of this stuff from the land of the Esquimaux years ago. The alchemists examined it and advised him to dump his cargo in the sea.'

I looked from Popham to Kendall, not wanting to believe what I was hearing. The one-eyed seaman nodded.

'It's true, lad. I've seen it myself, then and since. The alchemists give this stuff the name "pyrite" but some men call it "fool's gold".'

13

What potent forces disappointment can unleash. A hundred happy Englishmen, suddenly thwarted of the prospect of immediate and easy wealth, grew sullen and insubordinate. They fought among themselves, they became aggressive towards the natives and they looked for scapegoats. Some blamed Balthasar, some blamed me, some even blamed poor Jobson for the brutal murder of their hopes.

The mood affected their leaders. The new situation demanded another conference with the captains aboard the *Bear*. It was a stormy meeting: half of the seniors were for joining Popham in an assault on the kingdom of El Dorado; the remainder wanted to put Trinidad and the Orinoco behind them and to go in search of plunder among the Spanish settlements further north and west. Needless to say, no one now had any interest in the conquest of Trinidad. It was easy for them: they had not pledged themselves to the liberation of the Indians or claimed this island in the name of the Queen. They had not felt the thrill of possessing a new land, a land of as yet unexplored possibilities. As I explained the advantages of making good our claim to Trinidad I could see that I was talking to men who listened only out of deference to my position.

'This island will be a secure foothold for England on the Main. It has good harbours. It can be made impregnable.'

'You tell the men that's a good enough reason for risking their lives. I cannot.'

'Cannot or will not, Jobson?'

'The agreement was that we would take possession of Trinidad if we found gold. Well, we haven't found gold.'

I felt anger rising within me and clenched my fists.

'Agreement? You do not talk to me of agreement! Have you forgotten who leads this expedition and owns these ships? If you are so interested in agreements, what about the agreement we made with the Indians? Afraid to face your own men with my orders, are you? Then I doubt you will find the courage to walk into the midst of five hundred Arawak warriors and say "We have decided to leave you to the mercy of the Spaniards. When we have gone away de Berrio's men will probably come and burn your villages and slaughter your women and children because you helped us. Let that be a lesson to you not to trust the word of an Englishman".'

Angry shouts and protests greeted this outburst. It was Benjamin Wood whose mournful voice calmed us all.

'Surely we only need to postpone the raid on San José while we go in search of El Dorado. If we can reach this kingdom of gold or at least get close enough to prove to ourselves that it exists we shall have good reason to seize and garrison Trinidad. By that time, if the Lord wills, Raleigh and his men will be here. Together we will have no difficulty in capturing San José and with a bigger fleet we can bombard Port of Spain.'

The thought of having to share command with Raleigh was repugnant but Wood's words made sense.

'Who is for El Dorado, then?'

Half-a-dozen heads nodded. Popham had been eagerly canvassing support for an Orinoco expedition and had convinced some, but equally persuasive had been the fearsome tales told by our hosts of the terrible Carib cannibals, giant crocodiles and the man-eating fish supposed to haunt the delta's riverain maze. Peter Vincent, thin featured, with sleek black hair like an otter's, spoke for the dissenters.

'You said, Master Dudley, that you would force no man to accompany you up the Orinoco.'

'Nor will I, Peter. I take it you have no stomach for a river trip.'

'I prefer to take my chances at sea. The Spanish silver fleet will be assembling at Nombre de Dios now. There'll be mule trains moving along the coast, perhaps a straggler or two when the fleet sets sail.'

Mule trains and straggling ships! Those words seemed to sum up English naval tactics for two generations. What was needed now was a fresh approach. To me the new strategy was obvious but could I expect these sailors of the old school to understand? It was worth a try. I took my great Atlantic chart from the drawer and spread it on the table.

'Look, all of you. For twenty years and more England has had the finest ships, the best sailors and the boldest captains in the world. And, like a swarm of bees they have been attacking Philip of Spain – here, around his own coasts, here and here, the Azores and the Canaries, but mostly here, along the Main. Sometimes they have stung him badly, sometimes they have been swatted. But always the survivors have had to return to the hive. And the hive is here, England, nearly two thousand leagues away. With our own base we could wage incessant war against the Spanish treasure fleets, establish control along the coast, even take a stranglehold on the scrawny neck of the Panama isthmus.'

Jobson shook his head.

'There's nothing new in that, Master Dudley. Drake and Raleigh both had the same idea.'

'Yes but Drake's Nova Albion was too far away and the Virginia project was bungled. We must learn by those mistakes, not be deterred by them.' I stared round helplessly at their un-convinced frowns. 'Gentlemen, we must look to the future. It is not just our venture that is at stake.'

After a long, embarrassed silence Nick Wyatt said he was in favour of Captain Wood's compromise. Most of the others agreed with him but Peter Vincent was adamant in rejecting the Orinoco venture and he still carried two of the masters and a colonel with him. I had to bow to the inevitable and I had to do so in a manner which gave no hint of weakness.

'Captain Vincent, I give you command of the two caravels. You may take twenty men in each and try your fortune on the Main. You will rendezvous with me in this bay three weeks from today and may God fare you well. The *Bear* and the *Fury* will move across to the mainland as soon as all the victuals and equipment are reloaded. When we all reassemble here it will be for an assault on San José de Oruña. And now, gentlemen, I bid you goodnight.'

I rose and left the cabin, allowing no opportunity for further discussion.

I slept on board that night and next morning I had Balthasar rowed out to me. As he sat in the great cabin he looked uncomfortable; his usual smile was not in evidence and his head twisted in sudden, alarmed jerks at every creak and movement. Obviously he distrusted this strange floating house. I tried to put him at ease by showing him my spinning terrestrial globe. I took him on deck and demonstrated the astrolabe. Nothing seemed to awake his childlike curiosity. Then I thought of Will Bradshaw's drawings. The lad had a thick sheaf of pictures of parrots, wild pigs, trees, people and other Trinidad phenomena. They were kept in a chest in my cabin. Now I brought them out and spread them on the great cabin table. I pointed to a portrait of Chief Mointiman. Balthasar gasped and grabbed up the paper. His face lit up with delighted recognition and he turned the paper over, expecting, I suppose, to see the back of the old man's head. I showed him the picture of a fat Arawak elder who had obviously amused Will. Balthasar laughed.

By the time we had worked through the whole pipe, the Indian's fear had evaporated and the time seemed ripe to tell him why I had summoned him to the *Bear*. Balthasar listened quietly as I explained that I had postponed the raid on San José. I told him that first I must find gold for my men and that I was going to look for it along the big river, Orinoco.

At that he frowned, shook his head furiously and took hold of my arm.

'You must not go there. It is a bad place. The people are bad – cannibals. There is much forest, very dark and full of dangers.'

'Brave men do not fear the dark Balthasar.'

He hung his head.

'You will die. You will not come back. You will not free my

people from the Spaniards.'

'I will come back, Balthasar; that I promise. And I will fight against the Spaniards with you.'

'That is not what you said before.'

'Sometimes great chiefs have to change their plans. When they do, their warriors have to obey them without question. The warriors cannot always understand what the chiefs decide.' It was like talking to a child and, indeed, there was in the eyes of that simple savage a child's accusing innocence.

For a long time Balthasar sat motionless and very quiet. The stillness emanated from him seeming to clasp shackles on my limbs so that I, too, could neither move nor speak. At last he stood up and came round the table towards me. With careful fingers he detached from my jerkin the half-feather, which I was always careful to wear when he was with me.

Was he telling me that our bond was broken? Fear that it might be so filled me with a despair amounting almost to nausea. But the ceremony was not finished. Balthasar stood in the middle of the cabin. He unfastened his own white slither and held the two halves aloft between the thumb and forefinger of one hand. Without a word he let them fall. Pirouetting and slipping from side to side they fluttered separately to the scrubbed boards. They lay still. They lay one across the other.

With a whoop of delight the young Indian scooped them from the floor. His face had regained its radiant cheerfulness as he returned my symbol of brotherhood.

'You speak true. I will tell my chief what you say.'

In a single leap he was at the doorway. He turned.

'And I shall come with you to the land of the Caribs.'

Before I could reply he was gone. Before I was out of the cabin I heard a splash. When I reached the gunwale he was twenty yards away swimming strongly towards the shore.

On 12 February 1595 I added my name to the list of madmen who have gone in search of El Dorado. I like to think it was only a fortuitous sequence of circumstances that forced me to make that terrible journey but I suspect that I had been under the

Golden Man's spell ever since I cast my eyes on his image in Raleigh's library.

Because of the sandbanks and strong currents we could not take the ships close in shore. We were obliged to anchor ten miles off the delta and row the rest of the way, our three boats making hard work negotiating the unpredictable waves and swirling eddies. We toiled for most of the day to reach a strand which seemed to draw no closer no matter how hard we plied the oars. With officers and men alike sharing the work, we eventually ran the boats onto the beach at nightfall with scarcely any energy left for the necessary tasks of gathering driftwood, building a fire and posting sentries.

Embarking again next morning we rowed close inshore probing the flows and inlets of the serrated coastline until we found a wide, swiftly flowing stream. It was not the main outlet, the Manamo, but Popham was confident that it would lead us into the Orinoco's principal effluent, so we turned our prows against the current and pulled slowly into the shaded waterway. Immediately we were in a different world. Gigantic trees soared aloft, hanging their branches well out over the water. Between the massive trunks was a cavernous, greeny blackness, only relieved occasionally by a sliver of sunlight or a flash of brilliant plumage. The dense depths of intertwined foliage were alive with hidden movement and sound. Screeches and snufflings, rustlings and howls came clearly and frequently to our ears as we gazed into the forest. Sometimes we would catch a glimpse of a monkey swinging away among the branches into deeper cover. Sometimes a disturbed duck or heron would sputter the water with its wings and feet, then soar out across the river to seek sanctuary on the farther bank. Most of the time we were the only living creatures visible in that hot, airless, secret world. Watched but not welcomed, we profoundly felt ourselves to be the alien intruders that we were.

Avoiding the main current, we travelled close in to the right bank seeking a cross channel that would lead us to the Manamo. A dozen times we turned into broad avenues of river through which the water flowed swiftly and the bottom was deep. A dozen times we turned with difficulty and re-traced our path when the overreaching foliage choked the channel or fallen trunks of immense girth barred our way. To add to these delays I had to allow the sweating, bare-backed oarsmen frequent pauses to rest their aching arms and slake their thirst.

Around the middle of the afternoon we found a rare riverside clearing. One or two of the men were too exhausted to row any more and, as we were unlikely to find a better place I decided to rest there for the night. When the boats had been moored and the food and equipment carried ashore there was, at last, time to strip off our sweaty clothes, bathe in the cool water and lie in the patch of broken sunlight.

Afterwards I was sitting with Popham, looking at a rudimentary map he had made of the region when Nick Wyatt strolled across the clearing fastening his shirt.

'Is the whole country like this, Popham?'

He squatted on his haunches before us.

'The jungle spreads all over the lowland plane, but I gather from the natives that it disappears as you get towards the Guiana highlands.'

'Natives? What natives, Popham? There has been no sign of a human face since we entered this benighted country.'

'They're here, sure enough.' Popham glowered round theatrically and spoke in hushed tones. 'They're probably staring at us now with their great saucer-like eyes, foam dripping from their fangs.'

Wyatt laughed.

'Come now, you don't expect to frighten me with your wild travellers' tales.'

But Popham remained serious.

'Laugh while you can, young man. You'll not laugh when you catch your first glimpse of the Caribs. Ask that young savage, Balthasar. He'll tell you what fierce, evil creatures they are.'

Wyatt looked uncertainly from the elderly captain to me but I forced myself to keep a straight face. I even managed to sound apprehensive as I asked,

'Then, all that we have heard about these cannibals is true?'

'Oh yes, Master Dudley. Why I've seen a gang of them tear a man apart with their bare hands and eat his warm flesh on the spot.'

I gasped.

'How terrible.'

'Terrible's not the word for it, Master Dudley. It is the sort of sight that haunts men's dreams for years after. Yet even the Caribs are not as bad as the headless ones who dwell in the land beyond.'

Wyatt's eyes opened wide.

'The headless ones?'

'Aye, fearsome creatures whose faces are on their chests.'

'And they really are men?'

'Men? Nay, lad, giants rather. Why, I could tell you a tale ...'

At that point the look of credulous alarm on Nick Wyatt's face was too much for me. I laughed aloud and motioned Popham to silence.

'Enough, George. You will be telling us of centaurs and mermaids next. Come now, in your dealings with these Caribs how have you found them?'

He chuckled as Wyatt flushed with embarrassment.

'Well, Master Dudley, they are a fierce people and no mistake. Tall for the most part, and many of them have great rings of gold in their ears and noses.'

'How do they live in this forest?'

'Hunting and fishing and a very primitive kind of agriculture. They make clearings and build their huts. They farm the land for a year or two. Then, when it fails to produce a good crop they move on. This clearing here must have been a Carib village until recently.'

'Do they mine gold themselves?'

'No, as far as I can gather they get it by way of trade.'

'From the Guiana peoples?'

'Yes.'

'Then we need to find some of the Caribs who are willing to lead us into the hills and show us where their trading partners live.'

'As soon as we get into the main stream we'll find plenty of Carib settlements. Some of them will help us, especially if we offer them hatchets and knives. They have very few iron tools of their own.'

'Can we trust them?'

'Can you trust any savage? We'll have to watch them night and day, of course. But they are our only hope of threading this maze of rivers and finding the forest paths that will lead us to El Dorado's kingdom.'

'If it exists.'

'Would you really be sitting here if you thought it did not, Master Dudley?'

'And how far up river do we have to go before we reach the highlands?'

Popham stared at the map. His finger hovered uncertainly over a section of the river where a series of tributaries joined it in suspiciously parallel lines.

'These streams come down from the Guiana highlands.'

'But you have never been anywhere near this section of the river. This map is nothing but a copy – and a very poor copy – of the Spanish map you captured and gave to Raleigh.'

'Well, that's partly true, Master Dudley, but the Spaniard who made that map, he had been right up the Orinoco. He'd seen the land of El Dorado.'

'Had he met the Golden Man?'

'No, but ...'

'I know what you are going to say. He had not met the Golden Man himself but he knew someone who had. What a surprising number of people there are who know someone else who once saw a man who had seen El Dorado!'

Nick Wyatt had been listening carefully to this exchange. Now, he picked up the grubby piece of paper with its untidy delineation of coastline and river.

'Just how far along the Orinoco have you travelled, Popham?'

The old captain laughed but not very heartily.

'Come, come, lad, you sound like someone in the pay of the Inquisition.'

'I would like to know the answer to Nick's question, too.'

Grumbling, Popham spread the paper out again.

'Well, it's difficult to say. I came straight up the main channel last time. But I suppose I got to about here.'

I looked at the point he was indicating.

'Ah yes, about forty miles up river. And the Guiana highlands could be as much as four hundred miles from the coast. It looks rather as though your experience will be of limited value.'

Nick Wyatt raised his voice in indignation.

'You're an imposter, Popham. You told us you knew where El Dorado was; that you could lead us to him.'

I cut short Popham's angry reply.

'Gentlemen, you will please behave civilly to each other in front of the men. The next few days are going to be quite hard enough without divisions among the officers. As for maps drawn more from hope than knowledge, I've never had any confidence in them. We are pioneers, Nick. No one has charted the route for us or catalogued the dangers. We must discover them for ourselves.'

The following morning we, at last, found a channel which brought us to the Manamo, a broad, green-brown river with a slower current which made rowing easier. For three days we journeyed steadily. As Popham had forecast, we saw many native villages along both banks as well as several dug-out canoes plying between them. However, we did not stop, except occasionally to barter for food. I knew we would have to go a long way upriver before we could find guides with any knowledge of the hill country far to the south.

The morale of the men was good. They rowed by turns on a strict rota system. During their off duty spells and when we stopped to cook dinner or make overnight camp there was much to interest and occupy them. They fished or pursued birds with fowling pieces and improvised nets. They were fascinated by the agile monkeys and the ugly, vicious-looking crocodiles. And there were always those aspects of the daily routine which were faithfully observed: every evening I led the crew in prayers and psalms, and on Sundays our chaplain celebrated Holy Communion. Jobson held regular pike practice, impressing the men with the possibility that they might soon be going into battle against a native army. Thus were our days occupied and our men kept content. I was careful to make sure that none of them knew how far upriver lay the golden land of El Dorado and, for the time being, they were willing to endure the hardships of the journey for the sake of the glittering rewards awaiting them beyond the fringes of the jungle.

By noon on the fifth day (17 February) we had travelled by my computation some hundred and thirty miles. Still there was no change in the scenery: we seemed to be on an endless river flowing through infinite forest. It was then that we were suddenly aware of a new sound. Above the steady splash of the oars and the animal sounds of the jungle there arose a deep, rhythmic booming. At first it was very faint, but it grew rapidly louder. The men rested on their oars to listen. The sound identified itself as the beat of a single drum from somewhere on the left bank. Peering into the trees I glimpsed a movement along one of the channels. I ordered the oarsmen to back paddle. When the boat was parallel with the outlet I could see some hundred yards along the tributary to its first bend.

Around that bend swept a canoe but not a canoe like any we had so far seen. It was very long and propelled by at least twenty Indians who knelt as they plied their paddles in time to the drum beat. There were more men standing along the centre of the boat, tall men, profusely painted and decorated with necklaces and bracelets. Each held a long bow and carried a quiver of arrows on a strap over his shoulder. The canoe came swiftly towards us. Following it round the bend came another, and another, and another. There were six vessels in all, and every one carried a full complement of warriors.

I was suddenly aware of a moaning sound beside me. Balthasar had thrown himself down in the bottom of the boat, where he lay trembling and muttering, 'War canoes! They will kill us! They will kill us!'

I ordered the boats to come together and every man to have

his weapons to hand. We were ill-prepared for trouble. Most of the men had discarded their armour and helmets because of the sticky heat. In all the boats there were only four ready-primed arquebuses. The rest of the firearms together with the powder and shot were stowed under waterproof covers in the prow of Kendall's boat. We were appallingly vulnerable to those deadly bows. But as the canoes swept majestically out into the mainstream the Caribs showed no sign of raising their weapons.

Out of the corner of my eye I saw one of our soldiers lift his gun to his shoulder. I shouted so loud that the poor man almost dropped his weapon overboard. Until we knew the Indians' intentions we dared offer no provocation.

At a distance of about twenty yards from us the first canoe stopped, the beating of the drum ceased and the oarsmen feathered to hold the boat's position. The orders were given by an imposing figure seated in the stern. He now shouted to us across the water. I hauled Balthasar to his feet and asked if he could understand what the Carib chief was saying. The young Indian's eyes were glazed with fear. He shook his head, jabbering that these were wicked people and that he did not know their language. As calmly as I could I pointed out to him that if we could not communicate our peaceful intentions to the warrior leader he would very probably order his men to kill us.

Nervously Balthasar stood up and shouted some words in dialect. The exchange was brief. The chief's barge pulled away up river to the renewed sound of drumming. Balthasar crouched disconsolately in the dirty water slopping around in the bottom of the boat and spoke with eyes downcast.

'We must follow him to his village.'

I looked around at the other Carib canoes. They were taking up their stations beside and behind us. Our host clearly did not intend his invitation to be declined.

It transpired that we had fallen in with Chief Tivativa, the most powerful man in this part of the delta, who was returning from a raid on some less powerful neighbour. We could see the captive men and women bound hand and foot in the bottom of his canoes. During the brief journey to Tivativa's village I had the rest of the firearms distributed and made sure that every man carried at least one weapon. On arrival we moored the boats close together and I left fifteen arquebusiers to guard them. The rest of my troop I formed up into two ranks of pikemen and thus we marched into Tivativa's capital, our drummer beating a martial step and our standard bravely displayed.

But there was no sign that the Caribs intended us any harm nor could I detect any trickery in the chief's attitude towards us. He had us conveyed to two large huts at the centre of the village. There we were left and presently some of the women came bringing food and jars of a very bitter, fermented drink which I ordered my men not to touch until we had obliged one of the women to take a draught from each container. I positioned a row of pikemen before our guest quarters. The rest of us sat on the ground outside the huts and took stock of our surroundings.

I have read books by Spanish and English travellers, some of whom have never been within a thousand miles of the Orinoco, which describe the Caribs as monsters and beasts who can scarcely be considered human at all. If such fable-mongers are to be believed, these creatures festoon their bodies with the bones and entrails of their enemies. Like dogs, they do not know the meaning of discreet privacy, and perform all their bodily functions in public. Why capable geographers should insist on peopling the little-known parts of the earth with freaks and semi-human inhabitants I do not know; the truth is always less fantastic and much more interesting.

The truth about Tivativa's followers is that they were, to outward appearances, very little different to the other Carib and Arawak people we had met. They were tall, and the younger men were daubed with the vivid panoply of war. If it seems strange to the European mind that a warrior should decorate his own skin with bands of red and blue paint let him reflect for a moment how our own troops go forth to battle – the feathered plumes, the gaudy standards, the coloured sashes. Nor is it long ago that our fathers donned shields, surcoats and helms whose brilliant devices were governed by the strict law of heraldry. Whatever the medium, the objective remains the same – to strike fear into the hearts of the adversary. One encouraging feature about the decorations worn by Tivativa's people was the generous use they made of gold. Both men and women wore bangles of gold on their wrists. Some sported circlets in their ears of such incredible weight that their lobes were stretched until they touched their shoulders.

Some of the Caribs gathered around to stare at us but most of them were more interested in the triumphant procession of the victors. Tivativa had taken his seat under a thatched awning at one end of the open space in the centre of the village. Before him the warriors paraded, each one pushing before him the prisoners he had taken. Tivativa examined each of the women captives and selected some for his own use. These were led away to the royal enclosure behind him. The others, presumably, remained the property of their captors. The male prisoners were herded together into a simple pen to the right of the chief's pavilion.

When the procession was over Tivativa seemed to take notice of us for the first time. He sent a message that I was to join him. With Kendall, Popham, Jobson and Wyatt I walked across the 'forum' with a small escort of pikemen in order to make as brave a show as possible. The chief motioned me to sit beside him. I did so and gave orders to the others to stand behind us. Tivativa made no objections to this. Indeed, he scarcely seemed to notice: his attention was fixed on the next part of the celebrations. A fire was lit in the centre of the arena and the warriors formed a wide ring around it. Drummers took up a fast and exciting rhythm on a variety of instruments most of which were made from hollowed trunks and branches. Other musicians began a low kind of wailing chant. Then the painted men of battle began to dance. They circled one way then the other. They executed in unison wild leaps and intricate steps that were clearly part of some ancient ritual. From time to time an individual would jump into the centre and perform an elaborate mime intended, I imagine, to demonstrate some personal feat of bravery performed in the recent campaign.

I watched, fascinated. Perhaps 'entranced' would be a better word; the monotonous frenzy of the drums, the rhythmic swaying of the onlookers, the sinuous contortions of the dancers' bodies, glistening in the firelight – all worked like a sorceror's spell, depriving me of the will or power to move. As evening shaded into night the excitement of the Indians grew more intense. Most of them had drunk heavily of the native wine which seemed to have the effect of sharpening all their senses. The dancing became faster, building up to an eagerly awaited climax. All eyes were turned on Tivativa and an insistent chant arose – 'Gutmok! Gutmok!' At last the chief raised a hand. His gesture was greeted with a wild cheer. From the prisoners' enclosure a man was dragged forth by two Caribs. He did not struggle or cry out as he was thrown to the ground in front of Tivativa; I suspect that he was drugged. At a further signal from the chief, the victim was rolled on to his back and his throat was cut. The corpse was dragged to the fire and expertly dismembered with hatchets and long knives. The crowd watched, eagerly, greedily as the separate organs and limbs were spitted and roasted over the flames. There was, I reflected, little difference between these savages and a London mob congregating at Tyburn to see a traitor hung, drawn and quartered.

More captives were despatched in the same way and meanwhile the dancing continued, the women now taking part for the first time. It was a woman who presently came forward and knelt before Tivativa. She proffered a wooden dish on which lay, very lightly roasted, a human heart. The chief took the morsel, put it to his mouth, tore a large bite from it with his teeth – and then handed it to me.

14

I looked from the steaming viand in its moat of blood to the dark eyes of Tivativa who watched closely for my reaction. Beyond him I could see my own men, their fire-lit faces all turned in my direction. My head ached. I felt in my throat the first constrictions of impending nausea. I knew I could not make the gesture clearly expected of me even if the lives of myself and my companions depended on it. But how could I avoid it without giving offence?

No plan came to me with a blinding flash of inspiration; the solution evolved as I desperately played for time. Assuming what I hoped was a look of pleasure and gratitude, I took the platter and placed it on the ground in front of me. I knelt as if in prayer and at the same time muttered to one of the men behind me, 'Fetch Balthasar'. Then I began to rock backwards and forwards gabbling I know not what but conveying, as I hoped, some kind of devotional ritual which should not be disturbed. My impromptu act had the desired effect; I was conscious of a ring of brown and white faces watching me closely. I kept up my incantation for what seemed an age. Just when I was wondering whether my Trinidadian friend had escaped and run off into the forest I heard a whisper behind me.

'The savage is here, sir.'

I lifted my head. Slowly and deliberately I dipped my finger in the blood, raised it to my forehead and made there the sign of the Cross. I muttered, *'In nomine patris, et filii et spiritui sancti'*. I know not why. I suppose it seemed appropriate at the time. Solemnly I lifted the dish and handed it back to Tivativa with a slight inclination of the head. Then, while my audience still gave me their full attention, I turned deliberately to Balthasar.

'Explain to the chief that I and my men have made a vow to our God to eat no flesh until our journey is over.'

I smiled lightly at Tivativa as my interpreter fumblingly found words to express my message.

He looked puzzled. Had he misunderstood? He asked a question. Balthasar falteringly replied. The chief looked at me. He nodded. He spoke a few words to the woman. She hurried away and returned seconds later with another dish on which were stacked discs of the flat hard unleavened substance which serves the Indians as bread. Behind me Abraham Kendall exhaled a long sigh of relief.

The feasting and dancing went on far into the night and I am sure that Tivativa's guests were as exhausted as his dancers when he eventually declared the celebrations at an end. It was not until noon the following day that I felt presentable enough to send Balthasar to offer my compliments to the chief and request an audience. Back came the answer that the chief was resting. I could well imagine it. The next day Tivativa could not see me because he was going hunting. Twenty-four hours later my request for an interview was again refused, this time without a reason being given. We were well looked after but the delay was extremely frustrating. We still had a long way to go up river and then, after we had found El Dorado, we would have to face the return journey. We would undoubtedly be late for our rendezvous with the *Bear*, and Captain Wood could not wait indefinitely for us.

On the fourth day after our arrival Chief Tivativa at last consented to speak with me. He received me and my officers under the same thatched awning from which we had watched the dancing. He sat, as before, on the ground and with him sat some of the elders of the clan. The conversation which ensued was not an easy one: I had to phrase my thoughts in Spanish, of which language I was by no means a master as yet, Balthasar then had to make the conversion via Arawak into Carib, a tongue which, though similar to his own, held many pitfalls for him. The gist of the dialogue was as follows. Tivativa, as protocol demanded, spoke first.

'You are welcome here if you come in peace, Chief Dudley.'

'I come in peace, Chief Tivativa.'

'We have seen other men of your tribe, from time to time. They came in search of gold. Is that why you have ventured so far from your own people?'

'The other men you have seen are not of our tribe. They are our enemies. But we do, indeed, seek the same thing. Can you trade gold with us?'

Tivativa reached a hand into an earthenware pot beside him and threw something onto the ground in front of me. I picked up three large crescents of gold, each weighing almost a pound. Jobson gasped. He and Kendall exchanged excited glances. Wyatt said under his breath, 'So it is true!'

I was as excited as they were. It seemed we really were on the threshold of the golden land.

'These are beautiful. Do you have much gold here? Do your people mine it?'

'No, it comes from the land of Chief Armago.'

He pointed in the direction from which the river flowed.

'This Chief Armago, is he the one people call the Golden Man?'

Tivativa looked puzzled. I told him the legend of the king whose body was powdered with gold and who did homage to his god by plunging into the great lake of Manoa. The old chief seemed to find such behaviour very amusing. For several minutes he and his advisers chuckled at the thought of such strange antics.

'I would like to trade with this Chief Armago.'

Tivativa shook his head.

'No need to trade. You and I will raid Armago's land and take whatever we want.'

'No, Chief Tivativa. My queen desires friendly and peaceful relations with all the people of this land.'

He brushed my objection aside.

'You have brought many weapons with you and I have a hundred fine warriors. We will easily defeat Armago. We will go tomorrow.'

Having decided the matter, the chief, tall and erect despite his years, stood up. I was determined not to allow him the last word. As I rose to my feet, I said, 'I will discuss the matter with my officers.'

Tivativa smiled.

'We will go tomorrow.'

I strode down to the river bank taking Kendall with me for company because I needed someone to complain to.

'We cannot allow him to dictate terms to us. We represent a kingdom ten thousand times bigger than this petty Indian chiefdom. That fellow does not even know there is a whole world beyond his river. By God, I will not be forced into risking my men in a feud between two savages.'

'What will you do then, lad?'

I sat on a tree stump and stared away up river.

'Suppose we just leave; carry on till we find Armago. Then we can trade with him.'

'Do you think Tivativa will allow us to go to his rival? He's bound to send his war canoes after us.'

'As he himself said, we have guns.'

'H'm, suppose we did beat them off, what would happen when we came back down river? Tivativa could choose his own spot for an ambush.'

'You think we should fight his sordid little war for him, then. You think I should put free-born Englishmen under the command of a heathen cannibal to help him satisfy his bestial appetite for human flesh.'

Kendall leaned his massive shoulders against a tree.

'I think if we anger him we may end up on his next banquet menu. On the other hand, if we seem to go along with his plans who knows what may happen when we get to the territory of this Chief Whatsisname.'

'What do you mean?'

Kendal came and crouched on the ground before me. He dropped his voice to a whisper although there were no natives within earshot and if there had been they could not have understood what we were saying.

'At the moment we need old Beaknose [this was Kendall's name for our host]. Without his friendship we shall be lucky to get back to the ships alive let alone find any gold. But Beaknose needs us, too. I reckon this other chief . . .'

'Armago?'

'That's right. I reckon he's a pretty powerful fellow, and Beaknose is counting on our guns to win the battle for him.'

'Yes, you are probably right.'

'Well then, what happens when we reach Armago's place? We shan't have any need for Beaknose and his men then.'

'You mean . . .'

'I reckon Armago would take it as a great kindness if we were to rid him of his rival for good and all.'

I shook my head.

'No, Abraham, you are asking me to behave dishonourably. You forget that I represent the Queen of England and that we are the first Englishmen to come here. What chance will there be of establishing good relations for the future if we behave treacherously now?'

Kendall spat.

'I was brought up poor, lad. I could never afford this luxury you call "honour" and I never saw it do anyone any good. Do you think old Beaknose knows anything about "honour"? Do you imagine he will let us go back to our ships once we've won his battle for him? No, as soon as we've outlived our usefulness that will be the end of us.'

Kendall's words made sense but it was hard for me to admit it. It went against my entire upbringing.

'You may be right, Abraham, and you may be wrong.'

'Can you afford to wager the lives of your men on the chance of my being wrong?'

'I suppose it may do some good in the long run. It may show these Caribs that Englishmen are not to be trifled with.' The fact that I was already searching for excuses was proof that Kendall had, as usual, won his point.

We embarked the next morning in two contingents. I had insisted that my boats were kept separate from Tivativa's and the chief had not objected. Indeed, the battle tactics he proposed depended on it. The plan was that I and my men should go on ahead to Armago's. The chief would not expect any trouble from a small party of foreigners. Tivativa's canoes would moor a short distance down river and the warriors would make their way through the forest. When Armago was distracted in welcoming us his enemies would burst forth upon the village. Armago would then be caught defenceless between two bodies of attackers.

It was a good piece of tactical scheming but the version of the project that I put to my officers contained some amendments. As soon as we landed I proposed to go straight to Armago and, with Balthasar's help, warn him of the impending attack. When Tivativa and his men arrived they would, therefore, find a reception they had not expected. I hoped that I would be able to ensure that the battle was not too bloody. In that way I might placate my not-wholly-convinced conscience.

The crews of our three boats were in jubilant mood as we pulled against the sluggish current, a hundred yards or so ahead of the five war canoes. The oarsmen sang in time with their work. Others sharpened swords or checked harness in cheerful anticipation. At first I thought it was being on the move again and escaping the apprehensions of Tivativa's village that had put heart into the men. Nick Wyatt told me the real reason.

'They've heard about the gold.'

'What have they heard? I gave orders that the men were not to be told about Armago's gold mine. It might be another myth.'

'Oh, they know nothing about that. It's all rumour. They reckon you wouldn't be issuing weapons and leading them into battle if it wasn't to seize a fortune in gold.'

The gruff voices rose in a raucous, good-humoured crescendo.

'I hope they will not be disappointed again.'

We had been rowing for almost two hours when the Carib we were carrying as guide stood up in the prow of Jobson's boat and pointed to where the river turned sharply to the left about half a mile ahead. Jobson ordered his rowers to stop. Kendall and I did the same in our boats. Helmets were donned, armour adjusted and weapons held at the ready. Astern of us Tivativa's canoes pulled in towards the larboard bank. The Carib guide slipped over the side and swam to rejoin his colleagues. When all was ready the oars were taken up again and we rowed at a brisk pace towards Armageddon.

Beyond the bend the village came into view, much the same as all the others we had seen. As soon as the prows touched the bank I leaped ashore with Balthasar. While Kendall and Jobson formed the men into battle array we went in search of Chief Armago. It was the middle of the day and most of the villagers were resting as was the universal custom in those parts. However, our arrival caused considerable alarm. Women ran screaming into their huts. The older children and some of the men ran up to ask who we were. I could see only a few painted warriors about and that worried me greatly.

To Balthasar's repeated question, 'Where is Chief Armago' we only received the repeated reply, 'He is sick'. At last one of the village elders came forward who obviously grasped from our behaviour that we had an urgent message. He told us that the chief was, indeed, in his house gravely ill, unable to move. I asked who was in charge and waited with growing panic for the cumbersome process of translation to convey my meaning. Apparently no one was in charge. Where were the warriors of the village? Some were hunting, some were fishing, some were resting. I told him that he must muster as many armed men as possible to defend the village immediately. I told him Tivativa was coming.

At that he moved. He set someone to beat a drum and someone else to run around the huts arousing everybody. In a few minutes thirty or forty men had assembled armed with bows and knives. I indicated the direction from which the attack would be made. Everyone fell silent and listened. I could detect no sound above the usual noises of river and jungle but presently one of the warriors shouted something and pointed. All the bowmen fitted arrows. My men had been formed up in two ranks, arquebusiers at each end and pikemen in the centre. The river was on our left flank, most of the village huts behind us. In front lay a clearing some thirty paces across. Beyond it was the forest from which Tivativa's warriors would burst at any moment.

The expectant silence was long and profound. We stared so hard into the green depths of the undergrowth that it began to swim before our eyes. Then suddenly the forest fringe was filled with archers. They loosed off a shower of arrows then rushed forward, whooping and screaming. Men on our side were screaming, too, some with pain. There was an immediate answering volley of arrows and a ragged crackle as the wheel-locks were fired. A dozen of Tivativa's men crumpled and fell. The advance was checked. More exchanges of arrows. The second rank of arquebusiers fired while their colleagues reloaded. For some minutes we held off the charge then the attackers poured forth brandishing knives and hatchets. Our pikemen charged rapidly turning the enemy's right flank and cutting him off from the river. Now it was hand-to-hand fighting in the middle of the clearing. Tivativa's men were virtually caught between the English soldiers on their right and Armago's men on their left. A gap developed as part of the defenders' line gave way. Jobson immediately sent a dozen men with swords into the breach.

The invaders were now completely encircled. Tivativa's losses had already been heavy. The combatants were stumbling over bodies and slipping on the bloody grass. It would soon be over. I turned to my trumpeter to order him to sound retreat.

An arrow hummed past my shoulder. It took one of the pikemen in the neck. He spun round and fell on his face, writhing and shrieking. I turned to see three Caribs running between the huts and shooting their arrows as they came. Had Tivativa sent some of his men to attack from the other side? Then I saw the small, dead animal that one of them carried at his waist and I realised that these were some of Armago's returning hunters. I waved to stop them and then threw myself to the ground as another arrow flew through the air. More hunters arrived. Seeing strangers with helmets and armour fighting in their village, they threw themselves upon them.

The result was catastrophic. My men found themselves attacked by Caribs on all sides. They could not tell friend from foe and lashed out against everything with a brown face. Confusion was complete.

'Back to the boats, Master Jobson!'

I ordered the retreat to be sounded, then leaped into the fray to clear a path for my men back towards the river. Slowly the Englishmen extricated themselves from the mêlée. A line of pikemen formed and the survivors withdrew behind it. Jobson led a slow advance to recover the wounded. Then the English force backed towards the boats. The Caribs, now one cohesive mass of men, advanced shouting angrily, waving their weapons and sporadically firing their bows.

We tumbled into the boats. The injured were roughly laid in the bottoms. Weapons were thrown down. Oars were seized and the three vessels gained the middle of the river as quickly as possible. Out of range of the Indians' arrows we rested on our oars and let the boats drift downstream. No one said a word. We unbuckled harness and removed helmets. We tore up shirts to make bandages and tourniquets for the wounded. I took a roll call. We had lost twenty-two men. Three more died within the hour. Nick Wyatt had a nasty shoulder wound and Popham was bleeding profusely from a gash on his cheek.

I looked around at the remnants of my brave expedition. I listened to the groans of the dying. And I knew that my quest for El Dorado was at an end.

> Come, Sleep; O Sleep! the certain knot of peace,
> The baiting-place of wit, the balm of woe,
> The poor man's wealth, the prisoner's release,
> Th'indifferent judge between the high and low:
> With shield of proof shield me from out the press
> Of those fierce darts Despair at me doth throw:
> O make in me those civil wars to cease;
> I will good tribute pay, if thou do so.

How fervently I echoed that prayer of my late cousin, Sir Philip Sidney, in the nightmare days that followed. We found a spot ashore to bury the three dead men. Those that perished later we had neither the energy nor the time to inter; they were weighted with their armour and lowered into the Orinoco. We abandoned one of our boats and rowed the others rapidly seawards, shunning all native settlements and keeping a nervous watch for pursuing canoes. We spent our nights in the boats moored at small islands we had carefully checked for any sign of human occupation. It was uncomfortable wedged into a small place on the damp boards but I do not think that I could have slept had I been bedded on a mattress of the softest down. The sights and sounds of that hideous battle re-enacted themselves within my throbbing head. The resentment and hatred of my weary, disillusioned crew enveloped me like a suffocating blanket. The responsibility of getting the remnant of my men safely back aboard the *Bear* weighed heavily upon me.

And then Balthasar deserted me. It happened during our first night ashore. We had put five days rowing between us and the land of Tivativa and Armago and I considered that we could safely indulge the luxury of making a camp on dry land. Being able to stretch their legs, light a fire and cook fresh fish did slightly lift the men's spirits. After the meal and our evening prayers most of the company rolled in their blankets around the embers. I captained the first watch. Making my rounds of the sentries shortly after nightfall I came suddenly upon the young Arawak crouching by the water's edge. We had scarcely exchanged a single word since the battle. I imagined he was very frightened and rather homesick. I laid a hand on his shoulder.

'Courage, Balthasar, you will soon be home now.'

For a long time he did not reply. When he did it was without looking up.

'And when we get back will you fight the Spaniards for us?'

'I have given my word, Balthasar.'

He sprang lightly to his feet and we stood face to face. The moonlight scooped deep shadows from his features and gave the highlights a purplish tinge. It sparkled on the twin rivulets which ran from the corners of his eyes.

'You gave your word to Chief Tivativa and then you betrayed him and killed his people.'

'That is different...'

He stamped a foot like a petulant child.

'No, Master Dudley, it is not different. Tivativa was a man and you are a man and I am a man, and vows between men should be honoured. But I know what your people say: they say "He is only a savage; we do not need to keep our word to him". The Spaniards say that, too; you are all the same. You will promise anything for gold and when you do not find gold you are angry and you kill, kill, kill!'

I set my lamp down and took him by the shoulders.

'It is not like that, Balthasar.'

But his fury and despair were too deep for comfort, too well-rooted for reason. He shook my hands off, and made no effort to control the tears and sobs.

'How can I go back to my people? I told them to trust you. Many chiefs did not want to go with white strangers. I told them you were a man who keeps his word. The chief said I am young and not wise in such matters, and should not speak in council of elders. But I did. I made them believe in you. Now I can never show my face among my people.'

He turned away and stumbled into the darkness. Next morning he was gone and there was half a white feather beside my pillow. For three hours we searched among the massive tree trunks and intertwined undergrowth but in vain.

With Balthasar's disappearance our certainty of finding our way through the maze of the delta also disappeared. The closer we drew towards the sea the more the river shredded itself among islands of every shape and size. Two days after losing our guide we were, ourselves, lost. Following what seemed to be the main channel at a point where the waterway branched into five streams, we persisted until the banks had narrowed to less than fifty yards across. Realising our mistake, we turned and, as we thought, retraced our path but we never found the junction of the five streams. A dozen times we tried other rivers and a dozen times we were forced to change our minds. When we pitched camp that night some of the men were close to panic. We stood in a circle at a place where a recently fallen tree had carved a small hole in the forest, and we recited the penitential psalms.

'Out of the deep have I called unto thee, O Lord...' Were we to perish here for our sins; here in this dripping, green hell? It seemed that we were: that evening we had scarcely anything to eat. Our ships' victuals had long since been consumed but we had been able to rely on the abundance of river and forest, supplemented by fruit and bread bought from the natives. Now, suddenly, our fishermen and hunters ran out of luck; our supper table was graced by three small, brown rodents which yielded scarcely a mouthful of meat for each man.

When we resumed our journey all we could do was to try to navigate by the compass, choosing channels that seemed to be flowing the way we wished to go. Unfortunately, every stream pursued a course so tortuous that it was impossible to divine its overall direction. Time and again this policy led us through waterways squeezed into rushing rapids by their converging banks and through others blocked by fallen trunks and foliage. On these occasions we had to haul the boats out of the water and hack a way along the bank until the obstacle had been passed. The same manoeuvre might be necessary half a dozen times in a mile of river. It was crippling work but I suppose fear lent us strength. We knew that we must escape from that dreadful place while we still had the strength to do so, and already we could feel the weakening effects of hunger. We stopped as little as possible; rowing until nightfall, and beyond if the stream was clear, setting off again at first light. For two more of our wounded companions the strain of all this was too much. After the briefest ceremony consonant with respect we committed them to the river.

The one shred of comfort we had during those fearful days was the knowledge that, though food might be scarce, we would not run out of water. It was some time during the third day of our wandering in that liquid labyrinth that Nick Wyatt scooped a drink from the river with his good hand, sucked it up greedily and spat it vehemently back overboard.

'Salt water!'

He swore and rubbed his lips with the back of his hand.

The rowers stopped to stare at Nick and to assess with their now sluggish minds the implications of this latest development. It was George Popham who saved the moment.

'Salt water, lads! The sea! Not far to our ships now. Come along, one last pull. Put your backs into it.'

Dully the men bent to their oars, absolved from the effort of thought, following their leaders not out of loyalty but because they lacked the energy to do otherwise. I stared round at the horribly familiar broad tree trunks, the green-brown water and the matted creepers. I guessed we must be within twenty miles of the coast but would we find our way to it before thirst took its inevitable toll? It was frustrating to think that somewhere close at hand Captain Wood might well be searching the shoreline for some sign of the boats and wondering whether he should wait any longer.

We had now found our way back into a broad channel and could make as rapid progress as our weary limbs allowed. Hour after hour we rowed through daylight and darkness. At last I slept fitfully in the stern. I was awoken at first light by an urgent hand shaking my shoulder. Hazily I was aware of Tom Jobson's large face. He was pointing and saying something. But his voice was drowned by a raucous and ragged noise. Gradually I became aware that the noise was cheering. I struggled to a sitting position and followed the direction of the soldier's pointing finger. Ahead of us the forest had opened out like the jaws of some great beast and there, pearl grey in the dawn, stretched the level horizon of the ocean.

Our troubles were not over. We had to fix our position and then make our way against wave and current to the appointed meeting place. But now we were back in an element we knew. We had shaken off the horrors of the Orinoco jungle and this fact refreshed us and steeled our wills. The daylight was almost gone before we spied the *Bear* and the *Fury*. An hour later and we were being helped aboard by willing hands. I often found Benjamin Wood's pious language a little annoying but I never heard sweeter words than the captain's effusive thanksgiving to God for my safety.

15

A commander should never allow his own moods and feelings to interfere with his decision-making or his relations with his followers. I know that now; I did not know it then. For three days I wallowed in the profoundest melancholy. I kept to my cabin and brooded on the errors of judgement and the lack of resolution that had resulted in the death of twenty-seven good men. Wantonly I had widowed their wives and orphaned their children. And with what results? I had achieved nothing. I still did not know whether El Dorado and the kingdom of gold existed or not. To make matters worse, the *Regard* and the *Intent* had failed to keep their rendezvous. There seemed every likelihood that they, too, had come to grief.

Two events lifted me out of my lethargy. The first was the reappearance of my two caravels. They sailed into Pelican Bay on 10 March bringing with them a Spanish merchant ship of some 300 tons that they had captured off Hispaniola. It was outward bound from Europe with a mixed cargo for the colonists. I had to emerge from my cell to congratulate Vincent and examine his prize. She proved to be a well-found vessel and the contents of her hold – pewter plates, iron pots, bales of cloth, barrels of olive oil, timber and furs – were such as would fetch good prices in England. Since I did not now have enough crew to man all the ships, I decided to scuttle the *Intent* and transfer everything of value from her to the merchantman which, in defiance of fortune, I renamed the *Mermaid*.

This and the revictualling of the fleet for the return voyage took all my time and left me no leisure in which to mope. There was still no sign of Raleigh, and without his support I lacked the manpower for an assault on San José de Oruña. I do not know whether I was glad or sorry to abandon my commitment to Balthasar's people. I could blame my broken pledge on changed circumstances and I no longer had any need to dragoon an unwilling crew into a hazardous military enterprise. On the other hand I frequently recalled that proud, hilltop moment when I had claimed this island for England and become the youngest adventurer ever to found a new colony. I promised myself that I would return with a larger expedition and make good the boast engraved in copper on that plate which I could still see from my cabin window. Then I told myself not to make any more easy promises.

The second event was, on the face of it, trivial. I was on the main deck of the *Mermaid* watching as the boatloads of barrels, bales, chests and kegs were ferried across from the doomed *Intent*. A stocky sailor with a green sea cap stretched over a bush of fair hair scrambled awkwardly over the side. He had a coil of rope slung over one shoulder and his right arm was wrapped round a bundle of pikes. As he stepped onto the deck some of the unwieldy fifteen foot shafts disengaged themselves and became entangled in the rigging. The seaman was caught off balance. He stumbled and with his arm grabbed at the nearest object for support: that object happened to be me and we both went sprawling on the deck amid a clatter of weapons. With a string of oaths the man jumped to his feet. Then with rather less fluency he turned to me and mumbled an apology.

'Beg your pardon, sir ... I ... very clumsy ... I ...'

He helped me to my feet and brushed me down. I could not help smiling as the red-faced sailor sputtered into silence while his friends laughed at his discomfiture.

'All right, Hewson. But see that you tie them properly in future. Here, you dropped this.'

I stooped to retrieve the green woollen cap. As I did so a much folded piece of paper fell out. As I handed it to Will Hewson he stared at it for a moment then for no apparent reason decided that I needed an explanation.

'Thank you, sir. It's a letter for Len Tyler's wife. He wrote it in the boat the day before he died. I promised to deliver it.'

I did not know what to say but knew I must say something.

'I am sorry about Tyler, Hewson. Was he a close friend of yours?'

To my surprise the swarthy face grinned.

'Nothing to be sorry about, sir. His wife led him a dog's life. He only came on this voyage to get away from her. He wrote this letter as a sort of joke: "My darling Joan," he says, "I'm dying so you can't torment me any more".'

Strangely, his laugh did not sound callous.

'Well, Hewson, you will soon be able to deliver the letter. We sail for home tomorrow.'

The sailor surprised me again. Instead of registering pleasure, he looked genuinely alarmed.

'Oh no, sir, not home already, sir.'

'I thought you would have had enough fighting for one voyage, Hewson?'

He shrugged.

'It just seems a pity now we're here on the Main not to have a go at Spanish ships or ports, sir.'

Then he caught sight of the master bearing down on him.

'Best be getting on, sir.'

He touched his forehead quickly, then stooped to gather together his scattered burden.

I discussed this incident later with Kendall and Wood as we toured the deserted *Intent* to make sure that nothing of value had been left aboard.

'Is that really what they want? Is Hewson typical? Would they not rather be at home with their families, spending their pay?'

Wood opened the door of the small after cabin and peered inside.

'Not while there's a chance of filthy lucre, Master Dudley. All the hands know that this is the place where money's to be made, here on the Main. They would think it a sin to return home without at least trying to relieve King Philip's subjects of some of their ill-gotten gains.'

'I see. And is that a view you would share, Ben?'

He turned, his long face set in its perpetual mask of humourless earnestness.

'I cannot help thinking of what happens to every ounce of gold that leaves Nombre de Dios. It goes to support the regime of Antichrist; to pay for soldiers, spies and assassins to send into England and the Netherlands.'

Abraham Kendall emerged from the hold carrying a lantern.

'We are at war with Spain. Some would say it is our duty to do all the damage we can while we have the chance.'

'Do you really think that the men want to go on serving me after ... well, after these last three weeks.'

The two mariners exchanged looks of genuine surprise.

'Don't you worry about that, lad. Most of 'em have seen worse disasters. They might have grumbled at the time but now that the danger's passed and their bellies are full again ... Are we leaving this old falconet?'

He swung the small cannon on its swivel mounting.

I nodded.

'Are you sure ...'

'They'd follow Old Nick himself if they thought there was money in it. That's right, isn't it Ben?'

Wood frowned but nodded.

'Young Vincent says most of the treasure fleet has left the isthmus to assemble in Havana; a hundred and fifty sail in all. They should be departing from there in a few days. With four sound ships and our crews well rested we should be able to achieve something there if God prospers us.'

It was the familiar pattern: Philip II's silver convoys gathered every spring and set out across the Atlantic under the protection of as many warships as could be spared. And every spring the predators converged on the Main – some of them privateers with letters of marque from the English government, but most of them adventurers and cut-throats, the scourings of the prisons and gutters of England, France and the Low Countries. They sought the treasure fleet and pursued it, hoping to cut out some bullion-heavy straggler or to encounter a defenceless merchantman separated by storms from its companions. And now my officers and crewmen were hoping that Robert Dudley's grand expedition to the New World would peter out in just such a conventional pirate raid. A tag of Virgil came into my mind, one dunned into me years before by a childhood tutor. '*Auri sacra fames*, O cursed lust for gold, to what can you not compel the hearts of men'. I quoted aloud, but my companions, ostentatiously busy about their work, showed no sign of having heard.

On Wednesday 12 March 1595 the *Bear*, the *Fury*, the *Mermaid* and the *Regard* sailed out of Pelican Bay, across the Gulf of Paria, through the Dragon's Mouth, which yawns between Trinidad and the mainland, and set course north-westwards for Havana.

As we were borne gently across the Caribbean Sea by a following wind I was able, for the first time, to reflect on this Odyssey of mine. What had I learned that might be of benefit to future travellers? I had made new charts and rutters. I had explored Trinidad and journeyed up the Orinoco farther than any man before me. All my newly-garnered information would be available to my fellow countrymen on my return.

Yet even more important to my impatient young mind were the things that I had learned about ships and the men who manned them, things that annoyed me and that I now saw must be changed. Who was in command of a naval expedition? Was it the admiral? Only if he had the strength of character and the ruthlessness to impose his will on his officers. Was it the council of captains and senior mariners? They were too often at loggerheads among themselves. Where was the line drawn between the authority of the admiral and that of the general or colonel commanding the land troops? And the sailors; how could England hope to gain and keep the mastery of the seas when her ships were manned by a mixture of pressed men, criminals and vagabonds who could find no other work? How could a systematic policy of overseas expansion be implemented when its agents were buccaneers interested only in booty? What England needed was a permanent navy of trained, disciplined sailors adequately paid for the dangers and hardships of life at sea. And the captains and masters; there was need for a new breed here also. No man should be allowed to take a ship to sea who was not well versed in mathematics, astronomy and the latest developments in navigational techniques.

And what of the grand maritime strategy? I had even developed strong ideas about that. Colonisation was the answer; but not the hazardous, private kind of colonisation founded on a sudden inspiration, such as Raleigh's Virginian fiasco. My system had definite stages. First there would be garrisons established in places like Trinidad; easily defensible territory having good harbours and well maintained supply lines with England. These garrisons would be centres for conquest and exploration. The next stage would be civilian settlement – farmers, miners, merchants and essential manufacturers – under royal chartered companies, in those areas where there were natural resources to exploit and where good relations had been established with the natives. By my calculation such a policy would sweep away all the ill-organised Spanish settlements of America and the Indies, and would make England the master of the New World within ten years or twenty at the very most. These, I decided, would be the ideas I would canvass when I reached home. There must be someone at court who would listen – Robin, Charles Howard the ageing Lord High Admiral, Burghley or, more likely, Robert Cecil, the son Burghley was grooming to take his place. Strange how, after an absence of only a few months, these once familiar men were now mere names to which it was difficult to put faces.

There was one name of which that certainly was not true. I saw Margaret's eyes in the sparkling blue waters, her hair in the tumbling clouds. Her mischievous smile looked up from my charts and at night her oval face glowed in the moonlight on my cabin wall. My longing for her became more intense as the days passed. When I heard sailors singing about their women or telling bawdy stories of past exploits I felt an almost physical pain. I wanted desperately to know that she was well, wanted to hear her say that she missed me, wanted to be sure that her father had kept his word and not married her off to Wingfield as soon as I left the country. But what if she were still free; would I be able to keep my part of the bargain with Richard Cavendish and foreswear all maritime adventure in the future? There was so much still to be done: Drake, Frobisher, Gilbert and others had laid a fine foundation but a new generation of mariners and navigators had to build on it. I wanted to be a leader in this exciting and important work. And then, I reasoned, perhaps it was not necessary for me to go to sea. The new age would need planners, men of vision with the influence and wealth to realise their vision. Now that I had experienced at first hand the problems of exploration and deep sea navigation, it might be that I would be more useful at home, organising expeditions, designing ships, framing colonial policy. These were some of the ideas that occupied my mind and filled my notebooks during those days of hard sunlight and soft breezes – days which came to an abrupt end on 25 March.

We had passed safely through the hazardous straits between Puerto Rico and the small island of Mona and anchored for the night off the Atlantic seaboard of Hispaniola. In the morning we found ourselves smothered by a dense fog. For two days we could see nothing beyond our dripping shrouds. We dared not move and we could only maintain contact between the ships by trumpet signals. On the afternoon of the third day the veil of mist was torn to shreds by a freshening breeze from off the land. This served us scarcely better than the fog. Hardly had we weighed anchor and set off on a westerly course, than the wind, growing in intensity by the minute, forced us around several points towards the north. We made for the coast of Florida from where I decided to patrol the thirtieth parallel around the point at which Philip's treasure fleet must cross it on their way to the Azores.

I should have learned by this stage that admirals do not make decisions: the best they can do is propose courses of action and pray that God does not overrule them. In this instance God did overrule.

We were some hundred and fifty miles off the North American mainland and the weather had eased when I went to my bed on the night of 5 April. I was roughly awakened by Will Bradshaw in the middle of the second watch.

'Sir, sir, come quickly! We're on fire!'

As, still half asleep, I swung my feet over the edge of the bed, the floor came up to meet them. The cabin lamp, which Will must have lit, was swinging wildly. Its glow was momentarily lost in a hectic flash of lightning, followed immediately by the thunderclap. I struggled into my boots.

'Fire, Will? Where?'

'On the masts, sir. Come and see.'

I wrapped a heavy cloak around me and staggered outside. The deck was inches deep in rushing water and every lurch brought more cascading over the gunwale. Storm lines had been put up and the drenched sailors clawed their way along them as they obeyed the orders shouted by Kendall above the shrieking and clashing of the tempest. Every stitch of sail had been taken down and there at the mastheads were the peaks of fire that had so terrified my page. They sparkled and crackled alarmingly. Though I had never seen this strange sight before I recognised it from old books and mariners' tales. There was no time to explain to Will that it was St Elmo's fire, a phenomenon noted by mariners ever since the Phoenicians in stormy weather. I hauled myself up the companionway to the poop deck and found Benjamin Wood there. Beyond the ship nothing could be seen; rain, starless night and the overhanging ridges of the waves made an opaque barrier.

'Where are we, Ben?'

The captain's answer was partly whipped away by the wind. '... took ... cross-staff reading ... four hours ago ... thirty-two and a half degrees ... making at least six knots with this wind ... off Bermuda ...'

Bermuda! We were, then, being carried far to the north-east into one of the most notorious zones of the Atlantic. Countless ships had foundered about those islands and in the weed-strewn seas surrounding them. It was a region of unheralded, violent storms where vessels vanished suddenly and without trace. Inevitably, it was peopled in the mariners' imagination with devils, sirens and sea monsters. The men dragging themselves along the storm lines would already have divined from the St Elmo's fire

234

that ours was a doomed ship. A flash of lightning lit the whole sky and I gazed quickly round for some trace of my fleet. I had little hope of seeing anything save a brief expanse of foaming peaks and that was all I did see. If the other ships were still afloat they would also be running before the storm at their own speed. Since they were not as trim as the *Bear* they would almost certainly be many miles behind.

The gale continued with varying ferocity for twelve days. When the skies cleared and we were able to take instrument readings again we found ourselves in forty-three degrees, not far from Sable Island. Had we been driven much farther north we should have found ourselves on those Newfoundland sandbanks where the hapless Humphrey Gilbert's last expedition had come to grief.

We were only given a brief respite. We altered course in order to seek a haven on the North American coast where we could rest the crew and carry out vital repairs. But after only a few hours the wind veered to the north-west and steadily increased in ferocity until we had no alternative but to run once more before it. From the Atlantic chart it was obvious that our best hope now was to make a landfall on the Azores, some one thousand, seven hundred and fifty miles due east. We were under half sail and Kendall and I agreed that unless the wind abated we would reach Flores in about thirteen days. We were there in ten. There could only be one reason for this discrepancy: the chart, one of the ones most frequently used by English deep-sea navigators was wrong.

We anchored off Flores, replaced torn sails and broken spars, pumped out the bilge and checked the condition and stowage of the cargo. With my expedition reduced to one ship and fifty weary men there was no question of landing on the Spanish-owned island. As soon as we had put the *Bear* to rights we set sail for England.

After four days of indifferent and variable winds we were scarcely two hundred miles nearer home. At three o'clock in the afternoon the lookout in the crow's nest spied a sail. Most of the *Bear*'s canvas was already set but I had the main to'gallant broken out and slowly we gained on the other vessel. As the speck grew in size and took on a recognisable shape Wood, Kendall and

Jobson joined me at the poop deck rail to play out the ritual always observed when another ship was sighted.

'She's a fair size,' said Kendall, 'about five hundred tons.'

'Nearer six hundred,' Wood corrected him.

'French?' I suggested.

'More likely Spanish,' said Jobson.

'Spanish, certainly,' Wood confirmed. 'She's too high in the stern castle for a Frenchman.'

'Show colours then, Master Wood, and man the guns.'

'Aye, Master Dudley.'

Jobson leaned forward on the rail.

'Perhaps she's one of the silver fleet separated by the storm.'

Kendall shook his head.

'That's too much to hope for. She would have waited in the Azores for the rest of the fleet.'

Wood returned from giving his orders and joined in the debate.

'A warship; probably a thirty-gunner.'

I looked anxiously along the main deck at our eight eighteen-pounders. I had had the rest of the guns stowed away during our stay in the Azores in order to increase stability. There had seemed little point in continuing to clutter the deck with ordnance; the chance of action on the last leg of the voyage was slight and, in any case, much of our powder had been dampened in the storms. With only eight main guns and the bow and stern chasers we were no match for a well armed Spanish galleon. Yet, not for one moment did I consider the possibility of avoiding an engagement, nor, I am sure, did any other man aboard the *Bear*.

The Spanish ship was closer now. Her white sails with their religious emblems were clearly visible. The Hapsburg blue and gold fluttered defiantly from her maintop. The evening sun illumined her stern castle with its gilded emblem and decoration.

'Bring us within hailing distance, Master Wood.'

My eyes were fixed on the other vessel as the distance between us closed to a few hundred yards. Her decks were swarming with men – a large crew. Her gunports were open and now I could clearly count fourteen cannon on each side. Every detail of her decoration, much of it freshly painted, glowed and was reflected in the water. Now I could make out the gilded figure on her stern. I gasped.

'Kendall, Jobson! Look! Surely it cannot be.'

But there was no mistaking the female figure with the large spiked wheel – St Catherine. We stared in silence for several moments, awe-stricken witnesses of a very unwelcome resurrection. I recalled the sight of the dismasted hull settling lower in the black water of Santa Cruz harbour, her fate settled by a score of gashes in her bottom.

'They must have managed to beach her before she filled.'

Kendall looked personally affronted by Wood's suggestion.

'They'll have had a hard job, then. My men did their work well. She was settling fast in ten fathoms when we left her.'

Jobson smiled at his companions.

'Then we must thank the Spaniards for their industry. They have provided us with a fine prize. Just get me and my men aboard her and we'll soon have a different flag flying at that masthead.'

I could not fully share the colonel's confidence but I applauded his spirit.

'Well said. Abraham, you wanted to take her in Tenerife; now you have your chance. Hail her, if you please, and demand her surrender.'

Kendall cupped his hands and bellowed across the water.

'Ahoy *St Catherine*, dip your tops'l to the Queen of England.'

The galleon continued on her way. I repeated the demand in Spanish. For reply there was a puff of white smoke at the *Santa Catalina*'s stern and a small shot whistled over our foremast. A shiver of excitement went through my body. I was to have my first full naval battle. The conflict this galleon had denied me on our first encounter was now forced upon her. Despite all her captain's wiles he had fallen into my hands at last. There was an almost divine predestination about it. I ordered my bow saker to return the Spaniard's defiance.

But there would be little fighting that night. The sun had already settled below the horizon. It would be a question of keeping our quarry in view during the hours of darkness and manoeuvring to a position of advantage at first light. I personally supervised all the preparations. Balls, shot and powder were stacked in piles on the deck; firearms were distributed; grappling ropes and irons were made ready; the *Bear* was dressed overall in blazon of war – a large royal standard at the stern, the cross of St George at the fore and mizzentops, my bear and ragged staff amidships, my green and gold pennant at the prow; and from the maintop the long swallow-tailed pennant which fluttered far out over the ship's wake and occasionally dropped to dip its tip in the waves. When all had been made ready I doubled the second watch and ordered the bow saker to be fired every hour just to remind the Spaniards that we were still there.

For me sleep was impossible. I had been given a second chance to prove myself and I was determined not to waste the opportunity. When the *Bear* and the *Santa Catalina* had clashed before I had let the enemy escape and nearly wrecked my own ship into the bargain. Now my officers and crew would be watching to see if I could do any better at the second attempt. I spent the night in my cabin going over and over my tactics, trying to remember all I had learned about how a small ship could successfully come to terms with a larger, better-armed vessel. Keep to windward, do as much damage as possible with your small, long-range cannon then work in close to hit him near the water-line.

An hour before dawn the crew were fed and prayers said. There would probably be no time for either over the next few hours. When the sun came up ahead the two ships were level with three-quarters of a mile between them. I watched from the poop as we opened our account. Calmly, steadily and in order our larboard cannon crashed out. The master gunner, John Brewer, watched for the water spouts and moved from position to position adjusting the charges. Within minutes we had found our range and could see holes in the galleon's sails. The answering shots from the *Santa Catalina* all fell short.

'Master Brewer, fire on the downward roll!'

'Take in the foretop!'

The master's shouted orders were designed to keep the *Bear* on a parallel course with the adversary and direct our fire at her sides rather than her rigging.

'Veer two points to starboard!'

The *Santa Catalina* had turned to close the range. A cannon ball whistled into the sea a dozen yards away showering the fore-deck with water. We kept our distance. The Spaniard suddenly struck all sail and fell quickly astern. In order to maintain the action we had to make a wide circle to starboard, a long and laborious manoeuvre in the light southerly wind which was blowing. It even meant taking men off the guns to help with the flapping sails.

'The crafty knave!' Kendall growled as he looked towards the galleon.

I followed his gaze and saw the *Santa Catalina*'s white canvas rapidly unfurling.

'What's he doing? Is he going to make a run for it?'

'Not he. He's trying to steal our wind. See he's veering hard to starboard.'

'He will gain on us and come in close.'

Kendall swore.

'Sweet Jesu, Wood, can't you bring her round any faster!'

We had turned through almost a hundred and eighty degrees and were now head on to the wind and facing the *Santa Catalina*. Her sails were full and she was bearing down on our starboard bow. On her present course she would cut across in front of us and pass larboard to larboard at about a hundred yards range, giving us a full broadside from her fourteen great guns. That would hurt us badly and probably give her time to come back and grapple. There was only one way to avoid that and surprise the Spaniard. It would demand accurate timing and call for all the *Bear*'s manoeuvrability.

'Hold her there, Master Wood. Take in fore and main sails.

Aloft, sailors sat astride the yards and pulled in the folds of canvas. The *Bear* stood still with only her mizzen hoisted in the path of the advancing enemy.

'Master Wood, when I give the word loosen mainsail and put her over hard to larboard.'

'Do you mean "starboard", Master Dudley?'

'No, larboard, Ben.'

'That'll take us across the Spaniard's bows.'

'Which is the last thing her captain will be expecting. He will have her larboard guns primed and loaded and all of a sudden we shall be on her starboard beam.'

'More likely we'll be under her prow. She'll ram us amidships.'

'Not if we are quick. Have all the men on their mettle, ready to let go sail as soon as they hear the order. Come with me.'

I ran up to the foredeck. Wood and Kendall were beside me and every eye in the ship was fixed on the sharp, high prow of the galleon as it bore down upon us.

'Watch her closely, Abraham. She will cross our bows then she must turn a few points to larboard. That's the moment we must move.'

The *Santa Catalina* passed in front of us about a quarter of a mile distant. She gave us a raking musket fire as she passed across our bows but I ordered no retaliation. I needed every man concentrating on the manoeuvre. The precision and teamwork had to be faultless. The galleon's stern-post passed in line with our bowsprit.

'She's beginning to turn.'

'Now!'

The mainsail rattled down its mast. Expert hands made fast the sheets. The *Bear* veered across the path of the oncoming ship. The lateen mizzen felt for the breeze. Pray God it did not drop now! The mizzen filled. The mainsail too caught some wind. But not fast enough. We were now looking up at the galleon's bow. Men were running around her foredeck shouting confused orders. The mizzen flapped as the bulk of the big ship stole the wind. But the *Bear* was making way now. Our foredeck passed almost under the *Santa Catalina*'s bow. We could see sky and waves beyond. We turned aft. For a moment it seemed the enemy's bowsprit must pierce our mizzen. Then we slipped into clear water and the galleon lay astern.

'Full sail, please, Master Wood! Hard to larboard! Larboard guns ready. We'll have a broadside as soon as may be, Master Brewer.'

The *Bear* came round sweetly and ran before the wind rapidly overhauling her adversary. All was still noisy confusion on the galleon's decks but it would not be so for long. If we were to give her our four guns at close range we must do it quickly.

'Master Jobson, arquebus fire at will!'

The crackle of hand guns filled the air as the two ships drew alongside. I returned to the poop deck and as I reached it the *Bear* rocked sideways under the recoil of her own broadside. The gunners hurried to reload, anxious for another round before we drew away. I was caught off balance and stumbled against the gunwale. It was at that moment that the staff I was carrying was suddenly wrenched from my grasp as though by an invisible hand and fell, shattered, in the scuppers. A spatter of musket fire rattled around the poop deck. Beside me a soldier fell, clutching his leg. Singly the larboard guns roared again, then the *Bear* turned her back on the *Santa Catalina* and drew rapidly away.

It was only then that I saw the damage we had inflicted on our foe. She was badly scarred along her side and had a large hole abaft near the waterline. There was another jagged gash where one of her gunports had been. Her foretop had gone and her foresail was in shreds. All her sails were sprinkled with shot holes. A number of men were lying on the deck being tended by their comrades.

At last the *Bear* shook with the impact of the thunderous cannonade as the *Santa Catalina* brought her starboard guns into action. But only one or two balls found their mark in our stern castle. The rest whined past and plunged into the sea ahead. By the time the Spanish gunners had reloaded we were out of range. I hailed the galleon again.

'*Santa Catalina,* surrender now and avoid further suffering and damage!'

Once again the guns spoke her answer.

Kendall came up the companionway.

'They're uncommonly brave for Spaniards.'

'Perhaps their captain has not forgiven me for waking him so rudely in Santa Cruz.'

'If he's trying to teach you better manners, lad, he very nearly succeeded. If he'd come in on our windward side just now we'd be fighting for our ship with drawn swords this very moment. That was a brilliant piece of sailing, lad. Even Drake couldn't have done better. Thank God we've got youngsters like you to take our places in the years ahead.'

It was a long speech for Kendall and it was delivered in a voice full of emotion.

'Thank you, Abraham, but the day is not won yet.'

'Only a matter of time, lad. She won't risk another move like that. She'll have to give in sooner or later.'

'What do we do, stand back and pound her with our culverin?'

'No need to risk getting in closer. She's leaking already. I'll wager an angel she's ours by nightfall.'

I looked up at the sun and realised for the first time that it was well past its zenith. One mile away the *Santa Catalina* lay limp-sailed and weary on the swell. She had lost her arrogance if not her pride and I thought Kendall's money was probably safe.

Appearances are deceptive. For a further four hours we fired our long-range guns into the galleon and she could do nothing to us in return. But she would not surrender and night found the battle unresolved. I assembled the men and congratulated them and they gave me three cheers. I promised them victory on the morrow if they fought as well and bravely as they had already. Then I went to my cabin for a private supper and a much-needed sleep.

As I lay in the dark listening to the peaceful sounds of lapping water and creaking timbers I was happy in the knowledge that I should soon have my first prize of war. Even if the *Santa Catalina* succeeded in slipping away towards Spain in the darkness – and I had given strict orders that the watch was to maintain contact by sight or sound – I would soon overhaul her the following day, she was so badly crippled. Nothing could deprive me of my trophy now – nothing.

I was thrown violently out of sleep by an explosion which rocked the *Bear* like a tidal wave. It was still dark but as I stumbled about the cabin a glow from the window painted the furniture with red edges. Men were shouting and running about the deck. Were we on fire? Had the treacherous Spaniard come up on us in the dark? I hurried outside, and stared at the tall, twisting flames.

It was not my ship that the Spanish captain had set on fire; it was his own. She was ablaze from stem to stern, filling sea and sky with garish light. Now and again an explosion threw sparks and flaming timbers into the air. For ten minutes, fifteen perhaps, she glowed and crackled, and the *Bear*'s crew, lining the rail, could feel the heat of her. Then, hissing and roaring, she sank into the Atlantic, leaving the night unnaturally black and empty.

In the morning we searched the floating debris for survivors but there was no Spaniard, living or dead, to be seen. We knew then that the captain and his crew must have taken to the boats and set off by oar and sail for Spain, some six hundred miles distant. They had scattered kegs of powder through the *Santa Catalina* and had lit slow fuses before leaving. I felt cheated and I was angry but I could not find it in my heart to wish that my adversary and his men would not make port.

For our part, we made port two weeks later, returning to England as we had left England – in foul weather. Midst driving rain and sleet we passed between Land's End and the Scillies and gratefully slipped into the first Cornish haven we could find. It was St Ives.

16

I took the *Bear* to Bristol. There were two reasons for this: Bristol was a city of merchants and chandlers where I could easily dispose of my cargo and surplus supplies; it was also at one end of the Great West Road, and near the other end lay Windsor where, as I gathered from quayside gossip, the court was paying an unexpectedly early visit. It was, thus, at Windsor that I fervently hoped I would find Margaret. As quickly as possible I concluded my business and paid off the crew. Then, with Will Bradshaw and two servants leading the pack horses, I rode eastwards.

The closer we drew to Windsor, the more nervous I became. Would she be there or had her father married her off despite his promise? Would she be well; it was the worst time of year for plague, and my imagination easily conjured up terrifying pictures of Margaret on a wide bed, tossing and turning in a hot fever. Would she have found someone else to love? Six months was a long time in the life of a passionate young woman. Those six months had altered me, too. The whispy beard I had always found difficulty in cultivating had burgeoned into a quite luxuriant growth and my complexion had been tanned by sun and wind to a most unfashionable hue. And the changes were not only external. Whether I was a better or more mature man than the Robert Dudley who had set out from Southampton in November I knew not. What was quite certain was that I was not the man Margaret had fallen in love with.

It was an odd feeling to move among the merchants, servants, suitors, soldiers and grand personages thronging the outer ward of Windsor Castle and to feel no longer a part of the busy life of the court. It was odd and rather annoying to have to argue with the Gentlemen Pensioners on guard at the inner gatehouse before gaining admission. It was odd and amusing to hail an old colleague in the herb courtyard and to be greeted by a brusque 'Well, what is it, fellow' before he recognised me and clasped my hand with mingled pleasure and disbelief. He insisted on taking me straight to his chamber and hearing all my news. It was an hour and several cups of wine later before I was able to ask.

'Is Margaret Cavendish at court?'

My friend was a natural courtier, one of those men who live on gossip and thrive on intrigue. He smiled broadly and winked.

'So, it is still Margaret, is it?'

'I hope so. Is she here?'

'Yes, she is here.' He sniggered. 'And still unwed. Shall I go and tell her of your arrival?'

He jumped up and moved towards the door, his eyes alight with excitement. He was savouring with the utmost relish his possession of a unique piece of news and he could not wait to be off round the passageways and chambers – 'Robert Dudley is back. And what do you think he has been telling me . . .' Yes, the work of exaggeration, distortion and romanticising had begun. But that was not how I wanted Margaret to hear of my return. I moved across to stand in front of the door.

'Martin, wait!'

'Wait? Why man, do your arms not ache to hold her again?'

'Yes, but they do not ache to enfold the whole court – I do not want everyone flocking around me.'

'My dear fellow, as if I would . . .'

I grinned at him.

'As if you would not. Listen, I want an hour alone with Margaret somewhere and no one else must know I am here. Can you arrange that?'

Martin leered and waved an arm towards his velvet-hung bed.

'My humble abode is at your disposal.'

He stepped around me towards the door. My hand detained him.

'Martin, I want to surprise her. Tell her a messenger has arrived with news of my expedition.'

He nodded and took a step forward. Still I held him.

'And then not a word for at least an hour; do you understand?'

He looked reproachfully at me.

'My dear fellow, you know me. A secret is safer in here,' he tapped his head, 'than in the Tower.'

I laughed.

'I know you, indeed, Martin. Which is why I am making you promise.'

'Oh, very well, then. I promise.'

He frowned good humouredly, then bounded away self-importantly on his mission.

I called Will and had him carry up one of the chests I had brought from Bristol. When he had gone I took from the coffer my sea cloak and woollen cap. Martin had a fine Venetian mirror hanging on one waiscotted wall and with its aid I adjusted my clothing. The cap came low on my forehead and my new beard covered the lower part of my well-weathered face. I did not think Margaret could possibly recognise me when she came in.

If she came. Perhaps she would keep a messenger from Robert Dudley waiting a couple of hours or even send someone else to see to him. I wondered whether I could measure her love in the number of minutes she kept me waiting. I walked impatiently around the room. Martin had been allocated excellent quarters, but then he usually contrived to acquire the best by one means or another. The chamber was small but the bed felt very comfortable and the view southwards across the Thames valley was beautiful. Sunlight slanted through the casement and gleamed on a chased ewer and goblets standing on an inlaid Italian table, obviously a present from Martin's father who was one of the City goldsmiths. The wall behind them was hung with a small Flemish tapestry depicting the return of Odysseus.

'How appropriate,' I thought. 'How tasteful, cosy and appropriate.'

The door opened.

Margaret's simple low-necked white gown was embroidered with gold lilies and blue cornflowers. The inner sleeves were of the same blue and she had plaited real cornflowers into her hair. The scent of musk filled the room.

I made an awkward, seaman's bow.

Margaret closed the door and leaned against it, breathing heavily. She had obviously been running.

'You have a message from Master Dudley?'

She scrutinised me. I lowered my gaze and spoke gruffly.

'Yes, Madam.'

'Is he well?'

She stepped lightly towards me.

'Yes, Madam.'

'Then you will give him a message for me?'

With a force that almost knocked me over Margaret threw herself into my arms. She squeezed her body against mine and covered my lips with kisses. Between them she whispered, 'Tell Master Dudley, "I love you. I love you. I love you".'

'Trust Martin to give me away.'

'Martin? My darling, did you think I would not recognise you. I would know you under a hundred disguises. Oh, my darling, it is such a relief to have you back.'

We clung together without speaking, repossessing each other, our hearts aching with joy and delight. At length, I seated her on the bed and walked over to the chest.

'See what treasures I bring from the corners of the world to lay at your feet.'

One by one I set before her items I had acquired on my travels by barter and robbery – a gold falcon clasping a small emerald in its beak, which had once been destined for the wife or mistress of the *Santa Catalina*'s captain; a bale of rich damask from a Santa Cruz warehouse; a fan of parrot feathers given to me by Mointiman. Margaret's eyes were wide with surprise and delight as these and other gifts were uncovered. She knelt beside me on the floor surrounded by my offerings, demanding to know the story which attached to each.

When all had been seen and examined and praised Margaret kissed me again.

'They are all wonderful, my darling, but the best of all is to

247

have you home again.'

'The best present of all I have yet to give.'

'What is that?'

I whispered the answer in her ear.

Margaret giggled and blushed with pleasure.

'Wherever should I put it?'

But we soon discovered that she had a casket into which my gift fitted very snugly, as though it had been made for it.

Sparkling green eyes and the deeper green of the counterpane; inlaid ebony on the headboard in striking accord with her black hair; boars and harts looking down on us from the moulded ceiling; indifferent swallows swooping past the lattice intent on their own love play – the images implanted in those moments of heightened awareness remain ever crisp and clear.

Afterwards the floodgates burst releasing upon us a torrent of friends, congratulating, back-slapping and begging me to tell my story over and over again. After a while Margaret drew me from the throng.

'The Queen, you must go to the Queen. She will be furious if she finds she was not the first to hear your report.'

She need not have worried; Elizabeth was in the Council Chamber closeted with Burghley, Essex, Robert Cecil and her other leading advisers. I waited half an hour or more in the antechamber with a motley crowd of petitioners and hangers-on. At last she emerged leaning on Robin's left arm with the hunch-backed Cecil on her other side – Essex and Burghley's son, they were the new rivals, now that Raleigh, still at sea, had slipped from favour. The Queen moved slowly down the line of bowing courtiers. When she reached me her eyebrows rose in surprise and what I hoped was pleasure.

'So, the brave captain is returned?'

I kissed the proffered hand, then turned to Robin who put an arm round my shoulder.

'Welcome home, Bear cub!'

The Queen frowned.

'Not so warm in your greeting, my Lord. We have yet to be convinced that Master Dudley has earned it.'

She turned back to me, inscrutable behind her set, cosmetic mask.

'We understand that you did not proceed according to our charter.'

It was the accusation I had feared and I had long since prepared my answer.

'Everything I and my men ventured was for your Majesty. If your Majesty will be pleased to read this there will be no need of further proof of my loyalty.'

From Will Bradshaw, standing behind me, I took the folio volume which contained the *Bear*'s log. It was no ordinary ship's journal. It was neatly written in my best hand and illustrated by maps, charts and some of Will's most striking sketches. But it was the cover which drew a smile of appreciation from the Queen, as I had hoped it would. Among the spoils of Santa Cruz had been a large, cedarwood crucifix set with jewels. From this my ship's carpenter had fashioned two boards. The blacksmith had overlaid these with gold from melted-down Spanish coin and another member of the crew, with fastidious care, applied a bold pattern in emeralds and pearls. The chronicle of my voyage was bound between them and it was this volume that I now placed in her Majesty's hands to the admiring gasps of those around.

Elizabeth ran her fingers approvingly over the smooth surfaces and glanced through the book's pages.

'Your father always had exquisite taste in giving,' she said softly. Then brightly, almost coquettishly, 'But we would hear of your adventures from your own lips.'

She passed the present to one of her attendants and laid a hand on my right forearm.

'Come, my brave captain, let us leave my Lord of Essex and Master Cecil to burn in their own jealousy. You and I will walk on the north terrace alone and you shall tell me all about the curious people who put paint on their faces and feathers in their hair.'

For an hour or more the Queen and I paced to and fro along the paved walk, high above the thatched roofs of Windsor and the sunlit treetops. She probed minutely into every detail of my voyage revealing a far greater knowledge of nautical matters than I had supposed she could possibly possess.

'And now, tell us what you have discovered about this "Golden Man" of whom Raleigh speaks so passionately.'

'There is no Golden Man, your Majesty.'

I said it lightly, and immediately realised my mistake. The Queen looked disappointed and annoyed. No more than other people did she enjoy having her illusions shattered.

'You sound very sure of yourself, Master Dudley.'

'Your Majesty's reproof is just. I cannot say that El Dorado is a myth with a conviction born of experience but I have travelled sixty leagues and more up the Orinoco and there the people have not heard of a king who rules a land of enormous wealth.'

'You found no gold mines?'

'Gold there is, your Majesty, and therefore must there be gold mines, but where they are and how abundant I could not discover. This much I can report: whoever will seek the mines must fight his way through the worst country and the most bloodthirsty savages in the world.'

'You think such a task impossible?'

'Nothing is impossible to captains inspired by devotion to your Majesty. Yet such an expedition must be very carefully planned and will demand many ships and men.'

I outlined my scheme for an assault on Trinidad, and the establishment of a military colony which should serve as a base for the plundering of Spanish settlements and convoys as well as the extension of English rule to the mainland.

'And you would like to lead such an expedition?'

'I would consider such a command a great honour.'

'And how do you suppose this venture would be financed?'

We talked for several minutes of ships and supplies, of potential backers and the prospects of a good return on investment. The Queen considered shrewdly all I said and stored it away for further reference but she did not commit herself. Instead she took her hand from my arm and stood for some moments silently appraising me. At last she sighed deeply.

'Yes, Robin is right: you are the Bear's cub and grow more

250

like the old Bear every time we see you. He, too, possessed more valour than prudence.' She stared wistfully across the battlements towards a distant glint of river far below. 'He found it hard to follow the lead of older, wiser men.'

'Older men are not always wiser, your Majesty.'

She glanced at me sharply.

'That, young man, is a dangerous philosophy.' But she did not disagree. 'And now, if we do not return to the others they will suspect we have been indulging in all manner of dalliance.' The coy smile was incongruous on the thin lips.

With a surge of panic I realised that my opportunity was almost gone. There was something I had to say and there would never be a better time. I braced myself.

'Your Majesty.'

'Well, my Bear cub, what is it?'

'May I have leave to ask a favour?'

'Everyone at our court does little else. What is your desire?'

'I would beg leave to marry one of your Majesty's maids of honour.'

She frowned deeply.

'So, like other men, your protested love for us is only flattering.'

'Not so, your Majesty. But only the gods may dwell for ever on Olympus. Mere mortals must be content to worship from afar and satisfy themselves with simple pleasures.'

'Very pretty, very pretty.' Her chuckle resembled the cry of a startled pheasant. 'Mistress Cavendish, is it not?'

'Your Majesty sees into all hearts.'

'We see those that are worn on sleeves readily enough. Young Margaret has been melancholy and moonfaced ever since you left. What a troublesome thing is love. The girl was promised to Sir Anthony Wingfield. It would have been most suitable. Then no doubt she filled her head with poet's nonsense and she must needs fancy herself in love. Would that she were proof against men's stratagems, as we are. However, Mistress Margaret Misery is no use to us in her present mood. In God's name take her, Master Dudley. And be happy with her if you can.'

251

It was the only kind of royal blessing we received but it was enough and we laughed long over it later that day.

Margaret and I were wed on a moist, warm morning in late June at Trimley, her Suffolk home. Richard Cavendish spared no expense in providing food, drink and diversions for his guests and in setting us upon our married course in a riot of dancing and merriment which lasted for three days. If he still had misgivings about his son-in-law he never voiced them, nor was anything said of Sir Anthony Wingfield (I later heard that the corpulent knight had solaced himself with the middle-aged widow of a London mercer who had left her with a great deal of money and seven children).

Robin came down with a crowd of friends from London to make sure that, as he said, 'the cubs were properly mated' and after all the drinking of the night before the ceremony it is a wonder that I was able to take any coherent part in it. Reluctant as the revellers were to allow me to get to bed, they were eager to drag me from it in the morning. They roused me with a fearful cacophony of sound from trumpets, drums, viols and sundry improvised instruments. When I retreated beneath the sheets, the coverings were dragged off and I sat in my night shirt holding my hands over my ears while they cavorted around the chamber making enough noise to rouse the county. At last, I virtually had to throw them out so that my servants could wash and dress me. When peace had descended I could hear shrieks and giggles from Margaret's nearby room and knew that she was being similarly attended by her companions.

An hour later Robin and the others were back to escort me to the church. One of the Cavendish women presented me with a bunch of rosemary and tied it to my sleeve. The short pathway from the hall to the lych gate was lined by cheering villagers who threw flowers as we passed. The curate who was standing at the church door was an earnest young man who gazed askance at the not completely sober company. I turned at the sound of music and renewed cheering. The bride's procession was coming through the gateway. First to appear were the hired players, capering

252

in time to the sound of their shawms, tabors and viols. After them walked a boy, face lined with concentration, as he carried before him a great silver loving-cup filled with muscadel which slopped over the edge despite his efforts. Then, in the midst of female friends and relations waving silken streamers, Margaret came with her father beside her. A garland of leaves and wheat-ears gleamed against the raven black of her unbraided hair. Her russet gown was loosely sewn with knots of white ribbon and the colour was repeated in the little bunch of flowers clutched in her gloved hands. She seemed to radiate a peace and happiness strangely at variance with the jangling merriment surrounding her.

The parson waited in vain for the throng to subside into a respectful silence. At last, in a loud, slightly nervous, voice he began the ceremony.

'Dearly beloved friends...'

Somehow Margaret and I found solemn peace and profound meaning in the old words.

'Wilt thou have this woman... love her, comfort her, honour and keep...?'

'Wilt thou have this man... obey him, and serve him, love, honour and keep... '

We pledged ourselves to each other and then followed the parson into the church where the effigies of long-dead Cavendishes reclined in carven piety. Despite the fidgetings of the congregation, the service of matrimony was concluded at a leisurely pace and the communion began. When it came to the sermon the young preacher, presumably believing the presence of so many fine ladies and gentlemen called for his best oratory, launched into a lengthy diatribe on some abstruse point of theology. He lost himself, but not before he had lost his hearers. The whispered remarks from behind us were good humoured but they certainly were not very reverent.

At last the closing moments of the ceremony arrived. Margaret and I drank sweet wine from the great cup which was then carried to the guests. The parson began to stammer out a blessing but before he could finish there was a whoop from behind and Essex and his friends were upon us. Laughing and jostling they grabbed their 'prizes' to stick in their hats – the lovers' knots from Margaret's dress, her garters and the points of my doublet. When they were satisfied I took my bride's hand and led her back down the church. As we walked, our feet squeezed fragrance from the roses and lilac strewn along the aisle, and petals marked our path all the way back to the door of Grimston Hall.

At the wedding banquet our healths were drunk a hundred times and there seemed no end to the meat and poultry, the pies, junkets, cakes, comfits and sweetmeats. Robin made a speech in which he vowed that no man in England kept a finer table than our host and promised that the Queen should know as much the moment he returned to court. Sir Richard looked delighted despite himself and said how great an honour it was to have the Earl and so many other great ladies and gentlemen beneath his roof. After the feasting there was dancing on the lawns and after the dancing more feasting and then a masque and a mime performed by the hired players (who were reputed the best outside London) and still the company had no mind to cease their revels. Sometime late that night Margaret and I tried to creep away to avoid the traditional last ceremony. But we were seen. Our friends flocked around us, lifted us shoulder high and with much telling of old jokes and singing of bawdy songs brought us to our bridal chamber. Only when we had drawn the curtains of the great bed did we find the privacy to clasp each other in happy, exhausted embrace. And still the sounds of merrymaking rang through the house.

A week later we left Trimley and I took my new bride on a tour of all the estates of which she was now mistress. She was delighted with everything, and everyone – bailiffs, neighbours, servants, tenants – was delighted with her. We came at last to magnificent Kenilworth. Famed though it was, ever since my father's extensive rebuilding, it took Margaret completely by surprise. She was at first bewildered to find over a hundred indoor servants and an army of gardeners, grooms, foresters, watermen, shepherds, drovers, huntsmen, falconers, husbandmen and labourers at her command but she did not allow herself to be overwhelmed. Each morning she set out to explore a different part of the ancient castle. Each afternoon she and I would ride out to inspect some of the forests, farms and chases which lay within the estate's twenty-mile circumference or take a boat across the lake to examine the heronry, the hunting lodge, the trout hatchery or one of the other delights which made Kenilworth the envy of many a noble and gentleman.

I loved Margaret all the more for her genuine delight in this beautiful place. When we entertained, as we frequently did, the neighbouring gentry or friends from the court, she would point out with ingenuous enthusiasm the beautiful stained glass in the great hall windows, the slender bridge over the lake which Leicester had built for the Queen's visit, the rich carving of the fireplaces or the fine view from the top of Caesar's Tower. There was no trace of possessive or superior pride, such as most hostesses would have demonstrated; she simply longed for others to share her ever-fresh pleasure in these things.

Visitors were not the only ones to come under her spell: Margaret taught me to love Kenilworth and I think she taught Kenilworth to love me. I suppose it was my childhood experiences which gave me a profound loathing for large, empty, echoing buildings, and my great castle had always struck me as imposing yet forbidding. Whenever I had visited it before, it seemed to frown on me in a dignified, aloof fashion and merely to tolerate my residence. But when I came with Margaret by my side it welcomed us and revealed friendly arbours, cosy rooms, intimate corners and secret nooks which I had never seen before.

The summer passed quickly and happily but we were not so starry-eyed as to imagine that our extended honeymoon could last for ever. People and news from the outside world came frequently to our doors. Most important to me was the news of my ships. All of them came safe home in June and July. Monk had set sail with Raleigh in February but had grasped the first opportunity to break away from the fleet and had taken the *Bear's Whelp* privateering on my account in the Canaries and Azores. He returned to Southampton with two merchant prizes. The *Regard* and the *Mermaid* were both badly battered by the Atlantic storms but they returned separately to West Country ports where they were able to discharge and sell their cargoes (George Popham and the *Fury* had performed another of their celebrated disappearing acts). So, my West Indies venture which had started so disastrously ended by showing a very respectable profit.

One warm afternoon at the beginning of August a messenger came to Kenilworth bringing a small package. Margaret and I were just setting out for our daily excursion and I stuffed the parcel unopened into my purse. The day's outing was to be to the heronry, one of Margaret's favourite haunts. We had for weeks been following the progress of a family of newly-hatched birds from a hide built by one of the foresters. The nest was a platform of sticks and fronds well concealed in the reeds on the far side of the lake. We had seen the chicks grow from noisy, food-frantic balls of down into small, gangling replicas of their parents. We had watched the daily dramas of hunting, feeding and driving off predators. Now we were hoping to see the first flights of the young herons. But, when we reached our hide, nosing the flat-bottomed boat quietly in among the reeds, we found we were too late; the nest was empty. Margaret flumped down on the cushions, pouting.

'Oh, how unfair of them. After all the trouble we have taken over them they might have waited.'

I laughed.

'Not even the mistress of Kenilworth can command the birds.'

'You must not tease me, Robert. You know I did so want to see them fly.'

'Never mind, my darling, there will be more herons here next year. We will spend the whole summer here. And I will have a bigger hide built so that you can watch them in comfort.'

She looked up at me uncertainly.

'Robert, are you teasing me still.'

'No, I promise. We will come here and watch the herons together.'

As if on cue there was a commotion of splashing water and beating wings: four of the ungainly grey and white birds rose above the waving spikes of reed and soared into the air far out over the lake. Margaret stared, enraptured, until they had disappeared from view.

'Oh, I do love them so. I think it is because they are beautiful and funny at the same time. Let us go up to the far end and see if we can see them again.'

The boatman eased us out from the reeds and poled us slowly over the surface of the water. For some time we lay side by side watching the ducks and moorhens fussing about the bank while the grey bulk of the castle grew smaller and smaller in the distance. Suddenly, and for a fleeting moment, I was back on the Orinoco, sweating in the humid heat, hearing the raucous screeching of parrots and feeling panic in my stomach. I must have shivered or exclaimed because Margaret turned to me in alarm.

'What is it, Robert?'

'Nothing, I was just remembering another place.'

'Do you miss your ships and your foreign lands?'

'Not if I can have you instead.'

'Very prettily said, my lord. But seriously though.'

She propped herself on one elbow. Taking my hand in hers she drew off the ring she had given me at our wedding. Quietly, she read the inscription engraved on the inside.

' "Love me and leave me not". Was it unfair of me to ask that?'

'Silly, what makes you say that?'

'You talk very little about your voyage now but I know you think about it often; sometimes your memories take you by surprise, like just now. You said you were going to write a book about it but you have not started yet. Why not? Is it because of me? Is it because you are afraid of getting the urge to travel again?'

'What your father calls "sea fever"? No, it is not that. Every new experience is an exploration. It is not necessary to go half way round the world to find adventure. And now I am happy exploring a new life, with you.'

'And when you have explored that fully? Will you be looking for new adventures?'

257

She slipped the ring back on my finger and I held her hands in mine. I wanted so much to explain what I felt about her and our future and the vast, exciting, world of which Kenilworth was only a minute part. I had walked in places where no Englishmen had ever been before. How could I describe the thrill of that?

'My darling, I cannot know whether I shall ever want to go adventuring again. But I do know that I have discovered a new purpose, a new meaning for whatever I do.'

I floundered for words.

'That purpose is all about you, and Kenilworth, and our children, and our children's children. Does that make sense? I must fulfil myself for your sake. It is not a choice between Margaret and exploration; they are both ... Oh, I know not what ...'

I stuttered into silence. Margaret said nothing but I knew she understood. She would always understand.

My hand brushed against my purse and I remembered the package. I pulled out the little bundle sewn in cloth.

'Let us see what this is, shall we?'

When I had slit the stitches with my knife a small, rather dirty note book was revealed. There was a letter with it.

To the right honourable Master R. Dudley.

My respects to your honour. You must forgive these simple words but being of little education I cannot write prettily. I am shipping with Sir Francis Drake and Sir John Hawkins for places you and I know well so I shall not see you before you write the story of our recent voyage to the Indies and I must send you the enclosed which I hope you will find useful. I hear you are newly married and I wish you and your wife much happiness. Your honour's to command in all humble services,

Abram Kendall

I opened the book. It was the pilot's rutter that he had kept carefully throughout the journey. I showed it to Margaret, deciphering for her some of the nautical expressions and explaining the diagrams. She looked puzzled.

'Why did he write it? He must have been very busy helping to run the ship yet he obviously spent a lot of time on this book. He seems to have noted every astrolabe reading and even every change of wind direction.'

'Most mariners make their own rutters when they travel in little known waters. Then they can be copied or printed to help other sailors who voyage the same way.'

'Then you must have it printed for Master Kendall and you must write your own account and print that, too. You must start at once, today. It will help you to get the sea fever out of your blood.'

She smiled, but there was a trace of anxiety in her eyes.

It was an anxiety I shared when I was honest with myself. I had assured Richard Cavendish that my seafaring days were over and at the time I had meant it. Nor had I any cause to regret my decision; these past weeks with Margaret had been the happiest of my life. All my revolutionary ideas about naval organisation, colonisation and strategy seemed far less urgent now than they had done during those months when I brooded on them in my cabin aboard the *Bear*. All those memories and plans belonged to another world. Yet it was a world that would not keep itself apart; it intruded, unexpected and unbidden, into the world I shared with Margaret, like the hidden brown trout which suddenly appeared among the weed in the lake shallows.

I did write my account of the voyage and I had every intention of publishing it, bound in one volume with Kendall's rutter. I did not do so; or, at least, I did not do so until many years later. The reason was Sir Walter Raleigh's return. He was back in London in October, boasting of his achievements and taking every opportunity to pour scorn on my expedition. *Master Dudley* had gone to Trinidad and claimed it for the Queen but *he* had overrun the Spanish garrison of San José de Oruña and captured de Berrio, the governor. *Master Dudley* had travelled up the Orinoco making war on the Indians whereas *he* had patiently established good relations with all the people he came across. From what *he* had seen and heard from the natives he could confidently reveal the truth about the kingdom of Guiana and the surrounding country.

He even wrote a description of this land in a book he hurried to the press:

> I never saw a more beautiful country, nor more lively prospects; hills raised here and there, over the valleys, the river winding into different branches, plains without bush or stubble, all fair green grass, deer crossing our path, the birds towards evening singing on every side a thousand different tunes, herons of white, crimson and carnation perching on the river-side, the air fresh with a gentle wind, and every stone that we stooped to take up promised either gold or silver.

The man's audacity was breathtaking. From some of his men I learned that Raleigh had penetrated only a little farther up the Orinoco than I. He had reached the forest fringe and seen something of the highlands beyond before rapids and cataracts had forced him to turn back. He had certainly discovered nothing which justified him describing in detail the vast territory of Guiana and extolling it as a land ripe for conquest and colonisation. Yet that is exactly what he did: his book contained glowing descriptions of the salt lake of Gran Manoa around which were the towns of 'that mighty rich and beautiful empire of Guiana, that great and golden city which the Spaniards call El Dorado'. And there were maps, confidently set forth for all to see, on which were located not only the fabulous kingdom of the Golden Man, but also the land of the fierce women warriors called Amazons, and the place where the Ewaipanoma lived – weird creatures who have no heads but 'eyes in their shoulders, and their mouths in the middle of their breasts'. I could only laugh aloud when I read Sir Walter's serious account of these ridiculous stories whose only origin (if they had any origin at all) was in Indian folklore.

And, of course, everybody laughed; everybody except the wilfully gullible. The great mariner who had found a land flowing with gold, silver and precious stones and yet returned empty-handed was the laughing stock of the court. Some wits who knew Raleigh to be no sailor even suggested that he had not gone to the Indies at all, but had hidden himself somewhere in Cornwall and there made up his incredible story. Margaret and I were now back at Bedford House and many friends from London and Westminster came to talk with me there and ask what conditions were really like along the Orinoco. I was able to give the lie to almost every one of Raleigh's far-fetched anecdotes. Sir Walter's fury, as I heard from many lips, scarcely knew any bounds. He traduced me as a traitor, deserter and a mere 'sea scavenger'. We did not meet face to face in those months and it was as well that we did not: any confrontation must have resulted in a duel and the death of one of us. Had I thought that anyone took Raleigh's accusations seriously I would certainly have challenged him. As it was, the more angrily he protested, the more people ignored him. He was certainly in no position to do me any real damage for, though he was no longer excluded from the court, he was far from being fully restored to royal favour and was not permitted to resume his office of Captain of the Guard. The only annoying outcome of this charade was that it dampened all enthusiasm for a proper expedition to the Orinoco and precluded any serious discussion of English colonisation in the West Indies. The very words 'El Dorado' were enough to bring a smile to the lips of influential men who, under ordinary circumstances, might have considered backing a major expedition to the region. And so my manuscript and Kendall's rutter were locked away in a chest with other relics of the voyage to await a more propitious time.

There was another reason why the assembling of a fleet for the Indies was out of the question in the winter of 1595–6: Philip of Spain was preparing another invasion armada. Since 1588 scarce a year had passed without rumours of a fresh Spanish attack but this time there was no doubt. From spies, merchants and foreign visitors came news of ships being gathered in all the major ports of Spain and Portugal, of troops being levied and mercenaries hired, of money raised with the German and Italian bankers, of agents from Madrid ranging far and wide to commission meat, grain and wine for a great enterprise. In November the English shire levies were raised in all the southern counties and contingents of veteran soldiers sent to the principal coast towns to help organise defence. Despite these precautions a small force of Spanish galleys managed to attack Penzance and reduce part of the town to ashes. Throughout the country there was panic and, mingled with it, the resentment always engendered by such emergency measures as the billeting of soldiers on peaceful citizens and the taking of breadwinners away from their homes. For most Englishmen these were hard times; for three successive years harvests had been poor and I knew from my own tenants all about low grain yields and high flour prices. Merchants, too, found cause for complaint; the government forbade the movement of large ships which might have to be commandeered for the defence of the realm.

But what strategy was the government adopting for the coming conflict? The truth was, of course, that the Queen and her Council were at loggerheads. This was common knowledge in the society of the capital but, from time to time, I received inside information from Robin. Our meetings were infrequent now that I was not often at court but they were none the less cordial for that. Sometimes he would arrive unannounced at Bedford House and stay talking or playing cards far into the night. I think he found our home one of the few places where he could relax. Margaret and I belonged to his world and we had many friends and acquaintances in common. Yet, at the same time, we were apart from the strains and tensions of the personality conflicts and intrigues in which he was so deeply involved. He knew that with us he had no need to guard his tongue. Whatever the angry outburst, political confidence or outrageous opinion, it would go no further than the walls of Bedford House. He also knew that we accepted him in all his moods. For Robin, the passing years did not bring wisdom and discretion; if anything he seemed to grow even more unstable. Whenever he was shown into our parlour Margaret and I never knew whether we would find him elated or depressed, angry or melancholy, jubilant or indignant. During that December and January he vacillated so wildly that at times I feared for his sanity. Yet I had to admit he had some cause to be disturbed: the discussions in the Council about how to deal with the national emergency were long, frequent, and noted more for their heat than their sense of direction.

'It is the same as ever, Bear cub, if I suggest any policy it is opposed as a matter of principle by Burghley.'

We were sitting at supper a few days before Christmas in the new small dining-room. Margaret had had extensive changes made at Bedford House. The old hall had disappeared and this much more comfortable chamber was one of the suite of rooms which had replaced it. I looked up from my plate at the mention of Burghley's name.

'Surely he rarely comes to Council meetings now. He is a sick old man.'

'Oh, *he* is hardly ever there but his son is – the little hunchback – and he does as his father tells him. The Cecils and their friends control everything. You know what that means: every issue has to be considered in terms of money. It matters little if a course of action is right or wise or honourable; the question which must be asked is "Is it expensive?"'

The servants cleared the platters and set before us a dish of partridges from Kenilworth, an eel pie and lampreys in a cinnamon sauce. Margaret used the interlude to prattle about a visit to some mutual friend who had recently given birth to a boy. I made a great issue of tasting the sauce and finding it deficient in pepper. It was no use; as soon as the door closed behind the servers Robert continued reciting his catalogue of complaints.

'The Queen either cannot or will not see what the Cecils are planning. They control parliament between them and every office that falls vacant is filled with their friends. They are working themselves into an unassailable position so that when the Queen dies they will be indispensable to whoever takes her place.'

'The Queen has not made Robert Cecil Secretary.'

Robin laughed scornfully.

'No I *did* manage to prevent that, thank God.'

For some moments we ate in silence. The firelight glinted on silver and polished oak.

'So there is no decision on the Lord Admiral's plan, yet?'

'Oh no, we must wait until the Spanish crescents are sailing up the Channel again before her Majesty and Burghley actually make a decision to do anything.'

He drained his goblet and Margaret took the opportunity to try turning the conversation again.

'What is the Lord Admiral's plan, Robert?'

'Howard believes – and so does anyone with any sense – that the only way to stop the invasion is to strike first, destroy the Spanish fleet before it leaves harbour, perhaps even capture one of the coast towns and hold it to ransom.'

'That will need a lot of ships and men, will it not?'

Robin nodded.

'Two hundred capital ships and supply vessels with their crews and an army of fifteen thousand. Of course, "moneybags" Burghley says...'

'But there should be ways of recouping the expense: captured ships and cargo, ransomed towns?'

'Of course there are, Bear cub. Howard and I have said we will pay for the men and ships so that the expedition can get to sea at no charge to the treasury. There is no doubt that we can beat the Spaniards *and* make a profit.'

Margaret was still looking puzzled.

'But where will you find all the men and captains. Drake and Hawkins are away and many leading mariners with them.'

Robin laughed.

'I see you are determined to make a sailor of her, Bear cub. Yes, my pretty Meg, that is a problem. The Netherlands will send troops and ships and as for captains, well, Drake and Hawkins are not our only great mariners, you know. This young husband of yours has proved himself a fine commander.'

Margaret turned to me in alarm.

'Would you go, Robert?'

'Of course he would go. Nothing would stop him, eh, Bear cub. Why it would be just like old times.'

Hours later when we were lying side by side in bed Margaret repeated the question. I held her closer.

'My darling, how could I not go? England will need every captain she has. Would it make you very unhappy?'

'Only a little. I should be sorry if you were not here when our baby is born.'

I kissed her softly.

'A baby? Are you sure?'

'Yes.'

'When?'

'July.'

'July is a long way off. I may have gone and come back by then. Besides, you heard what Robin said. If the Cecils get their way there will be no expedition.

It was a week later that a message came from Robin. The Queen had agreed to a fleet being fitted out under the leadership of the Earl of Essex and Lord Howard of Effingham for the invasion of Spain. As joint commander of the expedition the Earl of Essex was empowered to offer me the command of one of the Queen's own warships, the *Nonpareil* of 500 tons.

17

'A brave sight, Ben.'

It was a bright March morning. Ben Wood and I were being rowed down the Medway from Rochester. All along the channel as far as we could see from Gillingham Reach to distant Queenborough the English war fleet rode at anchor. Hull upon gleaming hull, they stood proudly in the water from the smallest pinnace to the magnificent 800 ton *Ark Royal*. Pride and excitement possessed me, too. I was going to command one of the Queen's own great ships in what would probably go down in history as the most important naval venture of the age. Even Wood's attempt to prick the bubble of my ebullience failed to have any effect as I gazed among the bare masts and fresh-painted stern castles for my first glimpse of the *Nonpareil*.

'Put not your trust in chariots, Master Dudley. If the papists are to be beaten it must be the Lord will do it, as in '88.'

Then the boatman pointed and spoke in a husky voice which sounded full of Thames fog.

'There she is, my lord, beyond the big *Repulse* – and no finer ship in the fleet.'

The opinion was offered with the well-informed gravity of a man hoping for a good tip. I was more interested in Wood's judgement. Having drawn his moral, the solemn captain stroked his long jaw and eyed the *Nonpareil* critically. Her new paintwork gleamed in the piercing March sunlight. Her dark rows of open gunports looked efficiently menacing.

'She's a stout ship with a fine record: she fought well in '88. Of course, she's not as fast or as trim as the *Bear*.'

No, she was not the same as the *Bear*: no vessel would ever replace her in my affections, but there was a pride and a grandeur about the old *Nonpareil*. She had been the first to follow Drake's *Revenge* into the fray on that day when Philip's great Armada, fleeing from the hell-burners, had been decimated by the English fleet off Gravelines. She had been second only in rank to that same *Revenge* on the Lisbon raid in '89. And she had been a member of the already legendary Azores voyage from which the *Revenge* and Sir Richard Grenville had not returned. She boasted forty guns and carried a crew of two hundred and fifty sailors. There were bigger ships in the English fleet, some almost twice her size, but as I swung over the rail onto her maindeck, the *Nonpareil* seemed enormous. I felt very deeply the honour and responsibility of commanding her.

On one point I was quite determined: she should have the best crew I could muster. No drunken ruffians, pressed in waterside taverns would serve on my ship. My first move had been to locate Ben Wood and persuade him to be master of the *Nonpareil*. I wished that I could have had Kendall with me on my quarter-deck and still hoped that he would return from the Main in time to join my staff. Wood found fifty or so of the sailors who had been with us on the Indies voyage and they gladly signed on with me again. These men had already arrived and they welcomed me with a cheer as I stepped aboard. The bulk of the crew would be assembled nearer the time of embarkation. Wood had already retained some sailors in Plymouth and London and I had been approached by several of my tenants and neighbours asking me to take themselves or their sons on my ship.

There was another familiar figure waiting to greet me. George Popham had turned up at Bedford House on a bleak January day with an even bleaker story. The *Fury* had been severely damaged in the storms off Bermuda and had limped homewards leaking badly through several weakened joints. It had taken all the seacraft of Popham and his crew to keep their ship afloat. Long before reaching English waters they had jettisoned cargo, spare tackle, cabin furniture and everything else not absolutely necessary to their survival. The pumps were manned continuously night and day by the half-starved mariners. Then, just when they were beginning to believe they would make harbour safely, they were beset by a sudden squall and the gallant, old *Fury* resigned herself to the waves. When the crew abandoned her they were actually in sight of the Irish coast. Popham and his men had had several more adventures among the bogs and rebels of Ireland before reaching an English garrison. Within days of his return he was standing in my parlour asking for command of a Dudley ship. I told him I was planning no new venture but that I would welcome him on the *Nonpareil* as a lieutenant. Whatever George Popham's shortcomings, and they were many, I knew he would be a useful man to have at my side when it came to battling with other captains over our share of the expedition's victuals, supplies and equipment. And so it proved: thanks to George Popham the *Nonpareil* set sail with more beer and salt meat per man than any other ship in the fleet, and I knew that whatever damage she might sustain in the forthcoming battles she would not want for canvas, timber, rope, pitch or iron bars to make repairs.

There was nothing about the proprietorial figure who strode across the deck to meet us to suggest that he was a man worsted by fortune, a man who had lost everything. He beamed his welcome and clasped my hand enthusiastically, for all the world as though this were his ship and I an honoured visitor.

'There you are, Master Dudley, there you are. Good to see you – and you too, Ben. Well, come along, come along. I've a bite of dinner waiting in the great cabin. But you'll be wanting to look around first.'

He swept us off on a conducted tour, pointing out the principal features as he moved to the foredeck, then aft to the stepped half, quarter, and poop decks.

'Main and fore both carry to'gallants... two sweet demi-culverin at the prow... lighter guns on the fo'c'sle and half deck ... look at those fine thirty-five pounders... six officers' cabins – all crew quarters below decks...'

'Yes,' he concluded as he ushered us into the great cabin, an exhausting quarter of an hour later, 'she's a good ship, Master Dudley. She'll serve you well.'

Wood agreed as we seated ourselves at the table.

'I gather she's vice-admiral of the squadron, Master Dudley.'

'Yes, Lord Thomas Howard, leads the squadron in *Merhonour*.'

Popham pushed a pewter dish of steaming mutton towards me.

'I'm afraid we must serve ourselves; no servants aboard yet. Who have the other main commands?'

'Well, the Lord High Admiral himself is overall commander, of course, and leads the first squadron...'

'I thought the Earl of Essex shared the command with Admiral Charles Howard.'

'Essex has control of the land forces and is admiral of the second squadron, George, but Lord Charles Howard has supreme authority at sea. The third squadron, as you know, is ours under Lord Thomas Howard. The fourth squadron is led by Sir Walter Raleigh.'

'Raleigh?' Popham sputtered food all over the table. 'How in the name of all the saints...?'

'I imagine the Council had decided it needs every available captain.'

'But to give him a squadron...'

Wood shook his head.

'The man's pride would have forbidden him to accept less.'

'Aye,' Popham gestured with his knife. 'He'll not be ruled, especially by Essex and Howard. We'll have divided councils and in a battle that means lives lost.'

I knew he was right and I knew how hard Essex had fought his appointment but somehow Raleigh had gained the ear of Robert Cecil and that man's support counted for a great deal. Not very skilfully I turned the conversation towards the practicalities of the forthcoming campaign.

'You know, then, where we are bound, Master Dudley?' Wood asked.

'No, Ben, that is a close secret. The official story is that the fleet is being sent to join Drake and Hawkins for an invasion of the isthmus of Panama. Of course, that's just to deceive the Spaniards. I have no information about our real destination.'

Popham spoke through a mouthful of mutton.

'A raid along the Spanish coast to burn some of the ships.'

Wood shook his head.

'That would delay the armada but not stop it, like Drake's "singeing of Philip's beard" in '87. No, it's more than that. The rumour along the waterfront is that we're to attempt what the Spaniards tried to do to us eight years ago.'

Popham dropped his knife and belched appreciatively.

'Invade Spain? It's not possible.'

'With God everything is possible. And I pray it may be so. We shall have no peace until we rid the earth of papists. The Lord is our shield and buckler. Beneath his banner we can drive Antichrist and all his devils from Spain, Portugal – aye, even Rome . . .'

'I doubt whether that is exactly what her Majesty has in mind, Ben,' I said, trying to bring the zealot back to earth.

'That I don't know, Master Dudley. But I do know there's many a true Englishman in this fleet longing to settle papist Spain once and for all – men whose fathers were burned or tortured by the Holy Inquisition, men whose brothers died in the Irish wars, men whose friends have been lured away from God by Jesuits and Catholic priests.'

Ben Wood was right; there were many Englishmen who saw the conflict with Spain in just such clear-cut terms. Unfortunately, for everyone in whom the fires of religious fervour and national pride burned strongly and who hurried to enlist in Essex's army there were ten who ran away to hide when the muster officers called. Recruitment was long and difficult during that early spring of 1596. The *Nonpareil* and her companions were re-caulked, overhauled and refitted long before any sailing orders were received. The Queen herself was another cause of delay. Now she was resolved to send the fleet forth. Then she considered it was best kept at home for defence. Now she approved the secret plans drawn up by Howard and Essex. Then she changed them. For some days in April there was serious talk of diverting the expedition to Calais which the Spaniards had placed under siege, but while the royal mind was being made up the town fell and King Philip had a secure foothold on the French coast not twenty miles from Dover.

As the days and weeks passed with no sign of the fleet getting under way I began to think that I would, after all, be with Margaret for the birth of our first child. I spent as much time as possible at home with her. One afternoon towards the end of April we were walking in our garden at Bedford House overlooking the river. It had been raining earlier and the smell of damp earth was still in the air but the clouds had retreated and the world was fresh, crisp-edged and aglow with bright colours. Margaret sighed contentedly, looking across the sunlit water to the fields of Lambeth.

'It is lovely here when we can get out of doors.'

'Yes, my darling, but soon, very soon, you must leave for Kenilworth.'

She turned quickly, her back to the river wall.

'Oh, no, Robert, not before you go. I want to stay with you as long as possible.'

'I want that too but you must not stay in London any longer. There have already been a few cases of plague and with all the soldiers in town it will probably spread more quickly than usual.'

'But Robert...'

'No, my darling, for your own sake and the child's you must go.'

'Can you not come too?'

I took her hand.

'You know that is impossible. The order to sail may come at any time. We must arrange for some of your relatives to come and stay with you when the baby is due.'

We fell to discussing these domestic details but had not been doing so for very long when a boat scraped against our river stairs and unloaded a passenger. As he mounted the steps and came up to us I recognised one of my sailors, a slender, dark young man named James Miller. He doffed his cap and stood awkwardly before us.

'Message from Master Wood, sir.'

'Yes, James, what is it?'

'It's news of the Indies expedition, sir, the one led by Sir

Francis Drake and Sir John Hawkins. Master Wood didn't know whether you had heard.'

'No, are they back?'

'Some of them, sir, about half of them. A lot of them died of fever – Drake and Hawkins were among the ones that died – off Puerto Rico.'

Margaret gave a little cry and gripped my hand tightly. Drake and Hawkins both dead! Probably England's finest and certainly her most famous mariners. For a quarter of a century they had been the scourge of the Main and now they lay beneath its waters for ever. It was a cruel blow at a time like this. I thanked the messenger and told him to go to the kitchens for some dinner. But he remained where he was, fiddling with his woollen cap.

'That's not all the news, sir. Abraham Kendall is dead – the same day as Drake.'

I sent the seaman indoors and stood for a long time leaning on the garden wall looking out on the busy river with blurred eyes. Margaret came and lay her head on my shoulder.

'Did he mean so much to you?'

I rummaged through the jumble of images in my mind and saw the one-eyed bully towering over the frightened ship's boy.

'When we first met I hated him, but I think I came to love him. In a way I suppose he replaced my father.'

'You told me once that your Indies voyage would not have succeeded without him.'

'Nor would it. He saved us more than once.'

I recalled Abraham's brutal tongue and strong right arm, his savagery towards idle and stupid sailors, his straight talking to me and his fellow officers, his loyalty to me even when he believed I was wrong. They all added up to a man of wisdom and experience, a friend I could ill afford to lose and a mariner such as England badly needed.

'Are we watching the end of an age, Margaret?'

I put my arm round her.

'Our great captains – Frobisher, Cavendish, Grenville, Hawkins, Drake – all dead. The gifted statesmen gone – Leicester, Walsingham, even Burghley at death's door. Only the Queen outlives them all and how old is she?'

'Sixty-three, but no one is allowed to remind her. I think she feels it, too, that she is outliving her own best years and those of her country. She once said she believed that she and Philip of Spain were destined to go on fighting each other on earth for all eternity, making their own hell, while all the soldiers, sailors, captains, generals and statesmen worn out or slaughtered in their service enjoyed the bliss of heaven.'

She paused and we watched a pair of swans building their nest on the opposite bank.

'The Queen's tragedy is that she never had a baby.'

'Why do you say that?'

'Because having a baby makes you think of the future, not the past. Life will go on whatever we say or do, so we must work to make it a good life.'

'Or fight to make it a good life?'

She sighed deeply.

'I suppose so.'

Two days later I packed Margaret off to Kenilworth with an army of servants, midwives, wet nurses and women to fuss over her and cosset her. Towards the end she grew quite exasperated with my over-zealous attention to detail.

'If you overloaded your precious *Nonpareil* with crew and supplies as you are overloading me she would sink in the harbour.'

Later that day my summons to rejoin the fleet arrived. Wood and Popham had embarked all the crew and had everything ready for departure. On 1 May the fleet sailed out of the Thames estuary bound for Plymouth where we were to collect the troops and rendezvous with the small Dutch contingent. Only one vessel was left behind in the Medway. She was the *Warspite* and her commander was having difficulty recruiting a crew. Her commander was Sir Walter Raleigh and it was three weeks before he rejoined us.

We were a month in Plymouth. It did not take that long to embark the six thousand troops: once again we had to await our final sailing orders from the Queen. But the time was not wasted.

The army was a mixed contingent of raw levies, English veterans and Dutchmen. It was no easy task to weld them into a manoeuvrable fighting force, and day after day was filled with drilling and weapon practice in the fields beyond the town. Robin was magnificent. He was a hard master but he was as severe with himself as with the men and they loved him for it. Even the most inexperienced eye could recognise the skill which transformed a throng of fumbling recruits into a co-ordinated, eager militia.

The royal will and the direction of the wind finally combined to permit our departure on 3 June. Squadron by squadron we paraded along the Sound towards Rame Head; a hundred and thirty ships of all sizes, as proud a force as had ever sailed out of England. Every captain was given sealed orders but was commanded not to open them unless his ship became separated from the fleet. Since we were blessed with fine weather and no vessel went astray, we sailed steadily south-west by south for ten days in total ignorance of our destination. Only the war council, which consisted of the supreme commander, the squadron leaders and the colonels knew the expedition's overall strategy and they did not reveal their plans until 11 June. On that day Admiral Howard made the flag signal which summoned the captains of all the great-ships to a conference aboard the *Ark Royal*.

With a feeling of awe I took my seat in the flagship's great cabin. This was where the tactics had been agreed which destroyed the great armada of 1588. Howard of Effingham had sat at the head of this long table then as he was sitting now, though then his hair and beard were probably not white.

'Gentlemen we are now in approximately forty-two degrees of latitude and thirty leagues off the coast of Portugal. From this position we will steer a course south by east which will bring us around Cape St Vincent. Our objective, gentlemen, is Cadiz. Our orders are...'

The admiral's words were drowned in a buzz of conversation. So it was Cadiz again, the most vulnerable and the most prosperous of Philip II's ports. Drake and Essex had both led raids against it in the last decade, but surely more than a raid was intended this time.

Lord Howard tapped the table with his staff of office. The noise was not loud but it was sufficient. The admiral had a presence which needed little reinforcing with words or actions. The murmur of voices died away. When he had complete silence, Howard continued.

'Our orders, gentlemen, are to capture the town and to commandeer for her Majesty's use such shipping as may be in the harbour.'

There was a spontaneous roar of approval from all the junior captains who were hearing the plan for the first time. Here, at last, was a bold enterprise. This would hit proud Philip hard. To take and hold Cadiz, as he had recently taken and held Calais; to cut out the merchant ships and men of war in the harbour; it could cripple his war effort completely and force him to a permanent peace.

'My Lord of Essex is more familiar with the layout of the port, so I will ask him to present the plan of campaign in outline.'

Robin, on Howard's right, stood up and spread on the table a map of Cadiz. There it lay, the familiar outline of the double harbour, with the town standing at the seaward tip of the crescent-shaped promontory, the outer anchorage guarded by the Matagorda and Hercules batteries and the entrance passage restricted by sandbanks.

'Simplicity, my friends; that is the key to success in this operation. We have land and naval forces the enemy cannot match so there is no need for subtle plans. We anchor here off the seaward side of Cadiz and we land our troops for a frontal assault.'

'Madness!'

Everyone heard Raleigh's retort but Robin ignored it.

'When we command the town and the garrisons, the fleet will be able to enter the outer harbour in safety and capture the shipping.'

'Which by that time the Spaniards will have destroyed rather than allow it to fall into our hands.'

Robin was about to reply angrily when the admiral held up his hand.

'Sir Walter, you have presented these arguments in the war

council and you have been overruled. Please keep silent.'

'By your leave, my lord, these brave captains here are risking their lives and reputations in this expedition. They have a right to know that they are being denied their proper place in the action so that the army can take all the glory. If my lord of Essex . . .'

But my lord of Essex was shouting to drown Raleigh's protest.

'We all know who is more concerned about glory than the success of the expedition. Sir Walter here sees himself sailing valiantly into Cadiz harbour at the head of the English fleet so that he can be the first one in among the prize ships. It matters little to him how many of ours get blown out of the water by the land batteries.'

'How many soldiers do you suppose will be cut down by the Spanish guns before they ever reach the walls of Cadiz?'

'Sir Walter, I have asked you to be silent. And you, my lord, I must ask you to keep a tighter rein on your tongue. Gentlemen, I think I should tell you that in the war council Sir Walter Raleigh put forward the proposal that the Spanish shipping should be our first objective. He suggested that some of the smaller warships led by his own *Warspite* should sail into the harbour and capture whatever Spanish vessels are there before moving to attack the town. The war council considered this scheme carefully but rejected it because of the danger to our vessels from the shore batteries. And now I will ask the Earl of Essex to continue to outline the agreed plan.'

I did not listen closely to all that Robin had to say. I was worried, and for two reasons: I feared that the personal differences between him and Raleigh might tear the expedition apart, and I believed that on the issue of the invasion plan Raleigh was right. As the meeting dispersed and the captains waited for their longboats I went up to Robin who was talking with a group of friends on the quarterdeck. He was in high spirits and greeted me effusively.

'Bear cub! How are you? How do you like your *Nonpareil*? Sorry I have not been to see you on board your ship. Come on, let me take you back there now in my boat.'

We slid rapidly and easily over the calm green water in the

boat with the vice-admiral's pennant at the prow.

Robin laughed aloud.

'I have Raleigh where I want him now. Admiral Howard detests him – only he is too well-bred to say so – and there are no Cecils around for him to go running to. He will do as I say or I will have him before a martial court.'

'You cannot, Robin; not a squadron commander.'

'Howard and I have the Queen's commission. It gives us full judicial powers – *full* powers. I hope Raleigh gives me an excuse to use them.'

'Oh, come, Robin, you go too far.'

'What is this, Bear cub? Are you coming to Raleigh's defence? Have you forgotten he tried...'

'I shall never forget all that Raleigh has tried to do to me. I have no cause to love him, nor he me. But he is of no account.'

'Then what are you looking so disapproving about?'

'I am not sure that you are right about the frontal assault on Cadiz.'

'Oh, do you know better than Lord Howard and my colonels, then?'

'It will need a flat calm to land the men safely and it will still take time. The Spaniards will have no difficulty in getting their men to the beach. They may even bring their galleys out. You will be under fire from the battery, and our ships will not be able to get close enough inshore to help you.'

He scowled sullenly.

'God's blood, Bear cub, one venture and you come back a strategist. Do you suppose I have not thought of all that? What do you imagine I have been doing these past months? I have this invasion worked out to the last detail.'

'Perhaps the trouble lies just there, Robin. All the great strategists I have read agree that a general must be flexible above all else. Why are you so determined to follow your plan – because you know it is the best plan, or because Raleigh opposes it?'

I had risked Robin's anger because I thought it important to do so but he did not fly into a rage, perhaps because he did not want to lose control in front of the oarsmen. He looked away from me and appeared to be examining critically the array of stationary ships that seemed to fill the sea as far as the eye could see. He spoke quietly.

'Have I not done enough for you over the years to be able to depend on your loyalty now?'

When the fleet dropped anchor on the night of 19 June we were only a few miles from Cadiz. From a captured merchantman we had learned the welcome news that the harbour was crammed with Spanish shipping – laden merchant vessels and several men o'war, including Philip's proudest galleons, the four Apostles. During the hours of darkness, harness and weapons were distributed, cannon loaded, and final orders were despatched by Howard. We were to sail on at dawn, get as close as possible to the town and send our boats ashore, loaded with troops. If we could act quickly we would have the full advantage of surprise.

Next morning we shaded our eyes against the sun rising immediately behind Cadiz. The soldiers were drawn up in ranks on the decks. The chaplains had said prayers. The boats were unlashed. As we drew closer to the shore we expected and hoped to see a quiet town deep in slumber. What we did see, deployed across the entrance to the harbour under the guns of the forts, was a line of six galleons and five galleys. As if that was not bad enough, a freshening wind began to whip up a choppy sea.

18

How the defenders had got wind of our approach I do not know but there was no doubt that they were ready for us and that there would have to be a change of tactics. I said as much to Wood and Popham as we watched from the quarterdeck. Popham pointed towards the beach where figures could now be seen as the shadows thinned.

'Cavalrymen and pikemen. They've made a barricade there, too. There'll be no landing troops on that beach.'

'No, George, it will have to be a naval action. We must fight our way into the outer harbour.'

Wood gazed at the Spanish warships stretched between the patches of lighter coloured water which indicated sandbanks.

'There's not much room to manoeuvre. The admiral won't be able to use his bigger ships.'

'We can get the *Nonpareil* in there. She has a shallow enough draft.'

The others agreed enthusiastically. Wood shouted to the lookout at the maintop.

'Any signal from *Ark Royal*?'

'No signal, sir.'

We walked across to the starboard rail. Half a mile away the flagship gleamed in the early sunlight. There was no sign of activity, no extra pennants, no boats putting off with messages. Popham drummed his fingers impatiently on the rail.

'He must give the order, soon.'

I looked down into the ship's waist at the ranks of shuffling soldiers and the sailors grouped round the boats, ready to launch.

There was little I could do without fresh orders but I could make sure the *Nonpareil* was ready for action.

'Master Wood, please have the soldiers returned to quarters, stow the boats and call gun crews to stations.'

But before the master could carry out these orders there was another shout from the maintop.

'Boats putting off from *Repulse*, sir.'

'What boats?'

'Three boats, sir ... no four, carrying troops.'

I exchanged horrified glances with Wood and Popham. Followed by them and the other officers, I rushed up to the poop deck. Surely Robin was not pressing ahead with the original attack. We stared out over the stern. It was true: four boats loaded with armed men were bucking in the heavy swell as they pulled away from Essex's *Repulse*. Other captains were now following the vice-admiral's lead; several ships were lowering their boats.

'This is suicide!' Popham muttered angrily.

There was a sound of hurried steps on the companionway behind us.

'Permission to disembark the troops captain.'

I turned to see the young colonel in charge of the soldiers assigned to the *Nonpareil*. From his fresh face and eager expression I doubted whether he had seen any action before. He winced at my shouted reply.

'No!'

But he stood his ground. One hand involuntarily stroked the scarlet sash slanting across his breastplate. His brow wrinkled. He was deciding to assert his authority.

'Captain Dudley, you have your orders. I insist ...'

'My orders do not include sending you and your men to your deaths. Come here, colonel!'

I pointed to a nearby group of boats. They sat heavily in the water and the oarsmen were struggling to make headway against waves which rolled them dangerously from side to side. Even as we watched one of them dropped into a deep trough. Water poured in on both sides and she capsized instantly. Men shouted and screamed. They struggled to keep their heads above water.

They grabbed at floating oars, at the overturned boat, at their colleagues. Several sank immediately, weighed down by their armour.

'Quick, Master Wood, have a boat away to search for survivors!'

I looked around the anchorage at a dismal and heartrending scene of confusion: boats setting out for the shore, boats turning back, boats floundering, boats overturning, boats holding fast to the protection of their mother ships.

'Wood, see what you can do for any of those poor devils who need help. Popham, Farroll, Winter, come with me.'

With my small escort of officers I had myself rowed across to the *Merhonour* to talk with the squadron leader. Lord Thomas Howard (who was only distantly related to our admiral) greeted me civilly on his own quarterdeck where he stood with his officers. He was a slight man, with a thin face and anxious, darting eyes. Strangers who met him for the first time sometimes mistook his unprepossessing appearance and brevity of speech for weakness. Nothing could have been further from the truth: he owned a wisdom beyond his thirty-five years and his bravery had been proved in every major naval campaign since the defeat of the Great Armada. I was relieved to see that he had not disembarked any of his soldiers.

'You have come to me for instructions, Captain Dudley?'

'Yes, my lord.'

'And what can I tell you; I am under the same orders as yourself.'

'Which you have not carried out.'

'Which I have not *yet* carried out.'

'But there can be no question of landing the army under these conditions.'

'As I have sent to inform the Earl of Essex.' He waved a hand towards the *Repulse*. I saw a longboat crossing the water between the two ships. 'I suggest we wait for my lord's reply. Have you breakfasted? No? Then perhaps you will join us.' He led the way to the great cabin.

The news from the *Repulse* arrived while we were still eating. Essex was holding to his original plan but had decided to wait until the wind dropped. Lord Howard received the information in silence and chewed thoughtfully on a leg of chicken. I must have shown more impatience than the others, who were used to Howard's ways, for he turned to me.

'That does not please you, Captain Dudley. Why is that?'

'I think we could wait days for the weather to improve, my lord. By then the Spaniards may have burned their ships, hidden their valuables or even obtained reinforcements.'

'I fear you are right.' He stood up quickly. 'I will go to the admiral.' He strode to the doorway. I hurried after him.

'My lord, would it not be quicker if our squadron began the attack . . .'

Howard smiled and laid a hand on my shoulder.

'It might. It might also be disastrous. If, through delay, we lost Cadiz, that would be an immense disappointment. If, through precipitate action, we launched a disorganised attack and lost half our ships and men, that would be an irredeemable catastrophe. Please finish your meal and then return to your ship. Rest assured that as soon as I have fresh orders you will know them.'

It was mid afternoon before those orders arrived. I was in my cabin writing my log when a servant came to report that the squadron leader's longboat was approaching.

'Very well, send the messenger in here when he arrives.'

I carried on writing but almost immediately the man was back, looking flustered.

'Sir, it's not a messenger; it's Lord Howard himself.'

I hurried on deck.

'Ah, Captain Dudley, I apologise for thrusting myself upon your hospitality unannounced.' Howard, dressed in undemonstrative black, glanced critically along the ranks of soldiers and seamen Wood had hastily formed up on the main deck. 'Very good, Master Wood, thank you, thank you. Now, Captain, if we might talk.'

Seated in my cabin and sipping sack, Howard explained his unexpected arrival.

'The admiral, after some persuasion, shares our opinion, Captain. The troops, as you will have noticed are all re-embarked.

We are to force the entrance to the harbour, deal with the enemy shipping and land our army on the landward side of the town. I am to lead the attack and, since my own ship is too deep in the draught I am transferring my flag to the *Nonpareil*. Captain Dudley you will be at the head of the invasion of Cadiz.'

I was going to lead the attack! The fleet was replete with experienced naval commanders but I was going to be the first in the battle line! The taciturn Howard might make it sound quite unremarkable but, in fact, it was an unprecedented honour. It took me completely by surprise and I made a mess of expressing my thanks.

A smile passed momentarily over Lord Howard's face.

'It is your due. You are an accomplished captain and you have made more impression than you realise on the leaders of the English navy.' He stood up. 'Come, Captain, we have work to do. The attack begins at dawn so the ships must be moved into position before nightfall. Oh . . . and I fear I must commandeer your cabin.'

I slept little that night and it was not Ben Wood's bed, whose owner I had in turn dispossessed, which was to blame. Having spent the hours of daylight checking guns, powder, muskets, grappling gear and everything else that could be checked, I passed the night going over in my mind all the details of the channel, tide, wind direction and sail-setting. The Spaniards had drawn their galleons and galleys back at dusk and I knew that all their laden merchantmen would have been moved into the inner harbour where they could be defended by warships and the Puntal garrison. It was there, at the mouth of the inner harbour that the fighting would be. Somehow, we had to find a way of breaking through that barrier. These were the problems which interlaced themselves with strands of sleep and which were still with me when I arose in the middle of the second watch.

It was Popham's watch and I found him talking to the fore-deck guard. We paced the deck together, swinging our arms to keep warm.

'All quiet, George? No sound of movement ashore?'

He hesitated slightly.

'No, no movement *ashore.*'

'What do you mean by that?'

'There seemed to be a lot of disturbance on one of our ships a little while ago – orders being shouted, men running about the deck, and I thought I heard an anchor being raised.'

'Probably some poor devil being marched away to be clapped in irons for falling asleep on watch. Unless, of course, George, you nodded off and dreamed it all.'

But for a few moments we both stood silently, straining our ears to detect the slightest sound and peering for any unusual movement among the thicket of black masts crowding the sea astern of us. The first suggestion of day outlined the landward horizon but it was still too dark to distinguish individual ships and from our position at the head of the column we could see no stern lights.

'Well, all's quiet now, George. We will have the crew roused at the next turn of the hour-glass. Better wake the duty cook now. I want something hot in the mens' bellies before...'

This time we both heard it and there was no mistaking the sound: the grind of ropes through pulleys, the rasp of spars against the mast; someone was hoisting a sail. Popham swore.

'Someone's leaving the line.'

'They must have been ordered away by the admiral.'

'Has Lord Howard said anything to you about sending ships somewhere else?'

'No.'

'No. I thought not.'

'What's the matter, George?'

'Perhaps I have a suspicious mind, Master Dudley, but it occurs to me that someone may be dissatisfied with his place in the battle line.'

Then we saw her. About half a mile astern the outline of a ship detached itself from the black mass of hulls and the tangle of masts and rigging. It was under a single sail and it was moving slowly towards us.

'Quick! Call the crew to stations! Send to rouse Lord Howard!

No, rouse him yourself; ask him if he will be good enough to join me on the quarterdeck.'

When, a few minutes later, Lord Howard stood beside me, a servant still fussing around tying his points and adjusting his cloak, the sky had lightened to a pigeon grey and the moving ship was fully visible bearing down on our starboard quarter. The other vessels were now alive with running men. From every quarterdeck the rebel was hailed as she passed. That was how I caught the name before I recognised the ship. I was not surprised. Nor was Lord Howard.

'So Raleigh feels himself cheated of the place of honour and is determined to go in first.'

'Permission to weigh anchor and hoist sail, my lord? The men are all ready. We can beat *Warspite* if we move now.'

'I think not, Captain Dudley. The channel is narrow and still shallow at half tide. If we race for it together one or both of us will end up on the sandbanks. That will block the entrance and none of our ships will be able to get through.'

'But we cannot allow Raleigh to flaunt his disobedience.'

'I fear there is little we can do to stop him without jeopardising the whole operation.'

Warspite was now drawing alongside us. I could make out Raleigh's figure at the quarterdeck rail. I could imagine the supercilious smile. Lord Howard cupped his hands and shouted across the water.

'Sir Walter, what is the meaning of this? I command the assault. Drop anchor immediately!'

The answer came back clearly in Raleigh's high, thin whine of a voice.

'Good morning, my lord. What is delaying you? Follow me and we will rattle these Spaniards out of their beds.'

The *Warspite* slid past and sailed towards the harbour. Rage, frustration and despair swept over me. It was not just the personal snub and the bitter disappointment which hurt so much; I was enraged that the petty rivalries and antics of popinjays like Raleigh should be able to upset carefully laid battle plans. Partly I was annoyed with myself, for I knew that, but for the restraining influence of my superior, I would even now be racing the *Nonpareil* against the *Warspite* for death or glory.

Lord Howard spoke quietly but with a precise venom which was the nearest he came to expressing anger.

'I could almost wish that the Spanish guns would send that fool to the bottom of Cadiz Bay.'

'Do we follow, my lord?'

'I *follow* Raleigh? No, Captain, our plan remains unchanged. If Sir Walter wants to take on the shore batteries and the four Apostles single-handed, so be it. Before the morning is past he may well be beseeching our help. That is a prospect I find rather pleasing. And now that that distasteful incident is over, perhaps we may eat. I take it you are not sending me into battle with an empty stomach?'

As we sat at breakfast we heard the cannon begin their dialogue. Howard was quite unmoved, even when a messenger came aboard from the admiral demanding to know why we had not yet engaged the enemy in strength. Only when he had satisfied himself that the crews were fed and ready for battle did he give the order to weigh anchor.

Sails bulging before an onshore breeze, the *Nonpareil* leaped forward eagerly like a young stallion given its head. She ran rapidly between the shoals of Las Puercas and El Diaman and drew abreast of Cadiz atop the cliffs to starboard. The guns of the harbour garrison opened fire. The water spouted around us. The artillerymen knew their range. All too vividly I recalled the fate of the captured *San Felipe* on the last occasion I had run this gauntlet seven years before. Every moment I expected to hear the hideous crack and to see a tangle of canvas, ropes and shattered timber come crashing to the deck. We did not return the fire: our powder and shot were reserved for a more vulnerable foe.

Then we were through and sailing across the broad waters of the outer harbour. It was empty and devoid of movement. All the action was confined to the point ahead of us where the wooded slopes closed in from both sides to the narrow Puntal gap. Across the gap the four Apostles, *San Andrés*, *San Mateo*, *San Felipe* and *Santo Tomás*, were anchored. They were firing intermittently together with the Puntal garrison. Their target was the *Warspite* which, displaying fairly considerable superficial damage, had drawn back out of range and was answering with occasional shots from her culverin.

Lord Howard, who had joined me on the foredeck, allowed himself a satisfied chuckle.

'Our impetuous colleague seems to have found the oven a little too hot for his baking. Now, Captain, have larboard gun crews ready, if you please. We will pass *Warspite*'s stern and swing to starboard. Continuous larboard broadsides as we cross the front of the enemy. Come across as far as possible to let our other ships follow.'

I gave the orders and *Nonpareil* veered close in to the larboard shore to give *Warspite* as wide a berth as possible. There was not much room and, as we passed her stern I had a fleeting but clear view of Raleigh standing on her poop deck and shouting at us. But there was no time to bother with Sir Walter's antics. I had to bring my ship hard round to starboard, keeping one eye on submerged rocks and the other on the formidable array of galleons.

We slewed across in front of *Warspite* and opened fire. So did the four Apostles. The uproar was deafening: thundering cannon, braying trumpets, men shouting and running, the whine of great shot and the crackle of splintering wood. I could scarcely hear my own voice when I issued orders.

'Master Wood, take her to within three hundred yards of the fortress and drop anchor.

'Boy! Tell the master gunner I must have more rapid firing.'

'Master Savage, get that wounded man below.'

There was little time to look at the enemy. Through the smoke I could see that all four ships had some damage. The *Santo Tomás*, I thought, was listing slightly. I felt a hand on my shoulder. A young officer was pointing to starboard and shouting excitedly.

'Sir, the *Warspite*.'

I hurried to the starboard rail. *Warspite* was moving again. Angry at being overtaken, Raleigh was thrusting his ship into the battle line. On her present course she must ram us amidships.

'Tell the helmsmen to bring her thirty degrees to larboard, quickly!'

'Master Wood!'

Benjamin clattered up the companionway. I pointed out the *Warspite* and our change of direction.

'Drop anchor before we run in too close to the enemy guns.'

Lord Howard came up to the rail as Raleigh's ship passed within feet, then veered to starboard, effectively blocking our path. The *Nonpareil*'s crewmen had to work like demons taking in sail and dropping anchor to keep us from ramming *Warspite*'s stern.

Howard swore.

'If it were not for the other men aboard that ship I would willingly sink Sir Walter with my own cannon. Captain Dudley go across and tell him that he is endangering lives unnecessarily and that I order him to withdraw.'

I was trembling with fury as I climbed up the *Warspite*'s side. I was taken to the quarterdeck and Raleigh was made aware of my presence. He glanced casually in my direction then ignored me completely. For fifteen minutes he busied himself ordering subordinates and talking with his officers. At the end of that time my patience snapped. I strode across, caught hold of him by the arm and shouted above the roar of the battle.

'By God, sir, you shall hear me!'

Raleigh turned upon me a look of utmost contempt and shrugged off my arm. I was forced to talk to his back.

'Lord Howard orders you to withdraw and to stop your hazardous, childish behaviour.'

This time Raleigh did deign to reply, though he still refused to face me.

'I am not under Lord Howard's orders.'

'Lord Howard has command of the attack.'

'Lord Howard does not command me or my squadron.'

'Sir Walter, will you withdraw? You are in the way. You are preventing my ship and others getting broadside on to the enemy.'

'My poor young man, if you cannot handle your ship you should not be here. And now that you have run your errand, you may hurry back to your master.'

'Very well and I will report that Sir Walter Raleigh is as incapable of commanding a ship in battle as he is of founding colonies or finding El Dorado.'

I turned and hurried down to the main deck but at the rail Raleigh caught up with me, his face contorted with hate and fury.

'Do not suppose because you are a relative of the admiral and one of Essex's cronies that you can insult me!'

'All I have said I am prepared to prove with my sword.'

'Then we shall meet later and I shall take great pleasure in killing you. I detest and despise you ...'

I turned my back and climbed over the rail, but as I descended the rope ladder and jumped into my waiting boat Raleigh leaned over screaming with such maniacal frenzy that his words carried clearly above the thunder of battle.

'You may have wealth and powerful kinsmen but they will not save you. You have crossed me once too often. You cheated me on the Orinoco. You tried to cheat me here. I deserve the place of honour ... I am better ... experienced ... soldier ...' His ravings were lost in the tumultuous cacophony of cannon, musket and drum.

The *Warspite* did not budge. As a result the battle lasted at least an hour longer than necessary since most of the English ships could not bring all their guns to bear with full effect. But the Apostles took more punishment than they gave. Their cannon fire became increasingly ragged and by one o'clock it had ceased almost entirely. Lord Howard ordered boats and boarding parties away. Minutes later I was in the stern of a brig being rowed across the debris-strewn water towards the *San Mateo*. Musket-shot flecked the sea all around us. Just in front of me a soldier jumped up with a hand to his throat. Blood seeped through the fingers as he toppled overboard. I got my fingers round his harness straps. As the rowers back-paddled, we drew the man inboard and laid him on the boards but we knew as we did so that the staring eyes would see nothing more in this world.

The musket fire ceased. As we pulled once more towards the *San Mateo*, the great galleon began to move. But it was not a directed, purposeful movement; the cables had been cut and the ship was drifting towards the rocks beneath Fort Puntal. Beyond her we could see a boatload of men disappearing across the inner harbour. Other soldiers and sailors were not so lucky. They swarmed to the side and slithered down ropes or threw themselves into the sea. Some reached the rocks and scrambled ashore. Some did not.

'Faster! Row faster! We must reach her before she runs aground.'

The sweating sailors put their backs into the work but still the great leviathan seemed to be moving more swiftly than us. At last we were alongside and swarming up ropes and torn rigging to the deck. Every moment I expected to hear the sound of tearing timbers as the *San Mateo* ran onto submerged rocks.

'Bosun, find the whipstaff and bring her prow round seaward.'

'You, take six men and search for prisoners!'

The young colonel from the *Nonpareil* ran across the deck.

'Your pardon, Captain, *I* will give orders to my men.'

I grabbed hold of the starboard mainsail brace which was hanging loose, and thrust it into his hand.

'Save your breath! Take hold of that rope and when the mains'l's up pull on it for all your worth.'

I left him and hurried away to organise two teams of men to hoist the mainsail. With much grunting and swearing we yanked the yard and its heavy weight of canvas aloft, then fastened the ropes to the kevels. I rejoined the colonel and helped him to pull the sail round. The *San Mateo* was almost under the lee of Puntal Head. There was no time to hoist more sail. I prayed that we had enough up to swing the unwieldly vessel away from the rocks. My eyes were fixed on the grassy bush-scattered slope dead ahead. It no longer appeared to approach us. Slowly it swung away to leeward.

A series of staccato explosions rocked the ship, tilting my field of vision at a sudden angle. Turning, I saw the *Santo Tomás* ablaze from stem to stern, a smoking hole where her forecastle had been. The Spaniards must have fired her before deserting her and the flames had reached the powder store. Minutes later the

San Felipe went up as well, showering us with burning fragments. By this time the *San Mateo* was gliding safely into the deeper waters of the outer harbour. I handed the rope I was holding to one of the seamen. A voice behind me spoke.

'We had better anchor, Captain Dudley. I know not if there were any of our men aboard the burning ships but we must stay and see if our help is needed.'

'Yes, my lord. I did not know you were aboard.'

Lord Howard laughed.

'Did you want *all* the glory for yourself.'

'No, my lord . . .'

'You have given an excellent account of yourself and I shall say so when I report to the admiral.'

I sent George Popham off with the brig to pick up survivors and he returned with six English soldiers and three prisoners. I reported to Lord Howard on the *San Mateo*'s high poop deck.

'Good, Captain Dudley, then there is nothing more we can do here. Have the galleon anchored in the middle of the harbour and then return to your ship. I must go back aboard the *Merhonour*. First, I thank you for your hospitality; I have found my stay most exhilarating.'

'It has been a pleasure to have you aboard, my lord. I presume we go on into the inner harbour now.'

'The orders were to proceed to invest the town. As you can see, my lord of Essex and several of the other commanders are already disembarking their troops.'

It was true. After the initial assault carried out by the smaller warships, most of the English fleet had come into the harbour. About half of the total force had now anchored and boatloads of soldiers were being landed on the shore between Fort Puntal and the town.

'But the way into the inner harbour is now open. There are forty or more merchantmen in there completely at our mercy. They are fine ships laden with money, military supplies and who knows what else. It will take a couple of days to breach the defences of Cadiz. By that time what will remain of the shipping?'

I pointed to the two blackened Apostles which had settled, still smouldering, in the shallows.

'Either way there is a risk: attack the town and we may lose the merchantmen; go after the shipping and reinforcements may arrive at Cadiz.'

'Why not divide our forces, my lord?'

Howard stroked his beard and gazed across the harbour.

'An excellently diplomatic solution but one unlikely to commend itself to Essex. You are a friend of his, are you not. Then, you know that "moderation" and "compromise" are words which have no place in his vocabulary. Doubtless the noble earl considers that the navy has had quite enough glory for one day.'

'Then we must land all our troops immediately?'

'Those are our orders.'

'And wait around out here doing nothing while the army invades and loots the town?'

Lord Howard turned to look at me, a faint smile on his face, his head on one side.

'As to what happens after the soldiers are disembarked, we have no instructions. Somehow, I do not see Robert Dudley waiting around doing nothing. Now, I must take my leave. Come, I will take you to the *Nonpareil* on my way back to the *Merhonour*.'

From the *Nonpareil*'s quarterdeck my officers and I had an excellent view of the sack of Cadiz. We saw the troops landed in good order. Too late, a detachment of Spanish cavalry swept down towards the beach from the higher ground. By the time they arrived Essex had the bulk of his men lined up in battle formation. A few furious salvos from the English musketeers sent the horsemen galloping back towards the town. The afternoon sun glinted on their armour as the army marched by companies up the slope towards Cadiz. At some half a mile from the walls Essex halted his vanguard and his trumpets blared defiance at the defenders. It was apparently an attempt to goad the Spanish garrison into a foolhardy foray and it worked. A small force came out from the town, engaged the invaders in a brief skirmish, then retreated at full speed. With a roar which carried clearly across the water the English force broke into a charge. Whether it was a planned assault or a breakdown of discipline I do not know but the vanguard rushed right up to the walls of Cadiz. We watched anxiously, helplessly, expecting to see our countrymen cut down by fire from the ramparts. But there was very little sound of gunfire and the next thing we saw was the St George being waved from the top of the wall. Somehow a way had been found into the town. The middle and rear guards advanced at the run and poured in through the open gates. I remembered Peniche and could imagine only too well what was now happening in the town. Essex's orders to the army had forbidden rape and any kind of violence to women, children and priests but six thousand men on the rampage could not be controlled, and the officers would be too busy taking pictures, ornaments, money, crucifixes, gold and silver plate, jewels and the rich merchandise from the shops of Cadiz to worry themselves much about the behaviour of their men.

'That was easy work and there'll be rich pickings for it.' George Popham spoke ruefully and there was a chorus of agreement.

I looked around at the officers. None of them said anything but I knew what they were thinking.

'You want to go and join in the fun, do you?'

It was meant to sound sarcastic but one of the junior officers took my words at face value.

'Yes, sir. It's not right that we should do all the work and the soldiers get all the booty.'

Wood pointed across the anchorage.

'Some of the other captains seem to have come to the same decision.'

Boatfuls of jubilant-looking sailors were, indeed, putting off from other vessels. In the waist of the *Nonpareil* groups of disgruntled men were murmuring together or looking pointedly up at the quarterdeck. It was time to make a decision.

'Very well, if booty and action are what you want you shall have them. All men to their stations please, Master Wood. Ready to weigh anchor.'

As soon as the ship was under way I brought her round to face the entrance to the inner harbour. If no one else was going after the merchant shipping then I would have to do it myself. I hoped that other commanders would follow my lead but as the *Nonpareil* slid past the wrecks of the two Apostles and the now-silent Puntal battery there was no movement among the fleet. Apparently everyone else was more intent on the easier rewards to be had in Cadiz.

It was a mouth-watering sight that met our eyes as we emerged onto the peaceful inner harbour: row upon row of anchored merchantmen together with three or four warships and some galleys. I looked round at my companions.

'The choice is ours gentlemen; which one shall we have first?'

Popham scanned the anchorage with an expert eye.

'Yonder fat-bellied argosy with the blue flag over on the starboard bow. She sits low in the water and she's the kind of ship I've seen in the silver fleets.'

'Very well, George, and if she is carrying nothing better than cheap Sicilian wine we will make you drink every drop.'

Ben Wood tapped my arm and pointed to the other side of the bay.

'They've let slip the guard dogs.'

With steady drum beats, two galleys were skimming rapidly towards us like multi-legged pond insects. It was my first sight of these vessels in action and I had never seen anything more menacing: the slim lines, the low, ram-shaped prow, the six long-range guns mounted on the fore-platform, the ranks of heavily-armed troops waiting to grapple and swarm up our sides. It was Wood who seized the initiative.

'Furl mains'l! Come round ten points to larboard!'

As the orders were carried out, the master explained.

'They'll try to come one each side. We must present our broadside and fire at them before they split up.'

For the first time since I had known him George Popham looked worried.

'We mustn't let them board, Master Dudley. They outnumber us heavily, and,' he looked around towards the harbour entrance, 'we're all alone.'

The larboard cannon crashed out in unison. The galleys opened fire at the same moment. A ball splintered the poop deck rail.

Another tore through one of the fore-deck gun crews. Water spouted up round the galleys. One of them had its leading oars shattered and slowed down. But still they came on. The faster of the two pulled away to pass round our stern.

'Hoist mains'l, Master Wood.'

' 'Tis no use, Master Dudley, we shan't outpace them.'

The stern chasers were doing good work: they silenced two of the bow guns on the leading galley but she continued on the broad arc which would bring her round to our starboard side.

'You see how it'll be,' Popham explained. 'They'll come in head-on from both sides, presenting the smallest possible target. Then they'll ram or grapple and board us over their prows. Shall I give out the muskets?'

'There must be something else we can do.'

'Very little. They're deadly efficient in packs or pairs against single vessels.'

In desperation I looked around the harbour. Still there was not a friendly sail in sight. Then a seed of an idea – it was certainly no more – fell into my mind.

'Master Wood, hold them off as long as you can. Popham fetch a dozen men and come with me.'

The brig was still attached to the stern by a painter. We pulled it alongside and dropped into it.

'Now for your fat-bellied argosy, George!'

The *Nonpareil* had anchored two hundred yards short of her intended prize. It was the nearest ship which was why I had chosen it. We all pulled at the oars and were soon bumping alongside.

'Any sign of life, George?'

With drawn swords we swarmed up the merchantman's side. As if to answer my question three Spanish sailors hurriedly rushed forward, took one look, dropped their weapons and threw themselves into the sea.

'Cut the cables, Master Popham! You two, up aloft and unfurl mains'l.'

The seamen lifted their eyes to the main yards and did not move. I followed their gaze. The yards were bare. The crew had taken down the sails to make capture as difficult as possible.

'Curse them! Have they left no sails at all?'

'Mizzen, sir.'

'Then why are you standing there, man? Hoist it!'

'You, there, see if there are any cannon.'

There were no cannon.

Slowly, very, very, slowly the sluggish vessel made way. I ran to the fore-deck to see how the *Nonpareil* was faring. I almost wished I had not. The galley to larboard of my ship was in great difficulty, badly crippled by cannon shot. But the other had successfully completed its manoeuvre. Its sharp prow was buried in the *Nonpareil*'s side. Spanish soldiers were streaming forward. Grappling ropes were flying through the air. Wood and his crew were keeping up an intense musket fire but they could not hold off the attackers for long. Almost imperceptibly the distance closed. Time and again I discharged my pistol at the boarders. It was little more than a gesture of frustration. With a bow chaser I could have blasted the Spaniards out of the water, for she was dead ahead. As it was, the ship was my only weapon – and she was too slow. Already there were a handful of attackers on the *Nonpareil*'s deck. We were going to be too late.

The merchantman may have been slow but she was heavy. Once under way she was difficult to stop. That quality was excellent for the role of battering ram I had decided that she should play. I steered her as close as possible to the *Nonpareil* and almost brushed her starboard guns. The Spaniards were engrossed in the battle. Many of them did not see us until it was too late. We struck the galley amidships. Wedged as it was against the *Nonpareil*, it could not float clear. It crumpled beneath our bow like a toy ship. The water was littered with splintered wood and screaming men. The merchantman rode obliviously on.

By the time I had brought her to a halt and gone back aboard the *Nonpareil* the fighting was over. Several of my men were wounded but a dozen Spaniards lay dead on the deck. The other galley was hobbling back towards the shore and there was no point in giving chase. No more opposition was offered. I put a crew aboard the prize and gave them one of the warship's spare mainsails. Then as the sun was setting I took my two vessels back past Fort Puntal. As we anchored once more in the outer harbour I went to my cabin and lay, fully clothed on my bed. Within seconds I was asleep.

But that was not the end of the day's events. My page, Will Bradshaw, roused me about midnight. I followed him on deck and looked towards Puntal headland. It stood, densely black, against a sky of vivid, garish, flickering vermilion – the glow caused by a gigantic bonfire of forty first class ships and their cargoes.

I examined the prize next day. She was the *Rosario* of Cartagena carrying pay and military supplies to the army at Calais. There were chests full of gold and silver coin, barrels of gunpowder, a whole armoury of swords and handguns and bales of cloth and leather for making shirts and jerkins. Later I went ashore. Making my way through crowds of jubilant and drunken soldiers I eventually found the bishop's palace where Admiral Howard had established his headquarters. I found him seated with several officers in a marble courtyard beside a pool with playing fountains. I presented my report and formally surrendered my prize ship. The old sailor listened courteously, thanked me and invited me to stay for dinner. Over the meal several of the gentlemen questioned me in detail about the action with the galleys and I asked them about the taking of Cadiz. One interesting item of news I heard was that Raleigh had been wounded in the leg and was confined to his bed. I reflected that he would have to wait until his limb was mended before he could avenge my 'insults'. I underestimated him.

We remained for about two weeks in Cadiz. Essex and his supporters wanted to stay longer and fortify the town so that it could be used in peace negotiations with King Philip. He suggested that it might be exchanged for Calais, which the Queen had always wanted to regain for England. But the curse of divided command fell once more upon an English expedition. The majority of the senior officers were only interested in getting home with all their loot. Essex was forced to yield and thus the second great opportunity was thrown away: first the merchant fleet, now Cadiz itself. There was nothing to be done but to tear down the walls, blow up the castle and the batteries and sail for home.

We had been at sea for some five days when I received a message that I was to go aboard the *Ark Royal*. As my boat threaded its way through the fleet towards the flagship I wondered, with growing excitement why I had been sent for. It was not a general council; no other captains had been summoned. I knew that in Cadiz several military and naval commanders had been knighted for their conduct in the battle. Had the leaders decided belatedly that some honour was due to me?

I was kept waiting for several minutes on the main deck of the *Ark Royal*. Then two soldiers escorted me into the great cabin. The whole war council was seated along one side of the long table, with the Lord High Admiral in the centre. I was asked to stand in front of them. The two soldiers remained behind me. The atmosphere in the room was one of great solemnity. I looked, puzzled and alarmed, along the row of set, unsmiling faces. The admiral addressed me.

'Captain Robert Dudley you must understand that this is a martial court convened in accordance with the authority vested by her Majesty in the Earl of Essex and myself.'

A court? A trial? I looked at Robin. His eyes remained fixed on the papers before him.

'You are charged with two offences prejudicial to the conduct of the campaign and the safety of her Majesty's subjects. My lord of Essex, will you read the charges?'

Robin cleared his throat. He still would not look at me.

'Charge one: that you did mutinously threaten a senior officer, thereby challenging the authority vested by her Majesty in that officer and inciting others to mutiny. Charge two: that you did, without orders, attack enemy vessels thereby hazarding her Majesty's warship *Nonpareil*, needlessly endangering the lives of her crew and prejudicing the success of the expedition.'

The Lord High Admiral leaned forward.

'Captain Robert Dudley, you have heard the charges. What do

you say to them?'

My mind was in a tumult but I heard myself answer, distantly. 'I say the charges are utterly false, my lord.'

'Very well. The court will now hear evidence. The prisoner may not question the witnesses but will be allowed to address the court at the end of the proceedings. Sir Walter Raleigh, will you speak to the first charge?'

I scarcely listened as Raleigh told a highly coloured version of our argument aboard the *Warspite*. I was too busy trying to understand what lay behind this absurd trial. The first charge must obviously be put down to Raleigh's malice. Yet I felt sure that he would not have been allowed to make such an issue of the matter if the second charge had not been agreed upon. Sir Walter's private vendettas were too well known.

Why, then, was I being blamed for my attack on the merchant shipping? The capture of the *Rosario* was the major achievement of the whole Cadiz campaign. The three prize ships and the Queen's share of the Cadiz plunder were all that Howard and Essex had to show for what was a very expensive expedition. For, although they had personally borne a great part of the cost, the government had advanced £50,000 on the promise of repayment out of confiscated treasure. If I had not brought out the *Rosario* she would have been burned with the rest of the shipping in the inner harbour.

Slowly the truth revealed itself: they needed a scapegoat. They had realised that the Queen and the Council were not going to be pleased with the outcome of the Cadiz venture. Embarrassing questions were going to be asked and the most embarrassing would be, 'Why did you not make sure of the Spanish merchantmen which would have more than defrayed the costs of the expedition?' Now they had found an answer: 'An irresponsible captain made a private attack on the ships and this frightened the Spaniards into setting fire to them.' I fought a losing battle against panic: I could cheerfully face my country's enemies; I was more than a match for jealous rivals; but political warfare, the subtle undermining of a man's reputation with no regard for truth, what defence was there against that?

Raleigh finished his story and then called in one of his officers who confirmed that I had threatened Sir Walter's life. I had also, apparently, vowed I would bring my own men aboard the *Warspite* and move it, if Raleigh refused to do so. Having disposed of that point the court went on to consider the second indictment. To my horror I heard Robin's voice reading the evidence against me. He had been my only hope. I had been sure that he would say a few words on my behalf. Had our recent argument so embittered him that he was prepared not only to sacrifice me, but to wield the knife personally?

'Captain Dudley, on 21 June in the afternoon you launched a single ship attack on the combined royal and merchant fleets in the inner harbour at Cadiz. As a result of that attack you suffered the following casualties: three dead and fourteen wounded. Her Majesty's warship *Nonpareil* also sustained considerable damage. This attack was launched entirely on your own initiative and without orders from your superiors.'

I opened my mouth to make some kind of defence but before I could do so Lord Thomas Howard intervened.

'That is not strictly true, my lord.'

He spoke in his usual, quiet authoritative voice. All eyes turned towards him.

'Captain Dudley was acting under my orders.'

Howard stared intently at me and the message I read in that look was, 'If you value your life do not contradict what I am going to say'.

'I instructed Captain Dudley to reconnoitre in the inner harbour. According to reports I have received from the captain and other members of his crew, the *Nonpareil* was set upon by two enemy galleys as soon as she passed the Puntal headland. In the ensuing, unprovoked conflict Captain Dudley not only destroyed one of the galleys and severely damaged the other, but he seized an extremely valuable prize. In this engagement he showed considerable personal bravery and imagination. Anyone who knows Captain Dudley well will testify that he has these qualities in full measure. I am sure my lord of Essex will agree. I am also sure that her Majesty reposes considerable confidence in this young man and would be distressed to be deprived of his services.'

Robin nodded and I read relief in his face.

Raleigh scowled.

'How much are you being paid for that pretty speech?'

Howard and Essex turned angrily towards him. Before either could speak, the Lord High Admiral said, 'The prisoner will leave the court but remain on board the flagship.'

I was marched from the cabin. Before I had gone a few paces across the deck I heard the voices raised in furious argument. Minutes later Raleigh came out, limping and leaning on a stick. He called for his boat and was immediately rowed back to the *Warspite*. Then I knew that my ordeal was over, although it was half an hour or more before I was summoned back to the court room to hear the admiral announce with ponderous solemnity that it had been decided that there were no charges for me to answer. As a face-saver he added an admonition that I should in future show more respect to my superior officers. Thanks to an honourable man who was ready to stretch truth in the interests of justice I had been vindicated. Yet my triumph was only partial; I knew that my services would have been formally recognised but for the slanders Raleigh had been spreading.

On the deck afterwards Robin came up and grasped my hand.

'I am sorry you had to go through that, Bear cub.'

'Thank you, Robin. In a way I am glad; it has taught me a great deal.'

And indeed it had: on that day I shed another protective layer of innocence.

19

It was a Sunday morning when the bulk of the fleet sailed into Plymouth. The quayside was thronged with citizens come to gaze on the victorious ships bravely flying all their flags, to welcome Admiral Howard and the other gallant nobles and gentlemen of his entourage, to search anxiously for loved ones among the ranks of seamen and soldiers, to take the heroes off to the city taverns and listen to their tales of brave deeds. The dealers and tricksters were there, waiting to bargain for foreign treasures and trinkets. The bawds were out in their finest array. The cutpurses and the professional gamblers were present in large numbers. For all of them, in their several ways, as for the returning combatants, it would be a day to remember. Certainly it would be so for me.

Priority was given to prayer and thanksgiving. The admiral ordered a procession of the whole company from the harbour to St Andrew's church. With drums and trumpets sounding, polished helmets and breastplates gleaming, and the officers in their most brilliant plumes and sashes, the long column wound all round the town and finally came to a halt in the square before the church. As many of the company as could find standing room crowded into the cool cavern of St Andrew's with the local worshippers, and a thousand voices were raised in heartfelt *Te Deum*.

'We praise thee, O God!' For what? I asked myself the question as I sat in my privileged seat in the chancel listening to the echoing chorus of gratitude. What did I want to render thanks for on that warm summer morning? For being back in England? For the prospect of being soon reunited with Margaret? For the privilege of having been able to serve my country? For success in battle? For living up to the standards I set myself as a Dudley? For comrades and friends? Yes, for all that and more I felt profoundly, warmly grateful. But above all, perhaps, for survival. It was not just the dangers of storm and battle through which God had brought me safely to this point: I had been protected from the assassins of honour, from betrayal by friends, from the obscurity of a bastard birth, from my own rashness and pride. Even when I had felt alone, desolate, neglected, there had been someone there to help, encourage, guide; some channel, perhaps, of divine grace. My father, Robin Devereux, Abraham Kendall, Balthasar, Margaret, Benjamin Wood, Thomas Howard – I remembered them all with gratitude. But would there always be someone there? 'We therefore pray thee, help thy servants whom thou hast redeemed with thy precious blood...'

The rest of the day was spent in noisy celebrations and it was late before I was rowed back to my ship. Will Bradshaw was there to help me undress in the welcome peace of my own cabin.

'There was a messenger here, sir, from Kenilworth. He had been waiting some days for your return. He left this. I did not want to disturb you with it earlier.'

Only then did I see that the boy was crying, and I knew, even as I broke the seal, what I should find within. The neatly written words were only a confirmation.

'Your wife... brought to bed... a boy... stillborn... several days... died peacefully... she spoke of you continuously at the last...'

Next morning the fleet weighed anchor for the Thames and a tumultuous welcome in London. I began the long journey to Kenilworth where the new herons would now test their wings unwatched.

Margaret had died on 2 July and they had laid her to rest in the parish church. The priest showed me the place in the chancel. No memorial yet marked it – they were awaiting my instructions, he explained – but the edges of the flagstones were still earth-stained and slightly uneven.

'It is the best position remaining in the church. I knew you would want that.' He was a little, fussing old man, anxious to please and blunted by experience to the grief of others. 'There is, of course, room for yourself beside your wife, should you wish to reserve the space. And over here, against the north wall, an ideal site, I have always thought, for a splendid family memorial. Of course, you may prefer something simpler, sir. It seems to be the fashion these days. It is the influence of these Puritans, you know. However, if you want my advice . . .'

'Not now, old man.'

'Sir?'

'If you do not mind, I would like to be alone . . . A short time in prayer.'

At last he understood.

'Ah yes, to be sure, to be sure.'

He went away muttering.

Prayer? I could not pray no matter how hard I tried; could not marshal my thoughts; could only let them tumble untidily through my mind. Ten months, a few days less, that was all we had had together. She had feared the day that I would not return from a voyage and now it was she who had left me. And she so young, so full of life. Left me alone just when I had hoped I had left loneliness behind me. Was I sorry for myself or for Margaret? I was sorry for the pity of it all. She had found such joy and delight in even the simple things and now all was taken from her. Yet miserable fools who had never learned to wonder kept for years their insensitive grasp on life. I knelt on the dusty paving and wept for the loss of the gaiety, the beauty, the gentleness that were Margaret.

Then I heard her – softly but quite clearly. The church was empty but Margaret was there singing. Against all reason I knew and I still know that the voice was not inside my own head. The notes and words of her favourite song filled the cool air and echoed from the whitewashed walls.

When timely death my life and fortune ends
Let not my hearse be vexed with mourning friends.

304

But let all lovers, rich in triumph, come
And with sweet pastimes grace my happy tomb.
And Lesbia close thou up my little light,
And crown with love my ever during night,
    Ever during night.

'Good night, my Lesbia.'

I had often whispered those words as I kissed Margaret's sleep-heavy eyelids during those brief ten months that she shared my bed. Now I spoke them softly to her eternal spirit and I know that she heard.

No further sound disturbed the profound silence but I felt peace envelop me as it might have been a cloak of some weightless yet warm and soft material. Still there was sadness, still longing but I knew that I could bear them and that I would not be bearing them alone.

I did not stay long at Kenilworth. It held too many memories. Margaret had made the place very much her own, more so than I had realised. An embroidered bedspread, one of the new Italian walnut chests-with-drawers, a Flemish tapestry of Moses in the bulrushes (part of her dowry), a forgotten glove, a bed of her favourite scarlet peonies, the sketch-plan for a knot garden – nowhere could I escape the touch of her soul upon the materials of which life at Kenilworth was built. As soon as I had made the necessary arrangements for dispersing Margaret's personal household and attended to essential matters of estate business I went to Bedford House.

Many friends and acquaintances called on me there to offer sympathy. When Robin came he brought Lord Thomas Howard, a visitor as welcome as he was unexpected. What a contrast there was between the two men. They were almost of an age yet each responded quite differently to my grief. Robin found difficulty putting his compassion into words and wandered nervously round the room until the conversation entered areas which caused him less embarrassment. Howard stood tall, straight, correct before the parlour fire, hands folded over the top of his gold-mounted cane. His condolences were immaculately expressed and formal, but there was nothing of cold conventionality about them. As soon as the demands of etiquette were satisfied I turned the talk to other matters.

'I hear you were well received in London, Robin.'

Howard replied.

'It was almost like a coronation. Everyone was at the thanksgiving service in St Paul's and afterwards crowds cheered him through the City.'

'Aye, the people love me well enough. They know how to show appreciation for loyal service if others do not.'

He slumped into a chair and spread his legs before him. Howard frowned.

'Come, Robin, you exaggerate.'

I waved Lord Thomas to a chair on the other side of the hearth.

'What is the matter?'

'Robin feels slighted because Cecil is made Secretary.'

'So Burghley has succeeded at last?'

Robin scowled.

'Yes, as soon as we had gone off to risk our lives at Cadiz the hunchback was raised to the highest office in the land. She dared not do it while I was still at court but as soon as my back was turned...'

Howard smiled reassuringly.

'Robin, you take it too hard. The Queen values you for other reasons. Little Cecil is meet to be a scribbler of letters and bills; you are a man for higher things. Upon my life, I do not envy the fellow.'

'You are wrong, Thomas, dangerously wrong. He is more devious than his father and much more inscrutable. He is totally lacking in passion and no man is his confidant. Can you understand him or fathom the secrets of those dark eyes? I confess I cannot. All I know is that he means me no good.'

I recognised only too well the onset of one of Robin's fits of raging melancholy.

'He cannot harm you while you have the Queen's love.'

'You never spoke more truly, Bear cub. But do I have the Queen's love?'

He rose and went to a buffet to pour himself wine.

'Oh, surely Robin . . .'

Robin snorted.

'You tell him how it is, Thomas.'

Howard nodded.

'It is true; the Queen has, perhaps, been less than generous.'

Robin spluttered into his goblet.

'Perhaps! We accomplish the most brilliant naval and military exploit of the reign. We bring Philip to his knees and put an end to this long, tedious war. In every capital of Europe they are shouting the praises of "Elizabeth the Great" because of what we have done at Cadiz. Yet all the Queen can do is quibble over the booty.'

I looked to Howard for elucidation.

'Her Majesty feels that some of her commanders enriched themselves at the sack of Cadiz instead of safeguarding her interests.'

If that was what her Majesty felt, her Majesty was right. I had seen the consignments of plate, pearls, gold ornaments, furniture, Turkey carpets, tapestries, wine, pictures and books being loaded into the holds of the English vessels. I had heard the captains clamouring to set sail with their treasures rather than stay to consolidate their strategic position.

'But surely she does not blame Essex for that?'

'The Earl of Essex and the Lord Admiral were in charge of the expedition.'

Robin stood in the middle of the room and waved his now-empty goblet at us.

'You know, both of you, how I urged the garrisoning of Cadiz and a foray into the surrounding country to destroy the crops, villages and bridges in case of a siege. And was it not I who wanted to lie in wait for the treasure fleet – which, by the way, arrived but two days after our departure. God knows I strove harder than any man to do the Queen good service. And what do I have for my pains? Complaints that we did not capture more shipping or bring back more plunder. Clearly, the way to earn Elizabeth's gratitude is to sit at home, flattering her, entertaining her and making sure she never has to open her purse.'

Robin subsided into morose silence. I rose to fill his cup and offer wine to my other guest.

'And what news of Raleigh?'

Howard sipped his wine fastidiously.

'His welcome at court still lacks warmth. He hobbles a great deal and leans on his stick and makes much of his wound but the Queen is not impressed. His profit from the Cadiz raid has gone straight into another Orinoco voyage.'

'He is planning another venture?' I was genuinely alarmed.

'"Venture" is too grand a word for it. He can only afford one ship. He is fitting it out in the Medway even now.'

'And he has no backers?'

'No, Sir Walter must finance his own dreams. The Queen will not, nor will any rich man I know.'

'I cannot understand the man's obsession. Either he is mad or he knows something I do not. However, let us not talk of Raleigh. Robin, my Lord Howard, you will, I hope, stay to dinner.'

Robin shook his head.

'Thank you, Bear cub, but I am commanded to dine with the Queen at Hampton Court. In fact, I must go. But I am sure Lord Howard will keep you company.'

Howard nodded.

'I shall be very happy.'

It was a quiet meal. I was still too bound up in my own thoughts and feelings to be a good conversationalist and there were many silences during the meal. Yet it did not seem to matter; Howard did not take offence at my dismal performance as a host and only broke in upon my reveries when he had something helpful to say.

'Can you accept, Master Dudley, that I know exactly how you feel?'

'If you say it is so, my lord . . .'

'I should like to hope that you regard yourself as one of my friends. They all call me Thomas.'

'I should count that a great honour . . . Thomas. I trust you will use the same familiarity with me.'

'Then, Robert, know that I, too, lost the wife of my youth. I was seventeen, Mary a year younger, scarce more than a child, and ours was a love match. She died of the plague when we had been married but six months. I was desolate, I believed I should never feel the same for another woman as I had felt for Mary.'

'And did you?'

'In time. It took time. Five years, and during those years I could scarce look at another woman. Of course, there were neighbours who wanted to arrange marriages for their daughters. I was very eligible and my own family kept pressing me to take a wife. But once you have wed for love it is difficult to contemplate a conventional marriage.'

'Yet you did marry again, and very happily, as I know.'

'Yes, at the end of five years love found me again and Catherine and I are, as you say, very happy. So you see, Robert, blind Cupid can stumble across your path more than once. But you must not go looking for him; you may find only disappointment.'

'No, Thomas, I shall not seek him. Yet I know not what I shall do to occupy my mind.'

Howard looked genuinely surprised.

'Surely you know that matter will be decided for you.'

'How so?'

'The Queen has marked your talents. All men speak well of your courage and success at Cadiz – except Raleigh, of course. You are a noted man. Our sovereign respects your grief and for that reason alone she has not yet called you to court. But I assure you, you will not be left much longer to eat your heart out in obscurity.'

That prophecy was not long in being fulfilled. The court returned to Westminster on 3 October. The next morning a messenger in the Queen's livery arrived bearing a summons to the palace. I was there in good time waiting in the antechamber among the crowd of men and women who had been ordered to wait on the Queen or who were hopeful of a chance to present their petitions. Since my marriage and my formal relinquishing of my place at court I no longer had automatic access to the inner sanctum. Several councillors, officials and favourites passed through and many of them stopped for a word with me. None of them could or would answer my question, 'Why am I sent for?'

A hundred times I ran through the possibilities in my mind. Was I simply being recalled to attendance at court? Did the Queen wish to tell me in person how sorry she was about Margaret's death? She had already sent a message of condolence. Was there the chance of a new naval command? Had Elizabeth decided to take seriously my plans for Trinidad? Had Raleigh been working some new mischief against which I should have to defend myself? I soon realised that speculation was pointless; there were many reasons why the Queen might wish to see me. Yet I continued to speculate.

I did not have long to wait. Soon the door opened and I was called into the Presence Chamber. There was the usual throng of gorgeously dressed ladies and gentlemen, the liveried servants and the Queen, today in a white gown sewn with pearls, on her raised chair of state. Essex and Robert Cecil stood, one on each side. I mounted the velvet-covered steps, knelt, kissed the Queen's hand and was bidden to rise.

'You have been too long absent, Master Dudley.'

'I fear I would have been sombre company, your Majesty.'

'My poor captain.' It was not said unkindly. 'As you grow older you will learn to live with grief. We too have lost lovers but we have never let that distract us from our duty. Nor must you.'

'Your Majesty will ever find me ready to serve.'

'We are well aware of your loyalty and that is why we have summoned you hither. Master Dudley, within the last two years you have added great lustre to your own name and to ours. You have fitted out at your own charge part of an expedition to explore the unknown regions of the Indies. There you rivalled the exploits of some of our most famous servants – Drake and Frobisher, Cavendish and Hawkins. In the recent campaign of our army and navy in Spain you commanded our great ship *Nonpareil*. In this position you exercised great personal bravery and devotion to our person. Had we not known and loved your father we should have greatly marvelled that one so young could achieve so much. Do you recall the first time you were presented to us at Tilbury?'

'Very well, your Majesty.'

'We thought you then a likely young man to serve us well and we were not wrong. You have brought fresh honours to an honoured name. Your father would be very proud of you. We thank you for your love and we have decided to reward it. Kneel before us, Master Dudley.'

Bewildered, I obeyed. I could see little more than the crimson covering of the dais and the white satin of the Queen's dress. Her voice came from somewhere above and seemed strangely distant.

'My lord of Essex, your sword if you please. As you have ever shown a special interest in this young man you shall assist us. And so shall Sir Walter for he is a fellow explorer. Where is he?'

I heard the tap of Raleigh's stick on the boards, saw his black hose and scarlet, buckled shoes as he ascended the dais beside me. I glanced up. Elizabeth held the rapier's jewelled pommel. Raleigh and Essex each rested a hand on hers. Lightly the blade touched my shoulders.

'Arise, Sir Robert Dudley.'

I do not know what I said. My eyes were blurred as I confronted my sovereign. Raleigh's face was turned away but I vividly recall Elizabeth and Essex smiling at me, their heads close together and she saying, 'We cannot call him Bear cub any longer, Robin. See how bold and fierce he is grown. We can have no better protector. From now onwards he shall be the Queen's Bear.'